ALSO BY AMY SANDAS

Fallen Ladies
Luck Is No Lady
The Untouchable Earl
Lord of Lies

Christmas in a Cowboy's Arms anthology

RUNAWAY BRIDES
THE GUNSLINGER'S VOW

AMY SANDAS

sourcebooks
casablanca

Published by Sourcebooks Casablanca, an imprint of
Sourcebooks, Inc.
P.O. Box 4410, Naperville, Illinois 60567-4410
(630) 961-3900
Fax: (630) 961-2168
sourcebooks.com

Printed and bound in Canada.
MBP 10 9 8 7 6 5 4 3 2 1

For Taylor, a girl who has always known her own heart and is not afraid to follow it. You constantly surprise me. I am so proud to be your mom.

ONE

Boston, Massachusetts
August 2, 1881

"Miss Brighton? Miss Brighton, did you hear me?"

Alexandra blinked away her shock to meet the concerned gaze of her unexpected suitor. "I...yes," she said finally, though her voice felt off—not quite her own. "That is, I believe so."

Mr. Shaw's worried expression smoothed into a handsome smile. "I have just declared that I would like to make you my bride, Miss Brighton."

His words were no less a surprise the second time around. Peter Shaw was the quintessential Eastern gentleman of distinction. Though only twenty-six, he was already gaining momentum in political circles. He was charming, attractive, full of confidence, and met every one of Aunt Judith's criteria for an advantageous match.

And for some inexplicable reason, he had just asked *her*, Alexandra Brighton, to be his bride.

She couldn't have heard him right.

Alexandra gave a tiny shake of her head to free

up some words. "I am sorry, Mr. Shaw. I am a bit stunned. I had not expected such an offer." Nor had she expected the creeping sense of anxiety that came with it, making her throat tight and her palms clammy. Had he been falling in love with her all this time, and she had never even noticed?

Despite her awkwardness, he was all grace and charm. "See, that is what I like about you, Miss Brighton—your innate modesty and lack of pretense. You are unlike other young ladies in town. Their perspectives are so narrow, so limited. Most of them have never experienced anything beyond our tight little social niche, let alone life outside of Boston."

His eyes were a soft brown in the light that extended from the ballroom just visible beyond the balcony doors. "I admire your story, Miss Brighton. It is my opinion that your...unusual childhood afforded you a more valuable view of life." He took a slow breath as he clasped his hands behind his back and lowered his chin, as if confessing some great secret. "I have ambitions, Miss Brighton, plans for my future—for the future of Boston and this great state of Massachusetts. In order to secure that future, it is imperative that I appeal to a broad audience." He smiled again, his eyes crinkling gently. "You can help me do that."

Alexandra released her breath in a slow decompression of tension.

Now it made sense. Mr. Shaw hadn't inexplicably fallen in *love*. He was proposing a business arrangement.

She should have known.

Shaw was a member of the elite Boston social group known as the Brahmins, and marriages amongst his exclusive set were not made out of such an inconstant, imprudent thing as affection. The acknowledgment cleared away some of her confusion, but had no effect on her growing sense of dread.

"You leave me in a state of suspense for your response, Miss Brighton," he teased. Despite his words, he was as self-assured as ever.

Alexandra smiled, but the act felt tight and forced. She would accept. *Of course* she would accept. Not a single person of Alexandra's acquaintance would understand if she refused. An offer from a gentleman such as Peter Shaw was everything her aunt had been grooming her for.

He was waiting.

"I would be honored," she finally replied. But as the words left her mouth, she felt a moment of panic and wished she could call them back.

What was wrong with her?

Now that he had her agreement, Peter gave no sign of joy beyond a shallow nod. He did not appear the slightest bit aware of her growing discomfort. She had no idea she had gotten so good at *maintaining a social face*, as her aunt called it.

"I have already spoken privately with your aunt and obtained her blessing," he said, "but I will come by tomorrow to finalize the details. I have no doubt this marriage will be a tremendous success."

Then he stepped forward and very deliberately propped his fingertips beneath her chin, tilting her face upward as he bent down to press a quick kiss to her lips. It was Alexandra's very first kiss, and was over just as soon as it began. The impact of it faded away almost faster than she could acknowledge its occurrence.

Peter offered his arm and flashed another one of his charming almost-smiles. "We had better return to the ball before people start to talk." He led her, unresisting, back through the crowd to where Aunt Judith stood with her group of friends.

Alexandra's stomach churned the entire way. The ballroom felt too cloying, too hot. She was assailed by a fierce desire to return to the fresh air on the balcony. Alone.

Stop, she thought, even as she fought to remember how to breathe. *Aunt Judith will never forgive you if you make a scene.*

It was becoming increasingly difficult to care about that—to care about any of the fine Eastern manners she had so carefully been taught.

Mr. Shaw offered a few complimentary words to the matrons gathered with Aunt Judith before he bade his farewell to Alexandra with another comment about calling the next day. Then he walked away. Alexandra barely caught sight of the triumphant gleam in her aunt's eyes before she was set upon by her two best friends.

Courtney Adams was a flurry of pink silk and lace, vivid red curls, and sparkling green eyes set within pert features that also boasted elegantly arched brows and impishly curved lips. She was beautiful, but it was her bright personality that most people were drawn to. Courtney stepped in close to Alexandra to murmur dramatically, "You and Mr. Shaw were out of sight for quite a while. I wonder what the two of you were up to."

"Hush, Courtney." This was from Alexandra's cousin Evelyn, or Evie, as she and Courtney called her.

At twenty-one, Evie was a year older than both Alexandra and Courtney, but in many ways, she was far more naive. Protected and guided by Aunt Judith her entire life, she had had few opportunities to experience anything beyond the small world she had been born into. Evie's older brother, Warren, had betrayed the family's dreams of becoming a prominent Boston social figure by becoming a doctor instead. With Warren off saving lives across the country, Aunt Judith was left to pin all her hopes for climbing Boston's social ladder on her daughter… and Alexandra.

"Shall we all go for some refreshment?" Evie suggested. Her motivation was clearly to distance them from her mother so they could talk more freely.

After making their excuses to Aunt Judith, the three young ladies strolled across the ballroom at a sedate pace, despite the energy bristling among them. Alexandra found she could breathe more easily now that she was away from both Mr. Shaw and her aunt, but that cloying dread was still there, hovering about her shoulders in a heavy cloak.

Once settled in a corner of a connecting sitting room, lemonades in hand, Courtney urged in tones of whispered excitement, "So? What did the renowned Mr. Shaw have to say?"

Alexandra hesitated over her response. The conversation on the balcony still did not feel quite real. "He proposed marriage," she answered quietly.

"I knew it!"

Alexandra looked to Courtney in surprise. "You did? How could you? He gave no indication whatsoever that he had such an inclination. We have spoken less than half a dozen times."

"Yes, but that is still twice as much as he deigned to speak with any other girl," Evie noted reasonably. "He was obviously showing an interest in you."

"I wish someone had told me. Maybe I wouldn't have made a fool of myself by being so surprised."

Evie's eyes grew wide. "I thought you knew."

"You said yes, of course," Courtney said. "Tell me you said yes."

"I did."

Her friend clapped her hands and gave a bright smile. "Excellent. Now we are both engaged. We just need to find someone for Evie, and we can all become brides together."

Courtney's excitement only accented the churning discordance that had taken up residence inside Alexandra. She should be thrilled by the prospect of becoming Mrs. Peter Shaw. Ecstatic, even.

Instead, she felt…dishonest.

And on the verge of serious panic.

"Alexandra," Evie said softly, leaning forward to place her slim hand on Alexandra's wrist. "What is the matter?"

Meeting her cousin's compassionate gaze, Alexandra sighed. "I do not know. Something just feels…wrong."

"How do you mean?" Courtney asked, a flicker of concern crossing her features.

"I do not know," Alexandra repeated. "I am not sure I made the right choice in accepting. What if I am not the person Mr. Shaw believes me to be? He barely knows me."

"You will get to know each other better during the engagement and after, once you are married," Courtney assured.

Alexandra looked between her two closest friends. One red-haired and vivacious, the other slender and elegant with pale-blonde hair and soulful eyes. They knew her as no one else on the earth knew her, and loved her anyway. She could be nothing but fully honest with them.

"The truth is," Alexandra admitted, "I barely know myself anymore. Evie, you remember what I was like when I first arrived from Montana."

"Yes, and you have come such a very long way since then."

"That is my point," Alexandra said. "I barely recognize that girl in comparison to who I am now. But it *was* me. She might *still* be me somewhere deep down."

Her friends exchanged a quick glance, but did not interrupt.

"How do I know all this is not just a false facade? How can I commit to a future as someone's wife when I do not even know who I truly am?"

"What will you do?" Evie asked in a low whisper.

Alexandra took a bracing inhale. "I must tell Mr. Shaw that I need more time before committing to my answer."

"It will shock him to his toes," Courtney declared.

"It might be too late to withdraw your response." Evie directed her pointed gaze across the room.

Peter Shaw stood nearby, looking dapper and fine

in a group with some of the most prominent gentlemen of Boston society. His smile was modest as he accepted toasts and congratulatory handshakes. The way the gentlemen kept sliding surreptitious glances toward Alexandra suggested that he had already announced their engagement.

Panic expanded through her, tightening her chest.

She was trapped.

But a small, defiant part of her whispered: *Or maybe not.*

They were not married yet. Some engagements lasted months or even years. She had time.

A fierce little flame of rebellion sparked in the midst of her panic. The more she focused on that flame, the greater it grew, spreading out like a slow-burning wildfire. She had become the perfect Boston lady, but after five years of learning to curb her impulses, Alexandra pushed all that careful training aside and embraced the reckless urging inside her. "I am going back to Montana."

Her words slipped free before she completely thought them through, but the moment they were uttered, she knew the rightness of them.

She was suddenly flooded with memories of her childhood: how the Rockies rose majestically beyond the plains, how wildflowers spread across the ground in spring, and how the land made one feel unbelievably small and infinitely powerful at the same time.

The compulsion to see it all again—to go home—was overwhelming. And perfect.

Evie and Courtney stared at her, wide-eyed and in shock.

Her cousin recovered first. "Mother will never allow it." Her voice was low and almost sad.

"Your new fiancé will never allow it," Courtney added with conviction.

Alexandra leaned toward her friends and lowered her voice. "That is why they cannot know."

"But how will you manage it?" Courtney asked, awed excitement creeping into her words.

"I have money tucked away. Father gave it to me before I left home. I never had cause to use it. Now I do."

"But why?" Evie asked. "Why go back now?"

Alexandra had to think of her reply. It mostly felt like an instinctive certainty. Before she could consider going forward, she had to go back.

"I must discover unequivocally who I am. My life has been split into two very different halves: my childhood in Montana and the five years I have been here in Boston. I need to know how much of my past is still a part of me…or if it is time to put it to rest for good." She lowered her gaze as another realization hit deep in her heart. "I need to see my father again."

Her friends were silent for a moment. Then Courtney said, "How can we help?"

Ideas and plans tripped over themselves in Alexandra's mind as she considered everything she had to do to make good on her escape.

"I will leave tonight. All I need is time to get away. I must rely mostly on you, Evie. You will have to tell your mother I was not feeling well—the excitement and all—and I decided to head home early. Then tomorrow, when she asks after me, you can say I

developed an illness—I don't care what, just something to keep me abed. She won't come to check on
me. We know how she detests being around anyone
who is sick."

Evie's delicate features were tense with concern.
Alexandra knew it went against her cousin's nature
to be deceptive in any way, especially toward her
mother, but she nodded in agreement and Alexandra
felt a rush of gratitude for her dear cousin's loyalty.

Looking to Courtney, she said, "Will you lend me
your carriage? I must return to the house to gather some
belongings, then I will need a ride to the train station."

"Of course," Courtney agreed readily. "I will go
with you to help you pack."

"No, you mustn't. If things go bad, you can deny
that you knew anything of my plans. At least Evie's
perfidy will be kept within the family. Can I trust your
driver to keep my activities secret?"

"Absolutely. Edward is as discreet and steadfast as
they come."

"Once it is discovered where I have gone and it is
too late to stop me, Aunt Judith and Mr. Shaw will
have no choice but to await my return. Surely, they
will eventually come to understand my desire to visit
the land of my childhood one last time."

The other women's expressions seemed dubious,
but Alexandra ignored their uncertainty. Her confidence was more than enough to sustain her. It all
made such perfect sense. Surely she wouldn't be able
to breathe so easily if this were *wrong*.

She should have realized long ago that she would
never truly be happy until she knew where she belonged.

With a swift round of hugs, Alexandra bade heart-felt goodbyes to her best friends. Then she rose and made her way toward a discreet exit while Courtney and Evie loitered with their lemonade to give her as much time as possible before going to inform Aunt Judith of her departure.

As she slipped from the grand Boston mansion into the fresh night air, Alexandra breathed deep and wide. Catching sight of Courtney's family carriage, she glanced around to make sure no one else was about, then she lifted the skirts of her ball gown in both hands and sprinted off into the darkness.

Montana was waiting.

TWO

Boulder, Colorado Territory
August 4, 1881

MALCOLM KINCAID WOULD'VE GIVEN ANYTHING TO send his fist flying into the face of the wastrel seated across from him. He didn't, because the grimy outlaw claimed to have information Malcolm needed.

But damn, he wanted to.

Freddie Golding had spent his life stealing from widows and orphans and every sort of poor soul in between. The criminal went by a thousand different names, which was how he'd managed to evade the law for so long, even though he was wanted in five counties through three different territories. That and the fact that he was so common in appearance as to be totally forgettable.

The outlaw was going by a new name in Boulder and had no idea Malcolm knew exactly who he was. The world would be a better place without him, but right now Freddie had something Malcolm wanted more than the bounty on his head.

They sat at a table in the back corner of John J's Saloon. It was late on a Saturday night, and the place was hopping with men who'd come in to let loose with a night of drinking, gambling, and whoring.

By the shake in Freddie's hand as he reached for his glass, his red, bulbous nose and bloodshot eyes, it was clear he was not a man who went long without his whiskey.

"You said you had information for me," Malcolm said tersely. "Get to it or I'm leaving."

Freddie leaned forward, his greasy hair falling around his face as he smiled wide enough to show three missing teeth. "Oh, I've got what you want, mister. But you're not gettin' it for free."

Malcolm narrowed his gaze. His hand itched to curl into a fist.

"I heard you been asking for this little tidbit for years," Freddie said smugly. "Somethin' like that's gotta be worth quite a bit."

"Tell me what you know, and I'll decide what it's worth."

The greedy man downed the last of his whiskey, then flicked his rheumy gaze over Malcolm's untouched glass. Noting the longing in Freddie's expression, Malcolm lifted his whiskey. He stared hard over the rim of the glass until Freddie met his gaze.

"Tell me where he is."

There was a flash of uncertainty in the outlaw's dark, beady eyes as he licked his thin lips. "Maybe another drink'll help me remember the details."

Malcolm set his drink down hard, causing liquor to slosh from the glass. All pretense was gone from his manner as he replied in a biting tone, "Maybe I'll haul you back to Amarillo or Silver City and see what *they* think a fair price for the information might be. Or maybe I'll just take you straight down to Pueblo. I heard the judge in that town is itching to have you back."

Freddie's eyes grew wide as his gaze darted about the saloon, as though he expected a cavalry to emerge from the dusky shadows to drag him to justice. "I don't know what—"

"Shut up, Freddie. The only thing I wanna hear out of your mouth is what I came here looking for."

Freddie turned his wary focus back to Malcolm as he leaned in across the table. "You gonna take me in?"

"Not if you spill what you know."

After another quick glance around the room, he said, "You lookin' for the Belt Buckle Kid, right?"

Malcolm nodded. It wasn't a secret. He'd been hunting the elusive outlaw for years and had gotten close to capturing him more than once in the beginning. But then the Kid stopped using his idiotic nickname. No one knew him by anything else so he'd basically disappeared. It had been years since Malcolm had gotten any solid information on the wanted man.

Freddie hesitated one final time before letting his breath out in a gust. If he made a run for it, Malcolm would have him pinned to the ground and howling in an instant. They both knew who held the power here. "His real name's Walter Dunstan. His daddy's got a spread outside of Wolf Creek up there in Montana."

The tightness that bound Malcolm's chest shifted just enough to allow one full breath before it squeezed tight again.

Walter Dunstan of Wolf Creek, Montana.

It was strange. The elusive murderer had been known only as the Belt Buckle Kid for so long that the new name didn't seem to fit. *Walter Dunstan* sounded like some graying old man, not a cold-blooded killer who couldn't be much more than thirty years old.

None of it changed the fact that Walter Dunstan had a death to answer for.

"How do I know what you're telling me is the truth?" he asked.

Freddie shrugged. "You don't. But I can tell you that I used to work for his pa years ago. I was even with Walter when he beat that boy with his belt and first gained the stupid nickname."

It could be true. And if it was, that meant Malcolm was finally getting close to seeing his vow of vengeance fulfilled.

"If you go after him, you're likely to be the one who ends up with a bullet in the gut," Freddie warned. "His pa's real powerful."

Malcolm shrugged. As long as he took the Belt Buckle Kid out first, it didn't much matter what happened to him. And now that he had what he needed, he no longer had any use for Freddie. "Get the hell outta here before I change my mind about taking you in."

As Freddie stumbled from the saloon, Malcolm acknowledged that he probably should have collected the bounty on the man anyway. Freddie was a menace. Just being in his vicinity put a bad taste in Malcolm's mouth. The information was enough of a boon, however, that Malcolm was willing to give the slimy weasel a head start.

He lifted the whiskey and drained the glass in one swallow as he considered what he'd learned.

He didn't trust Freddie any farther than he could spit. But if what the man said was true, after all these years, Walter Dunstan was as good as dead. He just didn't know it yet.

THREE

Rock Springs, Wyoming Territory
August 12, 1881

ALEXANDRA BRIGHTON CAME TO A SWIFT HALT FOUR
steps into the Painted Horse Saloon. Blinking a few
times to adjust to the dim interior, she took a measured look around.

As saloons went, it was nothing special. Not that
Alexandra had seen many—or any, to be honest.

Despite the early hour, the place was busier than
expected. Three men stood in hushed conversation
as they leaned against the bar running the length of
the wall to her left. Several tables filled the open area
to the right, where two separate card games were in
progress, and narrow stairs toward the back led up to
a closed second floor. An upright piano that looked
like it hadn't been touched in years stood lonely in the
shadows by the stairs.

Upon her entrance, everyone turned to stare at
her, yet only a handful of the men bothered to scrape
to their feet. Their expressions, ranging from mildly

curious to outright covetous, reminded her of what she already knew: a saloon was no place for a lady.

Alexandra steadied her chin as she stared coolly back. She did not have the luxury of fear. That would have been handy *before* she had left Boston. But now, she was too far from the place she'd called home the last five years to go back.

Her only option was to go forward.

Preferably as quickly as possible.

All she needed was one good man. One noble, honorable man who could escort her to Montana while keeping her free from harm. Was that too much to ask?

She feared it was, but Alexandra was low on options. And funds.

The stagecoach out of Rock Springs, Wyoming, was inoperable due to required repairs, leaving Alexandra in desperate need of another way to get to Helena. When the blacksmith mentioned a bounty hunter in town who was heading in that direction, she didn't stop to think about it—just headed off to the saloon where the man was said to be catching some respite.

It had been a long time since her reckless will had landed her in trouble, yet here she was, standing in the middle of a filthy saloon while men of all varieties stared at her in a way that made her feel like a sheep who'd wandered into the midst of a wolf pack.

Stiffening her spine and reminding herself of her purpose, she scanned the room again.

One of these men had to be the bounty hunter.

The longer she stood there, the cruder the gazes became. The nerves running along her spine prickled, and her palms started to sweat in her fine gloves. Time to see her business done so she could get herself out of there.

"Which of you is the man called Kincaid?" she asked in a tone that cut uncomfortably through the humming quiet that had taken over the place.

She hadn't intended to sound so imperious, but her courage was slowly ebbing away, and her voice tended to sharpen in compensation for a lack of confidence.

More than a few men glanced away, refocusing their attention on their drink or their card game or whatever conversation they had been in before her interruption. Others eyed her with a new level of curiosity or an odd dose of wariness.

No one answered.

She opened her mouth to repeat her question when the bartender, an aging man with a bald head and rotund belly, caught her eye and gave a sharp jerk of his chin toward a man standing in the shadows at the far end of the bar.

Bolstering her nerves, Alexandra started forward with long strides that caused her many-layered skirts to snap against her heeled boots. The stranger appeared as rough as the other men in the place, but there was something about him—something in the way he held himself—that struck her acutely even as common sense urged her to be extra wary.

Though he hunched forward to rest his elbows on the bar, there was no mistaking his height, or that his shoulders were broad and strong beneath his dark duster coat. A good layer of dirt covered everything from his scuffed boots to the bandana around his neck and the wide-brimmed hat tipped low over his face, supporting the fact that he'd just ridden into town.

It was more than his intimidating size and trail-worn appearance that set this man apart, however. Despite his relaxed posture, he seemed ready for action. And if that were not enough, he was the only person in the whole place who had not given her a second glance. He appeared intent on ignoring her and everyone else.

And everyone else seemed equally determined to ignore him.

If she were a sheep, and the saloon's occupants were a pack of wolves, then this man was the alpha.

Her steps faltered. What kind of stupid sheep walked right up to the alpha wolf?

Apparently, this one did.

The flash of caution had come far too late. Though she came to an abrupt stop, she was already too close to pretend that she had intended to speak with anyone else. Of course, there had also been the haughty way she'd loudly stated his name for all to hear.

Blast.

Maybe he wasn't Kincaid after all. Maybe the bartender just had a cramp in his neck he was trying to stretch out.

But she couldn't turn back now. Taking another step closer, she said in what she hoped was a confident and civil tone, "Mr. Kincaid?"

The man remained as he was, his gaze trained forward. His lack of response was unnerving.

Alexandra kept her gaze fixed on his profile, though she had to tip her chin up to manage it. Unfortunately, the wide brim of his hat threw most of his face into shadow. All she could discern was a jawline covered with the scruff of a dark beard and the long line of his nose. His hair, a few shades lighter than his beard, was as dusty as the rest of him, falling over the collar of his coat to brush against his shoulders. The man was in desperate need of a bath.

He didn't turn his head to look at her or move his hand from where it curved around a small glass of whiskey, but Alexandra got the sense all the same that her approach bothered him.

No, it irritated the hell out of him.

She almost turned away, but her frustration and impatience had been building, along with her trepidation, and kept her feet rooted to the floor, even though it was increasingly clear that Kincaid was not the noble escort she had hoped to find.

He was dangerous. A man not to be trifled with.

Before she could turn away, someone shouted from behind her, "If you don't want her, I'll take her."

The slurred words inspired some muffled laughter throughout the saloon. Alexandra stiffened. Before she could find her voice to form any kind of response, Kincaid turned his head. Sharp gray eyes pierced from the shadows of his hat, directed past Alexandra to the man who had spoken.

She had never seen such hardness in a man's gaze, and it momentarily distracted her from her precarious situation. There was no emotion there. It was all steel and granite. Her lungs stopped drawing breath. Her stomach twisted.

And he wasn't even directing that steely gaze toward *her*.

She didn't need to turn around to know that he'd gotten the attention of everyone in the place. The outspoken drunkard mumbled some incoherent apology under his breath before Kincaid swept that harsh glare over the rest of the saloon, which had fallen silent for the second time since she had entered.

Then, apparently satisfied, Kincaid shifted his attention back toward the mirror behind the bar as he lifted his glass for a drink.

Alexandra didn't move. Not even to breathe.

Maybe he was the man she needed after all. If he could silence a saloon with nothing more than a hard stare, surely he could get her safely to her father's place in Montana.

Gathering her courage once again, she asked, "Are you Kincaid?"

No response.

She waited a full minute…and nothing.

With a smothered sound of annoyance, she turned toward the bar. The moment her gaze found the mirror on the wall across from her, she was ensnared by the bounty hunter's sharp gray focus.

He was staring at her in the grimy reflection and had probably been doing so from the moment she'd approached.

An intrinsic sort of physical awareness lifted the hair on the back of her neck. It was a sensation not quite like fear, though it was awfully close to it.

For a few moments, she couldn't manage anything more than to stare back at him. His features were a fascinating collection of harsh angles and rough-hewn lines. The thick beard did nothing to disguise his hard, masculine jaw, or detract from the impression of his straight nose and those frightening eyes.

Still staring at her.

A strange sort of weakness infused her insides, making her belly quiver and her knees turn to jelly. That sensation spurred her to speak again. She hated feeling weak nearly as much as she hated being afraid.

"My name is Alexandra Brighton, and I find myself in need of an escort to Montana."

"No."

She'd barely finished before he gave his reply. One curt word uttered in a low tone that left no room for civility.

Alexandra frowned. Her fingers curled into fists in her soft, pearl-gray gloves. "I know you are heading in that direction. The blacksmith said as much. It is imperative that I make my way north as soon as possible."

"Not my problem, lady."

His rudeness set her back, but not enough to give up. "That is correct; it's not your problem," Alexandra replied. She heard the annoyance in her voice and swiftly softened her tone. "You *can* be the solution, however."

"No."

Her temper flared. The man was infuriating. "Why not?" she pressed stubbornly.

He lifted his glass to drain the last of the whiskey. His Adam's apple rose and fell above the edge of his bandana. Setting the glass back on the bar, he muttered, "You got the wrong man."

"You are Kincaid."

He clenched his teeth, hardening the already harsh

line of his jaw. "I'm no guide, and I'm damned sure no lady's escort."

Oddly, the more discourteous and aggressive he became, the more he made her want to dig in her heels and force him to be reasonable. "You are a bounty hunter, correct?"

No reply.

"You hunt down outlaws for a reward. I imagine it has taken you all over this country of ours. You are likely quite familiar with any number of roads and trails that stretch across the western territories."

No reply.

Alexandra sighed. "Look, Mr. Kincaid," she began, doing her best to formulate her thoughts into a convincing argument, "I understand I may not be offering you the type of work you typically accept, but you will be paid. Quite handsomely, actually."

She didn't bother to add that she wouldn't be able to give him his fee until they reached her father.

"No."

"But—"

"No."

He didn't raise his voice or say anything more. Just the one syllable. Then he shifted his gaze toward the bartender with a dip of his chin to indicate he wanted another pour, dismissing her.

He wasn't going to help.

An overwhelming dread and some other emotion filled her, tightening her chest and turning her legs to lead. What on earth would she do now?

"Excuse me, miss?"

Alexandra was so deep in her own head, she nearly

jumped at the words, even though they were spoken in an even tone barely over a whisper. She hadn't even noticed someone stepping up behind her.

She turned in place to see a man aged somewhere in his forties, dressed in a pale-gray suit and neat bowler hat. He looked decidedly out of place in his Eastern clothing and impeccably clean appearance. Even she had a thin layer of dust coating her boots and the hem of her many skirts, but not this man, who stood at least two inches shorter than her.

His smile was open and friendly, which was even more of a rarity here than his fine clothes.

"Please forgive my intrusion into your conversation, but I could not help but overhear," he continued. Deep creases formed at the outer corners of his warm brown eyes as his smile widened. "Am I correct in surmising that you are in need of an escort to Montana?"

Though she couldn't be sure Kincaid was watching the interaction, something in her sensed his continued focus despite what appeared to be a cold lack of interest.

"That is true," she replied.

"I happen to be heading that way myself, up to Bozeman, along with my brother and his wife. If you wish, you would be welcome to travel with us."

Alexandra hesitated, though she wasn't sure why, other than something seemed…off.

The petite man displayed a demeanor more suited to the world she had left behind in Boston, which was both welcome and strikingly incongruent. Perhaps she was simply thrown off by the juxtaposition of this man's manner after experiencing the rough intensity of Kincaid. He looked soft by comparison.

Of course, anyone would look soft compared to the bounty hunter.

It shouldn't deter her. Just because this fellow did not have the same air of danger and steely competence as Kincaid did not mean he was not fully capable of getting her to Bozeman. She would be traveling in a group after all. There was some safety in numbers, and from all accounts, the West wasn't quite as wild as it had been even five years ago. And Bozeman was very near Helena.

"That's a very nice offer, Mr.—I'm sorry, I did not catch your name."

The man blushed. "Oh, my apologies again, miss. I really haven't been out of civilization so long to excuse such a lapse in manners." He gave a deep bow of his head. "I am Cleveland Lassiter, named for the city where I was born and raised."

His self-deprecating tone managed to ease a bit of Alexandra's wariness, and she smiled back. "A pleasure to meet you, Mr. Lassiter. My name is Alexandra Brighton, recently of Boston."

"What a wonderful city," Mr. Lassiter exclaimed, his brown eyes widening. "I visited there once as a young man. So much culture and such fine society."

Alexandra continued to smile, but said nothing in response.

For the oddest reason, it seemed the longer she stood speaking with the newcomer, the more tension she felt radiating from the large man beside her. Clearly, the bounty hunter preferred to occupy his shadows alone.

Good. Let him be annoyed.

Mr. Lassiter held his smile as he continued, "I would hate to see you stranded here in town when we have more than enough room in our modest conveyance. My brother drives the team, and I am certain my sister-in-law would welcome having some additional company to chat with beyond myself. She's from the city as well, you see, and not at all accustomed to these wide-open spaces and sparsely populated areas. She tends to get bored easily."

Even her aunt might have approved of such an offer from such a man. Mr. Lassiter truly seemed to be the answer to her problem.

So why did she still hesitate?

Because she knew more than most Easterners, that along the trail, there were more dangers than a person could count. Despite his rude and rough manner, long-buried instincts told her that Kincaid was undeniably more equipped to get her north without incident than this fine gentleman. She had just received the perfect offer from Mr. Lassiter, yet she felt compelled to ask Kincaid one more time if he would take the job.

Against her will, she glanced at the tall bounty hunter. At that moment, Kincaid chose to straighten from his hunched position. As he lifted his arm to bring the whiskey glass to his mouth, the edge of his coat swung away from his side. The movement revealed a long and generously muscled body in a faded denim shirt and well-worn dark trousers. It also revealed the Colt nestled in a holster strapped to his left hip, handle forward.

The sight of the gun, close enough that she could

have reached out and touched the cold metal, sent a spear of memory and irrational terror through her body. Starting in her toes, rushing up through her belly, across the surface of her heart to the base of her skull, the fear pressed in on her like the icy waters of a mountain lake.

Of course, Alexandra knew that almost everyone in these parts carried some sort of weapon. She thought she was ready to face that, but she hadn't anticipated such freezing terror. Hadn't prepared herself for the rush of traumatic memories.

"Miss Brighton. Excuse me, Miss Brighton?"

Mr. Lassiter's gentle voice drew her back to herself.

She turned to look at him, doing everything in her power to conceal the fear in her eyes and the debilitating command that had taken over her body. Forcing a tight smile, she said, "I am sorry, Mr. Lassiter. What were you saying?"

"Only that we are planning to leave town within the hour. If you'd like to join us, I am afraid you will need to hurry."

Still reeling from her reaction, Alexandra nodded, letting propriety trump instinct. Lassiter was the better choice. He was polite and would prove to be far better company. Not to mention, there wasn't the slightest hint of anything dangerous about him. "I shall be ready and would be happy to accept your offer."

"Excellent," Lassiter exclaimed, sounding quite sincere in his pleasure. Then he gave a rather pained glance around him before he added, "Shall we step out into the fresh air and discuss a meeting place?"

Alexandra nodded and followed Lassiter from the

saloon, noting that the eyes of several men followed her. Just before passing through the door, she sent a quick glance over her shoulder.

Kincaid had returned his elbows to the bar. His focus remained on the mirror across from him. As she stepped onto the boardwalk, the bounty hunter faded swiftly into the shadows he obviously preferred and Alexandra experienced an odd tightening in her center.

It felt a little like disappointment.

Malcolm Kincaid scanned the length of the mirror behind the bar. His position gave him a perfect view of the entire saloon. A few patrons had followed the Eastern lady's exit with sharp gazes.

There was one man in particular who triggered a spike of alertness.

He was older, with a bushy, salt-and-pepper beard and the cracked, browned skin of a man who'd spent most of his life under the sun. Though he sat at a poker game, he'd lifted his eyes toward Malcolm and the Eastern lady a few times too many during their brief conversation for mere curiosity.

Malcolm had been waiting for the man to make a move, but nothing came of it. Still, he didn't relax his vigilant observation until Miss Brighton and her companion had been gone at least twenty minutes. Only then was he assured she wouldn't be followed.

Fool woman.

The second she'd entered the saloon, she'd become a beacon of temptation. A woman like that—all wrapped up in a fine blue dress that showed off the trim curves of her figure, with her fair skin untouched by the sun and her dark hair twisted up into that fancy configuration topped by a ridiculous hat—was not a common sight in these parts. Only an Easterner would be stupid enough to strut boldly into one of the roughest saloons in Wyoming and practically declare herself unprotected and in possession of money. Despite her haughty manner, not a man in the place wouldn't have thought of how easy it would be to set upon the pretty young lady and take what she offered. And then some.

Damned fool woman.

She was not his problem. It was a good thing that fellow had come forward. Let the woman be his responsibility. Malcolm didn't need that kind of hassle.

Especially now that he was finally closing in on the Belt Buckle Kid.

Eight years was a long time to hunt for revenge. With any luck, the Kid would soon join his fellows six feet underground, and Malcolm could finally hang up his guns, or die trying.

Either way, there was only one thing waiting for him in Montana—and it wasn't the likes of Miss Alexandra Brighton.

FOUR

Mr. Lassiter's brother, introduced as George Polk, was actually a half brother and the exact opposite of the small Eastern gentleman in appearance. Mr. Polk was large, with a barrel chest and thick arms. He walked in a lumbering stride, and his clothing, though nice enough, wasn't nearly as fine or well fitted as Lassiter's. After giving Alexandra a short nod upon being advised she would be traveling with them, he took to sending her swift, darting glances from the corner of his dark eyes as he finished loading the covered wagon that would be taking them north.

Alexandra tried not to put too much importance on Mr. Polk's odd manner. Not everyone enjoyed meeting strangers, though the opposite seemed to be true of the man's wife, who came forward with an eagerly outstretched hand and a wide smile on her round face.

"Please call me Mattie," she said, with pale-blond sausage curls bouncing against her cheeks. Though she looked at least ten years older than Alexandra, she possessed an exuberant youthfulness that was slightly disarming. "I am so thrilled that Cleveland found another woman to join our group. It will be wonderful to have someone to talk to besides these two fellows—and someone from the great city of Boston, no less. I am from Philadelphia, myself, though it's been many years since I was anywhere near the place I grew up. I cannot wait to get to know you better. Conversation makes long drives go so much faster, don't you think?"

It turned out that Mr. Lassiter had been telling the truth when he'd said they would be leaving town within the hour. As soon as Alexandra's bags were loaded into the back of the wagon, they all climbed up and took their seats. Mr. Polk drove the horses, with Mr. Lassiter seated beside him. There was a second row of seating behind them, and Mattie insisted the two of them sit together so they could chat more easily.

Alexandra had never been one to shy away from polite conversation, but after several hours of nonstop chatter, she couldn't wait to stop for the night. Surely, Mattie would have to stop talking to get some sleep.

Finally, as the sun neared the horizon, Mr. Polk pulled the wagon up along a swiftly flowing creek. Camp was a simple setup. Thankfully, Mr. Polk was efficient in starting a campfire, and they had packed a good amount of food into the back of the wagon, so there was no need for anyone to hunt for their supper. A good thing, because it did not appear that the Lassiter party traveled with a hunting rifle, or any kind of firearm at all.

Considering her reaction to the sight of Kincaid's Colt, she should have been relieved by the lack of weapons. Instead, Alexandra experienced yet another niggling of doubt. One of many she'd experienced throughout the day as Mr. Polk had continued to send her odd looks and Mattie had seemed extremely interested in Alexandra's life in Boston and her destination in Montana. Though she tried to convince herself there was nothing untoward about their curiosity, something urged Alexandra to keep her replies vague enough without appearing reticent.

Then there was the issue about sleeping arrangements.

Mattie clearly intended to make up a bed for herself in the back of the wagon while the men set up bedrolls beside the fire. Lassiter offered to set up a place for Alexandra near the fire as well.

"Thank you," Alexandra replied, "but I would prefer to join Mattie in the wagon."

The two men hesitated, then Lassiter stepped forward with a smile. "I don't know if there is enough room for the both of you, I'm afraid."

Alexandra knew exactly how much space was in the back of the wagon. She smiled back, keeping her tone polite, though she was feeling put off by Lassiter's response. "I won't take up that much space. I'm sure we can make it work."

"Well, I—"

"What is the matter with you, Cleveland?" Mattie exclaimed as she peeked her head through the back flap of the wagon. "Of course Miss Brighton must share the wagon with me."

Lassiter smiled again. "I apologize. Please make yourself comfortable, Miss Brighton."

Alexandra was grateful for the bit of privacy, though she found it difficult to relax enough to fall asleep even after she heard two sets of snores coming from outside—one deep and rumbling, the other a nasally whistle. With the woman beside her also deeply asleep, Alexandra listened to the night sounds around them—the soft flow of wind against the canvas covering of the wagon, the sound of crickets and night birds in the distance, and the gentle, constant tumbling of the creek—but none of it helped to calm the strange tension that claimed her.

She felt on edge, as though some peril hovered just beyond their camp. Or perhaps the danger was closer. She wasn't sure why she couldn't completely relax in the midst of her traveling companions, but something simply did not feel right.

It was several hours before she finally fell into a light sleep.

Everyone started moving about early the next morning. Camp was already getting packed up by the time Alexandra emerged from the back of the wagon. When she asked if they would be leaving right away, Mattie assured with a bright smile, "Oh, it won't be for at least an hour or more—plenty of time to freshen up down by the creek if you'd like to take some time to yourself."

As she left camp to find a private spot in the bushes that lined the creek, Alexandra wondered what they might have for breakfast. She was starving. Initially intending to head to the creek to wash up as Mattie had suggested, she decided she'd rather eat first. She returned to camp after only a few minutes away to find Polk hastily hitching up the horses while the others waited in the wagon.

"I am sorry. I thought we weren't heading out for a little while yet," she said as she approached in wary suspicion.

Lassiter looked at her with an almost pained expression. "We are heading out, Miss Brighton, but you are not."

Alexandra stopped, alarm sweeping through her. She glanced toward Mattie, who was seated beside Lassiter, but the woman kept her gaze trained forward. Mr. Polk just stared at her in cold-eyed silence as he finished with the horses and hefted himself up into the driver's seat. She looked back to Lassiter. "What do you mean?"

"Oh, for heaven's sake, just drive already," Mattie interrupted impatiently.

Her husband immediately obliged with a flick of the driving reins, and the wagon started to roll away.

This couldn't be happening. "Wait!" Alexandra shouted as she started toward them. "You can't just leave me here. What about my things?"

Mattie lifted her hand from beneath the fall of her skirts to point a long-barreled pistol at Alexandra's chest, stopping her cold. "Not another step. Your fancy things now belong to me. I would shoot you to save you the pain of starving out here all alone, but I can't afford to waste the bullet," she said with a wide smile. "You understand."

Alexandra couldn't move. The sight of the gun rooted her feet to the earth as terror overtook her just as it had in the saloon. Her tongue stiffened in her mouth, and her throat closed up so she couldn't even shout for them to stop as Lassiter turned to his companions and said, "I told you she wouldn't put up a fight."

"You do know how to pick them, darling," Mattie replied.

"Don't bother trying to walk back to town, Miss Brighton," Lassiter called over his shoulder in a tone that was almost gleeful. "We left the road many miles ago, so you'll only get yourself lost and exhausted for no reason."

All Alexandra could do was watch them drive away with the sound of Mattie's laughter and the image of Lassiter's sneering expression burning into her mind.

They'd left her.

They'd stolen her things and left her.

As the shock wore off, fury swept in to take its place.

How could they live with themselves? Clearly, this was not the first time they had preyed upon a hapless traveler. How many victims had they left stranded out in the wilderness before her? How could she have been so stupid? So trusting?

Her fury quickly turned in on herself.

She should have known better. Instead, she had ignored her instincts and had fallen right into their hands, like an idiot.

Panic pressed in against her anger, threatening to debilitate her as her heart started racing and sweat broke out on the back of her neck.

She was going to die out here.

No. She wasn't.

She took a sweeping glance around to see if anything had been left behind that might help her in some way, but Lassiter and his friends had been thorough.

He had said they were no longer on the road, but surely, someone would come by at some point.

Oh, why hadn't she paid more attention along the drive? Mattie's distracting chatter, that's why.

At least she had fresh water from the creek, and she had the clothes she was wearing. It was not much, but it was something. She just needed to find a place to sit that was out of the sun…and hope she didn't attract the attention of a hungry predator and that she would eventually catch sight of someone passing by.

No problem.

Except it was a problem.

Lassiter's wagon had faded from sight, and not another soul came into view.

For hours, she waited, until the gnawing hunger in her belly got to be too much and she made the decision to leave her post in search of something—anything edible. Not wanting to leave her water source, Alexandra walked along the winding creek for what had to be several hours before coming across some wild berry bushes. She ate several handfuls before she forced herself to stop. Too much of the slightly under-ripe berries was likely to give her stomach cramps.

Feeling a return of energy that had wasted away in the heat of the day, she decided to keep walking. Perhaps she'd eventually come upon a dwelling or some other kind of shelter. But with every mile she walked and every hour that passed, fear and desperation crowded in a bit closer.

Though she had inherited her father's eternal optimism and his stubborn refusal to accept defeat, both became difficult to maintain as the sun started to dip toward the horizon and Alexandra realized she would be spending the night alone in the wilderness. Panic threatened again at that point, but she held it at bay while she searched for a good place to make camp. Without a fire, she would not only be vulnerable to the colder temperatures of night, but she would also have no way to ward off wild animals who might come near.

Feeling helpless and exhausted, she sat down beneath some trees and almost gave in to the despair welling inside her. She thought of her father in Montana—so close yet still so far away. Why on earth had she though it a good idea to leave Boston? How could this trip have gone so wrong?

Tears burned behind her eyelids, but she refused to let them fall.

She would not give up. Somehow, she would make it through the night and tomorrow and the next day. She had to.

Lifting her chin, she watched as the last rays of the sun slipped beneath the horizon. Then she tipped her head back to gaze up at the darkening sky as stars slowly appeared. She had no idea how long she sat like that, but when she looked down again, darkness surrounded her, and for a flashing moment, she forgot where she was.

But the sounds of nature at night quickly brought her back to her full senses.

She was alone in the middle of nowhere.

Then again, maybe not. Suddenly, in the distance, she saw a flicker of orange light. It was small and very

far away, but as she held her breath and watched, the
light grew a bit bigger. Big enough for her to determine it was a campfire.

She was on her feet before she finished the thought.
Fire meant heat. It meant safety and people. Relief made
her steps swift and light as she crossed the darkness, but
as she neared, her pace slowed, and she quieted her
steps. For all her stupidity in trusting Lassiter, she was
not inclined to repeat the lesson. So, she crept carefully
up to the edge of the firelight, hoping to spy a glance at
the manner of person occupying the small camp.

FIVE

By the time Malcolm bedded down the first night out of Rock Springs, he was hungry and ornery, but more than that, he was damn tired. After making only a basic camp, he chewed on some of the jerky he had in his pack before he reclined against his saddle and tipped his hat over his face.

He was nearly asleep—the halfway awake, still-listening kind of sleep he had gotten accustomed to since taking up the mantle of bounty hunter—when he heard a twig snap in the underbrush not far away.

He made no move at the sound. His horse only briefly lifted his head, more in curiosity than fear, so he suspected it was a creature of the two-legged variety rather than a predator on the prowl for a meal.

That didn't mean the person creeping slowing toward Malcolm's camp wasn't dangerous and wouldn't be treated as such. He had developed the habit of sleeping with his gun in hand and was grateful for the weight of it resting atop his thigh beneath his palm.

He waited, giving no sign he was aware of the intruder or that he was awake at all.

And he listened.

Light steps. Slow and deliberate. Hesitant, but curious.

His caution turned to irritation. He doubted the newcomer was a threat, but that didn't mean they were welcome.

"Show yourself," he said, subtly shifting the gun until it was pointed toward the source of the noise.

Though he kept his voice low, the words still hung in the air like a challenge.

Silence was the only response. Whoever approached his camp had stopped moving when he'd spoken. Without shifting from his relaxed position, he tipped the brim of his hat up by an inch or so. Enough for him to scan the brush and shadows that extended past the reach of his low-burning campfire.

Nothing stirred.

"Come on out or I'll come looking for you," he added tersely.

More silence. Then what sounded like a slow inhale followed by a long exhale.

"I will be happy to join you, Mr. Kincaid, if you will please first holster your gun."

"Son-of-a-bitch." Malcolm did not holster his gun, but he did shift the direction it was pointing to one less threatening as he glared at the shadows, waiting for Miss Brighton to make her appearance.

She did so slowly. Her focus was trained on the weapon resting on his thigh as she emerged.

The woman was still dressed in the Eastern getup she'd had on the day before. Her blue skirts were dusty at the hem, but the shirt beneath her matching jacket glowed white in the night. She no longer had the ridiculous hat perched atop her head, and some wispy strands of dark hair had slid free of the twisted-up arrangement to brush against her face. Aside from that very slight bit of dishevelment, she looked as though she were stepping into some high-styled drawing room, rather than a one-man camp in the middle of the Wyoming wilderness.

Keeping a sharp and wary gaze on his Colt, she stepped up to the fire and extended her hands to the modest flames. It looked like her fine gloves had gone the way of her hat.

"Good evening, Mr. Kincaid."

Malcolm curled the corner of his mouth as her formal tone struck a chord somewhere between aggravation and amusement. The amusement surprised him. "What the hell are you doing here?"

She shifted her attention from his gun to his face. "I saw your fire and hoped it belonged to someone generous who might be willing to share the hospitality of their camp."

Malcolm was pretty sure he heard a note of censure in her tone—as though she was trying to say his hospitality left much to be desired. "I don't like company."

The woman flicked a sharp glance toward his gun, still in hand and resting atop the thigh of his outstretched leg. "So I gathered," she stated in clipped tones.

There was some sass in that reply. Malcolm narrowed his gaze. "Where's your escort?"

A pause. Then, "Gone."

Malcolm tensed. "Gone where?"

She looked back to the fire and straightened her posture before answering. "I don't know where. They left."

He took a moment to be sure he'd heard that right, but there was no mistaking the words for what they were. "They left," he repeated.

The fancy Miss Brighton executed a gesture halfway between a dismissive shrug and a frustrated sweep of her hands. "Yes, Mr. Kincaid, they left," she repeated. "This morning, while I took a few personal moments to myself, Mr. Lassiter, his brother, and his brother's wife—though I have some serious doubts those two were married or that they were any relation at all to Mr. Lassiter—decided to take possession of my meager belongings and left me at the side of a creek a few miles from here." She paused then to lift her gaze back to meet his. "Does that clarify my situation enough for you?"

It did.

It was not a surprising tale. Her vulnerability had been obvious to anyone who'd seen her enter the saloon yesterday. She was lucky she hadn't been shot, though it probably would have been a better fate than being left to die in the wilderness.

That an Eastern lady like her had managed to survive the whole day on her own was unexpected. That she barely looked worse for wear was practically unbelievable. That she appeared more angry than terrified was proof of the woman's pure ignorance.

Malcolm propped his thumb under the brim of his hat and lifted it a bit more. "You've been out here—alone—all day?"

"Not by choice, I assure you." Her reply was muttered from between tightly clenched teeth. The woman wasn't angry—she was damned near furious and doing her best not to show it.

"You're lucky to be alive."

That brought her gaze sharply back to him. "You think I don't know that?" she snapped.

Malcolm didn't think a reply was necessary. He could feel the woman winding up for a tirade. Seeing no point in trying to stop her, he eased back into a more comfortable position to wait it out.

She swept her arm out to encompass the expansive darkness around them. "Those…those cowardly thieves left me to die out here. For what? A handful of traveling money, some clothing, and a few personal possessions that won't matter a whit to them." Though she didn't shout, each word got more and more weighted with her fury. "If they expected to find a wealth in jewels or sacks of cash hidden in my valise, they'll be sorely disappointed. Still, it was all I had. I can't believe I was such a fool to trust them. And you," she added sharply, swinging her bright eyes back to him. "This all could have been avoided if you'd just agreed to escort me yourself."

Malcolm took a deep breath. The woman's wrath was something to behold, not unlike a summer thunderstorm sweeping in from out of nowhere, but he was not about to stand for having it directed toward him.

"What makes you think you'd be any safer with me?"

Her eyes widened at the hint of menace he purposely inserted into his voice. She folded her arms across her chest in a protective gesture, but then she lifted her chin and met his shadowed gaze with a defiant stare.

"If you intended to…attack me"—her voice caught

on the phrase before she powered through it—"you've already had plenty of opportunity."

Malcolm slowly curved his mouth in a smile. "Maybe I like my women warmed up a bit first."

She glanced toward the fire in front of her. It was just a brief flick of her gaze. In less than half a second, she was back to staring at him. "You wouldn't," she declared quickly, but her weight shifted in preparation for flight.

Malcolm waited long enough to see the wariness spread across her pert little features before he replied, "I might."

SIX

Alexandra was frozen in place.

Five years was a long time to be away from the lawlessness of this land where she had grown up, but it was not so long that she'd forgotten how some men tended to take what they wanted when there was no one around to tell them they couldn't—and often, even when there was.

She was proud of having managed to keep from being totally incapacited by the sight of the gun in his hand when she'd first stepped into his camp. Her unnatural reaction to his Colt was something she needed to get past. Her rational mind understood that, at least, but memories tied to terror had a way of getting past rational thought. She had to be stronger than her past. That she'd managed to speak through the fear that had gripped her was progress and had been possible partly because she hadn't believed Kincaid had any intention of harming her.

At first, she hadn't recognized the man by the fire as Kincaid. All she had seen was a large man reclining against his saddle, looking as though he were familiar with life on the trail. It certainly wasn't enough to determine if he was an honorable character or not. Although, considering her recent experience, she wasn't too sure she should trust an opinion based on appearances anyway. She'd stood in indecision, debating whether she should back away and take her chances alone, when he'd spoken in that low, growling voice she recalled from the saloon. Her immediate reaction had been one of immeasurable relief.

Now standing at the fire while he stared at her from the shadows beneath his wide-brimmed hat, his threatening words still hanging between them, Alexandra couldn't move. Not to look away, not to run, not even to speak.

Though Kincaid remained on the ground, reclining in a deceptively lazy fashion against his saddle, there was nothing restful in his manner. One leg was bent, with his boot planted firmly in the dirt, the other outstretched. His right hand still held his gun atop his thigh. Her attention fell to the Colt, getting caught for long seconds on how the firelight flickered over the hard metal, before she forced her gaze away.

She shifted her attention cautiously up along his torso. The strength across his chest and in the width of his shoulders was not the slightest bit muted by his thick leather coat. A physical readiness emanated from his person. He could be on his feet and within reach of her in a second if he chose to.

His head was tipped at a casual yet arrogant angle as he waited for her to finish her assessment. He had visited a barber since she'd seen him the day before. His hair still brushed past his collar, but his face had been shaved clean. Without the thick beard, the harsh angles of his face stood out even more. He didn't look a whole lot more civilized without the scruff of beard. Maybe even less so. It was an impression that was enhanced by the unexpected smile that curved his wide mouth.

Another wave of fiery heat rushed through Alexandra, making her belly swirl uncomfortably and her skin grow flushed.

No.

She would not be intimidated.

That's what he wanted. It's what he was trying to do with his dark, muttered threat. But Alexandra Brighton was made of sterner stuff than that. Her father had made sure of it before he'd sent her away.

Malcolm Kincaid was a dangerous man. There was no doubt he knew exactly how to use that Colt, and had done so frequently. His size and strength and raw masculinity were frightening in the extreme, when Alexandra had gotten so used to the refined physicality and controlled manners of Boston's upper class. This man disturbed her in a way she had never experienced before…but she did not believe he would hurt her.

She wasn't sure how she knew that. She just did. Some instinct inside her whispered that she could trust this man.

She decided to call his bluff.

"You won't," she finally replied and was pleased to hear her voice come out strong and confident.

His smile slid away, and his mouth straightened into a harsh line. The swift shift in his expression sent another trickle of caution across her nape. "You take a mighty big risk, lady."

"It seems I have no choice, Mr. Kincaid."

Everything about him was hard and unwelcoming as they stared at each other in tense silence. Though her body buzzed with anxiety and impatience, Alexandra refused to speak first.

"I'll take you to the next town. That's it."

Her relief was overwhelming, but she responded with only a short nod of her head.

Clearly deciding that was the end of the conversation, Kincaid slid lower against his saddle, leaned his head back, and drew his hat down over his face. The hand holding the gun still rested atop his thigh.

Alexandra found her gaze ensnared by the weapon once again as her thoughts grasped unbidden on a vision of red soaking through faded denim. She heard ragged gasps for breath and saw accusation, pain, and fear glittering from pale eyes. An icy chill swept down her spine, but she forced herself to continue staring at the gun, pushing past the terrifying memories. She reminded herself that out here, the gun was a tool of survival, not a promise of violence.

But still, it took several long minutes to bring her fear back to the point where she could look away. She suspected Kincaid had used that gun more than most people. He was a bounty hunter, an extension of the law, so it would make sense for him to possess an exceptional level of comfort with his gun.

Except he looked more like a gunfighter than a lawman, and she wasn't sure whether or not that was a good thing.

Either way, something had led her back to him, and it felt an awful lot like fate.

Finally warmed to the point that she was willing to step away from the fire, she settled down near enough to still benefit from its warmth and light. Propping her back against a tree, she brought her knees up against her chest and tucked her skirts securely around her ankles.

She doubted she would sleep much, but the rest itself would be welcome after walking as far as she had that day.

She glanced over at her reluctant companion, her gaze drawn to him against her will.

There was nothing at all soft or gentle about Malcolm Kincaid. He was made up of tough sinew and quiet, seething strength. She could see it even now. She had met men like him when she had been young. Men shaped by the land and by hardships and challenges no one from the East could ever fathom.

Though her father had grown to manhood in the luxury and comfort of his family's Boston mansion, he had been re-formed by his experiences out West. And he had raised his only daughter to appreciate a man and woman's ability to adapt and change and strengthen.

Randolph Brighton had faced unrelenting hardships as he carved out a new life for himself and his daughter. Yet he had always made a point to learn from his failures and never lost his idealistic optimism and love for adventure. Kincaid's manner suggested his experiences, whatever they may have been, had affected him very differently.

Rather than being molded by the environment, she fancied he had instead taken on its very characteristics. He looked to be made of the same hard, unforgiving

elements that shaped the Rockies. He was as cold and
distant as the starlit sky. In just the very brief interactions she'd had with him, she knew instinctively that
he possessed a relentless devotion to isolation. She
suspected his harsh exterior was designed specifically
to preserve that.

She understood that desire. The need to retain a
certain amount of distance from others.

Alexandra rested her head on the arms folded atop
her knees. She watched the steady rise and fall of
Kincaid's chest until her eyelids drifted over her gaze.

One thing was certain: he was not a man to do
anything he didn't expressly choose to do, yet he
had—reluctantly—agreed to see her to the next town.

She'd have to convince him that wasn't enough.

Malcolm waited until the woman was asleep before he
shifted his position to one that was more comfortable.

Her quiet surprised him. He'd expected to hear an
unloading of complaints once she'd gotten his agreement to help. But she never once asked for the use of
his bedroll, or for food, or anything else. She just took
a seat against the tree and settled her wide blue eyes
on him until she couldn't keep them open anymore.

She'd never suspected he'd been watching her as she
stared at him. Had no idea how her blatant interest had
tightened his muscles until they ached and made his
body harden with a wave of unbidden physical interest.
He'd had to grind his teeth to control the reaction.

This was not a woman he had any intention of

lusting after. Just because her pure blue gaze made his skin feel tight, and that damned lower lip of hers made his throat ache with the desire to draw it into his mouth, did not change the fact that he had no interest in distractions.

She was damned attractive. Too attractive to be roaming across the country with no protection. But he was not about to take on that role. She didn't belong with him any more than she belonged west of the Mississippi. He had something far too important to occupy his focus and was not going to find himself responsible for someone who was likely to be more trouble than she was worth.

She was lucky she'd made it this far and probably had no idea how utterly defenseless she was. It would've been entirely within reason for her to have shown up at his fire in a state of terrified panic after wandering about by herself all day.

Fury made his blood run hot as he thought of the Lassiter fellow. He really hoped he'd have the pleasure of running into that man again someday to give him a lesson in Western justice.

SEVEN

Alexandra was awakened as her stomach cramped in painful want of food.

The lack of anything more substantial than the couple of handfuls of berries she had eaten the day before was making itself known.

However, her hunger was not so intense that it distracted from her stiff, aching limbs or the soreness of her bottom from sitting on the hard earth through the night. She shifted her body slowly to unwind her arms and lift her head. A painful protest shot through the muscles along her spine.

She bit her lip as she glanced about the camp.

She was alone.

Before panic set in at the thought that Kincaid may have changed his mind about helping her, she saw his coat draped over his saddle where it still rested on the other side of the smoldering campfire, and the heavenly scent of coffee came from the small metal pot set in the coals.

He had not gone far.

Carefully rising to her feet, Alexandra tipped her

face toward the sun that was already warming the earth, though it was not yet high on the horizon. Reaching her hands above her head and arching her spine in a long stretch, she considered the time of year and estimated it to be about seven o'clock, then smiled to herself over the assumption.

It had been a long time since she had judged time by the path of the sun. She had no idea if her guess was accurate.

It was early, anyway. That much was clear.

After indulging in another body-stimulating stretch, she turned in place and nearly jumped from her skin. A choked little squeak of surprise escaped from her throat.

Kincaid stood barely four steps away.

His shirtsleeves had been rolled up to his elbows, showing tanned skin sprinkled with hair. The neck of his shirt was wet, as was his longish hair. He held his brimmed hat in his hand, so Alexandra got her first unimpeded look at his face.

The harsh handsomeness of the man had her breath stopping quick.

The hard edge of his jaw led her gaze to the very masculine shape of his mouth, then to the proud line of his nose and the heavy, brooding scowl that hovered over his gray eyes.

His strong, steady focus hit her like a blast of... something she couldn't quite define. It was hot and cold at once, a fiery chill that struck deep into her bones and sinew.

Before she could analyze it further, he made a low sound that rose from his chest in a quiet sort of grunt.

"Regretting your decision to approach my fire?" he asked, then turned and strode to his saddle.

Alexandra remained in place, struck dumb by the interaction. A heated blush rose in her cheeks as she wondered what she had revealed in her expression to prompt his comment.

"You've got a few minutes. Then we head out."

His words spurred her into action, and she took two steps toward the nearest bushes. Then she stopped and looked back over her shoulder.

He was already lifting the saddle to carry it to where his horse stood not far away. It took her a moment to drag her attention away from the shifting bunch and stretch of muscles beneath his shirt. But then her gaze dipped downward to the firm curve of his rear and his strong legs as he strode away from her.

If not for the urgency of nature's call, she might have stood there all morning, watching the man move.

She'd clearly gone a bit soft in the head.

Clearing her throat in an attempt to also clear her muddled mind, she asked, "You're not planning on leaving while I step away, are you?"

Kincaid did not bother to slow the rhythmic movements of his task as he cast her a dark glance over his shoulder.

No words were necessary. His scowl said it all.

Alexandra lifted her eyebrows in an equally wordless response, as if to say *do you blame me?*

He gave a jerk of his head, indicating she should go about her business, before giving her his back as he pulled the cinch tight.

She almost smiled at the bounty hunter's

determination to be as brusque and rude as possible. It didn't bother her any. In fact, she found it sort of humorous.

Still, she had no intention of pushing him when there was no point. She was in as much of a hurry as he was to be on her way.

When she returned to camp, he wordlessly handed her a tin cup filled with rapidly cooling coffee.

Alexandra muttered a quick thank you before she sipped, then gulped down the bitter brew. The coffee helped to warm her stiff muscles and awaken her sleep-muddled mind. Once finished, she walked to the creek to rinse out the cup and splash some of the cool water on her face.

It was still early, but the sun was making its presence known as the morning warmed quickly under its rays.

Kincaid had not bothered to put his coat back on, but had rolled it up and secured it behind his saddle instead. Alexandra watched the play of muscles through his body as he swung effortlessly up onto his horse. The sight of him sitting tall on the bay gelding—his shirtsleeves rolled up, his hat drawn low, a red bandana tied loosely around his throat—made her heart stutter.

He was an impressive specimen of a man. The perfect choice to be her guide and escort. She just had to get him to agree to that fact.

As she stood there, he urged his horse forward a few steps and held his hand down to her.

She offered him the empty cup, and he gave an odd little quirk of his brow as he slipped it into his saddle pack. Then he offered his hand to her again.

"Swing up behind me."

Alexandra looked at his capable, callused palm and wondered how it would feel to place her hand in his. Then she shook her head as she lifted her gaze. "I can't."

"You don't know how to sit a horse?"

The contempt in his voice was annoying. Enough to chase off the last of Alexandra's trepidation. As amusing as his rudeness might be, she was not accustomed to such constant derision. She swept her hand down in a wide gesture toward her many-layered and artfully draping skirts. "This skirt is not designed for riding astride."

"Hike it up."

"No."

He stared hard at her.

She stared hard back. This was a battle he would not win. It was not that Alexandra had a problem with showing a little leg—she had not exactly been raised a modest miss, no matter how she seemed now. But if she lifted the skirts high enough to sit astride, the layers of material in her gown would hinder her ability to keep her seat. It simply wouldn't work. She'd just as likely end up tumbling back over the horse's rump to the ground.

She would be happy to explain all of that to Kincaid if he bothered to ask, which she knew he wouldn't. So instead, the moment became a test of wills. If he couldn't trust her assessment of her own limitations, he'd have to deal with her stubbornness instead.

She could see the muscles work in his jaw as he ground his back teeth together and shifted his gaze to scan the surrounding countryside.

He was debating leaving her behind. She could see it in his sharp eyes.

She bit her lip, doubt overwhelming the brief flash of fire. She shouldn't have been so confrontational. Hadn't she spent the last five years learning how to curb that deeply ingrained impulse?

Aunt Judith had worked very hard to instill in Alexandra the gracious and temperate virtues of a modest, polite young lady. The finishing school had done the rest to smooth away the last of Alexandra's rough edges and wild impulses.

For some reason, this man just brought it all back.

After a moment, Kincaid turned to untie the coat from behind his saddle. He placed it in front of him instead to pad the area around the pommel and saddle horn in the V of his legs. Then he reached a hand out to her again. "Come on, then."

Realizing this was the only concession she'd be likely to get from the man, Alexandra put her hand in his. His grip was warm and secure around hers as he lifted her off the ground with barely any effort at all. She landed sideways in front of him with a soft grunt at the swift force of the maneuver and teetered for a bit before she got her balance.

Kincaid's arm was braced strong at her back while her legs fell over one of his thighs, and the saddle horn dug hard into her hip despite the extra padding he'd provided.

And seemingly, all around her, was him. His masculine scent, his strength, his heat. And his irritation.

It made her nervous, how intensely she could feel him—all of him. Her pulse quickened to a reckless pace as her stomach tightened and her skin tingled. She shoved aside her reaction. She was here now, in his lap, and unless she wished to walk to the next town, it was where she'd stay. There was no point in being skittish.

Alexandra squirmed as she tried to fit her bottom more comfortably in the limited space. The horse shifted beneath her, and she could practically hear Kincaid grinding his teeth in impatience, but she was not about to ride however many hours with a bruise forming on her hip because she had not bothered to adjust her position.

Bracing one hand on the hard surface of Kincaid's thigh, she lifted and turned just enough to bend her right knee over the saddle horn, which settled her rear more firmly into the V of Kincaid's lap and succeeded in making her feel much more secure on her perch once she tested it by shifting her weight a bit from side to side.

"Are you done?" His tone was tense, making it impossible to miss the irritation underlying each word.

His obvious aggravation helped to chase away the last of her self-consciousness at being tucked so intimately against his body.

"Yes, much better," she said brightly, only because she knew the happy tone would annoy him.

She really needed to stop doing that. Her temerity had always gotten her into trouble as a child. There had been a time when her father had encouraged such willfulness, though the older she'd gotten, the less he'd seemed to tolerate the fact that she preferred to speak her mind and do things her own way.

She couldn't imagine what he'd think of her leaving Boston as she had. He could be furious. He might even send her straight back East as soon as she arrived in Montana.

That thought had her stomach clenching with uncertainty. She hated that thoughts of her father and home had the ability to make her feel that way. It was part of the reason she *had* to go back, before she went through with her marriage and was trapped in Boston—and the person she had been forced to become in Boston—for good.

Kincaid kept his horse to a slow and steady pace. He had no intention of putting unnecessary strain on Deuce. The woman in front of him was small by most standards, but over time, the added burden would limit the gelding's endurance.

The sooner Malcolm could get the stubborn woman off his hands—and out of his lap—the better.

She had sent his body into a riot when she'd squirmed into place. She fit surprisingly well once she'd adjusted her seat, but that adjusting had nearly brought a halt to the whole thing. The fool woman didn't even know what she'd done to him when she'd planted her hand flat on his thigh and turned herself until her rear end fit snug to his groin. It took all his willpower to keep his rush of lust from becoming obvious beneath her gently rounded bottom. Even her many skirts and petticoats wouldn't have been able to disguise his reaction.

The smell of her alone was enough to make his belly clench. As soon as he'd lifted her up onto the horse, the scent of summer flowers had come wafting from her person. It wasn't a heavy, cloying smell like some dance hall girls wore, but something lightly teasing. It mingled subtly with that essence intrinsic to females and had his body tightening in an instant.

Kincaid often went months without a woman while he tracked down a bounty. He'd learned to curb his needs for the sake of his work. He was not one to spend time in a whorehouse, and he didn't exactly make many lady friends in his line of work. His interactions with females were brief and occurred only when convenient.

There had been a time in his younger days when Malcolm had been known as a charmer. He'd enjoyed the flirtation and anticipation of courtship, and the ladies had enjoyed *him*. That had been a long time ago. The day he'd found his brother's dead body, he'd made a vow to be vigilant and focused on seeking justice

Nothing else mattered.

But as the weight and warmth of the woman in his arms reminded him of how long it had been since he'd held anything so lovely, keeping his focus proved to be a difficult endeavor. Further proof that women were distractions.

And distractions were unacceptable.

They rode in silence for more than an hour. The only sounds were the woods around them, the creak of the saddle beneath them, and the occasional insistent grumble of the woman's stomach.

Kincaid wondered how long she'd endure the discomfort before asking for food.

He had some jerky in his pack, a can of beans he would have heated up at camp the night before if he hadn't been so tired, and some two-day-old biscuits. He didn't often travel with much, as he preferred to hunt for his food. Despite her obvious hunger, however, she didn't once complain.

Stubborn might be an understatement for this woman.

The farther they went into the morning, the more Malcolm became convinced that she wasn't going to ask for food at all.

Damned fool.

Didn't she know she needed her strength to make it across this rough country on horseback? She should have at least asked for water by now. She'd end up starving herself out of ignorance. That or she'd grow faint, lose her seat, and end up falling from the horse. Then he'd not only have a helpless woman on his hands, but also an injured one.

She was disgustingly ignorant of the many reasons she wasn't prepared for the kind of trek she intended to take. She'd be best off going back where she'd come from.

When her stomach grumbled for the fiftieth time, Malcolm gave a grunt of annoyance as he reached into one of the saddle packs.

She leaned forward when she felt him moving and looked over her shoulder at him in curiosity.

Malcolm was struck hard by those big eyes of hers, so close he could see the darker, cobalt-colored ring that surrounded all that shining blue. And when she noticed the jerky he had in his hand, the look of utter longing had him tensing from head to toe as thoughts of something a far cry from *food* came to mind.

"You trying to starve yourself?" he asked gruffly. "You should've asked for something to eat before we left camp."

Her fine black brows tugged low over her eyes as she met his gaze. "I wasn't sure you had anything to share. You may not believe me, Mr. Kincaid, but it is not my wish to be an undue burden."

He snorted as he handed her a piece of jerky.

"You know, you also could have *offered* me something earlier," she noted before she took a hearty bite of the tough dried meat.

Malcolm refused to acknowledge that point.

"Just how far is the next town?" she asked after a short while.

She was facing forward again, and before Malcolm answered, he untied his canteen and handed it to her, knowing the saltiness of the jerky would make her thirsty.

She muttered a thanks, and Malcolm watched as she brought the canteen to her lips and tipped her head back to take a drink. Wayward strands of dark hair brushed against his chin, making him breathe deep as her flowery scent assaulted him once again. For something so subtle, it packed a big punch.

Handing the canteen back to him, she repeated, "You said you would take me to the next town, right?"

"We'll reach South Pass City by nightfall." He took a drink from the canteen before adding, "If we keep a steady pace and don't overburden the horse."

"And what will I find in South Pass City?"

Now the woman seemed intent on talking.

Malcolm never used to mind such things. He had been as social as the next guy. But spending so many years alone as he crisscrossed the western territories had made him rusty.

He just didn't see much point anymore in getting to know people. He was never in one place long enough to bother. And he sure as hell didn't intend to be in this woman's company any longer than necessary.

"What you'd expect, I suppose. Hotel, stage stop, telegraph office." To tell the truth, he hadn't been through South Pass City in several years. On his last time through, the place had already started showing signs of a dwindling population after the gold that had brought everyone to the little town was no longer so plentiful.

"I see." The two words were quiet yet seemed to resonate with trepidation.

That's right. The Lassiter fellow stole her belongings, which included her money.

He should keep his mouth shut. It wasn't his problem. *She* wasn't his problem. "I'll get you a room and a meal. Beyond that, you're on your own."

"You would do that?" The smile she tossed over her shoulder had him tensing the muscles in his thighs. That was exactly why he hadn't wanted to say anything. He didn't want her gratitude. Didn't want any more of those damned enticing smiles.

He clenched his teeth to keep from answering in case he spontaneously offered up his horse too.

"Do you think I might find someone in South Pass City willing to take me up to Helena?"

He shrugged. Not his problem.

"Unless you've decided to change your mind..." she led with a cajoling note in her voice. "You will be paid well once we arrive, and anything you spend will be reimbursed, I can promise you that. Not to mention, you *are* going in that direction already."

Malcolm sat straight in the saddle, his gaze trained forward over her shoulder as he resisted the urge to shake his head in exasperation. The woman was persistent. "If there is so much money waiting in Montana, why not have some wired to you?"

She stiffened, and after a long pause replied, "I can't."

That was it. No further explanation was forthcoming. Malcolm did his best not to find that curious.

After a bit, she picked up again on trying to persuade him. "You would hardly even know I was with you. We would just need another horse and a few more supplies. The trip could be made quite easily."

"You know nothing about these territories if you think to say something like that," he argued.

She lifted one brow. "You might be surprised, you know," she suggested lightly. "I could prove to be an asset on the journey."

Malcolm couldn't hold back his snort of disbelief.

Her expression darkened. "Are you this dismissive and distrustful of everyone, Mr. Kincaid? Or have I unwittingly done something to reserve that honor all for myself? Is there some reason you don't want to take me with you?"

Fully exasperated now, Malcolm swept his hat off his head to run a hand back through his hair before resetting the brim low enough to shadow his eyes.

"Listen, lady," he said in a low and measured tone, "I told you I ain't no escort. I make my way alone. Period. Besides that, the western territories are no place for someone like you. It's no place for *most* people desperate enough to find themselves here. I'm just trying to do you a favor. Your best bet would be to head back to wherever you came from and give up on reaching Montana altogether."

She stared at him with her pert chin raised stubbornly and her spine straight and stiff. The sun had already started to pinken her fair skin, and a fine sheen of moisture coated the bit of her slim neck that showed above her buttoned-up collar. Her hair looked about ready to tumble down from its pins, but likely held on for fear of offending the woman with its desire for freedom.

She looked exactly like what she was: a prim little Eastern lady stuck in the middle of Wyoming Territory with no clue as to the dangers surrounding her.

He stood by every bit of what he'd said.

After a moment, she blinked, and her head tilted to one side. An odd little smile crept over her full mouth.

Malcolm stomped the urge to steal a kiss from those damn lips. He would *not* lust after this woman.

"I do believe those were the most words you've managed to string together since the moment I met you."

Malcolm frowned. "You'd be smart to heed what I say."

Her blue gaze slid down and to the side. She sighed. "Perhaps. You likely won't be the only person to think so. But this is something I need to do." She flicked her eyes back to his. "It's something I will do with or without you, Mr. Kincaid, though I do believe I will be much better off *with* you."

"That proves how little you know me," he said curtly as he nudged Deuce into a trot that had the woman straightening her seat and keeping her mouth shut for another blessed stretch of time.

EIGHT

THE MILES CONTINUED TO PASS BY WHILE THEY KEPT to a pace designed for endurance rather than speed, and Alexandra anxiously considered her options. If she didn't convince Kincaid to take her with him, she would once again be stranded, just as she had been when Lassiter had left her at the creek. A town wasn't a whole lot better when she had no funds to support herself.

Alexandra considered Kincaid's suggestion of sending a telegram to her father and asking for his help, but swiftly rejected the idea.

She was making this journey on her own. That was the stupid point of it. To prove that her life still belonged to her. To discover who she really was.

Alexandra had arrived in Boston five years ago at the age of fifteen, unknowingly desperate for direction and assurance. Life with her father had been an endless adventure, while life with Aunt Judith was based on wealth, privilege, and an infinite list of rules.

Rules for behavior, deportment, appearance. Rules for when to speak, how to speak, and who to speak to. Everything Judith Reed did, from the smallest task to the grandest plan, was performed with one goal in mind—to become accepted by the highest, most respected, and most discretely powerful social circle in the city.

The structure and routine of her aunt's household had been a comfort to Alexandra at a time when she had become unsure of herself and the world at large. Coming from a life where the only rules were what was necessary for survival, the constant reminders on how to behave properly, how to speak, sit, walk, dress, and manage all other aspects of daily life felt like a reprieve. She didn't have to make any decisions for herself or face any consequences of impulsive actions. A part of her had been quite happy to leave the reckless girl she had once been out West to become someone new.

Under her aunt's expert tutelage, Alexandra had been reshaped into a lady of fine manners and perfect deportment. A lady worthy of a marriage proposal from a gentleman belonging to one of the oldest, wealthiest, and most respected families in the entire state of Massachusetts.

Thinking of Peter Shaw triggered a wave of guilt. She couldn't imagine what he would think of her sudden departure, but she stood by her decision to return to the land of her youth, perhaps for the last time. She had to know who she was before she could figure out who she could someday become.

Despite the problems she'd faced since her train had pulled into the station in Rock Springs, she already felt as if she could breathe more deeply. Just the simple act of riding horseback through the wilderness made her more relaxed and comfortable than she'd ever been at any of the balls or dinner parties she'd attended in Boston.

Even when she took into consideration the fact that she was in the reluctant company of a curt and stubbornly silent bounty hunter.

A smile curved her lips at the thought of how easily annoyed he was. If she hadn't been so desperate for him to take her all the way to Montana, she might have delighted in seeing how far she could push him.

She wasn't sure why he was so adamant in his refusal. It seemed a simple enough thing. Of course, he had made it clear that he expected her to be more burden than companion on the journey. She supposed she couldn't blame him for that. He would have no reason to suspect she was anything other than the tenderfoot Eastern lady she appeared to be.

And she wasn't exactly sure why she didn't just tell him of the life she'd had before she'd been sent to her aunt. Maybe because that identity—those aspects of herself—had been tucked so securely away for so long she wasn't sure how much still existed.

A heavy sigh released from her chest and her shoulders fell. She didn't straighten, even though it caused her spine to curve back against Kincaid's chest. In all honesty, the contact felt nice, especially now.

Uncertainty. Fear. Helplessness. The three things Alexandra hated feeling the most. And she'd experienced all three since leaving Boston.

Perhaps the only thing this journey home would succeed in proving was that she truly didn't belong out here, exactly as Kincaid had declared.

Another sigh escaped, and this time she felt Kincaid stiffen as her posture softened even more into the curve of his body. His thighs tensed. His arm braced against her ribs as he held the reins straightened, and he sat just a bit taller, as though in becoming all hardness and resistance he could discourage her from finding comfort against him.

She smiled again as her eyelids drooped over her blurring gaze.

Too late.

The lack of sleep from the night before, the steady rhythm of the horse, and the security of her position in front of Kincaid lulled her into a state of relaxation she could not resist. Instead, she sank into it further, if only because she knew it would annoy the bounty hunter beyond belief.

Her last thought was regret that she would sleep through his inevitable irritation.

Malcolm knew the instant she fell asleep. Her breath slipped into a deep and even rhythm as her body became pliant in the circle of his arms and her head dropped back against his shoulder. He had known it was coming, had sensed her slackening awareness.

The only reason he didn't urge her to stay awake was because he could tell himself he was looking forward to the reprieve from her unwelcome chatter.

She still thought to convince him to take her with him.

She was going to be disappointed.

He shifted in the saddle and adjusted her in front of him so she settled more fully against his chest. It made it easier to ensure she wouldn't tumble from the horse, but also forced him to feel the steady rise and fall of her breath as her ribs expanded against him. He didn't want to notice how she fit so snugly in the curve of his body or how the scent of her tormented him with every breath he took. But he did notice, and he was not unaffected. It'd been a long time since he'd been close to someone so soft, so feminine. And even longer since he'd just held someone in his arms.

It called up a bittersweet ache inside him that he didn't want to acknowledge. Not now. Maybe not ever.

He could manage one day with the woman. As long as he kept them to a steady pace, they'd reach South Pass City by nightfall. From there, she was on her own.

NINE

ALEXANDRA WOKE JUST AS KINCAID BROUGHT THE horse to a gentle halt.

She blinked a few times in rapid succession to clear the sleep from her eyes as she straightened in the saddle, realizing immediately that she had been resting rather intimately in Kincaid's arms.

And that he had allowed it.

A faint flush warmed her cheeks as she glanced about to determine just how long she'd slept.

They had stopped along a river bank at a spot where the winding waterway curved in a deep C, creating an oasis of greenery. A few tall-standing cottonwood trees created a shady spot that looked refreshing and lovely. The sun was high in the sky, and judging by the state of her hunger, she would guess several hours had passed since she'd snacked on the jerky.

"Hold on," Kincaid muttered as he dismounted from the horse before reaching to grasp her about the waist. His eyes were sharp, his brows tugged low over his gaze, and his mouth was drawn into a harsh line.

Nothing new there.

She braced her hands on his shoulders as he brought her to the ground. Impressions of his solid, wide-shouldered strength, the warmth of his body beneath the cotton of his shirt, and the ease with which he lifted her from the horse combined to make her momentarily light-headed. Or perhaps it was the scent of him—male and natural—that made her feel so very feminine by comparison.

A breath caught in her throat, and she tipped her chin back to look at him, but as soon as her feet touched earth, he released her and her hands fell to her sides. She felt an instant loss at the broken connection as he reached for the horse's reins and walked away, leading it to the water.

After taking a moment to regain her equilibrium, Alexandra followed him to the river's edge. It was a slow, meandering channel, but the water was clear and fresh. Lowering herself to her knees in the grass, she leaned forward and cupped her hands in the cool water to take a drink. The act brought back memories of splashing and swimming in similar rivers when she'd been much younger. She smiled and tipped her face up to the August sun. The heat of the day had continued to strengthen while she had slept, and perspiration had dampened the layers of her clothing.

She wished she could strip down to her undergarments and wade into the water to wash away the sweat and sleep and worry that still clung to her. It's what she would have done as a child.

Instead, she settled for rolling up the sleeves of her gown and releasing a couple of buttons at her throat. Aunt Judith would have gone into conniptions over

Alexandra's blatant display of impropriety. A lady should never reveal so much of her skin in mixed company.

She slid a glance to where Kincaid crouched at the water's edge to refill his canteen. He wasn't likely to be offended by the sight of her bare arms and a glimpse of collarbone.

The sluicing of cool water up her arms and the splashes she brought to the back of her neck helped to relieve much of her discomfort, though she still would have been grateful for clothing that consisted of significantly fewer layers. Expecting to travel by train and stage, she had worn her best traveling outfit. Her stolen valise had contained similar attire. It would have been smarter to bring clothing more appropriate to the land she intended to travel through, but she had thought to impress her father by showing him what a lady she'd become.

None of that mattered now. She was likely to be in a frightful state by the time she reached Helena.

Shaking her head, she rose to her feet with a sigh and smoothed her hands over her hair. The chignon continued to loosen, and several strands had slipped free to fall against her face and the back of her neck. She did her best to smooth it all back, but it stuck to her damp skin.

With a mutter of annoyance, she gave up. What was the point?

After filling his canteen, Kincaid had moved back to his horse to rifle through one of the saddlebags. After a moment, he pulled out the jerky and stuck a piece between his teeth before turning to offer some to Alexandra.

She stepped forward and took the small hunk of salty dried meat, offering a smile of gratitude as she did so.

Kincaid's perpetually scowling face did not alter. He bit off a chunk of the jerky and began to chew as he turned back to the saddlebag.

With a sigh, Alexandra said lightly, "You might try to lighten up a bit, Mr. Kincaid, or I will start to think you have a serious issue against me."

His shoulders pulled back. Just a bit. "You're welcome to think that."

Humph. So much for teasing the man into a more pleasant mood.

Though she was insightful enough not to take Kincaid's attitude personally, since it was apparent that it was simply his nature to be curt, it still stung to be so blithely dismissed.

Retreating to the shade beneath one of the cottonwoods, she eased herself down to the grass with her legs outstretched and began to pull on the jerky with her teeth. It was tough, but tasty enough to be satisfying after going hours with no food. She looked around, wondering if there might be something she could add to the little meal, but she did not recognize anything edible.

Kincaid's bay gelding appeared to disagree as he finished drinking and moved off to nibble on some of the longer grass growing nearby.

Unable to keep from looking his way, Alexandra watched as Kincaid crouched once again at the water's edge. He had dunked his bandana in the water and now tied it back around his neck. The wet cotton immediately soaked the collar of his shirt. Alexandra wondered if more rivulets of water ran down his back beneath the material where she couldn't see. She imagined little trails of cooling water running in paths down a deeply muscled spine, skin tanned by exposure to the sun.

When he straightened from his crouch and rose to his full height with a long, unfurling stretch, Alexandra didn't even try to stop her gaze from falling to where his dark, fitted trousers formed to firm buttocks and hard, masculine thighs.

Her lips parted as heat that had nothing to do with the sun flooded her system.

Of course, Kincaid turned toward her at just that moment. Catching her staring at him, he came to a halt and arched a brow in his first display of an emotion other than irritation or impatience.

She didn't know quite what that arched brow conveyed—curiosity? amusement?—but it triggered a rush of self-awareness that warmed her cheeks even more. She quickly glanced down to brush some grass off her skirts.

When Kincaid walked toward her, she refused to look up at him until she knew her brief flare of embarrassment had been contained and she didn't have some moon-eyed expression on her face. She was not accustomed to being caught off guard, but this man seemed to do it easily.

The bounty hunter leaned his back against the trunk of another one of the trees and took his hat off, but he did not sit.

"This is only a short stop," he clarified. "We'll continue on in a bit."

"Of course. I understand you want to be rid of me as soon as possible." Alexandra's tone had gone stiff to conceal her inner discomfort.

He did not refute her, and disappointment mixed in with her distress. Why should she care what he thought of her? She tugged off another bite of jerky to distract herself.

It didn't work.

The man drew far too much of her attention.

What she needed to be doing was picking his brain for whatever she could find that might get him to help her.

Gazing out toward the river, she forced a more conversational tone. "Where in Montana are you going, Mr. Kincaid?"

"Not your business, Miss Brighton." Though it was the first time she'd heard him say her name, it did not come out sounding at all friendly.

Wrinkling her nose, she thought a moment, then changed tactics. "Are you on a job?"

His response was a curt grunt.

She glanced aside at him. "A bounty? Are you heading to Montana on the trail of a bounty?"

Something dark and sharp flashed behind his eyes as he kept his gaze angled straight forward. If she had hoped to warm him to her, it seemed she might have chosen the exact wrong thing to ask him.

"No," he replied in a voice that was as hard as his expression. "It is not a bounty."

Despite the warnings of her intuition urging her to let it go, Alexandra was compelled to know more. "What, then?" she asked, half wary of his reply.

Her fear was validated as he answered, "I am going north to kill a man."

Alexandra was stunned by the blunt admission. She saw the truth of his statement in the flat steel of his gaze, in the way his pulse beat heavily in his throat, and his gun hand twitched as though he were already imagining the cold revolver against his palm.

An odd sensation rolled through Alexandra as she sat looking up at the man. Though he leaned against the tree in an almost casual fashion, there was a constant air of strength and power in him. It was obvious in the width of his shoulders, the corded muscles of his forearms, the taut length of his legs. And in the harsh angles of his features and the deep-set eyes that sparked with danger.

The sight of him in that moment made the muscles along her spine tense while her belly fluttered strangely. "Does he deserve to die?" she asked just above a whisper. She hadn't intended to say anything. The words just slid from her lips without conscious intention.

The question drew his focus back to her, and as the full blast of his stare met hers, the flutter in her belly spread out to her fingers and toes in a fierce, tingling rush.

"He does."

TEN

THE NEXT FEW HOURS WENT BY AT A FASTER PACE AS Kincaid seemed even more determined to get to town—and get Alexandra off his hands.

They did not eat much throughout the day, and she suspected it was likely due to Kincaid not wanting to take the extra time to stop and hunt for something more substantial than the jerky and some dried biscuits he later pulled from his pack.

Throughout the afternoon, Alexandra continued trying to come up with some way to change his mind about leaving her in South Pass City. But any time she tried to start a conversation, it always went the same way—to a swift dead end.

It was frustrating and discouraging.

After a while, she even started to annoy herself with the useless attempts, and she lapsed into a period of silence. But this time, she was not able to relax enough to drift into sleep. She was far too alert and physically aware of the man seated behind her. Every subtle movement of his body transferred to hers, from the occasional brush of his chest against her back, to the way his hard thighs shifted or tensed beneath hers.

He rode a horse well. Man and animal were well attuned to each other despite the added burden they both endured. His hands were firm but forgiving on the reins, displaying the fact that very little was needed from him for the horse to follow his direction.

Clearly, they had been together a long time.

What kind of life did a bounty hunter lead? Constantly moving about, chasing after outlaws. Putting himself in danger at every turn, never settling into a peaceful existence. He knew the land; he was capable and confident. She had no doubt he knew how to use that gun of his with expert skill, or he wouldn't be successful at his chosen vocation.

Had his life hardened him into the man he was, or had he chosen the life that best suited his already harsh demeanor?

He might be a bit rude in his speech, but he wasn't exactly disrespectful. Aside from his not-too-subtle threat over the campfire the night before—which she was certain had just been an attempt at scaring her away—he had never once made her feel that he might take advantage of their circumstances.

She was not likely to be lucky enough to find anyone else nearly as suited to her purposes.

That thought doubled in conviction as they approached a town just as the sun was setting.

The closer they got, the more it became apparent that South Pass City was not the bustling stage stop Alexandra had hoped for, though it might have been at one time.

The town was nestled in a low spot amongst gently rolling hills. A handful of storefronts lined the dirt road that ran through the middle of town, and various other buildings were scattered beyond, many of which appeared abandoned.

Only a few townsfolk remained out and about in the dying daylight, casting warily curious glances as Alexandra and Kincaid rode past. Not surprisingly, the saloon showed the most life, with music and raucous laughter spilling out onto the street from its swinging doors.

Not far past the saloon stood a white-washed building that had faded to a weathered gray. It stood three stories and had a covered porch stretching across the front. Light shone from its windows, and a large sign over the front door declared it the hotel.

Kincaid brought his gelding to the hitching rail and dismounted. Without a word, he reached up to grasp her waist. Alexandra rested her hands on his shoulders as he lowered her to her feet. Her legs wavered a bit, having gotten stiff from being in the saddle all day, and his hands tightened their grip, holding her secure while she steadied herself.

He glanced toward the hotel. "I'll get you a room and a meal. Tomorrow, you'll be able to find someone to help you."

"But I've already found you," she insisted with a smile.

Her words brought his gaze swinging back to meet hers. They still stood close beside the horse, his hands braced heavy and warm on her hips, hers still resting on his arms. Something flashed in the steel-gray of his eyes.

Irritation, most likely.

Alexandra continued quickly, "Look, I know you don't want to help me. I appreciate that, and I am infinitely grateful that you brought me this far. But the fact remains that I need to get to exactly where you are already going." She took a swift breath and continued, already seeing the resistance forming in his features. "You will be paid generously, and I might surprise you by proving to be quite useful on the trail. I can—"

"Enough," he muttered as he stepped back from her and swept his hat off his head to run fingers back through his hair, casting her a dark look. "Why can't you get it through that head of yours that the answer is *no*?"

Alexandra lifted her shoulders in a brief shrug as a smile curved her lips. "I have a hard time accepting things I do not agree with. You are the man I need, Mr. Kincaid. We were meant to cross paths in Rock Springs—"

"You cornered me in a saloon."

"—and again after I was stranded by Lassiter," she continued as though he hadn't interrupted. "Sometimes fate is unavoidable."

With a low growl of frustration, he shoved his hat back on his head. "A room and a meal. That's it." Then he turned and strode into the hotel with determined steps.

Stubborn man.

She did not want to entertain the possibility that she would not be able to convince him, but she was seriously running out of time. Deciding to give him a moment to breathe, she waited with Deuce, murmuring soft words to the gelding as she tried to think of anything else she could do to change Kincaid's mind about her.

He came back outside within a couple of minutes, so fast that she feared there may not have been a room available. But then he handed her a key before he took up Deuce's reins.

"You're in room four at the end of the hall on the second floor," he said as he backed the gelding away from the hitching post. "A meal will be brought up to you unless you'd rather eat in their dining room."

"In the room is fine," she replied quickly. Dread and panic warred within her as she watched him turn and walk away. That was it, then? He just walked off into the night?

No. She couldn't accept that. "Kincaid," she blurted in a breathless sort of shout.

He stopped to look over his shoulder at her. There was a lot going on behind that hard, flintlike gaze. Alexandra wished she could decipher what it all meant. All she knew was that she did not want him to just walk away.

As he stared back at her in a stretched-out silence, something passed between them that had her toes curling in her boots and the hair rising on her nape.

"I'm not gone yet," he said then in a low voice that seemed as strained and tense as she felt. But it was enough to ease her sudden panic.

She watched as he led his horse around the corner of the hotel and out of sight, then released a heavy sigh. He was probably just settling his horse for the night.

No doubt he got a room for himself, and she would have another chance to speak with him in the morning.

He wouldn't just take off without a proper goodbye. His curt statement assured her of that if nothing else. Turning to the hotel, she thought of the soft bed and hot meal that awaited her and quickened her steps.

The hotel was nothing grand by any means, but her room was clean and in possession of the basic necessities. A bed, a bureau holding a small lamp and wash bowl, and a chair set before a window that overlooked the main street through town.

Alexandra gazed out the window. Aside from the lights and music coming from the saloon next door, the town was quiet. She didn't recall passing a stage stop on their way in. Considering how much of the town seemed to be permanently closed, she sincerely doubted it was still operational. Not that the stage was an option for her when she didn't have the money to purchase a ticket. Which still left her with the hope of finding someone who might be her guide. Someone with the skills and knowledge to get her to Montana. Someone she could trust.

Someone exactly like Kincaid.

Anxiety gripped her insides, and she swiftly reined it in.

She would not get all twisted up by the thought of being alone again. In deciding to leave Boston, she had accepted that there would be challenges along the way. She had, in fact, been looking forward to just that. If Kincaid did not come around and she found herself on her own again tomorrow, she would survive. She would get to Montana one way or another.

It was irrational, really, how single-minded she'd become regarding the bounty hunter. Considering he'd stated loud and clear from the start that he wanted nothing to do with her.

It must have been her stubborn nature asserting itself.

A knock pulled her from her worried thoughts. She crossed the room and opened the door to a slender young woman in a calico dress and white apron, holding a tray of savory-smelling food.

"I've got your supper here." The woman stepped swiftly past Alexandra to set the tray on the bureau. "It ain't much, but it'll fill your belly," she said with a brisk smile as she started back across the room. "My brother'll be up with your bath in a few minutes. We'll fetch everything in the morning so as not to disturb you again tonight."

"Wait," Alexandra said. "Did you say a bath?"

The woman stopped on the threshold. "Your man ordered a bath for you. Don't you want it?" she asked with a tip of her head.

"Yes. Yes, of course, I do," Alexandra replied. "Thank you."

"You're welcome. We don't get many travelers through here anymore, so you let us know if there's anything else you need. It's just me and my brother, Jim, but we'll do what we can for you."

"Thank you, ah…what is your name?"

"Oh, my name is Jane, miss."

"Thank you, Jane," Alexandra returned with a smile. "I'm sure I'll be quite fine."

Jane gave a nod and another quick smile before

heading off down the hallway. Within a couple of minutes, Jim arrived, carrying a copper hip bath. He couldn't have been more than sixteen or so. He was all lanky limbs and big feet, but he must have been stronger than he looked, since he took several trips up and down the stairs, lugging two full buckets of water each time to fill the tub, and never seemed to break a sweat or lose his wide and ready grin.

Just over an hour later, Alexandra's hunger was satisfied by a plate of roasted ham, little baked potatoes, and a wonderful blueberry cobbler. And the bath had been a heavenly surprise. Though she would have liked to luxuriate in the steamy water to ease the ache that infused her muscles, she made quick work of scrubbing herself clean—soaping and rinsing her hair twice—before wrapping herself in a towel and dunking her underclothes and blouse in the tub for a washing as well. She didn't put the dusty blue traveling outfit through the same regimen for fear of ruining it, but she brushed away as much of the dried dirt as she could manage.

By the time she had her wet things spread all about the room to dry and had finger-combed through her hair to release all the tangles, exhaustion claimed her, and she was more than ready to sink into the softness of the bed. She climbed between the sheets, still wrapped in the towel, and fell asleep with thoughts of Kincaid mixing haphazardly with memories from her childhood…while deep in her heart beat a fervent wish that the bounty hunter would still be there in the morning.

ELEVEN

MALCOLM STOOD ACROSS THE STREET FROM THE hotel, rolling loose tobacco into a cigarette, wondering why he was still there. She'd turned the lamp down in her room at least twenty minutes ago and was probably fast asleep by now.

He'd made no commitments to her. Just the opposite, in fact. There was nothing to stop him from walking away right now, getting on his horse, and riding out of town. Aside from the fact that Deuce needed the rest.

And the other matter.

Earlier, in front of the hotel when she'd called out his name, the look on her face had hit him like a bullet to the chest. He should have ended their association then and there, but he hadn't been able to do it and had reassured her instead.

He struck a match and lit his cigarette.

What the hell was wrong with him? He was not responsible for the woman. He did not *want* to be responsible for the woman. Not when the last person he'd been in charge of had wound up dead.

Yet, after settling Deuce in the stables past the hotel, he'd gone to the saloon. The bartender had been as knowledgeable as he'd expected, but the news had not been good. The town was on a swift decline, going from a couple of thousand people down to less than a hundred in the last decade or so. With their stage stop inoperable, they rarely saw any travelers passing through, and when Malcolm asked about any potential guides for someone wanting to head north, the bartender had just laughed and walked away.

Not good.

Not good at all.

Malcolm drew in a long pull on the cigarette, then exhaled in a trail of smoke that drifted up into the night. With a heavy frown, he glanced back at Miss Brighton's window.

Dammit.

The woman was going to get her way, and for some reason, that irritated the hell out of him. He was going against every vow he'd made since Gavin's death. He'd be taking on the responsibility of someone else's welfare. And that someone was a pampered lady with no idea what they'd be facing out on the trail. Malcolm would be responsible for every aspect of her survival and comfort.

It was enough to make him want to punch something. Instead, he stubbed out his cigarette and took angry strides back into the hotel, taking wicked delight in the idea of waking her from a peaceful slumber to tell her he'd be taking her to Montana after all.

He ascended the stairs two at a time, then stalked down the hall. Though he was in room one at the other end of the building, he walked right up to the door marked with a four. After knocking sharply, he lowered his chin, crossed his arms over his chest, and waited. He chose not to analyze why the idea of disturbing her sleep gave him a perverse sort of pleasure.

He was about to knock again, when the lock released and the door opened to reveal a very sleepy— and very undressed—woman blinking at him with wide blue eyes.

"Mr. Kincaid? Is something wrong?"

Wrong? Hellfire and damnation. Malcolm could barely think.

The foolish woman stood there in nothing more than a white towel wrapped around her body from chest to knee. The creamy skin of her limbs and shoulders was entirely exposed, and dark hair fell in heavy waves down her back. She looked soft and feminine and too damned enticing.

Lust swept hot and furious through him. He ground his back teeth hard to stop his body's instant reaction to the sight of Miss Brighton in such a state.

"What the hell are you doing opening the door like that?" Malcolm growled, glancing down the hall to make sure no one else was about.

Her eyes grew wider as she looked down at herself. A swift blush pinkened her cheeks, and she tried to step back around the edge of the door. "I was in a deep sleep," she explained. "I forgot I wasn't dressed."

"What if it hadn't been me knocking?" he asked angrily.

It was probably his tone that had her lifting her chin and narrowing her gaze. "Well, it is you, isn't it? And you still haven't told me *why* you have come to bother me in the middle of the night."

"It's barely ten o'clock."

Apparently over her embarrassment, she crossed her arms over her chest in a perfect copy of his own stance and lifted her brows in question. The action plumped the upper swells of her breasts, and Malcolm's mouth went bone-dry.

Forcing his attention back to her face didn't seem to help much. Not with her eyes all soft from sleep and those lips looking so damn kissable.

"I'll take you to Montana," he said abruptly, trying to shake himself free of the sensual snare he'd walked into.

Her mouth dropped open in surprise. "You will?"

Malcolm was tempted to back out then simply due to the strength of his unbidden desire. He did not want to entertain the idea that his attraction to her was growing stronger rather than fading. But it was the damned truth. The journey was going to be torturous in more ways than one. He had no intention of acting on the lust she inspired, but that didn't mean he didn't feel it, and it didn't mean he'd always be able to hide it.

But he couldn't in good conscience leave her stranded. Doing so would make him no better than Lassiter, and there was no telling what manner of character she'd end up in the hands of if he wasn't there to keep her out of trouble.

"We do things my way," he stated firmly. "No arguing."

She nodded vigorously. "Of course. Whatever you say, Mr. Kincaid."

Malcolm narrowed his gaze. Her ready agreement was suspicious, but he'd made his decision. "Malcolm," he muttered.

Her eyebrows lifted in surprise. Then she smiled, and Malcolm's gut clenched. The curve of that lower lip was going to be the death of him.

"All right, Malcolm." She unfolded her arms to extend her hand. "And you may call me Alexandra."

Malcolm knew he shouldn't take her hand. Not there in the dark while she stood in nothing but a towel, not when desire ran rampant through his blood at the simple sight of her. But she kept her hand extended and lifted a brow as though in challenge.

He took her hand in his, noting its softness and how easily it became folded up in his larger grip. His bicep tensed with the urge to give a quick and forceful tug so she'd tumble toward him until her breasts flattened against his chest, her thighs bumped his, and her breath spread across his throat. It'd be so easy to take her in his arms and claim her mouth.

But she was innocent and far too trusting—not to mention way the hell out of his class—and Malcolm had never taken anything from a woman that wasn't freely given. Miss Brighton was not for him.

Oblivious to his train of thought, she gave a surprisingly firm handshake. Her smile never wavered as she declared, "You won't regret this. I promise."

Malcolm released her hand and stepped back. "Be downstairs by seven o'clock tomorrow."

"I will. Thank you, Malcolm."

"And ask who's at your door before you open the damned thing."

Malcolm held his position until the door closed and he heard the lock click into place. Then he stalked down the hall to his own room, taking slow breaths to rein in his body's fierce and unwelcome craving. He'd need to see to his own relief tonight. There was no way he was going to start on the trail with that woman wound as tight as he was.

Not if he hoped to survive the journey.

TWELVE

ALEXANDRA STOOD BY THE DOOR, LISTENING TO Malcolm's booted steps retreating down the hall. Only when she couldn't hear him anymore did she release the breath she'd been holding.

Heat rushed through her body as she recalled the look on his face when she'd opened the door in her less-than-dressed state. The scorching heat in his eyes had shocked her from head to toe.

Alexandra had been the object of admiring glances and appreciative smiles from gentlemen in Boston. She knew she was passably pretty, especially when dressed up in her finery. But Malcolm Kincaid had stood, still as stone, while his focus slid over her body, leaving tingling chills in its wake. She had grown so accustomed to the polite and reserved manners of the gentlemen from her social circles out East that she did not know how to respond to such a bold perusal.

The intensity of his gaze had triggered an instant wave of self-awareness that had made her fingers and toes tingle while a fluttering sensation erupted deep in the pit of her being. It was a heightened sort of anticipation.

It was the oddest thing. Kincaid barely tolerated her.

Yet, there had been something akin to hunger in his gaze. And then the anger. Now that she thought about it, his gruff manner may have been an attempt at hiding his physical reaction. If he was attracted to her, he didn't want to be. That much was abundantly clear.

Kincaid had had plenty of opportunity to take advantage of her vulnerability. But he hadn't, and she trusted he never would. Kincaid might be harsh, ill-mannered, rude, and desperately protective of his desire for isolation, but he possessed a deep thread of honor that he would likely never admit to.

She had detected it in him from the start, and it had convinced her that he was the man she needed. She trusted him.

Her father might have argued that she trusted too easily. Perhaps it was true to some degree. It had certainly been more so during her youth, when she'd viewed the world as an inviting adventure and all its inhabitants as kindred souls…but this was different. This kind of trust went deeper.

She wondered what had changed his mind, but she was not going to press her luck by questioning him about it. He had agreed. That was the important thing.

The next morning, she woke with the dawn and dressed quickly before twisting her hair up as neatly as possible with the limited number of hairpins still in her possession. She paused for just a second to look about the room to make sure she hadn't forgotten anything, then recalled that she had nothing beyond the clothes on her back. It was direct evidence of how truly cut adrift she was from the many comforts and conveniences of her life in Boston. She was disconnected. On her own. The realization was disconcerting and freeing at the same time.

It was more than twenty minutes before seven o'clock, but as she entered the small dining room, she saw Kincaid seated at a table with his back to the corner. From his position, he could survey the entire room, as well as anyone entering or leaving through the front door. He was also in the perfect place to watch her approach.

Alexandra thought she had gotten past the previous night's incident.

Apparently not.

Her skin flushed instantly as she met his sharp stare. She recalled how his gaze had swept down the length of her body while she'd stood in nothing but a towel. That silver flame she'd seen in his eyes the night before was carefully banked this morning, yet it did not seem to change the fact that his gaze caused a rush of warmth through her blood.

Though he stood as she reached the table, he did not bother to pull out her chair. No matter. Such a thing would have brought them into close proximity, and she was not prepared for that just now.

"Good morning, Malcolm," she said brightly to disguise her awkwardness.

His response was a grunt, which was just as well, since she had no idea what else to say.

Luckily, she was spared the need for further conversation as Jane came forward from the back room. "Would you like some coffee, miss?"

Not sure if they had the time, Alexandra glanced

to Kincaid, and he gave a short nod. "Yes, thank you," she replied, grateful they would not be striking out immediately.

"Breakfast will be out shortly," Jane advised after she poured the hot brew.

After a lovely meal of eggs, ham, and fried potatoes—the cost of which Alexandra estimated and added to a running tally of what she would need to refund Kincaid once the trip was over—they left the hotel to procure a few supplies and another horse.

Alexandra could not help smiling as they walked down the boardwalk to the mercantile store they'd passed when they'd come into town. Sneaking a sidelong glance at the man walking beside her, she was surprised to discover that he was eyeing her suspiciously.

"What?" she asked.

"You're not gonna spend the whole day gloating about getting your way, are you?"

She lifted her brows, all innocence. "I haven't said a word."

He grunted, but she thought she saw the slightest twitch at the corner of his mouth. "It's written all over your face."

"Do you blame me?"

"We'll see."

"It will all be worth it once we get there." A sudden realization had her turning her head to look at him in surprise. "You know, you haven't even asked what you will be paid for your services."

"Doesn't matter," he replied as he suddenly grasped her elbow to assist her over a loose board.

"Thank you," she murmured after he released her

again, doing her best to ignore the way his strong but gentle grip had felt through the layers of her coat and the blouse beneath. She picked up the conversation where it had left off. "Of course it matters. Surely, that had an influence on your decision."

He did not reply, just kept his focus directed straight ahead. If not for the payment, then why? It certainly was not because he had grown fond of her. As Alexandra opened her mouth to press further, he jerked his head to the side.

"We're here."

The mercantile was of modest size, but was stocked with just about anything a person could need, providing everything from hair ribbons and dress material, to sacks of onions and flour, to hardware and weapons.

While Kincaid went straight to the young woman behind the counter, obviously needing no time to browse, Alexandra took the opportunity to wander around a bit.

She walked along rows of shelves piled high with food stored in tin cans, burlap sacks, and wooden crates. From there she found herself amongst dozens of bolts of fabrics. Cottons, calicos, wool, in an array of patterns and colors. A variety of ladies' bonnets and men's hats hung on the wall in neat rows beside racks of shoes suitable for everyone in the family, from the youngest to the oldest, from work boots to Sunday dress shoes.

Alexandra noted a pair of lightweight boots that would have been far more appropriate than the fancy heeled shoes she currently wore. In truth, it would be ideal to replace her entire outfit, which, although perfectly suited to train travel, would continue to be a terrible hindrance on horseback.

But without any money, she'd have to make do with what she had.

At least her clothes were as clean as she could manage. She would have to find a way to sit her horse safely, however. Perhaps she could cut away some of the draping fabric that drew her skirts back into their narrow silhouette. It would not be as effective an outfit as the pair of denim trousers she passed by, but the idea had some merit.

A twinge of deep regret stole through her as she thought about having to ruin such beautiful clothing. One of the first things Aunt Judith had done when Alexandra had arrived in Boston was to take her shopping for appropriate clothing. It had been a two-day excursion that left young Alexandra stunned by all the fripperies and unnecessary items she had apparently needed. It had taken some time to grow accustomed to the very different expectations for how a young lady should present herself—not just in manner, but in fashion as well.

And now, she was considering slicing through the skirts of her traveling gown to make it easier to sit a horse.

She shook her head.

Aunt Judith would think her crazy. Her friends would too.

They might be right. Just a little bit. Her determination to get to Montana was making her consider many things she wouldn't have imagined just a few weeks ago.

"I'm gonna go see about getting a horse."

Lost in her thoughts, Alexandra jumped at the sound of Kincaid's voice so close behind her.

She turned around to see him standing in the narrow aisle between the shoes and a selection of horse tack and supplies. Though it was full sun outside and the storefront boasted large windows, at the back of the store where they stood, only dim light filtered beyond the rows of shelves. Alexandra was struck by how out of place Kincaid looked amongst all the neatly stacked goods. He was far more suited to wide-open spaces, mountains, and fresh air.

He didn't move, but something must have shifted around them, bringing the scent of horse, leather, and man toward her. Alexandra breathed in deeply despite herself.

"Wait here. I'll return to bring everything back to the hotel."

She nodded. "Please keep an account of your expenses on this trip so you can be reimbursed."

He did not respond to that, only tipped his head before turning to stride from the store.

Almost as soon as Malcolm made his exit, two women entered the shop.

One of them glanced back over her shoulder with a pinched expression. "That must have been the bounty hunter I heard came to town last evening."

"Bounty hunter?" the other asked as they crossed out of view without even noticing Alexandra's presence toward the back of the store. They turned down the next row, and though Alexandra tried not to continue listening to them, it proved impossible, considering they didn't even attempt to lower their voices.

"Yes, and he rode in with a young…woman."

The hesitation was obvious. The choice of the word *woman* over *lady*, equally telling. Alexandra's skin heated at the suggestion in the prudish tone.

"Really?" came the astonished reply.

"Indeed. Apparently, they are traveling together. Just the two of them."

Alexandra turned her attention to the display at her right, but she didn't really see it.

"I'm sure I'd never have the courage to travel alone with a man like that."

"No *lady* would."

And with that, the two continued on and soon after paid for their purchase and left the store, while Alexandra made sure they didn't accidently catch sight of her. She would not say she hid exactly, just did her best to ensure there would not be an embarrassing confrontation.

Their gossipy comments had initially angered her, but then she wondered if she should have been shamed instead. Her actions since arriving in the West had broken at least a hundred rules of decorum her aunt had insisted she follow.

But life was different out here.

The two shoppers clearly questioned her respectability, but such things could not be allowed to hold you back from something that needed to be accomplished. Alexandra's father had taught her that. And he had once been one of the most respected gentlemen in Boston.

She would not let their comments bother her. She had more important things to worry about, after all.

Like getting to Montana and figuring out the rest of her future.

Shortly after the ladies left, the store clerk—a young woman about the same age as Alexandra, with pale, freckled skin and a ready smile—spotted her and approached. "Ah, there you are, miss. The mister says to get you some clothing more suited for riding horseback. I thought you might want to choose the items yourself."

Alexandra was surprised, though she probably shouldn't have been. Of course, he would think of everything.

Pushing aside any further concern over what she'd overheard, she allowed the clerk to lead her back to the ready-made clothing, where she selected a simple cotton blouse and a split skirt in serviceable wool designed for riding astride. When the clerk stated she was also to select a pair of proper shoes, she went back to the boots she'd seen earlier.

After Alexandra made her choices, the clerk left her to continue gathering up the rest of their order.

Pleased that Kincaid had thought to ensure she would have the right attire to make the rest of the trip more comfortable, Alexandra was smiling as she came back toward the front of the store. That was when a collection of rifles and pistols behind the cashier's counter drew her gaze.

Her steps came to a sudden halt as she stared at a particular model of handgun: a small Colt, suitable for a woman or a child. Once again frozen by the involuntary physical reaction, she could only stand in place staring at the familiar weapon, remembering its weight in her hand, recalling the sharp report it issued when fired, smelling the gunpowder filtering through the crisp air of an early autumn evening.

"Miss? Miss, are you all right?"

Alexandra was drawn from the suffocating memories by the clerk's concerned voice. She wondered how long the woman had been at her side, trying to gain her attention. Sensation swiftly returned to her muscles, and the iciness left her limbs in a whoosh that made her feel weakened but no longer frozen with fear.

"I've never seen anyone go so pale," the clerk said with concern. "It's like you seen a ghost or something."

"I'm sorry. I was lost in my thoughts for a moment." She smiled, hoping to assure the poor woman that she hadn't lost her wits.

To distract herself, she walked toward a counter display with a glass top. The case contained various knives arranged alongside leather sheaths in perfect rows. Fitted with brass guards, some handles were made of smoothed deer antler, while others were of polished wood that gleamed in the uncertain light. The sheaths were fine-crafted, the leather appearing supple yet strong with tight stitching along the seams.

A knife would come in handy in so many ways.

Her gaze lit upon one not quite as large as some others, but suitable for cutting through a young sapling or an animal hide. It possessed a smooth, sharp blade and a handle made with a wood so dark it looked nearly black. She'd had one very similar when she'd been young.

"Have you interest in a hunting blade, miss?" The

clerk set some supplies near the cash register and walked toward Alexandra.

"How much is that one there?"

"A fine piece, miss." The clerk smiled and retrieved a key to open the glass top of the case to withdraw the knife and hand it to Alexandra for her inspection.

The knife was beautiful. Perfectly balanced with a finely honed blade. Holding the familiar tool gave Alexandra a burst of confidence. It seemed to form a link between who she was now to the self-assured and ever-capable girl she had once been. Though she felt a prickle of guilt for her impulsive desire to add the knife to Kincaid's stack of purchases, she knew it was a sound and practical decision. A blade such as this had infinite uses on the trail and would allow her some means to contribute.

But Kincaid would surely notice the added cost. "Is there anything of equal value in the current purchases that I could trade it for?"

The clerk swept a glance at the gathered items from Kincaid's order. "Ah, the silver hairbrush, I suppose."

"Perfect," Alexandra replied. "I will take the knife instead." She could make do without a hairbrush—though she appreciated Kincaid's thoughtfulness in including it—but the knife suddenly felt far more necessary.

While Alexandra waited patiently for the clerk to finish wrapping their purchases into neat little brown paper parcels, she heard the fall of a familiar booted step on the wood-plank floor.

Kincaid had returned.

She covertly slid the knife between two of the wrapped parcels waiting on the counter.

She wasn't sure why she felt a need to hide the purchase. Maybe she did not want to hear the disdain in his voice when he argued that a knife would be nothing but a danger to *someone like her*. He had placed her firmly in the category of useless tenderfoot from the moment he'd first met her, and likely wouldn't believe her if she told him she knew well enough how to use it.

She could try harder to convince him that she had a childhood's worth of experience living in Montana, moving about with her father from one adventure to another. But the truth was that she wasn't sure how much of those experiences were still within her.

If nothing else, this trip would likely show her just how much of that girl still existed.

Placing her hand on the packages to keep anything from shifting, she turned to Kincaid with a lifted brow. "That was quick. Did you have any luck in securing another horse?"

He nodded and glanced at the clerk. "Everything all set?"

"Yes, sir, I believe this is all of it. Are you sure you wouldn't like more of our food stuffs? We have—"

"No. We're fine with this," he replied as he tossed a length of coiled rope and her new saddlebags over his shoulder, then tucked the sack of grain for the horses and a new bedroll under his arm.

Alexandra quickly scooped up the small stack of parcels that contained her hidden purchase. Kincaid eyed her curiously, since he could have easily carried all their meager supplies himself. "I told you I will not be an extra burden," Alexandra explained. "I can carry my weight."

With his characteristic grunt, which she was coming to understand as being his way of saying, "I disagree, but I'm not gonna bother to argue," he turned to leave without another word.

Alexandra thanked the woman behind the counter, giving a bright and sunny smile in the hopes of making up for Kincaid's rudeness, then she followed her escort out into the sunshine.

After she'd spent so much time in the dim store, the brightness of the day blinded her for a moment until her eyes adjusted.

By then, Kincaid was already securing their supplies to the saddle of the horse he'd acquired. The mount he'd chosen was a beautiful, light-chestnut mare, and though she showed some age, she was fit and stocky and obviously built for endurance.

Alexandra walked to the horse's head to introduce herself. Shifting the packages into one arm, she placed her hand on the horse's forelock. The mare immediately bowed her head and huffed a breath.

Alexandra smiled. They would get along just fine. "What is her name?" she asked.

"I didn't ask."

Frowning, Alexandra looked into the mare's dark eyes and whispered, "I will come up with something. Don't worry."

Kincaid came forward after securing their supplies and reached for Alexandra's burden.

She smiled sweetly. "I've got these."

With a shake of his head, he untied the horse from the hitching post. In addition to thinking her helpless and ignorant, the man probably thought her odd, as well.

She shouldn't let it bother her.

She'd spent the last five years worrying about how the people of Boston might see her. Though she never fully understood her aunt's overwhelming awe of the Boston Brahmins, she appreciated the desire not to be viewed as so very different from all of them.

Even though she was.

Only Evie and Courtney knew Alexandra was not the polished lady everyone assumed her to be. It was odd how the hard-earned qualities that had gained her acceptance among her aunt's people were a basis for derision from Kincaid.

He turned the horse and began to lead her down the road. "Let's get back to the hotel so we can be on our way."

"We are leaving town right away?" Alexandra asked as she rushed to catch up to him.

"There's still plenty of daylight left. We'll need to make the most of it."

"I see."

"Your mare is sure-footed. If you can stay in the saddle, you'll manage."

His assumption that she was worried about riding made her bristle with indignation, but she knew there was no point in trying to assert her abilities. He'd eventually have to change his opinion of her.

Wouldn't he?

When they reached the hotel, Kincaid stopped out front and nodded toward the building. "Get yourself ready. We head out in an hour." Then he turned and walked her mare toward the stables behind the hotel.

Alexandra sighed as she took her parcels up to her

room. As she began to unwrap the new clothing from the brown paper, she got excited about finally having attire more suited to her current needs.

Aside from the cotton shirt, split skirt, and boots that she had picked out, Kincaid had thought to include an oiled slicker lined with flannel, two large handkerchiefs that could be used as bandanas or for various other purposes, and two pairs of serviceable woolen socks.

She smiled at the thought of how aghast Evie and Courtney would be by her delight in such common items. Neither of her friends had ever existed outside their wealthy, privileged circumstances. They'd never even left Boston except for trips to New York City on shopping excursions.

After removing her tight-fitted jacket, fine-stitched blouse, and her many-layered skirts and petticoats, she stood in only her one-piece undergarment. Thank goodness she did not have a confining corset to contend with, having realized when she was preparing to leave Boston that she would not be able to manage lacing the garment on her own. She quickly redressed in the woolen skirt, plain cotton shirt, thick stockings, and the new boots. Then she took a deep breath that filled her lungs all the way to the bottom.

A curious feeling of liberation filtered through her, reminding her a bit of the freedom she'd enjoyed as a girl.

Using her new knife, she cut a few strips off one of the handkerchiefs, which she used to secure the knife's sheath to her calf above the edge of her boot where it would be in easy reach beneath her skirts.

Then she wrapped up her discarded petticoats and her fine blouse in one of the pieces of brown paper from the mercantile and retied it with twine. The petticoats and blouse were lightweight enough to add to her saddle pack and might come in handy along the journey. With a rueful expression, she looked at the fine traveling outfit she'd thought she'd be wearing when she arrived at her father's. She certainly wouldn't be making the impression she'd expected to, but bringing the weighty and cumbersome Eastern getup along would be the height of impracticality.

Her hesitation in leaving the gown behind was a little unexpected. She never would have been concerned with such fine trappings in her youth. It proved how much she had changed under her aunt's tutelage, but it didn't alter what she had to do.

She left the dark-blue skirt, matching jacket, and her elegant heeled boots neatly on the bed. Maybe Jane would get some use out of them. Scooping up the rain slicker and her package, she turned and left the room, bolstered by the feel of the knife against her calf and optimistic that her plan to leave Boston might have finally taken a turn for the better.

THIRTEEN

FIGURING IT WOULD STILL BE A WHILE BEFORE MISS Brighton showed herself, Malcolm leaned back against the hitching rail and folded his arms across his chest. The horses were fed, watered, and ready. All they were waiting on was the woman.

Alexandra.

Her given name danced through his mind. For the most part, it suited her. It was feminine and traditional, but it didn't do much to suggest the impish way her eyes lit up when she smiled, nor did it hint at the natural sensuality that eased from beneath her proper manners, rigid posture, and single-minded focus.

The stubborn woman sure had gotten what she wanted.

Now that Malcolm had agreed to take on the job, he wanted it started and done. He was not an impatient man, but he preferred to do things at a set pace. They'd already lost too many hours of the day.

The trip up to Helena would take a couple of weeks on horseback and required traveling through some rugged country. The way was made even more dangerous by the presence of wild animals, outlaws, and some bands of renegade Indians who hadn't been in agreement with the government's decision to force them onto reservations when they had once roamed the country at will.

He doubted his new companion would find much enjoyment in the travel ahead. For someone not used to it, spending day after day in a saddle could be hell on the body. But the woman was damned determined.

Malcolm shifted his stance against the rail. He was anxious to get going and had to fight against the urge to go fetch her, when the sound of booted feet crossing the porch had him lifting his head.

She'd stopped at the top of the two steps that would bring her down to where he stood. Dressed in a split skirt of brown wool, a cotton shirt buttoned to her throat, and serviceable boots, with the rain slicker draped over her arm, she almost looked prepared for their journey ahead. It was the twinkle of excitement in her eyes that threw off the look. If she had any idea what kind of hardships she'd be facing, she would not be so eager.

A blast of irritation shot through him. He should not be escorting this lady across the wilderness.

Neither of them said anything for a few moments. Then her gaze flickered briefly to the gun at his hip before she lifted her eyes again to his. He'd noticed that flash of fear before. It seemed to come up every time she caught sight of his gun.

Someone unaccustomed to the necessity of carrying a firearm would experience natural discomfort at the constant sight of a gun. But this seemed to go deeper than mere discomfort. It was damned near close to panic.

But then it was gone as she tipped her chin up and looked down at him with a slightly arched brow. "Are you quite finished with glaring at me, Mr. Kincaid? Or are you not ready to depart?"

Malcolm pushed off from the rail. "Just waiting on you, sweetheart."

She gave a little huff.

He grabbed the felt hat he'd set on the post beside him. Then he stalked forward to where she still stood at the edge of the porch. He placed the floppy, wide-brimmed hat on her head, making the mistake of meeting her gaze as he did so. He immediately experienced a fierce little stab in the center of his chest before a smooth glide of heat angled straight down. There was something about those blue eyes of hers. Clenching his teeth, he couldn't bring himself to look away.

He caught the faintest hint of her scent, clean and feminine. His body stirred to life with an attraction he had no intention of acknowledging. *Dammit.*

Being around this woman for the next weeks was going to be a very particular kind of hell.

"Thank you," she murmured.

The words drew his focus to that mouth-watering lower lip. She took a swift breath and seemed to hold it. Malcolm forced his gaze back up to meet hers again. "This ain't gonna be easy," he said sharply.

She let out her breath and nodded. "I know."

Malcolm lowered his brows, wondering just how much she did know. Not much, he reckoned as he felt his pulse quicken. "You do as I say. Every moment, not just when you feel like it."

She nodded again.

"You're gonna need to do your part."

"I said I would," she stated with a fierce frown.

"You have no idea what will be required of you over the next couple of weeks. I'll keep you alive and get you to Montana, but I'm not your servant. You'll be expected to do for yourself."

"Of course," she said stiffly.

He could see the hurt pride in her face, but he couldn't worry about that. She needed to know what to expect. He turned away. "Get on your horse and let's go."

He didn't wait to see how she managed to mount the mare on her own. Once he was in his saddle, he started off down the street that would take them toward the Wind River Mountain Range. It was not long before he heard her behind him. He hoped she'd stay back a bit, but she rode up alongside him anyway.

A prickle of awareness itched at the back of his neck. Malcolm sent a focused gaze along both sides of the street. There was barely anyone about. Just a few kids, an older woman carrying a basket of vegetables, and a handful of men hanging around near the saloon. No one seemed too concerned by their passing, but something felt off.

Malcolm continued to scan their surroundings as the town faded into the distance behind them. He noted no cause for alarm. More than likely, it was the unwelcome companion at his side that made him feel uneasy.

Malcolm chanced a glance toward the woman

beside him. She hadn't said a single word since they'd started off, but kept her horse at his mount's flank, refusing to fall into step behind him.

She sat a good horse. Her hands were gentle on the reins, though sure enough to maintain her control over the experienced mare. Her seat was relaxed astride the saddle and her feet secure in the stirrups. She moved with the horse in a rhythm that proved she was no stranger to horseback.

Of course, knowing how to ride did not mean she wouldn't feel the punishment of spending day after day in the saddle. For the moment, however, she looked far from uncomfortable.

The fool woman looked downright *joyful*.

She had pushed her hat back on her head. The cord tied under her chin kept it from falling off her head completely while she tipped her face up toward the sun. Her eyes were closed, and a smile spread her lips.

Malcolm narrowed his gaze.

He'd admit to himself, anyway, that she'd surprised him so far.

There had been plenty of opportunity over the last two days for her to start complaining or demanding accommodations he couldn't or wouldn't provide. Aside from her relentless desire to bend him to her will, she'd not been such bad company.

He didn't want to wonder what had prompted her to leave Boston and travel to Montana. For whatever reason, there was a near desperate determination in her, despite moments like this when she looked for all the world like she was on a pleasure outing. She had a purpose.

So did he.

He returned his gaze to the road ahead and redirected his thoughts to the Belt Buckle Kid, now also known as Walter Dunstan. The man who had murdered his brother and ruined his own life. Malcolm wasn't too familiar with the area around Wolf Creek, Montana, where Dunstan was supposedly hiding.

It didn't matter. Malcolm would find him, and the bastard would pay.

FOURTEEN

It was obvious Kincaid was not much for casual conversation, so Alexandra did her best to accommodate him. It took more effort than she had expected, but the bounty hunter had seemed exceptionally irritable since she'd come out of the hotel. Now that he'd agreed to take her north, she didn't want to do anything to make him regret it more than he did already.

She hadn't been a talkative sort while living in Boston, unless she was in the company of Evie and Courtney. With anyone else, she'd had no trouble following her Aunt Judith's dictates about holding her thoughts and opinions to herself. During those first few years, Aunt Judith had been terrified of what Alexandra would say, ever fearful of what she might inadvertently reveal about her unusual upbringing. Being vigilant in how she presented herself became second nature.

But out here, under an endless blue sky with the raw beauty of nature extending in all directions, Alexandra felt that ever-present caution sliding away as memories from her past came floating back. Memories of things she once knew. Things she'd once loved.

She and her father used to tell stories to pass the long days on the trail. Or they would point out interesting landmarks and discuss the various flora and fauna they observed. But most of the time they talked of what they might find in the next town or over the next rise in the landscape. Even as a young girl, Alexandra had recognized those discussions as being metaphors for their lives in general.

Randolph Brighton had not been a man to stay in one place for long. His soul yearned for new experiences. He reveled in discovering the unknown and rarely planned anything in advance, preferring to trust in where the winds of fate blew him. He'd instilled that same appreciation for exploration in his daughter. Alexandra had thrived in the freedom of such an existence.

When she'd left her father and the land of her childhood at the tender age of fifteen, her thoughts and feelings had been in a turbulent state, but she had never considered the possibility that she might be leaving Montana for good. She hadn't known then that it had probably been her father's intention all along.

Though she'd reached a point of contentment with her life in Boston, Peter's proposal had triggered a deep longing for home—a yearning to reconnect with the life she'd loved before it was possibly lost to her forever.

So here she was, riding alongside a reluctant, bad-tempered guide as they headed into the wilderness. Though she would have preferred to fill some of the long hours on horseback with a bit of conversation, there was plenty along the trail to catch her eye and entertain her thoughts. She had forgotten how it felt to be out in the open air, on horseback, with a long road ahead and no regrets behind. A familiar sense of adventure swept through her, filling her heart with renewed optimism.

It was enough to get her through the hours until they stopped to make camp for the night well before sundown. They had just reached a small lake at the base of the mountains. Bringing his gelding to a halt at the edge of a pine forest that extended from the lakeshore, Kincaid dismounted without a word.

Alexandra suspected Kincaid would have ridden a bit longer if he had been alone. That he stopped on her account sparked a contradictory response of both gratitude and annoyance.

Gratitude because, although he had not set a particularly grueling pace, it had been years since she had spent so much time in the saddle, and her body ached in ways she'd never known.

The annoyance came in with the fact that he'd never asked her how she was faring, and throughout the day, he'd cast her several dubious glances, as though he expected her to fall from her horse at any moment. Yes, she was sore and tired and hungry, and the thought of stretching out on a bedroll beside a warm fire inspired a special kind of yearning. But she would have continued if he'd asked.

At least, she thought she would have.

Probably.

Alexandra frowned as she swung down from the saddle. As soon as her feet hit the earth, her legs turned to jelly and crumpled beneath her. Even though she gripped the saddle horn with both hands, she could not prevent herself from falling.

But she didn't hit the ground.

Kincaid grasped her from behind. His strong arms wrapped around her middle just below her breasts as he brought her back to standing. He loosened his grip once she found her feet, but her strength wobbled, so he didn't release her completely.

Though her exhausted, aching muscles screamed in resistance and his secure grip momentarily crushed her ribs, neither were the cause of the hard breath she sucked into her lungs.

It was the unexpected and frightfully intense rush of heat that claimed her from head to toe while she stood with her back hard-pressed to Kincaid's chest and his forearms propped beneath her breasts.

Where did all that heat come from? Her ears burned, and her belly felt lit with some internal fire.

Then he released her and stepped away, taking his heat and strength with him.

It was all she could do not to sag against the side of her mare, and she forced her breath to a steady rhythm.

"Be more careful," he ordered as he turned to grasp his horse's reins.

Alexandra watched him lead the bay gelding to the lake's edge to drink. If she weren't so tired and hungry, she might have been amused by his perpetually gruff manner.

"I'll tend the horses," he said without looking at her. "You gather what firewood you can find."

His words did not allow for any argument. Running

her hand over Sibyl's forelock, she murmured some soft words of praise to the mare before turning away. The bounty hunter had given her an odd look the first time he'd heard her use the name she'd chosen for the horse, but Alexandra thought it suited her just fine, and the mare seemed to like it well enough.

Luckily, the forest was littered with dead branches and twigs, making her task quite easy, and the more Alexandra moved about, the more her muscles loosened and shook off the stiffness that had formed from a long day in the saddle.

After her fifth trip into the forest, she returned to camp to find that Kincaid had finished caring for the horses and was already starting a fire with the wood she'd gathered.

She added her current armload to the neatly stacked pile of firewood then watched as flames flickered to life beneath Kincaid's expert ministrations. "What else can I do?" she asked.

He didn't bother to look up as he added more wood to the growing blaze. "Set up your bedroll and keep the fire from dying." He stood and grabbed the rifle that had been strapped to his saddle. "I'll be back."

Then he strode from camp and disappeared into the trees.

She understood what he was doing—making sure she knew not to expect any coddling from him. He needn't worry. Alexandra's father had made sure any thoughts of coddling were eliminated from her head years ago. In her youth, there was no time for gentle lessons and long explanations. If something needed doing, you just got started and figured it out as you went.

Knowing it would cool significantly once the sun dropped below the horizon, she collected her bedroll and laid it out just far enough from the fire so as not to be at risk of catching any sparks. Then she added a few of the larger branches to the flames before turning to the saddlebags with the intention of digging out the small canister of coffee she knew he carried.

She felt a twinge of discomfort searching through Kincaid's saddlebags without asking. But it was a tiny twinge. Privacy was not a luxury afforded on the trail.

She found the coffee quickly enough and the small kettle to cook it in, but as she drew it out of the bag, something else came with it, falling to the ground before she could catch it.

Curious, she picked up the small tintype photograph. Though it was worn and cracked, she could still make out the image of two young men standing on what looked like the front porch of a house.

The younger man of the two—barely more than a boy, really—stood tall and lanky. His face was slightly blurred, suggesting he had moved during the exposure of the film, so it was difficult to see much of his features, but there was no mistaking his wide grin as he looked at the man beside him.

That man stood with one booted foot propped up on a wooden crate as he leaned back against the porch post in a casual but commanding pose. His arms were folded across his chest, and his eyes—Kincaid's eyes—were focused straight at the camera as though he were urging the photographer to get the whole thing over with. He looked several years younger in the photograph and did not yet seem to possess his perpetual scowl, but the familiar intensity in his gaze was unmistakable.

The two men resembled each other enough to be brothers, which left Alexandra wondering where the younger man might be now. The worn condition of the photograph suggested Kincaid had been carrying it with him for some time. She would never have taken him for being the sentimental type, yet this image clearly meant something to him.

The discovery left her with a deep sense of melancholy.

After carefully slipping the tintype back into Kincaid's pack, she fetched water from the lake to make coffee. Once the pot was set on the coals to brew, she returned to the lakeshore to wash her face and arms and filled both of their canteens with fresh water.

Nearly an hour later, she had a nice bed of coals ready for cooking. She'd found a can of beans in Kincaid's pack, and after a few minutes of debate, she had decided to use her knife to open it up and set it in the coals to warm up. If by chance he was unlucky in finding game, at least there would be something hot to eat when he returned.

Soon after, she heard two shots in quick succession, signifying the beans would likely be an accompaniment to whatever Kincaid brought back. Filling a tin cup with some of the steaming coffee, she settled down in the center of her bedroll to await his return.

The sun dropped behind the mountains, casting the land around camp into thick darkness, and she started to worry that something might have happened to delay him.

Finally, hearing a twig snap, she instinctively reached for the knife tied to her calf as she rose smoothly to her feet. Then a whistle sounded gently from the night, and Kincaid's horse gave a soft huff of welcome, followed by Kincaid's voice answering in a low murmur.

With a breath of relief, Alexandra sheathed her knife and sat back down.

A moment later, Kincaid stepped into the circle of firelight with two rabbits in hand. Seeing her seated on her bedroll, he stopped. Something curious flashed in his eyes. It was immediately followed by a tensing of his jaw and a familiar darkening of his brow.

It looked an awful lot like regret.

Though he hadn't initially wanted to take on the task of being her guide, she'd hoped his changed mind had also signaled a change in heart. Judging by the revealing shift in his features at the sight of her, that did not seem to be the case, and it hurt more than she wanted to admit.

"Do you need help with the rabbits?" she asked, her tone sounding stiff and haughty.

"I've got it," he replied as he came forward and set his rifle aside before crouching before the fire. The flicker of the flames threw a fascinating dance of light over the angles of his face, rough-hewn and handsome despite his glowering expression.

Alexandra's breath tightened. Malcolm Kincaid had a peculiar effect on her. There was no denying it. She wished she didn't find his harsh demeanor so intriguing. It seemed the more curt and gruff he became, the more she wanted to tease a smile out of him. She also wished his raw masculinity didn't appeal to her nearly as much as it did. But if she were to be honest with herself, she had to acknowledge her physical attraction to the man.

She didn't, however, have to let *him* know how he affected her.

"I found some beans and made some coffee, but I wasn't sure where you'd want your bedroll," she said helpfully, trying to shake off the tension that had settled across her shoulders.

He glanced up at that. His wolfish eyes found hers over the flames.

She got an immediate sense that she could have placed his bedroll right alongside hers and he wouldn't have argued.

She had no idea where the thought came from. It was just suddenly there, along with a heat that infused her body from head to toe, making her feel all lit up inside, like a storm of excitement, fear, and something else were all swirling together.

Then he looked back to his task and the moment was over…but the heat remained.

After setting the rabbits to roast over the flames, Kincaid laid out his bedroll and propped his saddle against a fallen tree across the fire from where Alexandra sat. Then he went to check on the horses.

Alexandra was pensive as she stirred the beans and turned the rabbits.

It was strange to think she'd been with Kincaid for two full days already, and there were still so many more stretched out in front of them before they'd reach Helena.

Her throat tightened at the thought of her father.

After he'd sent her to live with his sister, their only contact had been through letters. In five years, he never came east to see her and never asked her to come back to Montana. Not even for a visit.

She'd sent letter upon letter describing her new experiences, trying to see them as another adventure. But his replies, though prompt and heartfelt, did not regale her with the same level of description. As the years passed, despite how close they had been, Alexandra realized they were becoming strangers.

After a while, she had started to wonder if he blamed her for what had happened.

It seemed possible, considering how quickly he'd decided to send her away—and the fact that he never once suggested she might return home someday. The times she'd asked outright if she could return, he'd ignored her.

Was he right?

Had she been at fault for walking home that day by herself?

She'd done it so many times before. It was just a couple of miles, and her father had been sending her on errands by herself for years. When the two men had ridden up to her, had she said something—done something—to make them think she'd welcome their attentions?

Anger twisted inside her like wildfire in the wind.

No. She had done nothing. She knew it was true.

Yet her father had sent her away. He had been her world and then he'd discarded her. She needed to know why. Why had he sent her to Boston rather than stand by her side to face the consequences of that day?

She needed to look him in the eye and see that he did not blame her. She needed to understand what had motivated his decision to send her away, fracturing her life into two pieces.

"If you're hoping to kill that fire, you've nearly done it."

Alexandra blinked and lifted her gaze to see Kincaid leaning back against his saddle, his legs stretched out in front of him and crossed at the ankles.

"What?"

He nodded toward the fire, and she looked down to where she had been jabbing into the flames with a stick, causing the burning logs to break apart and sparks to fly into the sky.

With a disgusted noise, she tossed the stick into the fire and leaned back.

"I hope it wasn't something I did that lit your temper."

She was surprised to detect a hint of teasing in his tone. Smiling bright and false, she met his gaze as she replied, "Not yet."

The sound he made sounded suspiciously close to a chuckle.

FIFTEEN

The next day, Malcolm set a more arduous pace. He'd taken things easy the day before to give Miss Brighton a chance to become accustomed to the physical demands of traveling on horseback, but any more days like that and it would take twice as long to reach Helena.

To be fair, the woman seemed to be managing well enough.

Just as the day before, she remained quiet throughout the day, keeping her focus stretched out around her. She seemed to be soaking everything in with her deep, steady breaths and her wide blue eyes, sighing in wonder over an endless patch of wildflowers, or gasping softly at the flight of a falcon swooping close to snatch a meal before rising again into the sky.

The total lack of caution in the woman riding beside him seemed to inspire an overabundance of the stuff in himself. He found himself constantly scanning for potential dangers as they made their way. It was damned exhausting.

By the time they stopped for camp that second night, he just wanted to bed down and sleep.

But there was a meal yet to provide.

Leaving her with the instruction to take care of the horses and make camp, he headed out with his rifle. He managed to scrounge up some supper and return in less than twenty minutes.

She was still caring for the horses as he approached, speaking to them in low, murmured words as she brushed the dirt and sweat from their coats.

She knew her way around horses. Not what he'd expected, but not that unusual. He walked to where she had laid the saddles and packs. Setting aside the ruffed grouse he'd scared up, he went about gathering firewood. By the time he came back with a good armload of dried branches, it was to find Alexandra already starting a fire with some dried grass, small sticks, and tinder from his matchbox.

He stood and stared at her, watching as she knelt beside her little fire and struck the match. After carefully setting fire to the tinder, she leaned forward to blow gently across the flicker of flames, coaxing them into greater life until they expanded to engulf the pile of sticks. Then, one by one, she added some of the larger pieces of wood she'd set beside her, making sure not to overwhelm the fire before it could gather enough strength.

"You've done that before." It was stating the obvious, but Malcolm found himself forming the words before he could think better of it.

She looked up with a smile that held just a touch of smug pride. "Does it surprise you that I can start a fire?" she asked.

Malcolm dropped the armful of wood he'd gathered into a pile before he began preparing the birds for roasting. "I don't know of another Eastern lady who would've been able to do the same."

"You've known many Eastern ladies?"

He looked up from his task to see her fine brows arching in question. His breath hitched at the sight of her curved lower lip resisting a smile. She was teasing him.

He narrowed his gaze and gave a slow smile of his own. He was pleased to see her eyes widen in response. "A few," he replied simply.

He could see she wanted him to elaborate. She even opened her mouth a bit, as though she was going to say something. But she didn't. Instead, she pushed up to her feet in a way that revealed the stiffness and soreness of her muscles after two full days on the trail. Without a word of complaint or even a quiet groan of discomfort, she went to fetch their bedrolls. She dropped his to the ground at his side before going around to the other side of the fire to lay hers out on the dirt.

"I haven't always lived in Boston," she said after she'd been sitting in silence for a little while.

Malcolm had been wondering how long that would last. He speared the grouse on sticks and came forward to crouch before the fire. Propping the birds against some rocks so they could slow roast over the low flames, he shifted his attention to the woman across the fire.

She seemed lost in her thoughts. Sitting with her knees drawn to her chest, she'd wrapped her arms around her legs, linking her fingers over her ankles. Her gaze was directed toward the fire, but it was unfocused. As he watched, she expanded her chest in a weighted sigh. He wasn't sure if it was a sound of sadness, regret, or something else, but it was heavy and went deep. She didn't speak again, and after a bit, his curiosity got the better of him.

"Why'd you leave?"

Her blue eyes met his, and the emotion in them hit hard to his gut.

"Boston or Montana?" she asked softly.

Suddenly uncomfortable with how personal the conversation had become, Malcolm shrugged. He wasn't sure which option might be the less intrusive of the two.

"There was a time I thought I'd live my entire life in Montana. If you've ever spent any time there, you'd know it is beautiful country." Her eyes went dark as she stared into the flickering flames, and her voice lowered with memory. "When I went East, I didn't want to like Boston. It hadn't been my choice to go. But I made friends, which is something I didn't have much of in my childhood, and I started to appreciate the opportunities a big city could offer."

She laughed, a warm sort of throaty chuckle. "My aunt Judith scolded me countless times for my curiosity. I had a ceaseless compulsion to explore every corner of the city, the culture, the people. So very different from what I'd known before, but beautiful in its own way. Eventually, I came to love Boston."

"More than Montana?" He shouldn't want to know. He wasn't even sure where the question came from.

Her eyes met his. Gold flames danced in the blue of her gaze. "I guess that is what I am hoping to find out."

Malcolm looked at her. Really looked at her.

Her boots were dusty, as was her split skirt and the shirt she wore under the oiled slicker he'd bought her. She'd pushed the wide-brimmed hat off her head, and it hung down her back by the thin cord around her neck. Her dark hair was just barely secured at the back of her head in a loose knot that allowed fine wisps to fall against her face and neck. She had dirty hands and a weary gaze, yet she displayed the hint of a smile about her mouth.

Despite her dishevelment, the fine Eastern lady who'd boldly strode into the Painted Horse Saloon was still there. She was present in the woman's elegant posture and the refined way she spoke. In her quiet dignity and feminine softness.

It's just that Malcolm was seeing something else besides all that. A light of adventure in her eyes, competence in her manner, and a deep, barely perceptible yearning.

There was more to this woman's story than he'd first suspected. And even more going on in that head of hers than what she shared with her deceptively easy manner and light conversation.

After a few moments of returning his silent stare, she broke eye contact with a flutter of thick eyelashes and an almost rueful curl at the corner of her lips. "What about you, Malcolm Kincaid?"

He leaned back and eyed her with a lifted brow. "What about me?"

"Where do you come from?"

"Are we sharing our life stories now?"

Her gaze flicked back up to meet his. "I don't need to know *everything*, but a little something wouldn't hurt. We are going to be together for a couple of weeks, after all. Is there a reason we must remain strangers?"

Malcolm felt a rush of heat though his blood. Her innocent words reminded him of just how much he'd like to get to know her. Just not in the way she meant. And not in any way he intended to explore.

No matter how badly he wanted to taste that sweet mouth of hers.

He cleared his throat. "I ain't got much to tell."

"I don't believe that."

"Not much I *want* to tell."

She smiled. "That sounds more truthful. You like your privacy. I understand. Perhaps you can just tell me how you came to be a bounty hunter."

Malcolm shook his head. The woman was relentless.

"I am not going anywhere, Malcolm. You may as well open up a bit."

Damn him, but he liked the sound of his given name on her lips. "I just sorta fell into it," he answered gruffly.

"How?"

He tossed her a heavy scowl for her persistence, to which she responded by grinning widely.

"I was looking for someone else when I happened upon a man I'd seen on some wanted posters in the last town. I wouldn't have bothered with him, but he issued a challenge I couldn't refuse. He lost, and I claimed the bounty."

"Why on earth would he challenge you?"

Malcolm shrugged. "He said he didn't like the way I talked."

"Idiot."

He smiled at her incredulous tone. "Why? You like my Texas drawl?"

Her expression lit up at the confession. "I should have guessed. I once met a man from Houston, and you do have a similar manner of speaking."

"Houston is a far cry from where I grew up."

"And where was that?"

He stiffened. It had been years since he'd thought about the cotton farm where he'd grown up. He and Gavin had basically agreed when they'd left that there was no reason to ever bring up the subject of their beginnings.

"Doesn't matter," he said with a tight jaw.

"But—"

"Leave it."

She closed her mouth sharply and stared hard at him across the flames. Darkness had fallen while they'd talked, and the night was close around them. The fire lit her face and cast sharp shadows beyond. It was clear that she wanted to press the matter, wanted to insist he tell her everything. The woman's curiosity ran as deep as her stubborn nature. But his past was something Malcolm preferred to leave alone. There was nothing but pain and loss behind him.

After a bit, she lowered her gaze. "All right, I am sorry for prying." Her blue eyes lifted again to catch his, and something in her expression twisted around his insides. "But yes, I do like your drawl."

That night, Alexandra had trouble sleeping.

After the grouse were eaten in relative silence, Malcolm left camp for a bit. He didn't say where he was going or why, just muttered something about being back soon before he slipped off into the night.

Alexandra didn't think he'd go far or for long, since he left with nothing but the gun on his hip, but she lay staring at the flames until he returned. She did not bother to feign sleep and watched him openly as he settled down across the fire, lying back against his saddle and tipping his hat forward to shadow his face. He didn't once glance in her direction.

Alexandra continued to watch him until his breath eased to a slow and steady rhythm and then for a while beyond that.

She wasn't sure why she kept trying to envision him as the young man in the photograph. Though he still possessed the same intense focus and the slight air of arrogance, there was a weight in his manner now that had not been apparent in the image from his past. She wanted to know if it had to do with the other young man. Was he a brother or close friend? Why did the mention of his origins make him so uneasy?

Why couldn't she just let him be?

She understood the need to leave the past well enough alone, yet she felt compelled to understand his. Probably because it distracted her from thoughts of her own history.

With a sound of disgust, she rolled to her back and stared up at the sky.

An infinite array of stars spread out overhead, stretching from one horizon to the next. The night sky was so wide and encompassing that the world beneath her seemed to drop away, leaving her floating out amongst those tiny points of light, with no direction and no purpose.

It felt like a metaphor for her life, which was both comforting and disturbing at the same time, because one question repeated through her mind as she slowly drifted to sleep.

Where did Peter Shaw belong in that vast sea of stars?

SIXTEEN

THEY DEVELOPED A ROUTINE OVER THE FOLLOWING days. Most of the aches and pains eased to a fading memory. Since conversation was kept to a minimum, Alexandra filled her time in the saddle by reveling in the sights around her. The Rockies rising to the west, ever majestic and awe-inspiring. The wildflowers and winding rivers. The fresh air, late summer sunshine, and the occasional glimpses of wildlife.

The landscape they passed through was truly beautiful, and the farther north they went, the more it started to resemble the home she remembered.

Each night, when they stopped to set up camp, Alexandra would take care of the horses while Malcolm went hunting in the last light of the day. Most often, she'd also have wood gathered and a fire started by the time he returned. More than once, she'd offered to help prepare the small game he never failed to come back with, but he'd just given her a dismissive look and gone about the task himself.

She sometimes wondered if he purposely took his time while out hunting. She told herself it wasn't her company specifically he wished to avoid, just people in general, but she wished he would have gotten more accustomed to her presence after spending a few days together. Aside from that night when she'd tried to learn more about him and was effectively denied, they hadn't spoken of anything on a personal level.

Unfortunately, the lengthy silences and lack of distraction often lent her too much time to delve into her own thoughts, which inevitably ended up bouncing between worries about how her father would react to her return and concern over how to handle the Peter issue.

Every time she thought of her engagement, it was with an uneasy tightening in her chest.

She did not want a loveless marriage as the wife of an ambitious, albeit charming, politician. She did not want to forever cover up the aspects of herself that had been cultivated in the wilds of the western frontier.

Peter's offer had forced her to face the truth that although she had become comfortable in her aunt's world, she was not certain it was where she belonged. She shouldn't have left town without a word to her betrothed, but she had been a coward. Her only thought had been to return to Montana. And she had no idea how her father would greet her.

Would he even let her stay?

It was the question she most pondered during the long days in the saddle. And it was the one thing she could not answer.

Malcolm preferred to keep a distance from the more well-traveled routes. Again, something she attributed to his preference for solitude. They rarely saw evidence of other travelers except at a distance: the dust cloud from a small group on horseback racing across an open plain, a wagon and four stopped near a dried creek bed, and once, a small band of Indians watching their passing from a hilltop.

When Malcolm saw that she'd noticed the Indians in the distance, he explained that they were passing through the Shoshone–Arapaho reservation, and as long as they kept moving, there should be no cause for concern. His assurance proved to be accurate, and soon it was just the two of them again for as far as she could see.

Late in the afternoon on their eighth day of travel, a town came into view in the distance. When they continued toward it rather than veering around, Alexandra glanced at Malcolm. "Are we stopping?" she asked, holding her breath hopefully.

It had been years since she had been so grimy and dust-covered. She'd give anything right then for a thorough washing. She couldn't imagine Malcolm didn't feel the same. His beard had grown back in over the last several days, though it was not as bushy as it had been when she'd first met him. He lifted his hand to scratch along his jaw. Perhaps he was looking forward to cleaning up as much as she was.

"I figure we can make use of the hotel in town for tonight."

Alexandra couldn't hold back the little sound of delight that bubbled from her throat, and he flicked a sharp look in her direction. "Don't get too comfortable. One night, then we're off again, first thing in the morning."

"Even one night in a real bed again would be heaven." She sighed deeply at the anticipated pleasure of it. "Not to mention a steaming hot bath with real soap."

His expression shifted at her words. His eyes narrowed, their steely light becoming shadowed beneath a heavy brow. His mouth drew taut as the muscles in his jaw tensed.

Then he looked away.

Alexandra was left feeling confused, curious, and a bit breathless. She wasn't sure what had crossed his mind in that moment, but she would have given anything right then to be able to hear his thoughts.

They fell into silence for the remainder of the ride into the town, which was identified by a rough wooden sign posted at the outskirts: COULSON, MONTANA.

Seeing the sign, Alexandra turned to Malcolm. "Why didn't you tell me we'd crossed into Montana?"

He glanced aside at her. "Didn't think it mattered. We've still got several days before we reach Helena."

Alexandra frowned. It did matter. She'd been so determined to get back to this land where she and her father had roamed from one corner to the other, that she sort of figured she would know it when she'd finally arrived. She shook off the notion, not wanting to dwell on thoughts of what that might mean, when it likely meant nothing at all.

Coulson proved to be a bustling town with people crisscrossing the street in every direction. She counted no less than five saloons, two dance halls, and at least three restaurants with the most heavenly scents wafting toward them on the early evening breeze.

The hotel was a large building painted white with

black trim. It looked newly built. A sign out front boasted in-room baths and an on-site restaurant with fine dining. Though Alexandra wouldn't have cared just then how fine the dining was as long as it went beyond small game roasted over a campfire, she was thrilled that she wouldn't have to go to a public bathhouse to wash away the layers of dirt she'd accumulated.

After settling their horses in the livery right next door, they carried their saddlebags to the hotel. Malcolm got two rooms and requested baths right away. Alexandra couldn't keep from smiling, and her steps were light as they made their way up to the second floor of the hotel where their rooms were situated right next to each other.

They stopped outside the first room, and Malcolm handed her the key. Alexandra didn't realize how close they stood in the narrow, dimly lit hallway until she had to tip her head back to meet his gaze. When she did, warmth spread through her, making her stomach tighten as she parted her lips to draw a swift breath. She had become accustomed to seeing him beside her on his horse or reclining across a campfire. This—standing nearly toe to toe within the intimate confines of walls with a ceiling overhead, close enough to catch a hint of his masculine scent—was decidedly different.

"There's a laundry down the street," he said curtly as his brows lowered to shadow his eyes. "Have you got something else to wear?"

Alexandra took a moment to locate her voice. "I could manage," she replied.

"Set your dirty clothes outside your door, and I'll take them down for a washing."

"Thank you."

He stared at her just long enough for her breath to catch again and her skin to start tingling, then he gave a nod and continued down the hall to his room barely six steps away.

Not wanting Malcolm to look back and see the blush she feared was coloring her cheeks, Alexandra hastily entered her room and closed the door behind her with a slow release of breath.

The room was a comfortable size and contained everything she could have wished for right then. A large bed took up the corner and was covered in a pretty blue and yellow quilt. A rug covered the wooden floor, and an oversized copper hip bath stood in the corner behind a dressing screen. Though there was no fireplace, a small woodstove emanated heat, and the room was warm and secure.

Her bathwater was brought up almost immediately, accompanied by a plush towel and a cake of soap that smelled like wild honeysuckle.

After the last of the steaming buckets of water was poured into the tub and the door was securely locked, she impatiently removed her clothing then made quick work of unpinning her hair. She was desperate to ensure the steaming water didn't cool before she managed to sink into it.

Wrapping herself in the towel, she gathered her soiled clothing and went to the door to listen for anyone who might be out in the hall. Confident no one was about, she opened the door and dropped her clothes in a neat pile on the floor before scooting back into her room and turning the lock again.

She approached the bath with a delightful burst of anticipation. It was only when she stepped behind the privacy screen that she noticed the door tucked into the corner of the room. Her heart tripped over itself as she realized it connected to Malcolm's room.

Heat chased across the surface of her skin. Flashing visions of him undressing as he prepared for his own bath made her knees weaken. Before she realized what she was doing, she'd walked up to the door and held her breath as she pressed her ear to the door's surface.

Silence echoed from beyond. Just before she would have drawn away again, a self-chastising comment flying through her head, she heard his booted feet crossing the floorboards in his long, easy stride. A moment later, his steps sounded out in the hall. He stopped at her door, assumedly to scoop up her clothing, before he continued down toward the stairs.

Only then did she release a shaky breath, feeling more than slightly disappointed.

What had she been hoping for exactly?

With a huff of self-directed annoyance, she dropped her towel and got into the tub, determined to put thoughts of the ornery bounty hunter with steely gray eyes completely out of her mind for the duration of the night.

It was not so easy when not much later, as she soaked in the cooling water, Malcolm returned to his room. She surrendered to the image of his long, muscled body folded into the hip bath, soapy water sluicing over his broad back and down his lean torso.

Goodness, what had gotten into her? She had never had such thoughts back in Boston.

But then, she had also never met a man with so many characteristics to inspire those thoughts. And there was something to be said for being out on her own, away from all the strictures of her aunt's world and back in the wide-open spaces where one could breathe deep and feel free.

After her bath, she dressed in a very wrinkled petticoat and fine blouse that had been stuffed into her saddlebag for more than a week, grateful she'd thought to bring them along. She pulled on her extra pair of woolen stockings to keep the chill from her feet, then used her fingers to work through the length of her hair so it wouldn't dry in a tangle.

She was standing in front of the woodstove, hoping the heat would dry her hair more quickly, when a sharp knock startled her into a squeak of surprise.

Surprise, because the knock had come from the door connecting to Malcolm's room.

Her heart beat double time as she stared at the door, wondering if she'd imagined the sound.

When it came again, less patient this time, she rushed to push aside the privacy screen. The smell of honeysuckle wafted from the cooling bathwater as she turned the lock and opened the door.

Malcolm stood tall and imposing in the narrow door frame. He'd changed into fresh denim pants that fit perfectly to his lean hips and muscled thighs, and the cotton shirt he wore was an exact match to his eyes. He had left the top buttons undone, and his throat was still damp from his bath. His hair was finger combed back from his handsome face, which—no big surprise—displayed a heavy scowl.

"You didn't ask who it was," he accused. His voice was dark with disapproval.

Alexandra took a step back and crossed her arms over her chest. "Why should I? I knew this was your room."

His gaze dropped momentarily to where her breasts were pushed up by her crossed arms, and Alexandra realized that without a camisole beneath, her fine blouse did not provide proper cover. Before she could shift her arms to cover herself, his eyes lifted back to hers.

His scowl had deepened. "I could have been anyone."

Alexandra frowned at his stubbornness. "But you weren't," she argued. Then she added, "You shaved."

He blinked at the swift shift in topic, his tense expression sliding away in an instant. "Look, I figured you wouldn't be dressed for going down to the restaurant, so I arranged to have some food brought up here." He paused to glance back over his shoulder. "I've got a fire going, and a table has been brought up."

Her eyes widened in astonishment. "Are you asking me to dine with you?"

He hesitated, his body taut, as though he wished to take back the invitation. Then he let his gaze meet hers, and something sharp and hot struck her right below her sternum. The sensation was instantaneous and intense, then diffused to a wave of warmth before she could fully analyze it.

"If you don't—"

"I'd love to," she interrupted with a wide grin. She was not going to let him take that back. The idea of a nice meal at a table, accompanied by the possibility of conversation, was too enticing to lose.

"Just let me, ah…" She glanced back over her shoulder. "I will be just a moment."

She headed back into her room and grasped a light blanket off the bed to draw it around her shoulders. As a shawl, it was imperfect, but at least it provided some modesty.

He was still standing in the doorway when she stepped back behind the bathing screen.

"Ready," she said, her voice a touch breathless.

He didn't move at first. His eyes seemed to consume her in silent consideration until a knock on his other door signaled the arrival of their meal.

SEVENTEEN

Dinner was a huge mistake.

Malcolm knew it the moment she opened the door, with her hair falling lush and wavy down her back, wearing little more than a white cotton underskirt and a thin blouse that did little to conceal the shape of her breasts. But he'd gotten snared again by those blue eyes of hers and found himself inviting her to his room for dinner. Now they sat across from each other at a little table with a warm fire to one side and a bed to the other.

The food was unmemorable, but that could have been because he kept getting distracted by the woman across from him.

"Have you been to this town before?"

Malcolm paused in the act of bringing a forkful of food to his mouth. She was determined to have a conversation, even though at that moment he wanted nothing more than to escape from the way her casual proximity was affecting him.

She blinked, waiting for an answer, but he could barely find the proper words to respond as the blanket she'd tossed around her shoulders slipped down once again. He refused to lower his gaze toward the lovely shadows beneath the nearly transparent material of her shirt.

But that meant he had to look at her face.

She looked younger with her hair loose and tousled down her back and falling over her shoulders, her manner soft and relaxed. The sense of intimacy she invoked had him wishing for things he hadn't thought of in years. Though Malcolm was finding the effort to ignore his lusty thoughts almost more than he could take, it was the quiet longing inside him that bothered him most.

"Have you?" she prompted.

"Once or twice," he replied before filling his mouth with food. "A few years back."

Before she could ask another question, Malcolm stood. He had intended to wait until later to partake of the whiskey he'd picked up at a saloon after dropping off their laundry, but his mind needed a little dulling. Returning to the table, he poured himself a drink.

When she pushed her own glass across the table with her slim fingers, he lifted a brow in surprise.

She smiled at him from beneath a veil of thick lashes. "May I share?"

He gave her a pour. Half of what he'd given himself.

"You have traveled a great deal, I suppose," she ventured as she drew her glass back and lifted it to take a sniff of the hard liquor.

Malcolm leaned back in his chair. "You could say that."

The whiskey was good, but he wasn't exactly

drinking for the pleasure of it tonight. He watched as she took a tentative sip. Her eyes went wide and teared up a bit, but she didn't start coughing. After a moment, she took another sip.

He resisted the urge to shake his head.

The woman was damned determined to prove herself. That much was obvious. Though what exactly she was trying to prove and to whom was unclear.

He didn't want to be curious about her.

They were still a week or so out from Helena, and once they got there, he would wash his hands of her. Walter Dunstan was hiding out farther north, and Malcolm was anxious to get to him before the fugitive caught wind of his approach.

That had happened more than once in the first years of his pursuit. Malcolm would get to within a day's ride of the man, and somehow, the Kid would hear news of the relentless bounty hunter on his trail, and he'd have just enough time to slip away.

The quicker Malcolm got to him, the faster he would finally have the justice he'd been after for so damn long.

He watched as Alexandra took another sip of the whiskey. Her eyes drifted closed, and she swirled the liquor in her mouth before swallowing. Malcolm's belly tightened, sending jolts of need to his loins, making him hard and aching in an instant.

Apparently, justice was not all he wanted.

But it was all he was willing to take.

He downed the last of his whiskey, then shoved his plate away before he poured himself another glass. His insides were too uncomfortable to finish the meal, despite how hungry he'd been only an hour before. The hunger he felt now wouldn't be satisfied by anything on the plate.

"Why do you want to kill that man up in Montana?"

Malcolm tensed. The liquor had certainly loosened her lips, though it probably hadn't been needed. The woman had a disturbing tendency to want to know too much.

She had also finished eating and sat leaning forward with her elbows resting on the table. She idly turned her glass, making the whiskey spin in a slow swirl, while her gaze remained locked on him, as though he were the most interesting thing in her world just then.

And maybe he was. Maybe her curiosity was fueled by boredom. Or maybe it was the whiskey making her look at him like that. Whatever the cause, he felt her focus like a bullet straight through his middle. "He is a murderer."

"Who did he kill?"

"More than one person, according to the tales I've heard."

Her eyes narrowed just a fraction, and she tipped her head to the side, causing a fall of dark hair to slide over her shoulder and caress her cheek. "But only one person that matters, I'd wager."

Malcolm didn't answer. It didn't seem necessary.

"What if you don't find him?" Her question was soft, but it hit him with the force of a steam train.

He tipped another healthy dose of the whiskey down his throat. A vision formed in his mind: Gavin lying in that dirt alley with a pool of dried blood surrounding his lifeless body. "I will," he vowed. "If it takes me to my dying day, I'll find him. And I'll kill him."

"And after?"

Malcolm tightened his grip on his empty glass. *After* was a vague dream of a notion. "After doesn't matter," he muttered.

"What about a wife? Children? A home somewhere?"

Her words sent a swift kick of pain through his insides. There was a time he'd imagined having those things. In a "someday" sort of way. But everything changed when he'd let his brother get killed. Gavin had been his responsibility—his family, his blood—and he'd failed him.

He looked at her then, his jaw aching from being clenched so tight. Her gaze was expectant. Her pretty features formed into an expression that was somewhat sad, somewhat fascinated. He didn't like it. He didn't like how her questions made him feel. "Such things ain't for me."

"Never?"

"Nope."

Malcolm didn't deserve some cozy little life while his brother had nothing but the cold ground. Vengeance. Justice. Those were the things that mattered.

For some reason, his answer frustrated her. He could see it in the way her black brows drew together and her chin jutted out just a bit farther. She sat back and crossed her arms over her chest.

"So, you will just keep riding back and forth through the territories until you die. Alone."

He shrugged. Eventually, his work would lead to a bullet in his chest. It would be a fitting end.

"I find that a terrible waste," she said in a low voice.

Malcolm pushed to his feet. "Then it's a good thing it ain't your life. Dinner is over. Best get some sleep. I will bring your clothes first thing in the morning. We head out early."

He stood stiff and still beside the table as she slowly rose to her feet. Before she turned away, however, she picked up her glass of whiskey. Rather than taking another small sip, she tipped the glass and drained the last of the liquor in one large swallow.

Putting her glass back on the table, she pinned Malcolm with a steady stare. "Sleep well, Malcolm."

Then she turned and walked sedately across the room to the connecting door, looking every bit the fine lady, despite her unbound hair, underclothes, and stocking feet…until the moment she turned in the doorway.

She glanced back over her shoulder, eyes bright.

Malcolm wasn't sure what he saw in that look, but it made his body go into a riot of need while his heart thudded heavily against his ribs. It scared him, to be honest. He needed to get some distance between them—and a closed door—before he gave in to the urge inside him to keep her near.

Dammit.

It was all he could do to stand there as his blood thundered through his veins, his insides knotted, and all the muscles in his body gripped tight to his bones. His desire for her was a painful thing just then.

As though she knew what he was feeling—or perhaps because she felt just a drop of it herself—her lips parted on a breath that went deeper than a sigh.

"Go to bed, Miss Brighton," he said, his voice harsh and heavy.

She stood there for a second longer, and he wondered if she'd refuse. He had never known the kind of anticipation he felt in that moment while she seemed on the verge of coming back to him. His mind raced through the scenario as though it played out in front of him.

She'd let the blanket fall from her shoulders as she approached. He'd lift his hands to brush her hair back so he could see her face and reveal more of her subtly concealed body. Then she'd place her hands against his chest as he leaned forward to finally get a taste of those lips.

His musing was cut short by the sound of the door clicking shut. With her on the other side.

Malcolm swept up the whiskey bottle and took a healthy swig. He'd need all the help he could get to fall asleep tonight.

EIGHTEEN

THE WHISKEY DIDN'T HELP.

Malcolm spent most of the night fighting not to hear every blasted sound she made the next room over. From the soft slide of the bedcovers to her low, even breath once she drifted off to sleep. It didn't help that he'd decided to nurse the bottle of whiskey from a chair he'd placed right beside the connecting door.

He told himself it was to make sure she was safe.

He'd gotten used to having her close. Without being able to see her tucked in her bedroll across a campfire, he felt a need to ensure her presence another way.

That was how he noted the subtle shift when the gentle sounds of slumber turned to something else. At first, the low murmur only brought him to his feet. He paused to listen for any further evidence of distress. Then he heard her cry out, as though in pain or fear.

He didn't hesitate. Not even considering that she may have locked the connecting door—she hadn't—he charged through it, searching for her in the darkened room.

The bed was easy enough to spot, and her small

form was right in the center, twisting in the blankets as she thrashed about in her sleep. There was no one else in the room, no evidence of any outward danger.

Just a dream.

Malcolm was about to leave when she cried out again, her hands grasping and shoving at the twisted bed covers as though they attacked her. The word *no* tumbled over and over from her lips in a warped litany.

He glanced back to his own room. This woman's dreams were none of his business.

But the longer her nightmare went on, the more pitiful and frightened her whimpers became. She was fighting a demon in her sleep, and that demon was winning.

"Don't touch me," she nearly shouted, the words dissolving into heavy sobs.

He'd had enough.

He strode forward and reached for her shoulders to shake her awake. At his first touch, she jolted violently, her breath hitching in her chest. He jostled her again, saying her name quietly but firmly to reach past the boundaries of sleep.

She reacted with a whimper, then a fierce growl as she struck out at him, throwing her fists wildly toward his chest.

Then she suddenly sat straight up in bed, her hair a tangled mess, sweat coating her skin, her eyes wide with terror. "I didn't mean to," she whispered, her voice thin and scared. "I swear, Papa, I didn't mean to."

Malcolm stiffened. She was still trapped in her dream. "Alexandra. *Alex*, wake up. It's me."

She blinked a few times and her eyes slowly began to focus on him in the dark. They were still haunted, and her breath was still swift and shallow, but she was fully awake now.

"Oh my God," she murmured before her entire body began to shake.

Malcolm had no idea what to do, but then the matter was taken out of his hands as she launched herself against his chest. Her hands curled tightly into the material of his shirt, and her face tucked in at his throat.

He sat on the bed, holding her like that for several minutes, feeling awkward and useless.

She didn't cry, though by the degree of tension in her body, he knew she could have. Instead, she just took long and steady gulps of air, pressing her slight form against him, silently demanding he keep her safe in the circle of his arms.

After a bit, she seemed to calm down.

"You all right?" he asked.

"I'm sorry. I haven't had that nightmare in years."

"Must've been the whiskey."

"You called me Alex," she muttered. "I like it."

Malcolm didn't reply. He wasn't sure what had prompted the nickname, but he liked it too. It denoted the same strength and determination as her given name, but was less refined, less rigid. Truer to the woman he'd started to see her as.

After a moment, she drew back just enough to tip her face up to his. Nighttime shadows played gently over her face, making her eyes seem even more beseeching, and her mouth that much more inviting.

He didn't want to think of her mouth.

He didn't want to think of her body either, all warm and pliant, but he had no choice, when every second made him more and more aware of how her soft curves fit against his hard angles, and how her breath carried the faint scent of whiskey, while her hair smelled of wild honeysuckle.

Sweet elegance and fire.

That's what she was.

As he sat there, resisting the urge to explore more of what she was made of, down to every secret little detail, she brought one of her hands up to brush her fingertips along the side of his jaw.

A flare of need angled to his groin. He ground his back teeth together in resistance. He should stand up and get the hell out of there.

"Thank you," she murmured, "for coming to me."

He made the mistake of watching her mouth as she spoke, the way those lips shaped the soft words, and all hell broke loose inside him. It was the catalyst he needed.

Releasing her, he rose to his feet. "Go back to sleep." Then he walked back into his room and closed the door hard behind him.

He didn't sleep a wink.

The next morning, Malcolm waited under the extending eaves of the livery next door to the hotel. He'd had breakfast sent up to Alexandra's room with her freshly laundered clothes. He had grabbed only a quick bite himself, feeling a need to get out of his confining room and into the fresh air.

He was on edge.

To be honest, he had been on edge from the moment Alexandra Brighton had approached him in that saloon. Every day since, the discomfort had only dug deeper.

Leaning his shoulders back against the wall, he pulled his tobacco pouch from his pocket and rolled a cigarette. The morning air was crisp, though the sun shone bright in the sky. It was late August, and though autumn was still a little ways off, the days were getting cooler. So were the nights.

He took a long draw on the cigarette. He refused to think of the ways to make nights warmer on the trail, but his body responded to the subconscious suggestion anyway. With a sound of frustration, he tossed the half-finished cigarette to the dirt and ground it out with his heel.

What the hell was taking her so long?

He glanced up to scan the road in front of the hotel. Townsfolk passed back and forth on the boardwalk as they went about their daily business. A few kids were playing in the street, chasing after a mangy dog. Two older men stood outside the barber, chatting with their lips clamped around cigars and their hands tucked into the pockets of their trousers.

It was a typical scene. He swept his gaze up and down the street once more.

When an old man with sun-browned skin and a bushy gray beard stepped out from around the corner of the restaurant down the road, a prickle of unease danced down the back of Malcolm's neck. There wasn't anything particularly alarming about the man, but he looked damned familiar.

Then Malcolm recalled where he'd last seen him—in the Painted Horse Saloon the day Alexandra had walked in seeking a guide.

Where she had called out his name for all to hear.

Dammit.

It wouldn't be the first time Malcolm had been tailed. In his line of work, there would always be someone wanting revenge for a bounty he'd turned in to the authorities or had been forced to kill. Malcolm preferred to wait it out until they approached him, ideally when he wasn't in town where innocent bystanders could get in the way of stray bullets.

But he'd never had anyone traveling with him.

This was exactly the reason he hadn't wanted to take on the task of escorting her.

His annoyance almost had him striding across the street to confront the man then and there just to get it over with. Before he could, the old man started walking across the street toward the hotel.

Malcolm stiffened.

No, not toward the hotel. Toward a bigger, younger fellow with a great barrel chest and long arms who happened to be leaving the hotel. The two of them met not far from where Malcolm stood in the shadows, exchanged a few short words that he couldn't make out, then turned and headed off toward a couple of horses tied up in front of the saloon. Within minutes they were riding out of town.

Coincidence?

Maybe. Maybe not.

"There you are. Are we ready to head out?"

Malcolm turned to see Alexandra striding toward

him, once again dressed in her split skirt, serviceable cotton shirt, and the lined rain slicker. Her hair was twisted up and pinned beneath the hat he'd gotten for her. He almost wished she'd left it free down her back as she'd had it last night, but gave himself a mental kick in the ass before he could completely form the thought.

Her sunny smile said she wasn't any worse for wear after her fitful sleep last night. In fact, she looked perfectly well rested and too damned pretty.

She stopped within a few steps of him, her expression shifting into a frown. "You appear to be in a bit of a mood today. Didn't you sleep well?"

"I slept just fine." He didn't, of course. "Come on. The horses are waiting."

She gave him a narrow look, one he assumed meant she was about to say something he didn't want to hear, so he took ahold of the saddlebag in her arms and started around to the front of the livery where their mounts stood saddled and ready. Thankfully, she didn't protest.

He kept his gaze scanning both sides of the street as they headed out of town. There was no sign of the two men.

Malcolm wasn't sure if it was just his surly mood in general that had him convinced there was going to be trouble that day or some instinct he'd developed over his years chasing outlaws, but something was not sitting right in his gut.

They rode for several hours before stopping to take a rest along the Yellowstone River and eat some of the cold chicken he'd gotten from the hotel restaurant.

He sat his horse for a few minutes, watching as

Alexandra dismounted and led her mare to the river's edge. Her movements were natural and easy. She had adapted well to the trail in a surprisingly quick amount of time.

"I'm gonna go scout around," he said.

"Why? Is there something wrong?"

"You hired me to make sure you got to Montana safely, so let me do my job. Sit tight and eat your lunch. I'll be back."

Malcolm rode to higher ground to get a better view of the trail lengthening ahead. There were signs of others having passed the same way recently, but nothing to support his growing sense of foreboding. Still, he remained on high alert throughout the day as he continued to scout ahead and check behind them every so often to ensure they weren't being followed or heading into any kind of ambush.

He could see that his behavior made Alexandra nervous. If it weren't for her, he wouldn't have bothered with the extra precaution. He'd have continued on his way and dealt with whatever came at him when it came. No one lived forever. His only regret would be in failing to avenge Gavin's death.

But with the woman riding alongside him, everything changed. Even if the men were only after him, she could get caught in crossfire. And if he didn't make it out the other side of a gunfight, she'd be left at the mercy of those who did.

He couldn't let that happen.

As the bright-blue sky was brushed with the softer hues of a descending sun, Malcolm began looking for a place to make camp for the night. Someplace easily defendable, where they couldn't be snuck up on unawares.

He found a good spot against a large, rocky outcropping that prevented any approach from nearly three full sides. With only some scrub brush and a few random trees in the landscape extending from their fire, he'd be able to see anything that moved.

The nearest water source was a bit of a walk, but it was early enough that he managed to fill their supplies and get their horses watered long before dark settled in around them. Dinner was meager, since he didn't want to go too far on a hunt, but they still had some chicken left over, along with some bread and a small tart from the restaurant that had been wrapped carefully in cloth and then brown paper before being tucked into his saddlebag.

The look on Alexandra's face when he set the sweet treat on a flat rock and began to unwrap it was nearly enough to make him forget about his worries. He'd never seen anyone so damned excited for food before. He had to fight back the smile threatening to curl the corners of his mouth.

"Where did you get that?"

"The restaurant in town," he replied.

"You carried that with you all day?" Her tone was flabbergasted.

He shrugged. "I guess I forgot about it."

"I do not understand you one bit, Malcolm Kincaid," she said as she scooted up to sit beside him, gazing at the tart display in the flickering firelight. "Who in their right mind could forget such a delight?"

Malcolm slid his gaze over her profile, unable to

keep from admiring the line of her pert little nose and stubborn chin, or the way her lips rolled in to be wet by her tongue. Her hair had loosened from the pins throughout the day, and once she'd tossed her hat onto her bedroll, some sweeping locks had slid free to brush against her temple and cheek.

"Are we going to eat it or just admire it all night?"

Her inquiry drew a chuckle from him before he could stop it. The sound had her looking at him in shock. "Now, what on earth was *that*?"

He drew a knife to cut the tart perfectly in two. "I do know how to laugh," he muttered.

"I guess I'd figured it was impossible."

Malcolm handed her one half of the tart before taking his portion for a bite. Sweet and creamy with the taste of fresh berries. It was good, and in two more bites, it was gone.

Then he noticed Alexandra staring at him, her eyes wide and stunned.

He lifted a brow in question. "What now?"

"I cannot believe you just wolfed it down like that. Didn't you want to savor it? Did you even taste it?"

He flicked a glance at her tart, where one small bite had been taken. "Life doesn't always give you time to savor the good things. They can be gone before you knew what you had. Best to take your pleasures when you can."

He shouldn't have met her gaze when he said that. Once he did, he found it hard to look away. Whatever made her eyes sparkle like stars in the night had him suddenly thinking of one pleasure he hadn't indulged in for a long while.

"Why do I get the sense you don't allow yourself many pleasures in life, even when they are available?" she said softly.

"I haven't time for such things."

"You should make time."

He rose swiftly to his feet. That was enough conversation. "When you finish that thing, you'd best get to sleep."

Stalking across camp, he took a seat with his back resting against a large boulder, where he could look out over the valley. Anyone approaching their camp would have to come from that way.

He heard her moving around behind him. "You haven't laid out your bedroll yet. Are you planning to sit up all night?"

Was there a hint of testiness in her tone? He'd annoyed her. It didn't matter. "Yep."

"You are? Why?"

He debated a moment on what to say. His concerns could be nothing. There was no point frightening her for no reason. "Just a precaution. Go to sleep."

Thankfully, she did as he said. And Malcolm settled in for another sleepless night.

NINETEEN

THE MORNING DAWNED BRIGHT AND CHILLY WITH A clear blue sky and a sharp wind coming in from the north. Though the evening had been still beyond the movement of nighttime creatures, Malcolm hadn't shaken the sense of disquiet that had him itching to get going.

He stood at the edge of camp with a hot cup of coffee in his hand as he scanned the land laid out before them. Alexandra was starting to stir behind him, and he resisted the urge to rush her.

He took another sip of his coffee, then stiffened as he caught sight of some movement along a ridge not far away. It could have been a shadow created by the shifting clouds that had started to blow in, or an animal, or nothing at all. He couldn't remember the last time he'd been so on edge. He wouldn't be surprised if he was starting to see things.

"Is everything all right?"

Malcolm turned to see Alexandra standing beside her bedroll, watching him with a wary expression. "Take care of your needs and start packing up."

Her brow furrowed in question, but she started doing as he said anyway.

He returned his attention to that ridge. The subtle, shifting shadows had taken on a more definite shape. "Dammit," he muttered.

"What is it?"

"Do as I said, and fast," he said sharply, hoping she wouldn't question further. "We've got company approaching."

As he spoke, he tossed the remaining contents of his cup into the fire, then kicked the logs to spread out the heat so they'd die down faster. Both horses were fed, watered, saddled, and ready. He just needed to load up the last of their belongings.

As the growing cloud of dirt drew nearer, he made out the shapes of three men on the approach. Not terrible odds. But he'd never had a liability like this *woman* who walked up to him looking as fresh and pretty as the morning.

He threw her a fierce frown as he tied her bedroll to her saddle. "Take your horse and get out of sight behind those rocks over there. You're gonna stay hidden no matter what." He set her wide-brimmed hat on her head, wishing he could say something to take away the pale fear that had settled on her face. "If things go bad, you get on that mare and ride back to Coulson like the devil's at your heels. The sheriff can help you from there."

"Who are they?" she asked, her eyes wide. "What do they want?"

Malcolm's gut clenched with a sick kind of dread he'd never experienced before. "Don't know." But he was pretty damn sure they weren't approaching for a bit of friendly conversation. "Get hidden."

Turning away, he did his best not to let his worry for the woman cloud his awareness while he got the rest of their stuff tucked into his bags.

By the time the three riders reached camp, Malcolm was leaning back against the rock again, smoking his cheroot tobacco. He wore his coat, but had left it open with the one side tucked behind the holster of his gun, keeping the weapon accessible and visible. He noted with little surprise that the bushy-bearded fellow from town was among them, as was the barrel-chested man he'd seen in the street outside the hotel. The third rider was unfamiliar, but he eyed Malcolm like a snake preparing to strike.

He sure as hell hoped Alexandra stayed out of sight. Though his every gut instinct told him these men were trouble, he hoped for the sake of the woman behind him that they had not come to camp with any malicious intent.

Usually, if someone came looking for Malcolm Kincaid, it was with the hope of getting revenge on behalf of someone who'd met their end by his hand. There had also been the occasional gunfighter looking to make a name for himself by challenging Kincaid to a draw, but a show such as that was usually done with witnesses to spread the tale. These three men approached him in the middle of nowhere and seemed awful casual in their manner.

The old man even smiled, deepening the cracks in his weathered face. "G'morning to ya. It's a mighty fine day."

Malcolm gave a short nod. "Sure is."

"You headin' west?"

"I was just packing up," Malcolm replied, avoiding the question.

The old man shifted in his saddle. "I'm afraid I can't let you run off just yet."

Malcolm flicked a glance to the barrel-chested man, who turned to spit a stream of brown tobacco juice into the dirt. The one with the snake eyes stretched his neck as he darted his gaze about the camp behind Malcolm, as though looking for something.

"You're Malcolm Kincaid, aren't ya?"

Malcolm looked back to the spokesman of their group. "I get the sense you already know the answer to that."

"And right you are, since I heard that pretty lady call you out in that saloon down in Rock Springs." The old man chuckled, a rough sound of genuine amusement. "I could barely believe my luck. My boss has men scattered all over these territories watching for you to show up after he sent Freddy to feed you his location. All I had to do was make sure you were heading in the right direction and wait for my friends here to join me."

Fury boiled in Malcolm's blood. Freddie Golding had been sent by Dunstan. It had been a setup from the start.

He glared at the old man. "Don't count yourself lucky just yet."

Another grating chuckle. "I heard you were fast, but you ain't fast enough to shoot all three of us before one of us puts a bullet in you."

"Try me," Malcolm stated, his voice low and challenging.

"Hot damn," the barrel-chested man snorted, "this just got interesting."

Malcolm made note of his meaty hand inching toward his gun. Snake Eyes was sitting straighter in his saddle, his body tense and alert, but the old man remained relaxed and smiling. He was clearly the most dangerous of the trio.

Malcolm hoped Alexandra stayed hidden and was ready to ride off at the first shot. There was a damn good chance of catching a ricochet amongst all that rock. Her best bet was to get as far away as fast as possible. Malcolm just couldn't leave any of these three alive to chase after her.

"Don't worry, Kincaid," the old man said. "You're not gonna die today. These two are just messing with ya. Boss wants to kill you himself. Whoever delivers you to him alive gets a mighty fine paycheck."

"Mighty fine," the barrel-chested man repeated with a grin.

"Now, I'd like to do this in as civilized a manner as possible, but I've heard tales of how fast you are with that gun, and I don't intend to get shot in the process. So, I want you to take that Colt out with two fingers of your left hand and toss it into those bushes."

Malcolm hesitated. If he were alone, he'd do just what these men said. Dunstan wanted to meet him face-to-face? That suited him just fine.

But not while Alex was in his care. There was no way in hell Malcolm was going to let her fall into the hands of these men.

He shook his head. "My gun stays with me. Ride on back to your boss and tell him I'll be there as soon as I finish up some business."

"Is that what you call that little lady of yers?" Snake Eyes asked, his gaze once again darting around the camp. "We know you've got her tucked away somewhere."

Malcolm tensed. The man's slippery tone made him sick with rising fury. Snake Eyes would be the first to die.

"Don't mind my friend here. He thinks he has a way with women. I'm just here for you," the old man advised. "You do things my way, and this doesn't have to get ugly. Boss wants you alive. He didn't say you couldn't be bleeding, and not every shot kills."

"They do when I make 'em," Malcolm replied.

"Dang, Stu," said Snake Eyes, "shoot him and be done."

"You just want his woman," the barrel-chested man complained.

"Hell yeah, don't you?"

"Enough," the old man said, putting a stop to their argument. "You're coming with us, Kincaid. It's up to you if you want to do it with bullet holes or not."

"I choose bullets." He didn't even finish speaking before the old man went for his gun.

He didn't clear the holster before Malcolm drew his Colt, fired one shot at ol' Snake Eyes and a second straight into the old man's chest just as he was pulling back on the hammer. Both men hit the ground before the big guy managed to lift his gun.

Malcolm's hard gaze froze him in place. Small,

dark eyes darted toward his fallen comrades before he dropped his pistol to the dirt and slowly raised both hands. "Don't shoot. I ain't armed."

"Ride back to your boss and tell him I'm coming for him."

The man nodded vigorously and pulled hard on his reins to turn his horse and ride off the way he came.

Malcolm didn't waste time checking to see if the other two still breathed. He knew his shots were true. Holstering his gun, his only thought was of getting Alexandra out of there.

He turned to see her coming out from behind the rock, clutching the reins of her horse in a white-knuckled grip. The terror on her face caused a sickening feeling in his gut. "You all right?" he asked as he walked toward her.

She blinked a few times, then tipped her chin up to meet his gaze. Her eyes were bright with fear and something else.

"Alex," he said sternly as he lifted his hand to her shoulder.

In a flash, her gaze cleared and refocused. But she wasn't looking at him—she was looking past him. He turned, catching sight of the barrel-chested man aiming a rifle at his back. Before Malcolm could go for his own gun, Alexandra already had it drawn and lifted in both hands. Two shots sounded at once, and a searing hot pain slammed through Malcolm's shoulder.

The other man fell to the ground, his rifle hitting the dirt beside him.

Jesus Christ! She'd shot him right above his sighting eye at nearly forty yards.

He looked back at the woman next to him. She stood stock-still with his gun still raised in both hands, though her arms were starting to shake. Her face was blanched as white as flour, and her eyes held a look unlike anything he'd ever seen before.

Malcolm lifted his hand slowly to place it on top of hers, forcing her to lower the gun. It took only the slightest bit of urging, and he had the gun out of her hands and back in his holster. That brought her attention to him, but not in any natural way. Her blue eyes were wide and unfocused, like she wasn't sure where she was or what had just happened.

Then a strange, strangled sound struggled up through her throat.

Malcolm followed her gaze to where blood was rapidly soaking the gray cotton of his shirt. He checked the back of his shoulder, and his hand came back with more blood.

The bullet had passed through.

Aside from the initial blast of pain, he didn't feel much. He'd been shot before and knew that the shock would wear off soon enough and he'd be hurting. Before that happened, he needed to get them moving and find a safe place to hole up. If the old man had been telling the truth about Dunstan having men out looking for him, there could be others heading their way already.

"Alexandra."

She showed no sign of hearing him, her gaze refusing to budge from the red stain spreading over his shoulder.

"Alex," he said again, more forcefully. It managed

to bring her eyes up to his face, but the lost and haunted look was still a veil over her usually direct focus. "Get yourself up on that horse. We gotta ride out. Now. You understand me?"

She gave a tiny bob of her head, but she made no move to mount her horse.

With a muttered curse, Malcolm grasped her shoulders to turn her around, then planted his hands around her waist and hefted her up toward the horse's back, hoping she would do the rest.

Thank God she did, because the effort was enough to send a fresh flow of blood down his arm in a blast of throbbing pain and fire.

After making sure she was settled, Malcolm scooped up the extra guns and went around to the three rider-less horses to quickly gather other useful supplies from their saddlebags. He secured everything to his saddle, then swung up onto his own horse, and with only a passing glance toward the three bodies being left behind, he led them from camp and took off at a swift lope, heading straight into the mountains.

TWENTY

ALEXANDRA WAS LOST.

Lost and stumbling through tormented memories of fear and pain and blood. The recollections rushed at her from all directions, as immediate and detailed as they had been on the day it had happened.

She hadn't expected to be so affected by the sight of those two bodies lying in the dirt. It had been all she could do to hold the old, debilitating fear at bay as Malcolm approached, appearing unhurt.

But then she'd seen the one he'd sent off, creeping back around the edge of camp. When the man lifted his rifle to take aim, she'd acted without thought, grabbing Malcolm's gun and firing. It had been instinctive, just like five years ago. The feel of the weapon in her hand, the way the shot reverberated through her arms and down through her belly to where her feet were rooted hard into the ground…it was all too familiar.

This time, however, it was Malcolm who ended up with the dark stain spreading across his chest. Seeing the blood was too much. Past and present became twisted together as she remembered the face of another man who had stared at her with shock and tearful agony as the life seeped from his body to stain the ground.

She tried to close her mind to the memories, to stay present and in control as Malcolm grasped her shoulders and shouted at her. She knew he needed something from her, but she couldn't respond, couldn't grasp ahold of the current reality when the past had become so real again.

The next thing she knew she was up on her horse and they were riding, hard and fast. Across open land with wind whipping at their faces, then scrambling along narrow, twisted passes, through rocky terrain as they went up, up into the rugged mountains.

Unable to do anything but hold on and keep up, Alexandra followed, her gaze hard on Malcolm's back where at least the stain had stopped growing.

For hours, they didn't slow their pace. She was grateful for the physically grueling ride, since it forced her to bring her awareness back to the needs at hand: staying on her horse and keeping the mare from stumbling over the rough terrain. The past faded once again as her focus became trained on accomplishing the current goal.

She had no idea where they were heading, but it soon became clear that their mounts wouldn't be able to take much more. Still, Malcolm kept pushing ahead, taking them higher into the mountains and farther from the common trails. He seemed determined to get them somewhere in particular.

After riding most of the day with little rest and no talking, they entered a small valley. A grassy hill sloped down to a creek, and a thick forest of tall pines and Douglas firs crawled up the mountainside beyond. Tucked in beneath a small grove of aspen trees sat a little cabin.

Malcolm rode straight for it.

Alexandra's relief was intense.

He had not taken even a moment all day to address his gunshot wound. He was bound to be hurting, and for the last leg of their ride, he had started to sway in the saddle. He needed to rest as badly as their horses did. Alexandra didn't realize just how badly until she came to a stop beside him in front of the cabin and saw the hard grimace of pain and exhaustion etched into his features.

He said nothing as he leaned over the pommel and swung his feet to the ground. He gave a short grunt and stumbled hard against his horse's shoulder.

She quickly dismounted and came around her horse to his side. Though the bleeding had stopped at the back of his shoulder where the bullet had left his body, the same was not the case at the entry wound. His whole side was soaked in red beneath his coat. He had lost a terrifying amount of blood.

She swallowed back the lump of distress that rose in her throat and did her best to settle the churning in her stomach. Weary panic threatened again as those dark, persistent memories pushed forward. She refused to acknowledge them. Now was no time to sink into the mire of old trauma.

Malcolm needed her to be strong. "That doesn't look good," she muttered.

"It feels worse," he replied through gritted teeth.

Still holding the pommel, he looked down at her with the heavy shadow of pain in his eyes. "I'm gonna need your help."

She swallowed hard and nodded, stepping forward with the intention of slipping her arm around his waist to help him into the cabin.

"Take care of the horses. See they get water down by the creek and some grain. There's a shelter 'round back." He pushed away from his mount to stand upright as he tossed his saddlebags over his good shoulder. He paused, looking down at her as though he wanted to say something. But no words came. Instead, he clenched his jaw and turned to make his way up the two steps of the small, covered porch into the cabin.

Alexandra stared at the darkened doorway he'd passed through, biting her lip. She didn't want to leave him, but the horses had endured a grueling day and needed to be cared for.

The creek ran clear and swift only a short distance down the hill. After the horses got a nice drink, she led them behind the cabin to where a lean-to extended from the back. A rough wooden trough was built against the outer wall of the cabin, and after pouring some grain on the ground for each of them, she went in search of a bucket to fill the trough with water. She didn't have to go far, and within another thirty minutes, she had them both unsaddled and brushed down.

Confident they would be fine for the night, she rushed back to see how Malcolm was faring. The bed-rolls and saddlebags she'd left outside the front door had already been brought in. She hoped that meant his injury wasn't as bad as it had looked.

She held on to that hope for all of twenty seconds as she stepped into the cabin and saw the truth.

The shelter was as small on the inside as it looked from the outside: just a single room with two small windows to let in the dying light. A narrow bed was pushed into a far corner, and a stone fireplace was centered on the opposite wall. A pile of wood was stacked up beside the hearth next to a bucket of dry kindling. Malcolm had already started a healthy fire, and warmth spread through the small space. In the center of the room, Malcolm stood beside a single chair in front of a rickety wooden table.

He had taken off his coat, leather vest, and hat. His gun belt had also been removed and was slung over the back of the chair. On the table stood a bottle of whiskey next to a large copper bowl filled with water. His blood-soaked shirt was unbuttoned down the front, exposing his lean, muscled torso smeared with the rusty color of dried blood.

He didn't look up as she entered the cabin. His movements were unsteady as he attempted to peel the material of his shirt away from where it had gotten stuck to his wound. Weariness curved his spine and bowed his head as he focused on his task.

"Let me help," she offered.

"I'm fine."

He wasn't fine. That much was clear, but she bit her tongue against pointing that fact out.

"Are the horses settled?" he asked.

"That's what you told me to do, isn't it?"

He looked at her then with a lifted brow at the

testiness of her tone. She didn't apologize for it. Her worry set her on edge. A gunshot wound was a serious thing. It was good that the bullet wasn't still lodged in his shoulder, but there was no guarantee against infection or other complications.

She'd seen an infected wound once when she'd been young. A man at the mine where her father had worked for a short time had a deep gash in his leg after a fall. They ended up having to cut away much of the infected flesh to halt the spread of gangrene.

The thought of cutting into Malcolm's shoulder made her hands tremble. But the wound needed to be cleaned of any dirt or debris as quickly and thoroughly as possible.

He muttered a curse and reached for the bottle of whiskey, lifting it to his mouth for a quick swig. His exhaustion was obvious. He'd already lost a lot of blood, and it would do no good for him to waste what energy he had left when he would need it for recovery.

"Sit down, please, before you fall over," Alexandra directed, her anxiety making her voice sharp as she strode forward.

"I'm not gonna fall over."

"That's right," she agreed, "because you're going to sit. Now."

He gave her a warning look, but the pain in his eyes kept his expression from being very intimidating.

She smiled tensely. "I said please."

His eyes narrowed, but he lowered himself to the chair anyway. He remained still and silent, aside from some harshly drawn breaths as she carefully tried to lift the edges of the shirt away from his shoulder. The dried blood had plastered the cotton to the wound. His tugging had already started some fresh bleeding, and she was reluctant to force any more.

"Are there more cloths somewhere? Medicine or bandages?"

"There are some rags in the cupboard over there. No medicine beyond this." He lifted the bottle of spirits in a half-hearted gesture.

Alexandra worried at her bottom lip with her teeth as she considered what she would need. "You'll have to be patient as I look about for a few things. Can you manage that?" she asked.

He gave a nod. "I'll just sit right here and drink until I pass out."

She frowned. That certainly wouldn't help. She'd need him conscious if she was going to get anything accomplished.

"I was kidding," he said with a curve to his lips. "Fetch what you need."

She started with the cupboards built along the wall beside the front door. "What is this place, anyway?" she asked. "How did you know it was here?"

"It used to belong to a sort-of friend of mine."

In her search, Alexandra came across two large iron kettles for cooking, some utensils, and some tin dishes. There was also a sack of flour, some salt and sugar, a jar of honey, a few cans of beans, and a small collection of spices.

It was more than she'd expected.

She also found a stack of old rags, but they were not anything she'd want to use to clean an open wound. And there was no medicine to be found.

She would have to make do.

A bucket of water that Malcolm must have brought up from the creek while she was stabling the horses sat beside the door. Alexandra used it to fill one of the kettles that she hung on a hook over the fire. Then she went to her saddlebags and pulled out her petticoat and handkerchiefs. One of the handkerchiefs was well-used, but the other was clean enough. Using the knife strapped to her leg, she immediately went about slicing the fine material of her petticoat into strips for bandages.

"You're mighty handy with that knife," Malcolm said, his voice heavy but not slurred despite the doses of whiskey he'd consumed. Alexandra looked up from her task to see him turned in his chair to watch her. "I didn't know you had that on you."

She refused to feel guilty for the secret purchase. "There is much you don't know about me, Malcolm Kincaid."

"I'm guessing that is as true a statement as any," he said in a tone that suggested he maybe wished that wasn't the case.

She gave him a curious look, but he'd already glanced away.

When she had enough bandages, she tucked the remainder of her petticoat away. After refilling the copper bowl with hot water from the kettle, she returned to Malcolm's side and muttered a swift prayer that she remembered enough about treating a wound to do no more damage than what had already been done.

She considered having him move to the bed in case he lost consciousness—from the pain or the whiskey— before she'd finished. But she had much better access while he sat in the chair. If he were lying in the bed, or even sitting at the edge, her task would be more difficult.

She would have to be quick and efficient then.

If only her cousin Warren were there. He had gone to medical school in Pittsburgh before settling out in Wyoming a couple of years ago, to run a small medical practice. She realized with some surprise that they had probably passed not too far from where he lived near the Shoshone Mountains with his wife and two children.

Unfortunately, Warren was too far away to come to their aid now, even if she knew how to contact him. Or any other doctor, for that matter.

It seemed Malcolm only had her, and though she'd learned how to deal with a variety of injuries during her time with her father, she'd never had to tend to a gunshot wound.

"Ready?" she asked.

Malcolm tightened his hand around the neck of the whiskey bottle and gave a short nod. "Go on."

Using the water-soaked handkerchief, she drenched both sides of his shoulder where the shirt had dried to the wound. After a little while, the material began to loosen, and she was able to gently lift it away and slide it down his arm. Fresh blood oozed from the angry wound at the front. The exit wound was not so bad, though both areas were surrounded by puffy red skin that was hot to the touch. The heat and redness extended up the side of his neck and down his chest.

"What do you think?" he asked, looking at her face rather than his shoulder, where he could likely see well enough the damage that had been done.

"It's not good," she answered. The redness and

heat bothered her. She hoped it didn't mean what she suspected.

"Can you handle it, Eastern lady?"

She lifted her chin to give him a narrow-eyed look. "I can handle it, bounty hunter."

"That's what I figured," he replied before his eyelids drooped a bit over his gaze.

"But you must stay upright and alert for me," she said sternly. "Do you understand?"

He nodded, but said nothing more.

Alexandra worked quickly after that, keeping her focus on the injury as she wiped away both the dried blood and the fresh. He barely flinched as she diligently flushed out the wound, first with water, then with the whiskey. When she felt she had gotten it as clean as possible, she gave it a critical look. It needed some stitches to close it off, but she hadn't found anything in her search that even remotely resembled a sewing needle. Instead, she pressed a folded bit of cloth tight to both wounds and wrapped his shoulder securely with the strips of her petticoat before tying off the ends.

He remained silent while she worked, setting aside the whiskey about halfway through.

As she finished off the last bandage, she asked, "Can you stand? The bed looks clean enough, and you desperately need some rest."

"So do you, sweetheart." His words were delivered in a low drawl; the whiskey finally seemed to be having an effect.

"I'll be fine," she replied, though she wasn't. She could feel the exhaustion pressing in around the edges of her awareness. Her focus on Malcolm was the only thing keeping it at bay. "Come on. We've got to get you settled. If you end up falling on the floor, that's where you're going to stay."

He braced his good hand on the table and pushed to his feet, swaying a bit when he straightened.

Alexandra tucked herself along his side, fretting over the heat that emanated from his body. He was weak and unsteady, but they managed to get him to the bed. She drew back the woolen blanket just before he sat down.

"All the way," she urged.

He obliged without argument, lying back as she lifted his feet onto the bed. After tugging his boots off, she covered him with the blanket but only to his waist, not wanting to make him too warm.

"Just gonna rest a bit. Then we'll be off again." He made a sound almost like a sigh, and his head fell to the side.

Alexandra stepped back but didn't turn away. She stared at his large, muscled form laid out on the narrow mattress. His skin was covered in a fine sheen of sweat, but not as much as she'd expect for the amount of heat burning beneath the surface. And that deep, angry redness extending from his shoulder was getting worse.

Cleaning the wound wasn't going to be enough. She needed something to kill any infection that might have started to spread.

Yarrow. Or bee balm.

Glancing out one of the cabin's small windows, she saw the low slant of an evening sun. She would have to go now before it got too dark.

After making sure the fire had enough wood, Alexandra stepped outside. She hoped she'd still be able to recognize the right plants. It had been years since she'd had to gather such things, and she had no idea how prevalent they might be in this area.

But she had to try.

TWENTY-ONE

ALEXANDRA SPENT THE NIGHT IN A WRETCHED STATE of worry and exhaustion.

She found the herbs she needed and used the honey as a base for a poultice. Malcolm had barely stirred when she'd unwrapped his bandages and spread the mixture over his shoulder. It had been a challenge to get him to roll to his side so she could get to his back, but she managed it with gentle shoves and firm-voiced commands.

Unfortunately, it was no longer just the area around his wound that burned so hot. A fever had taken hold of his body.

Aside from the poultice, she'd also brewed some herbs into a tea to help fight infection from the inside, but he was too deeply unconscious for her to have any success in getting the tea down his throat. By then, her fatigue made it so that she could barely even think straight. She had to hope the poultice and rest would be enough.

Her body aching with exhaustion, she curled up along Malcolm's side in the narrow bed. The sound of his breathing lulled her swiftly to sleep.

It could not have been much later that she was awoken by deep, guttural sounds of distress coming from the man beside her. The first thing she thought as she reached full consciousness was that she had somehow contracted a fever as well. She felt as though she were roasting on a spit.

But in the next moment, she realized all the heat was coming from Malcolm.

Turning on the narrow bed, she smoothed her hand over his chest, then up to the side of his face. It didn't seem possible for a human body to exude so much heat. The light of the dying fire showed his features pressed into a hard grimace as he turned his head to avoid her touch.

The fever was consuming him.

Despite the stiffness of her limbs, she rose from the bed and stoked the fire just enough to provide more light and reheat the tea. Once the herbal drink was ready, she poured some into a bowl and set it on a chair beside the bed, along with another square of cloth from her petticoat. Using all the strength she had, she lifted his shoulders from the mattress enough to where she could ease her body between him and the wall at her back, allowing him to recline against her in a slightly more upright position.

The heat and weight of him took her breath until she managed to shift to a better angle where his head rested against her shoulder and her arms were free to administer the tea.

Then she soaked the cloth in the herb-steeped brew and brought it to his mouth, allowing the drops to ease between his lips in tiny doses. She continued the painstaking process until the bowl was empty. It would take a few hours before the tea would have any effect, but hopefully it would bring on perspiration to release the heat from his body.

By the time sunrise started to flow into the shack through the open door, he seemed to be more comfortable.

But it was a temporary reprieve.

He began a pattern of fever spikes and restless sleep followed by a period of calm and quiet. Alexandra spent most of that day alternating between administering cooling-cloth baths, easing drops of the tea between his lips, and switching out old poultices for new. She caught fitful naps at his bedside and ignored the growing hunger in her belly until it got to be too much. She then warmed a can of beans over the fire.

When Malcolm settled in for what she hoped would be another stretch of calm sleep, she decided she had better see what else she could find to eat before the sun set again.

Earlier, she had snooped more about the cabin. In a small trunk that had been pushed under the bed, she found some men's clothing made for a frame larger than hers, though not nearly as large as Malcolm's, and a small cake of soap wrapped up in burlap.

After spending the last few days in the same clothes, she was grateful to borrow the stored attire that was much more suited to her current situation. Her split skirt and cotton shirt were in desperate need of a washing, as were her underclothes. Though the pants were a bit baggy and had to be held up by a strip of rope, and the flannel shirt hung down to her knees until she tied the ends at her waist, at least the clothing was clean.

At some point, she would wash their clothes in the large washtub she'd also found under the bed, but for now, finding more herbs and some food were more vital priorities.

It was a relief to have something more appropriate to wear while scouting the land around the cabin. On her way out, she passed by Malcolm's Colt, still slung over the back of the chair. She had a sudden unexpected urge to take the gun with her before the familiar fear swept the thought away. She'd been able to raise the gun to protect Malcolm in a moment of instinctual reaction. But to intentionally take up the weapon…she couldn't.

She would be fine without it.

Careful not to venture too far from the cabin, she still managed to make wider circles than she had done the prior evening.

She was delighted to find some wild mushrooms and wild onion and greens that could be added to a soup. It would not be terribly filling, but it was better than nothing. Based on the animal tracks she'd seen, she decided that if they were going to be staying for a while, it would be a good idea to set some snares. When he made it through the infection, Malcolm would need something more substantial than watery soup to help him regain his strength.

Thank goodness her father had always been so determined to learn all there was to know about surviving off the land. As a child, she hadn't thought twice about the knowledge she'd soaked up at his side. He'd made sure she knew all the various uses of local plants and herbs, how to hunt with bow, pistol, and rifle, and how to fashion a snare or a rudimentary fishing pole out of whatever was at hand. She'd never considered the skills anything other than necessary... until she was sent east, that is, and discovered how odd such skills were considered amongst her aunt's people.

Peter had said he appreciated the ways she was different from other young ladies in his set. What would he think if he saw her now?

In truth, it didn't matter. She would still do what she had to do.

When she returned to the cabin, it was to find Malcolm in another fever peak. This one was different, however. Sweat soaked the sheets as he moved in fitful, thrashing movements beneath the blankets. Perhaps the fever was finally breaking.

Hopeful relief rushed through Alexandra, chasing away any lingering exhaustion. She quickly went about making him as comfortable as possible, bathing him with wet cloths soaked in water from the creek. After a while, he seemed cooler to the touch, and his restlessness calmed to the point that she was able to change his bandages. The wounds were still swollen and red. A slightly discolored fluid leaked from the entry site.

She applied the poultice, making a mental note that she would need to make more the next day.

Filling the two iron pots with water, she set them both over the fire. The smaller one would hold the soup, and the larger was for washing. Though washing with a cloth was not going to be nearly as satisfying as sinking into a bath, at least she had the chunk of soap, and she'd be able to dunk her head in the tub to wash the dirt from her hair. She would just have to be quick about it, since the cabin offered nothing by way of privacy.

She glanced at the man sleeping somewhat peacefully in the bed. She hoped it wasn't wishful thinking that he seemed to be resting more comfortably. After checking on him one more time to find that his skin was damp and much cooler to the touch than it had been, she began the process of preparing the items she'd brought back from her scavenging expedition.

First the soup, then the bath.

If his fever was truly on its way out, he might be waking soon. And after two days with no more sustenance than herbal tea, he was going to be famished.

Malcolm felt like hell.

His body ached from head to toe, except for his shoulder, where it seemed like a burning hot stone was pressing down on him, making it impossible to move his arm without shooting pain.

He tried to turn his head, but everything hurt too damn much. He was as weak as a child.

A moment later, a cooling hand pressed to his forehead, and he heard the low murmur of a familiar woman's voice. He tried to focus on that voice but couldn't grasp a firm hold. Unable to resist the weight of his exhaustion, he slipped helplessly back beneath the dark waves of sleep.

The next time he woke he felt a bit stronger and managed to open his eyes enough to see the flicker of firelight against a plain wooden ceiling. He shifted, and deep, throbbing pain rolled through his shoulder and down his arm, making his stomach turn.

And he remembered. Dunstan's men riding into their camp. The shooting.

Alexandra drawing his Colt and killing that man with an expert shot.

And the bullet that went through his shoulder.

Thank God they hadn't been far from Yellow Tom's cabin. They were damned lucky Malcolm managed to get them here, though he barely remembered the details of that day.

Giving up on trying to sit, he turned his head, expecting to see Alexandra nearby, probably scared out of her wits at being left alone to tend an unconscious man.

The cabin was dimly lit by a low fire burning in the small hearth, and the gray light of a cloudy day could be seen through the small windows. Clothing had been draped over the chair and the table, both of which had been pulled closer to the fire for drying. He noticed the split riding skirt, the cotton shirt, stockings, and fine white underthings.

But no Alex.

With a grunt of pain, he tried to lift himself higher against the pillows.

Where the hell was she?

Glancing about, he got the sense that she hadn't been gone long. The fire was well tended, and a strange smell hovered in the room, earthy and medicinal.

As he lay there, struggling to prop himself up on

his good arm, the cabin door opened, and Alexandra stepped through. She wore baggy woolen pants, with her knife strapped to her hip, and two dead rabbits hung from a rope in her hand. Her blue gaze swept to the bed where he lay, and her lips parted on a swift indrawn breath.

"You're awake," she exclaimed in a low voice as she laid the rabbits beside the door and approached the bed.

He grunted, the sound passing harshly through his parched throat. "You might call it that," he muttered thickly. "Not sure I would."

"Let me get you some tea."

He didn't feel the slightest craving for tea. Whiskey would have been more welcome, but she was already headed to the fire.

She took off her coat along the way and tossed it onto the chair seat, followed by her felt hat. Along with the oversized woolen pants, she wore an old, faded flannel shirt that was way too big for her, and she had braided her hair into a long rope hanging down the center of her back, leaving the end to swing against the bunched-up seat of her pants. She looked nothing like the woman who had barged into the saloon a couple of weeks ago.

The transformation was unsettling.

She returned to his side with a battered old tin cup. Steam rose from its depths. "I brewed this fresh this morning." She flashed a quick smile. "I will heat up some soup when you feel up to it."

"How long have I been out?" he asked. The words felt like sandpaper passing through his throat.

"This is our third day here at the cabin. I thought you might wake up last night, but it seemed you needed another night of rest."

He tried to push to sitting again, but weakness and the pain in his shoulder made his jaw tighten with the effort.

"Here. Let me help."

She set the cup down on the floor before leaning forward to slide her arm and shoulder around behind him. Leveraging him with very little disturbance of his arm, she efficiently rearranged the pillow to give a little added support. It wasn't quite sitting, but it would allow him to drink the tea without pouring it all over himself.

"You've done that before," he stated as she settled herself at the edge of the bed and reached for the cup again.

She tossed him another smile. "A time or two."

It galled his pride that she'd had to play nursemaid to him. He was supposed to take care of her, not the other way around.

"Drink this, please. It will give you some strength."

He took the cup from her hand and sniffed the fragrant steam. It smelled of soil and rain and some unidentifiable element.

He must have made a face, because she gave a soft chuckle, bringing his eyes back to hers. "It's not nearly as bad as what I had to give you the last two days. You are lucky you've been unconscious with fever."

"You been trying to poison me?" he asked with a lifted brow.

She gave a snort. "Hardly."

He took a drink of the watery brew, then another. The heat of it soothed his throat, and the taste was not nearly as bad as the smell. As he sipped, she returned to the fire where she crouched beside an iron pot swinging from a hook attached to the wall. She drew it out from over the fire and stirred its contents.

She moved about the cabin with a quiet sort of ease and confidence that he hadn't noticed during their days on the trail…though if he were honest, he would have to admit that maybe it had always been there and he just hadn't been paying attention. He recalled the many times she'd offered to assist with various tasks, only to have him shut her down. He'd assumed she'd only offered out of some obligation of manners.

But maybe she did know how to properly dress a bird and skin a rabbit.

"I need to check your shoulder," she said as she returned to his side. Her hip bumped against his as she sat beside him on the stiff mattress.

She displayed no prudish hesitance at being so near to him while he was naked from the waist up. She'd apparently had time to get used to it and didn't even seem aware of the impropriety of the situation.

He was aware.

Even though he ached from head to toe and his shoulder throbbed and burned like the devil, he was damn sure aware of her. Her nearness, her scent— more earthy and fresh, but still sweet—her warmth, and the way all those things made him feel deep down in the dark hollow of his being. Days of fever hadn't been enough to lessen his attraction to her.

It possibly only increased his desire. It had been

easier to ignore when she'd been so obviously out of reach. But the woman beside him was not a stiff and proper high-stepping lady.

This woman was all ease and comfort and feminine capability.

He watched her face while she started to release the bandages wrapped around his shoulder. Her expression was intent, her eyes focused. Her hands were warm and her fingers deft as they brushed his tender skin. He clenched his jaw to keep from flinching when the final layers of the cloth were removed, leaving his wound unprotected.

She probed gently around the area. She did not hesitate in her actions and gave no indication of being repulsed by the damaged flesh.

"The area has cooled, and there is no more dis-colored fluid draining from the site," she murmured thoughtfully. "But there is still a great deal of healing to be done."

Lifting her gaze to meet his, she stilled. The black centers of her eyes expanded, contracting the blue around them. Her lips were parted as though she had intended to say something but couldn't manage to get it out, and Malcolm suspected he knew why.

While she'd been tending him, she'd leaned in close to conduct a thorough examination, and when she'd finished, she'd laid her hand on his chest, just over the spot where his heart beat heavy and strong. It seemed a natural action at the time, but when she'd lifted her eyes, she had clearly been surprised by the intimacy of their position.

He couldn't stop the subtle curling of his lips. "A

bit different now, isn't it?" he asked, keeping his voice low, not wanting to spook her.

She took a slow breath, then let it out on a shaky little sigh before she drew back and lifted her hand from his bare chest. "A bit," she answered before she rose to her feet with a blush that told him she wasn't entirely unaffected.

Malcolm regretted her retreat. He liked having her near, having her hands on him, even if it was in the capacity of nurse rather than lover. He didn't want to think about the other things she made him feel, deep down where he'd buried old expectations for a future home…and family of his own. He shouldn't associate such thoughts with her. She was a fine Eastern lady— except she wasn't. She was *Alex*, and that meant a helluva lot more than he'd ever thought it could.

"Finish that tea," she said as she moved across the cabin to a cupboard on the far side. "I am going to make up another poultice before replacing your bandage, and then we can talk about heating up some soup."

Malcolm did as she instructed, the pungent brew getting better as he drank it. And all the while, he silently watched her.

As she selected from a store of fresh herbs and ground them into paste in a small bowl.

As she deftly used her knife to cut more strips of soft cotton from her petticoat to use as bandages.

As she hung another black kettle over the fire to heat the soup.

As she sat beside him on the bed once again and applied the poultice and bandages with efficient skill, giving him a soft nudge or a low-spoken word when she needed him to move this way or that.

When that task was finished and she would have stood to move on to something else that needed doing, he stopped her. Resting his now-empty cup in his lap, he reached out with his good hand, placing it on her forearm before she could move away.

"Thanks."

Her eyes brightened as her lovely mouth curled with amusement. "Did you think I'd let you die?" she teased. "I need you, remember?"

He sent a swift glance about the cabin before bringing his gaze back to hers. "You seem to have managed just fine without me." Her glowing smile had his belly tightening. He needed to shift focus before he did something he shouldn't. "Now, what was that about soup?"

TWENTY-TWO

He insisted on eating at the table rather than in the bed like an invalid.

Alexandra refused to allow it, but he just started getting up anyway, and she had to rush to his side to add her support in case he wasn't as up to the task as he thought himself to be.

Gratefully, he made the few steps with minimal assistance. She would have liked to give credit to her teas, but she suspected it was just him.

When she commented on it, he shrugged. "I've always been able to bounce back real fast after catching sick. One day I'd be laid out in bed, feeling near death, the next day I'd be running around, climbing trees."

Alexandra liked imagining him as a rowdy little boy, dirt-covered and unable to sit still.

"Well, don't overdo it," she warned. "You may have recovered from the fever in record time, but that gunshot wound is nowhere near to being healed."

"But it will heal," he said. "Thanks to you." He lowered himself into the chair beside the table. "How'd you know what to do with the herbs and all?"

"My father had a passion for knowledge about the land we traveled and how to survive on it. You could say he was a bit of an adventurer. He made a point of learning all he could about a place, its people, the jobs they did. I was always at his side, so I guess I soaked up that knowledge along with him."

"Is he the one who taught you to shoot?"

She stiffened and met his sharp and steady gaze. Awareness mixed with uncertainty slid through her. Now that he was awake, it was unnerving to be so close to him while he remained dressed only in his pants and bandages made from her underthings. And his voice, quiet and deep, did things to her.

"He is," she replied before turning away, hoping he wouldn't ask any more questions along that track. She had very purposely not thought about what she had done when she'd seen that man pointing a gun at Malcolm's back, or how she'd felt at the sight of the blood spreading across Malcolm's shoulder.

Stepping away, she busied herself with fetching a bowl of soup, starting with mostly broth for the first helping. If he did well with that, she would get him a more substantial portion. When she set the bowl in front of him, he looked up at her, his expression indicating he was unimpressed by the watery broth.

That morning she'd found a patch of wild carrots and managed to identify several other plants with roots that could be dug up to add more nutritional elements to the stew she planned to make with the rabbits she'd caught. But that would have to wait until later. For now, it was the mushroom and onion soup with steeped greens.

"Just to start," she said. "You haven't eaten anything beyond the tea for two days. I don't want to overwhelm you."

He gave a grunt in response but picked up his spoon anyway.

He was obviously not adept at using his left hand, and Alexandra had to bite her lips against offering to help.

Leaving him to it, she went about pulling the sheets from the bed. They needed a good washing, and she had found a second set in the small trunk with the clothes. She supposed Malcolm might enjoy a more thorough bath as well, considering she had been limited in what she could do with a wet cloth while he'd slept. Straightening with the load of linens in her arms, she turned to see Malcolm watching her.

Her heart gave a little flip at the predatory nature of his gaze. She was reminded of how she'd once felt like a sheep to his alpha wolf. In that moment, she wished she were more wolf than sheep. An equal to him. In his eyes, at least.

"What?" she asked, needing to break the strange tether he'd tied around her chest with that look.

He just shook his head and went back to his soup.

After dropping the soiled linens in the washtub and remaking the bed, she scooped up the bucket she used to haul water from the creek and headed for the door. "I'll be right outside if you need me."

"Leave the door open," he said. "This place could use a little fresh air."

She hesitated. The rising sun had burnt away much of the early morning cloud cover, and it looked like it would be a clear day. There was just a slight autumn nip in the air, but it was more invigorating than anything. "I don't want you to catch a chill."

"I'll be fine," he said before he lifted the bowl to his lips and drank the last of the broth.

"Would you like more soup?" she asked, taking a step back into the cabin.

He rose to his feet with the bowl in hand. "I've still got one good arm, and my legs are working just fine. I can manage."

He was doing better than managing. Aside from a little weakness and being unable to use his right arm, he barely seemed the worse for wear. The strength would return once he got more nourishment in his body. It was a relief to see that he was likely going to be just fine.

More than fine. He'd probably be ready to ride out again in just a few days.

She wasn't exactly sure why, but that thought gave her a sharp stab of disappointment. She pushed it away quietly and went back to work.

Bringing the horses down to the creek with her, she tied them on long leads so they could graze. Just as she started heading back to the cabin with her bucket of water, Malcolm stepped out. He had slipped on a fresh shirt, though he'd only buttoned it halfway up, leaving the spread of his collarbone, the edge of his bandage, and a good portion of his chest visible. In his good hand, he carried the soup kettle.

Alexandra stopped to watch him stride strong and sure down the little hill toward the creek. Aside from the way he held his right arm bent and tucked in against his side, she never would have known he was injured. He paused beside Deuce to stroke the gelding's neck and mutter something only the animal could hear.

She felt warmed by the sight of him. It was strange, really, when she'd basically been looking at him non-stop for the last few days. But seeing him as himself again made her feel relieved yet oddly melancholy, proud but in a possessive sort of way, and ultimately… awkwardly besotted. Such a strange mixture of emotions. She had no idea where to start to make sense of it all.

While he had been unconscious, she'd been too concerned for his well-being to consider her attraction to him. But now…her awareness of him and the pure pull of his presence seemed to be stronger than ever.

When he looked up and saw her standing halfway up the hill just watching him, he raised a brow in silent question.

"Are you sure you should be moving about so freely?" she asked, saying the first thing that came to mind.

"I'm sure," he replied. "We can't stay here long. I don't have the luxury of acting the invalid."

She didn't reply to that and stood silent as he continued down to the edge of the creek. But when he started to wash out the kettle, having apparently eaten all the soup she'd made, she rushed to his side. "I can do that."

"So can I," he said stonily.

Alexandra clenched her teeth. She had thought him stubborn and terse before, but apparently, an injured Malcolm could be even more so.

Rather than argue with him, she headed back up to the cabin. Daylight and fresh air filled the little shelter, making it almost cheerful. It was quite a difference from the dark and quiet she'd been living in for the last few days.

After putting some of the water into the second kettle to heat over the fire, she started to fill the large washtub. She didn't see Malcolm on her second or third trip to the creek and assumed he'd stepped into the trees for privacy. But as she turned after emptying another bucket into the tub, she nearly bumped right into him.

He had come into the cabin so quietly that she hadn't even heard a floorboard creak.

He was close enough that she had to tip her head back to look into his face. He seemed to fill the little one-room cabin with his height and the breadth of his shoulders. His natural air of command and innate strength hadn't been diminished by his fever, and in the confining space, he presented an intimidating presence.

But Alexandra wasn't intimidated.

Rather the opposite. Everything about him drew her in.

Standing there with the bucket in her hand and a gasp of surprise on her lips, she had to fight the urge to sway into him, to become surrounded by that strength and revel in the undeniable maleness of him.

"You don't have to do everything." His voice was oddly intimate as he slid his much larger, rough-textured hand over hers to take the handle of the bucket out of her grip.

She kept her fingers curled tight.

"I don't want you to overdo it," she replied, wondering at the way the words had to fight their way up through a throat gone suddenly dry. "You've been very sick. You are probably still weak. Doing too much could reopen your shoulder."

He gave her a frown. "Let me decide what's too much."

"But—"

"Alexandra, I get it. You've proven what you're capable of."

Something in his words bothered her, dousing her rising heat with a wash of cold annoyance. She released the bucket to him and crossed her arms over her chest. "You think I took care of you to *prove* something?"

He lifted his brows. "You've been saying from the start that you wouldn't be a burden. I'll admit I didn't believe you. I can see I might've been wrong."

"Might have?" she interjected.

He said nothing to that, but she could see the muscles in his jaw tensing as he clenched his teeth. He was getting frustrated.

Well, good, because she was already there. She had reached her limit with his belittling tone, his skepticism, and his stubborn refusal to *see* her.

He couldn't just admit that he'd underestimated her? That maybe he had gotten her wrong?

Of course not. That would be too reasonable.

"You listen to me, Malcolm Kincaid," she said in a level tone, despite her rising irritation. "For fifteen years, my father and I lived all around the Montana Territory. Just the two of us most of the time. My father grew up in as fine a lifestyle as can be imagined, and when he got out here, he had a lot to learn. It wasn't easy for him, which is probably why he made sure such things were as natural to me as breathing. From the time I could toddle around on my own two feet, I started learning how to forage, how to fish, snare, and hunt. I didn't learn those things to prove anything—I learned them because it was necessary."

Her chest tightened as Malcolm just stared at her with an ever-darkening scowl.

"You want me to be some pampered lady? Well, I'm not. I never have been. I just learned how to wear the clothes, that's all. Everything I did here was because it needed to be done. And there're still things that need to be done. You want to do your part, fine. But I'm sure as hell going to do mine."

She turned away and headed for the door, swiping up an old sack from the cupboard counter as she passed. Before stepping outside, she stopped and looked back at him.

"I'm going to set some fresh snares, then I'm going to gather up some things for tonight's meal. You want to lug buckets up from the creek, go ahead. When you are done, you can wash yourself up, because frankly, you stink."

That parting shot was totally unnecessary—the man had been ill for days; was he supposed to smell like flowers?—but she was just angry enough to stoop that low.

As she stomped out into the woods surrounding the cabin, she couldn't help but realize she had over-reacted just a bit.

All right, maybe a lot.

She blamed it on a lack of sleep and the tension she'd been living with over the last couple of days as Malcolm fought through the fever. Surely, it wasn't because his opinion of her mattered so much.

She'd spent the last five years in Boston, covering up aspects of herself that would have been misunderstood at best, ridiculed and shamed at worst. For the last few days, though she'd been focused on making sure Malcolm made it through the infection, she'd also finally felt like herself again. All of herself. It had felt so right and easy to fall back into the way of life she'd been gone from for so long. So much so, that she hadn't even had to stop and think about it.

But now she did. Malcolm's careless words made her feel extremely self-conscious, just like she'd felt when she'd first arrived in Boston. As though she had done something wrong, though she couldn't understand what it was. Or more to the point, that *she*—the girl she was, the person she had become— was somehow wrong.

It had been confusing when she'd been fifteen, but it was possibly more so now. She knew what it was to act like the young lady everyone wanted her to be. But now she'd had a chance to relive the freedom and confidence she'd known as a girl, and she liked it.

Yet it still wasn't acceptable.

Well, too bad.

She stomped on a dry stick lying in the underbrush and snapped it in half, sending one end of the stick flying back at her shin.

"Blast," she cursed under her breath as she stopped to rub at the smarting injury.

She was done behaving in a manner designed to meet the expectations of other people. If Malcolm couldn't accept her as she wanted to be, then that was his problem. It was long past time that she stopped trying to please everyone else and finally accepted all of who she was. There would always be someone to find fault, but at least she would be real. She would be free.

TWENTY-THREE

ALEXANDRA RETURNED TO THE CABIN ALMOST TWO hours later.

Malcolm stood outside, leaning back against the frame of the open door. He had stepped out with the intention of tracking her down, certain she had gotten lost or injured somewhere.

Luckily, he'd heard her approach a full minute before she'd stepped into view and had enough time to appear more relaxed than he felt. After the earful she'd given him earlier, he had a feeling she wouldn't appreciate his concern.

As it was, as soon as she saw him standing there, her steps slowed a bit, giving him time to take note of her appearance.

She walked with long strides across the little clearing and carried a small sack filled with whatever she'd scrounged up from the forest. She'd bypassed her coat and hat, likely because she'd left in too much of a hurry to grab them. Her long, dark braid rested over her shoulder, and some loose strands brushed against her cheeks and throat. Her eyes were bright blue in the sunshine, and her skin was taking on a golden hue.

She looked damned appealing if he were to be honest with himself. But then, she'd attracted more than a passing notice from him the moment he'd first seen her. And every time after that. It was a force that kept expanding and going deeper. He was afraid that when he had to, he wouldn't be able to shake it.

Stopping in front of him, she gave him an expectant look. He knew it was probably because he was blocking the doorway, but he decided not to accommodate her just yet.

"I owe you an apology," he muttered.

She arched a fine, black brow in a skeptical expression he knew he deserved. "I underestimated you and offended you. I'll do my best not to do that again."

After a moment, she responded with a short nod and a pretty pinkening in her cheeks.

"I would have dressed the rabbits," he continued, "but couldn't quite manage it."

He wasn't about to tell her that just getting washed up and dressed had taken nearly an hour of grunting and wincing.

A frown tugged at her brows. "I didn't expect you to do that. I can dress the rabbits."

He grimaced. "I don't like not being able to do things for myself."

She released a heavy sigh of exasperation. "You are supposed to be recuperating. That's all you need to worry about."

"I'm hungry."

"Then let me pass, and I'll start our supper," she said with growing frustration.

He wasn't sure why he was baiting her like he was—it just felt like something he needed to do. To release some of the tension between them, maybe.

He pushed off from the doorframe to stand at full height.

She took a step forward, obviously expecting him to move aside right away.

He didn't, and she brought herself to an abrupt halt, visibly stiffening at their unexpected proximity. Tipping her head back to look up at him, she gave him a fierce little scowl that was far more attractive than it should have been.

Blood pulsed thick and hot through his veins, and his stomach tightened with a specific sort of craving. "I washed up," he said in a low tone, unable to completely keep the sensual suggestion from his voice, though he did his best to hold tight on the reins of his rising desire. "Even used soap and put on some clean clothes. Do I smell better now?"

She drew in a deep breath through her nose. It seemed to be an involuntary action, because as soon as she did it, a blush spread across the crests of her cheeks.

"You smell fine," she muttered quickly as she glanced to the side and lowered her chin.

It was difficult to hold back the chuckle, but he managed. "Glad you approve." Then he stepped to the side, and she rushed past him into the cabin.

He considered following her inside, but as she started emptying the items from the sack onto the table, he realized she'd be kept busy for a while preparing the stew. It was a good opportunity for him to do a little scouting of his own.

Besides, being in close quarters with her while his body was so primed with physical need was not a great idea. "I'm gonna take a walk around."

"Watch out for snares," she said without looking up.

He'd tried to get his gun belt strapped on earlier, but with his right arm practically useless, he'd given up. Feeling naked without his Colt, he'd tucked it into the waistband of his pants instead. He was a horrible shot with his left hand, but it was better than having no means of protection at all.

At least his legs could get him around. He was still physically weakened from the fever. The soup had helped, but he figured his energy wouldn't last much longer. He wanted to get a look around while he still felt able to do so.

Malcolm made several widening circles around the cabin, checking for any sign of human activity beyond Alexandra's movements. There was nothing to set off any alarms, but he knew he wouldn't be able to relax until Alexandra was safely in Helena and he was on his own again.

Once that happened, Dunstan's men could come for him anytime. It'd save him the trouble of having to explain who he was when he showed up at the man's door.

The sun was heading toward the horizon as he made his way back to the cabin, following the bubbling flow of the creek. Stepping into the little clearing, he came to a stop. She must have washed the bed linens while he'd been gone. They'd been slung over low tree branches to dry in the breeze. Something about the sight of the gentle-sloped hill leading up to the tiny cabin set beneath the aspens, smoke rising from the stone chimney, gave him an unexpected twist of discomfort in his gut.

The scene was too warm and welcoming. Too damned domesticated.

Shoving down the unexpected longing that rose to mix with eight years of guilt, he headed up the hill in long, careful strides. The little bit of scouting around he'd done had worn him out. If he didn't sit down soon, he was liable to fall on his ass.

They'd have to move on soon. But knowing Dunstan had men looking for him, there was no way he was gonna take a chance out in the open again until he had full use of his right arm.

He flexed and fisted his right hand as he tried to circle his shoulder. Pain shot down to his fingertips, and the fist he made was no stronger than a child's. At least Yellow Tom's cabin was tucked deep into the mountains, far from any town or common road. If Dunstan had more men out looking for him, they'd be unlikely to find them here.

He still couldn't believe the way Alex had pulled his gun and shot the man sneaking up behind him. There had been no mistaking the stricken panic on her face and the glassy, disconnected look in her eyes when she realized what she'd done. She'd been locked in pure terror.

But there was also no denying her skill. Her movements had been sure and steady, her aim undeniably impressive. Something had happened to create that fear in her. It hadn't always been there, or she never would have picked up a gun to learn how to shoot in the first place.

Entering the cabin, he was greeted by a wealth of delicious odors, rich and wonderful.

"Damn, that smells good," he said as he closed the door behind him, then slid his Colt back into the gun belt, where it hung from a nail beside the door.

"It won't be long." Her tone was light, suggesting she had gotten over her earlier irritation. He got the sense she wasn't one to sit and stew for long.

As his eyes adjusted to the dimmer lighting in the cabin, he saw her standing before the fire, stirring the contents of the kettle. The end of her thick braid swung against her hips as she straightened and looked back at him.

The top buttons of the flannel shirt were open, revealing her slim neck and the shadows of her collarbone, and her sleeves had been rolled up to just below her elbows. The heat of the fire had caused the wispy strands of hair framing her face to curl, and the fire reflected bright and inviting in her eyes as she favored him with a smile.

Malcolm felt like he had gotten kicked in the chest by a horse.

Heat unfurled in his belly, making him stiffen in resistance. The intimacy of their current situation was making it nearly impossible to keep to his vow not to lust after her.

Why exactly had he made that vow, again?

"Why don't you take a seat at the table?" she said with a tip of her head. "Since there was only the one chair, I pushed it over to the bed, so we can both sit while we eat."

Malcolm glanced at the table, which she had already set up with their dishes and utensils. "What can I do?" he asked, needing a distraction to pull his thoughts from the lustful turn they'd taken. "I'm feeling kinda useless."

She tossed another smile, this one containing a clear flash of mischief. "You're an injured man. You are useless."

He narrowed his gaze. "You're lucky you're way over there when you say that."

"I'm not stupid."

"No, not stupid," he agreed. "Maybe a might impulsive?"

She tipped her head in brief consideration, then shrugged. "Sometimes."

"More than a little bossy."

She narrowed her gaze at that, but it looked like she was trying to suppress a smile in the way she pressed her lips together. "When the situation requires it," she acknowledged.

"With more courage and grit than I expected."

She didn't reply to that, but he thought he saw a blush warm her cheeks before she crossed the room to the cupboards along the wall.

"Considering your expectations were set pretty low to begin with," she replied with an exasperated sigh, "I didn't really have far to go to surpass them."

He almost chuckled at her sass, but held it in, enjoying the game too much to give it up just yet. "How was I to know you had all this hidden beneath that fancy getup you wore?"

"Maybe you should not be so quick to judge someone by their appearance," she answered smartly as she returned to the table with the half-empty bottle of whiskey in her hand. "Are you going to sit?"

He looked at the two options then back to her. "Would you rather have the bed or the chair?"

As soon as he asked the question, his body tightened with that deep and delicious kind of ache that came with harshly suppressed desire.

Two images immediately flashed through his brain. One was of the two of them laid out on the bed with naked limbs tangled together and her hands running wild over his body. And the other was of them again, only this time he was seated in the chair and she sat facing him, straddling his thighs.

Both were far too erotic for his vulnerable state. He hardened in a fierce rush. Luckily, she had already turned to take a seat on the bed, allowing him to quickly lower himself into the chair so she wouldn't see his physical reaction.

She uncapped the whiskey and poured some into his cup.

"First you try to poison me, now you're trying to get me drunk," he commented. "You wanna get rid of me, lady?"

Her gaze slid slowly up to meet his across the table. "You're just so much easier to manage when you're unconscious."

He couldn't contain his chuckle at that. "I don't doubt that's the truth."

She poured a shot of whiskey for herself, then set the bottle down and lifted her cup to take a modest sip. She immediately sucked in a swift breath through slightly parted lips before giving a soft little cough as her eyes watered. "This is terrible."

She was right. Yellow Tom's whiskey was nothing like the bottle they'd shared in Coulson. "It's total rotgut," he agreed, "but it helps to dull the pain."

Her expression immediately turned to one of concern. "You should let me check it, in case the wound opened from all you've been doing today."

"Later."

His shoulder had started throbbing something fierce a few hours before. He'd managed to ignore it for a while, but it was getting steadily worse.

The look she gave him said she saw through his delay tactic, but she didn't press.

"Who's waiting for you up in Montana?"

The unexpected question had her tensing. Her gaze lowered to the table for a second before she brought it back up to meet his. "My father is there."

From what she'd said about her father being from Boston, he'd assumed that they had gone east together.

"It's been five years since I've seen him." Her voice trailed off, as though she were thinking of the last time she'd been in her father's company.

Five years was a long time. "What's bringing you home?"

Giving him a narrow-eyed smile, she said, "You're asking an awful lot of questions."

Malcolm shrugged. "I've got nothing else to keep me occupied."

"My story isn't that interesting."

"I doubt that," he replied and meant it. The more

time he spent in the woman's company, the more curious he became about her. "Is there something in particular you're leaving behind in Boston?"

She kept her mouth shut. Her reticence intrigued him.

"You got secrets you don't want to share, sweetheart?" he teased, the endearment slipping out before he could stop it.

"Everyone has a few secrets," she answered quietly. Those blue eyes of hers were steady and serious as she met his gaze. "Why are you heading north to kill someone?"

Malcolm hesitated. It wasn't that he had anything to hide. He wasn't ashamed of his intention to kill Gavin's murderer, but it was not an easy thing to discuss.

Shifting in his chair, he lifted his whiskey and downed it all in a quick swallow. Maybe the hard liquor gave him the courage to go back and relive the tragedy that had motivated him these past eight years. Or maybe it was just her.

He met her quiet gaze and saw something there he hadn't seen in a long time, maybe ever. It was gentle curiosity, a total lack of judgment or expectation, and an openness he didn't know quite what to do with. He'd never cared before if anyone understood what drove him, but he wanted her to understand.

That should have scared him. In fact, it terrified him.

He drew a long breath that burned in his tight throat, but the words flowed with surprising ease. "Eight years ago, only a week before his nineteenth birthday, my little brother was murdered for the winnings of a dirty poker game. He took four shots in the chest, and while he bled to death, four men rifled through his pockets then walked away, leaving him facedown in the dirt." God, it hurt to say it, to see it all again in his mind's eye. "When Gavin didn't make it home that night, I went looking for him. He was already long dead, his blood soaked into the ground around his lifeless body." He clenched his teeth hard to ease the thickening in his throat and the tightening in his chest. "I've been tracking down the men who murdered him ever since. There's one left. The one who pulled the trigger and put those bullets in Gavin's heart.

"For years, he stayed a step ahead of me. No one knew his real name, just the stupid nickname he went by. At first, I'd hear stories of the bastard bragging about being sought by a bounty hunter. He seemed to enjoy the notoriety. But after a few close calls where I almost had him, he must've gotten scared, because about five years ago he went into hiding." Malcolm fisted his hands and cringed at the pain shooting into his shoulder. "I finally have word on where he's been holed up. I won't stop until he's dead."

His breath was shallow and raw as he looked at her across the small table, unsure how she'd respond to the violence that seethed inside him.

Her eyes had darkened with sympathy, and anger perhaps, but she didn't appear frightened by his admission. She sat with her elbows on the table, staring at him thoughtfully. "Those men who rode into our camp…he sent them?"

"Yep."

"You would have gone with them if not for me, wouldn't you?"

He nodded, pouring another shot into his glass.

"If not for me, you wouldn't have resisted. You never would have gotten shot."

He looked at her sharply. "It's because of you I'm still alive."

"Yet, it might all be for nothing," she said with a frown. "This man…he is trying to find you first, so he can kill you before you kill him. Is that right?"

Malcolm nodded again.

"And after you leave me with my father, you're going to ride right up to his front door?"

There was no point in responding to that. He'd made it pretty clear that was what he intended to do.

"What if he's faster?" she asked. "Would your brother want you to sacrifice your life to avenge his?"

Guilt and anger thundered through him. The thickness in his throat made his next words tight. "It doesn't matter what he wants. He's dead."

She met his gaze for a moment, her eyes dark and stormy. "It matters to me."

The soft words and her compassionate, earnest expression immediately diffused the tangle of rage and regret inside him. He was left feeling weak and tired. It was not a state he relished. This was the reason he didn't get close to people. He needed the anger and the guilt. They fueled him and gave him direction. Without them, he'd be too tempted to start thinking of other things—like comfort and rest and a gentle companion who might have the power to loosen the cold fist of revenge around his heart.

Glancing down at his whiskey, he lifted his glass and tossed back its contents as she rose to her feet and picked up both of their bowls. "The stew should be ready."

There was a stretch of silence as they started their meal. Malcolm shoved down further thoughts of Gavin and Walter Dunstan. He didn't have the strength to stay long in the dark thoughts. Anger, pain, guilt, and vengeance were draining emotions, and he had little to give to them this night.

Slowly, by a mutual, unspoken agreement, they eased into more casual conversation. The stew was hearty and flavorful, and talk turned to stories of Yellow Tom.

Thomas Chilton had been a singular type of character. A gruff and cynical old man who had made his living trading furs, he had preferred to avoid contact with other human beings as much as possible and built this cabin toward that purpose.

"But how did you meet him?" Alexandra asked.

"I was passing through the area a few years back during a snowstorm so bad I could barely see my hand in front of my face. I'd been on the tail of a particularly violent criminal, wanted for killing two families down in Kansas, and I had refused to give up the chase, when the blizzard hit." He shook his head. "It was a stupid call.

"With the heavy snowfall creating a whiteout, I had no sense of direction. I figured I was going to freeze to death right there in my saddle, when I happened across this cabin out of sheer luck. I swear I had to bang on that door for twenty minutes before Tom decided I wasn't going away and finally let me in."

"He would have let you freeze?" she asked with wide eyes.

"Damn straight, if I hadn't been so persistent. In fact, after the storm had passed the next day and he kicked me out, I discovered something I hadn't been able to see the night before."

"What?"

"The murderer I was tracking…frozen stiff not far from the front door."

She gasped. "That's horrible."

Malcolm met her shocked gaze. "Not when you consider what he did to his victims."

There was a pause before she rose to her feet and gathered their dirty dishes from the table.

"So how did you end up considering Tom a friend?" she asked as she placed the dishes in the washtub and poured some water over them from the bucket by the fire.

"Before I left, I did some hunting and left the kill as payment for his hospitality, realizing how differently things could have ended up. And when I collected on that reward for the outlaw who led me to the cabin, I came back to give Yellow Tom half of the earnings. In return, he gave me a hot meal before I went on my way again."

"He sounds like a very interesting character," she said as she sat cross-legged beside the tub to wash their dishes.

"I stopped in a couple of more times when I was in the area. He'd grumble about it, but he'd still open the door to me. Last year, I found him sitting outside his front door, pipe in hand and a bottle of whiskey next to him. By the look of him, he hadn't been dead long."

"Oh no," she exclaimed, genuine distress in her gaze.

"As far as I know, he had no family. No one else he'd call friend. I buried him up on one of the mountain ridges where he liked to hunt, and took care to clean up his place. From the looks of things, no one has come by since."

"That's terribly sad."

Malcolm's mouth curved in a half smile. "He'd probably hate us staying here as long as we have. One night was all he'd tolerate."

She returned his smile. "It seems his little cabin has saved your life twice now," she said as she rose to her feet and returned the cleaned dishes to the cupboard.

Malcolm's gaze tracked her movements as she performed the very domestic task. A twinge of discomfort passed through him. The scene looked too damn right. It was going to be hard to come back here without thinking of her crossing the room in the flickering firelight or walking in the door with two rabbits in hand.

When she turned and saw him watching her, she stopped, her brows arching upward in question.

Malcolm forced his thoughts off the path they were on, landing on the first thing he could come up with as a distraction. "With a beard down to his belt buckle, it's too bad Yellow Tom isn't likely to have kept a razor handy," he said, rubbing his knuckles along the growth of beard that covered his jaw.

"But he did have a razor," she offered readily. "I found one in the bottom of the trunk where I got these clothes. It's practically brand new. I can dig it out for you, if you'd like a shave."

He would, to tell the truth. He could only leave

his beard to grow so long before it started to irritate him. Lifting his right hand, he flexed his fingers then curled them into a slow fist. The fist was weak, and the simple action sent fiery pain through his shoulder. "I don't think I could keep my hand steady enough not to risk cutting my own throat."

"I'll do it." She crossed to the old trunk in the corner of the room.

He narrowed his gaze. "I don't think that's a good idea," he said skeptically.

"Why not? I did it for my father plenty."

"We should wait until there's more light."

Her expression held more than a hint of mischief as she approached the table with a folded leather pouch. "You really don't trust me, do you?"

Malcolm ran his hand over his jaw and then down his throat. "It's not you I don't trust. It's your skill with a sharp blade."

Something rare and beautiful flickered in her bright gaze, and her lips curled deliciously into a smile that made Malcolm's blood run hot in an instant. "Just relax," she assured him gently. "It will be fine. I promise."

TWENTY-FOUR

ALEXANDRA BIT THE INSIDE OF HER CHEEK TO HOLD back her amusement.

Malcolm's discomfort was practically palpable. Finally, she had him at a disadvantage and she decided she liked it.

She'd shaved her father so many times growing up that even though it had been years since the last time, she was fully confident that she'd have no trouble. As she set a cloth that had been dunked in steaming water on his face to soften the skin and make the bristled hair more malleable, she met his cautious gaze.

And smiled.

There was a flash in the gray depths of his eyes. A promise of retribution if this didn't go well? And something else?

A tingling thrill danced through her center.

She examined the straight razor with a flick of her thumb across the blade. It was exceptionally sharp. It needed to be, since there would be no benefit of cream to ease the passing of the blade.

After removing the hot cloth, she brushed her

fingers over his beard. It had gotten pretty thick over the last few days. Almost to the point that it was starting to soften, but not quite.

"Are you sure—" he began, but Alexandra cut him off.

"I'll have no more doubts," she said in a tone that was both soothing and stern. "I just need you to remain calm and relaxed. Close your eyes if you must. I will be finished in no time at all."

His expression was a study in wary resistance, but she waited, staring at him with a lifted brow until he did as she asked. When he finally closed his eyes, he opened his mouth to say something. Alexandra stopped him with a press of her fingers over his lips. "And no talking."

She had intended the words to be a strict command, but they came out more like a soft murmur. The feel of his lips beneath her fingers had distracted her. The firm arches and masculine lines always appeared to hold such tension. To the touch, however, his lips were soft and warm, and she couldn't help but wonder how they'd feel pressed intimately against her own.

He cleared his throat, pulling her attention swiftly up to his eyes. He was watching her stare at his mouth. She blinked and glanced aside, her stomach flipping wildly. "Let's get started," she said curtly to hide her embarrassment, hoping he couldn't see the fierce blush rising in her cheeks.

She was relieved when he closed his eyes again. His eyes, much like his lips, tended to cause distraction, and she had no intention of proving his fears correct by drawing even the smallest drop of blood.

Picking up the razor, she began.

Memories of doing the same thing for her father assisted her as she progressed. It was easy enough to recall just the right angle at which to hold the blade against the skin, where to start, and how to maneuver over and around the trickier areas.

The only problem—and it proved to be a bigger one than she expected—was in the fact that this wasn't her father's familiar, smiling face under her hand. It was Malcolm's. With all its hard lines and unforgiving angles. Its roughness and strength and masculine beauty.

He remained still and silent as she moved around him, repositioning herself every so often to get a better angle, leaning in close. She was very careful to avoid hitting his injury, but more than once her legs bumped against his or her arm brushed his chest.

It did not take long for her to realize how completely she had failed to understand that he would not be the only one at risk. Alexandra was in danger of something far more significant than a nick to the skin.

By the time she reached his throat, she had developed a slight shakiness. Not in her hands, which were steady and sure, but inside. Deep inside. Her stomach was engaged in a strange little quivering dance, her legs felt like jelly, and her breath was tight, as though it came from too high in her lungs.

She was careful to ensure Malcolm could detect none of that. He had been reluctant enough to let her shave him. She had no intention of giving him a reason to regret his decision.

She focused on the movement of the blade, trying to zero in on her task and block out the distractions.

But when it came to Malcolm Kincaid, she was discovering that the man was made up of a variety of subtle and not-so-subtle distractions. From his eyes and mouth to his large, capable hands splayed atop the surface of his thighs. And his thighs—firmly muscled and spread to allow her enough space to stand between them.

"Tip your head back a bit, please." Goodness, how uneven her voice sounded.

He did as she asked, and after swishing the blade clean in the bowl of water she'd set on the table, she carefully applied it to his throat, using her other hand to draw the skin taut beneath her blade. It took only a few minutes, but she figured she must have held her breath the entire time, because when she was finished, she was quite light-headed.

With a long intake of breath, she stepped back. Tipping her head, she took a critical look at her work.

"Not a single nick to be seen," she declared with a triumphant smile. Despite her inner discomfort, she had managed very well.

He opened his eyes. "You're not finished."

She frowned, then widened her eyes in realization. "Oh. My father always preferred to keep a mustache."

"I'd like it gone."

"Of course," she murmured.

He tipped his head back but did not close his eyes. Though *she* held the sharpened blade, the look in his eyes made her feel as though she were the one in mortal danger.

The quivering in her belly took flight in a dance of fluttering wings. It was a delicious sort of danger.

And she found that she liked not knowing if she was safe from it.

She lowered her attention to his mouth. Just a small swath of hair remained there above his lips, but it suddenly seemed like the true test of her skill.

Steadying her breath, she lifted the blade once again, feeling his steely gaze while she worked.

After the second short pass of the razor, she shifted her weight, and her knee bumped against his inner thigh. The inadvertent contact was devastating to her nerves, and she bit the inside of her cheek hard to hold in the gasp that rose from her tight chest.

Another short stroke revealed the divot that bisected the space between his nose and his mouth.

Her belly flipped, then flopped, and she turned to rinse the blade and give herself a moment to force a longer breath. Turning back, she bumped his thigh again. This time, he lifted his hand and set it on the curve of her hip.

She knew it was intended to steady her. He couldn't have known that his touch right then would send a flood of melting heat through her center.

Her gaze flew up to his, and what she saw there made the heat inside her burst into a bright, burning flame.

Maybe he knew exactly what he was making her feel. His eyes held a hint of that raw hunger, and she was fairly certain the same hunger burned in her own eyes.

His fingers flexed over her hip, as though he would draw her in closer to him, but he didn't.

He didn't remove his hand either.

"Almost done," he said in a rough voice.

She suspected his words were meant to be

encouraging, but really, they just managed to make her even more jittery inside. Intensely aware of their proximity, of the warm weight of his hand on her hip and the fact that he watched her face with those intense, predatory eyes, Alexandra brought the blade up for one final pass.

But it was simply too much. The internal shakiness she had been battling from the start finally reached her hand. And as she brought the razor down over the outer edge of his mouth, the blade slipped—an infinitesimal amount, but it was enough to nick the skin above the corner of his lip.

Alexandra made a small sound of dismay as a red drop of blood formed. She swept her thumb over the spot, wiping it away. "I'm sorry," she said softly. "I almost managed it."

Without a word, he grasped her hand and brought it to his mouth. Pressing her thumb to his lips, he gave a flick of his tongue and reclaimed the drop of blood.

Alexandra's breath stopped the instant her thumb came in contact with his perfect lips, but the velvet texture of his tongue was nearly more than she could endure. Heat pooled between her thighs, and her knees locked to keep her from collapsing to the floor right there between his legs.

The second his lips closed over the pad of her thumb, Malcolm knew he'd made a huge mistake. But then he went one worse and had to taste her.

He wanted to do more. The look in her eyes suggested *she* wanted him to do more.

He released her instead. "Thank you," he muttered.

She didn't respond. As he rose to his feet, she took a few quick steps back. Good thing she did, or he might have put his arms around her. He might have cupped his hand over the curve of her buttocks to hold her against him while he discovered what her mouth tasted like.

"Sit back down," she said quietly. "I want to check your shoulder before you retire for the night."

"It's fine."

"I'll judge that for myself." She gave a tip of her head toward the chair. "Have a seat."

Though everything in him was tense and tight with the urge to get the hell out of there before he did something he shouldn't, he could tell by her expression that she wouldn't be put off. He lowered back into the chair while she moved around behind him, fetching the poultice and more bandages.

"We'll have to remove your shirt." Her words, coming from so close behind him, caused ripples of awareness through his blood.

In movements made rough and jerky by the desire he couldn't completely tamp down, he released the buttons of his shirt and shrugged it off. Then her hands were on him, roaming over his back and shoulder as she unwound the bandages. His stomach muscles tensed in resistance.

She got to him. Down deep in his core. Her scent, her soft hands, her bright, curious, devastating eyes. He'd managed to control his rising physical lust, but only just barely. He felt a yearning for something more. Something that went beyond hot, searching looks and brief brushes of her hands.

The worst part was that he knew—he felt in his bones—that she wanted him just as badly.

"Lean forward a bit, please," she murmured.

Once the bandages were removed, she smoothed her fingertips around the wound on the back of his shoulder, probing at the edges, then sliding away with a cooling touch. He sat stiff and silent as she worked, trying not to think about how it might feel to have her hands moving over his body for other reasons.

He could not allow himself to indulge in such fantasies.

When she came around to check where the bullet had entered his body, he tipped his head so he could consider her expression. The concentration and compassion evident in her gentle features nearly unmanned him.

In that exact second, he understood that this woman was more dangerous than he'd previously realized. It wasn't just physical lust that squeezed his chest tight. The dark, quiet longing inside him went beyond that.

He couldn't recall ever having anyone care for him with such intent focus. Such soft and tender regard didn't fit in with his life. He could barely remember a time when death hadn't claimed a permanent corner of his existence. Chasing Gavin's killers, hunting bounties, fending off attacks of retribution and glory seekers. There was always some reason to draw his gun, and he never knew if that draw would be his last.

He didn't know any other way to live, but he sure as hell didn't need to drag anyone else into such a life. Not when he couldn't guarantee he'd be able to protect them. His failure with Gavin proved he was unworthy of that kind of responsibility.

Hell, their current situation was proof of that.

Dunstan's men had nearly had him, and then where would Alex have been? She relied on him to protect her.

He'd done a crap job of it so far.

The train of his thoughts made his skin feel tight and itchy. His blood ran hot with the urge to move.

Thank God she was efficient and finished applying the new bandage within a matter of minutes. As soon as the ends were tied off, he stood and slid his shirt back on. He was heading for the door before he even finished buttoning it up. "I'm going to check on the horses," he declared before stepping into the dark of night.

TWENTY-FIVE

ALEXANDRA STOOD BESIDE THE TABLE, STARING AT THE cabin door long after Malcolm had passed through it. She released a long, shaky breath. Then inhaled slowly and released another one.

The time she'd spent nursing Malcolm's wounds and doing everything she knew to do to help him fight the fever had been draining and intense. But it was nothing compared to what it was like spending the day in and around the confining cabin now that he was fully awake and on his feet.

When he'd been unconscious, it had never occurred to her to consider the half-nakedness of his body as anything but necessary for the care she needed to provide.

But now...

Touching the man, even with the purest of intentions and her focus firmly directed at his injuries, had taken on a new layer of intimacy. His smallest movements bunched the muscles of his back, chest, and abdomen. The strength in his body was impossible to ignore, despite the wounds he'd suffered and the fever he'd just endured.

And his strength appealed to her.

It *really* appealed to her.

Alexandra finally turned away. She wasn't sure exactly what she'd been waiting for anyway. Unfortunately, her gaze then fell on the bed, and she realized with a rush of panic that there was only one. Bed, that is.

She may have shared the narrow mattress with Malcolm the last two nights, but that was because he'd needed her to soothe him when he grew restless and cool him when he became overly warm.

She'd just have to sleep on the floor.

Yes. That would be best. She gave a decisive nod. With his injury, he needed the bed far more than she did.

The decision made, she went about setting up her bedroll beside the fire. There was only the one pillow on the bed, so she rolled up her split skirt to tuck under her head. Her large coat would serve as a blanket when the fire died down and the cabin grew cold through the night.

It wasn't likely to be very comfortable, but certainly no worse than lying on the ground beside a campfire.

Of course, on the trail, there wasn't a perfectly comfortable bed within sight.

After adding another log to the fireplace, Alexandra lowered herself to the bedroll, kneeling in the center as she unplaited her hair. She was sitting there, running her hands through the tangles, when Malcolm returned.

When their eyes met, they both froze.

An odd, rushing force seemed to flow from his eyes straight into her body. For a bright moment, she felt as though she were sitting there waiting specifically for *him.* Not in any casual way, as in she knew he'd be returning soon, but in a deep-rooted, visceral, down-to-her-bones kind of way. As though his appearance somehow fulfilled every longing she'd ever had and so many more she didn't know had existed. The feeling came on in one consuming, flashing instant before his gaze darkened with a heavy scowl.

"What the hell are you doing?" he asked.

Alexandra blinked a few times, trying to clear away the strange reaction. Though her mind became more focused, it did nothing to help the way her body seemed to hum in anticipation under his steady regard.

"I'm...freeing the tangles from my hair before I braid it again," she suggested cautiously.

He came forward, stopping a few steps away, and looked down at her with a thunderous expression. "No. What are you doing on the floor?"

"This is where I am going to sleep."

"Like hell. I'll take the floor."

"No," she stated firmly. "You won't."

"You're sleeping in the bed, and that's that," he practically growled.

"You can glare at me all you want, but it won't change the fact that you're the one who is injured. It only makes sense that you take the bed. I'll be fine right here."

Suddenly, something shifted in his expression. His brows lifted, and he eyed her with a narrowed gaze. "Is that where you slept the last two nights?"

Alexandra stiffened. She hadn't expected that question.

"You slept on the bed, didn't you?" he said in a dangerously low timbre. "Beside me."

She felt a rush of heat across her cheeks. It annoyed her that she was embarrassed by her decision to stay close. "I…it seemed necessary at the time. I was so tired, and you stirred so frequently, it was just easier to be close by. I didn't think it would be an issue."

He said nothing at first—just stood there staring at her with his angled features set in a harsh unreadable expression, his eyes intense and unwavering.

"It's not an issue," he finally said in a dark murmur. "And it won't be tonight either. We'll share the bed."

Alexandra's shocked gaze swung toward the bed where it was tucked so harmlessly into the corner of the room, under the dark eaves, at the farthest reach of the firelight.

It was a terrible idea. Entirely inappropriate.

It was one thing to sleep beside an ill, unconscious man while tending his needs. It was something else altogether to contemplate lying beside that man while he was in possession of his full awareness. Not to mention the matter of how his very masculine qualities had been tripping her up all day. She was far too cognizant of his physical appeal, and of her attraction to him on a very personal and intimate level.

It was crazy to even consider it.

But she was considering it. She looked back to Malcolm, where he stood near the table. "It's not a very wide bed," she said finally.

"We fit together just fine the last two nights."

"I might hurt your shoulder."

"You can sleep on my left side."

"It's not proper," she finished weakly.

He gave her a look that suggested he was amused.

"You've been alone with me for more than a week, sleeping only steps away from each other over a campfire. What's so different about this?"

She looked at him in surprise. "Because it's a bed."

"That we've already shared."

"While you were unconscious and feverish."

He sighed and dropped his chin. "The truth is, I don't relish the idea of sleeping on a hard wood floor, and there is no way I'm gonna let you do that while I'm enjoying a soft mattress. I'm also getting mighty tired and don't want to spend the rest of the night arguing."

The fatigue in his voice was obvious. He was tired and undoubtedly in pain. And here she was fussing over where she was planning to sleep.

He was right—they had already shared the bed. Though she knew it was in no way the same as when she'd been nursing him through the fever, it seemed ridiculous to continue arguing. "Fine." She nodded. "We'll share the bed."

As soon as she conceded, he turned away.

Alexandra finished rebraiding her hair while Malcolm sat on the edge of the bed to remove his boots. She almost offered to help but bit her lip against it.

When he finished with his boots, he lay on his back with his injured shoulder practically pressed against the far wall. Bending his good arm to tuck his hand beneath his head, he closed his eyes.

She waited until his breathing settled into a steady rhythm before she rose to her feet and approached, feeling extremely self-conscious. Trying not to disturb him, she lay on her side with her back toward him.

After only a few minutes, her muscles began to ache

from how tensely she held herself. She was just too aware of him. His breath, his warmth, the knowledge that his large male body was stretched out only inches from her.

She'd probably get more sleep on the floor after all.

"Relax, Alex," he murmured behind her, his voice thick with sleep.

"I'm trying," she muttered.

She heard him chuckle before he reached down to draw the blanket up over them both.

Despite her exhaustion, it was a long time before Alexandra managed to ease the tension in her body enough to slip into sleep. Even though there was enough space in the bed to allow a tiny gap between their bodies, she could still feel him. The heat from his body reached out to her, only now it was not the unnatural heat of fever but a more beckoning sort of warmth. As the fire burned down and the chill of night seeped more steadily into the cabin, she yearned to make use of that warmth. But she resisted and curled more tightly on her side, drawing her legs up and tucking her chin.

She just needed to relax and sleep. It should be easy, but it was still a while before she finally released her hold on consciousness.

Sometime later, when she was disturbed by an increasing chill and was too sleep-addled to resist her instinctive desire for comfort, she turned toward the warmth beside her, pressing along his heat and lifting her hand to his chest where the steady thrum of his heartbeat lulled her back to sleep.

TWENTY-SIX

MALCOLM'S SHOULDER HURT LIKE HOLY HELL. THE throbbing reached down to his fingers and up through his neck, pulling him out of a deep sleep. Opening his eyes, he saw that the cabin was gently lit with the slow, easy light of dawn.

He'd slept straight through the night without waking. A rare occurrence.

He was lying on his back with his injured arm tucked in along his side. His body felt stiff and sore. He needed to move, but as soon as he started shifting, he felt resistance.

Alex.

He stopped moving—practically stopped breathing—as he soaked in the sensation of having her small, feminine form pressed so sweetly to his. Her hand rested over his heart, and she had one knee bent high atop his thigh.

His physical need for her came on him with the force of a locomotive. His body craved hers with a depth that dumbfounded him. During the night, his arm had come down to pillow her head and wrap around her slim back. He flexed his fingers over the curve of her hip. The longer he lay there, the more his discomfort grew.

He'd never allowed himself to be governed by his sexual needs, but this woman tempted him almost beyond reason. Grinding his teeth, he shifted his arm beneath her head.

She snuggled in closer, wiggling her hips and sliding her hand up along his neck until she pressed her palm against the side of his face. Then she sighed.

Holy hell.

Every muscle in his body was on fire in his effort to keep from rolling over and settling his body atop hers. He could already imagine her hands sliding down his back to grasp his buttocks and pull him into the cradle of her thighs.

"Dammit."

He didn't realize he'd muttered the word aloud until she gave a tiny jolt and lifted her head off his shoulder. He was suddenly staring straight into her gorgeously sleepy, stunned, and confused blue eyes.

Alexandra was instantly aware of several things at once.

One: She was lying full-length against Malcolm's side and had practically wrapped herself around him.

Two: He didn't seem to mind, since his arm was braced around her back and his large hand curved rather possessively over her hip.

Three: Their lips were inches from touching. Close enough that she could feel his breath on her face.

Four: The stark yearning in his eyes sent deep shock waves of sensation straight through her center and filled her body with the oddest, most wonderful urge to press herself closer and closer to him until she felt no separation.

"I'm sorry," she murmured, hoping words might create some necessary space between them. "I did not mean to…um, does your shoulder hurt?" she finished awkwardly.

"Like the devil." His voice was rough and low from sleep.

"You overdid it yesterday." She started to shift and push herself up on her elbow. "I should take a look."

"It's fine," he said gruffly, his arm tightening around her back, his hand sliding down to cup her rear.

She froze, partially looming over him, a swirl of delicious sensations erupting in her belly. His body was so warm and solid beside hers. His scent so masculine. She wanted to bury her nose against the side of his neck and breathe him in.

She blushed at the thought and shifted her gaze away from his face. Pressing her hand gently against his chest to prop herself up, she made another attempt at rising. "I should—"

"I know," he interrupted in a gravelly voice. Shifting his attention to the ceiling, he dropped his arm from her, allowing her to roll away and swing her legs to the floor.

The chill in the cabin made her shiver as she rose from the bed. Going to the fireplace, she added some wood to the glowing coals. The stack beside the hearth would need to be replenished today. Luckily, there was a healthy supply, cut and stacked back near the horse shelter.

Once the fire was going strong, she swept up her coat and risked a glance toward Malcolm.

She nearly lost her footing at the sight of him sitting on the edge of the mattress, his feet planted on the floor and his knees wide as he ran his hand back through his hair. She had a ridiculous urge to crawl into his lap and wrap her arms around his big shoulders.

He made some tentative movements with his right arm, testing his shoulder's abilities.

"How does it feel?" she asked.

"Stiff. And sore."

She got the sense that was an understatement. "If you want to fetch some water to start coffee, I'll go check the snares. After that, I'm taking a look at that shoulder. Whether you like it or not," she added when it looked like he might argue.

He gave her a narrow-eyed look before he rose to his feet and made a motion like he was tipping a hat. "Yes, ma'am."

Alexandra was distracted as she tramped through the woods. Her brain was still sleepy, and her thoughts kept getting dragged back to the cabin. She had been so nervous the night before about falling asleep beside Malcolm, she hadn't even thought about having to wake up next to him.

Part of her wished she could have stayed in the bed with him a little longer. All right…a lot longer—soaking up his warmth, sharing his strength, giving comfort.

But the sun had risen, and the tasks of the day were upon them.

She made her way around to her snares but found them all empty.

Disappointment pulled at her shoulders. Then she thought of the creek. Perhaps if they headed upstream far enough, they'd find a spot good for fishing.

On her way back to the cabin, she kept an eye out for Indian hemp, a plant with strong fibers that could be stripped from the bark to use as line. As she examined some tree branches, thinking they'd make perfect fishing poles, she heard the snap of a dried twig not far behind her. All her instincts shifted into high alert, and her pulse rushed like thunder in her ears. Her first thought was of a wild animal, though images of rough men sent to kill Malcolm tumbled quickly after.

Terrified, she slowly turned in place, wishing she had her knife in hand. She was almost relieved when she didn't see a hardened criminal coming at her through the woods.

Unfortunately, a mountain lion wasn't any better.

As soon as she made eye contact with the animal, it went as still as stone and stared back at her from behind a grouping of trees. The predatory gleam in the large cat's eyes went straight through Alexandra, chilling her blood and freezing her muscles.

Don't run. Their instinct is to chase.

The instruction filtered up from some long-lost memory, and she seized it, digging deep for more.

Do not appear to be prey. Become a threat. Make yourself not worth the effort to take you down.

How?

She did not want to look away from the animal. As long as she kept her awareness focused on the predatory cat, maybe it wouldn't see an opening to attack. But she needed some way to defend herself if it did. Her knife was strapped to her hip, but even if she could quickly get it in hand, she would need to allow the animal to come frighteningly close before she could use it.

Time and her surroundings seemed to slow to a crawl, while everything inside her raced at an unnatural pace. Her heart, her breath, the spinning of her thoughts.

Fear threatened to cloud her mind, but she shoved it down to the pit of her stomach. She would *not* become this animal's prey. Not while Malcolm still relied on her. Not before she reached Montana. Not before she discovered herself...

The lion took a slow, stalking step forward.

Alexandra was running out of time. She needed to act.

The animal took another measured step.

Alexandra instinctively shifted her weight to better ground. As she did so, her foot kicked at what might have been a fallen branch or a rock, and her balance faltered—it was just for a second, but it was enough. The cat lunged.

Driven by a very deep and pure desire to live, Alexandra crouched and grasped ahold of the object at her feet. Thank God, it was a thick, old tree branch. She brought it up with both hands just in time to take a wide and powerful swing while releasing a throat-aching yell of fear and anger and total desperation.

The branch hit against the side of the mountain lion's head and shoulder with enough force to knock the animal aside and send a numbing reverberation up her arms. The lion stumbled and took a few steps to the side, shaking its head before eyeing Alexandra again with a low growl.

Determined to fight with everything she had, Alexandra squared off and lifted the branch in preparation for another swing. "I won't stop fighting," she shouted. "So just go. Leave!"

She swung the branch in a wide arch in front of her, giving another yell, hoping it would be enough to scare the animal off.

The lion stepped back in reaction, its hindquarters lowering.

Alexandra didn't know if it was intimidated or if it was getting ready to make another leaping attack. "Get out of here!" she yelled again, feeling tears burning in her eyes. "I am not your prey."

With a quiet snarl, the animal spun around and took off back the way it had come.

Alexandra stood for several minutes, staring after it with the branch still raised and ready, her breath short and fierce, and her body humming with fear and the instinct for survival. Her ears strained to hear any indication that the animal might return. There was nothing. The forest had gone eerily quiet.

Her relief was weakening, but she didn't give in to it. Keeping a tight grip on the branch, she quickly made her way back to the clearing, constantly scanning her surroundings for a glimpse of pale-brown fur or predatory eyes. By the time she stepped from the forest, she was shaking. But it wasn't fear. It was an intense physical reaction to what she'd just done.

She had chased off a mountain lion. And though it was not something she ever wished to have to repeat, it told her something.

She had been terrified and uncertain, but she had managed to do what was necessary to survive. In a way, she had always done that: as a child learning about the world at her father's side, that day when she was fifteen and her life completely changed, and afterward in Boston.

But she didn't want to just survive anymore. She wanted to live. To take risks and be free.

It suddenly seemed so obvious that she could never go back to Boston. She would never again be the woman who had been so lost and afraid after Lassiter left her to die. That wasn't who she was. Not anymore. Maybe it never had been, though she'd almost convinced herself otherwise.

In the same way that Malcolm belonged out beneath the wide-open sky, breathing the air of the Rockies, so did she—unconfined by walls and rules created by others for their own comfort.

Here in the wilderness, she was liberated. She was home.

She decided not to tell Malcolm about the mountain lion. She didn't need him worrying about her safety any more than he did already. He would probably try to make her stay inside the cabin going forward, and she couldn't have that. Instead, she vowed to be more vigilant and look for fresh tracks when she went out to the snares. She wouldn't be caught so unaware again.

When she entered the cabin, it was to be greeted with the rich and wonderful smell of coffee and something else. Curious, she approached the table and saw a pan of fresh-made biscuits cooling.

"They should be good to soak up what's left of the stew from last night," Malcolm offered in explanation as he stood from where he was crouched beside the fire.

"They smell wonderful," she replied, turning to see him standing in the doorway. "I'm impressed."

He let the compliment pass without comment, giving a nod toward her empty hands. "Nothing in the snares?"

"No, but I was thinking maybe we could follow the creek to see if there is a good fishing hole somewhere nearby."

He tipped his head. "I know a spot." His eyes narrowed, and he gave her a questioning look. "Are you all right?"

Alexandra smiled. "Of course."

He seemed uncertain, but thankfully did not press the issue.

After breakfast, Alexandra sat him down to get a look at his shoulder.

The wound appeared much improved, but the movement of his arm remained stiff and limited. The muscle beneath would need more time to heal. She hoped there wasn't any permanent nerve damage. He had overdone it the day before, and she told him as much as she replaced his bandages with some of the last that she had on hand from her repurposed petticoat.

His reply was gruff. "I'll have to be able to do a helluva lot more before we leave this place. Unless you plan on strapping my Colt to your hip the rest of the way to Helena."

Alexandra tensed with a thousand words of denial on her lips. Her blood ran cold at the idea. Meeting his sharp, steely gaze, she forced herself to answer with a steadiness in her voice that didn't reach all the way to her core. "I have no desire to carry a gun," she stated, tying off the bandage with a bit more force than may have been necessary.

He lowered his chin and reached for his shirt. "Then you'll have to leave the shooting to me," he replied in a milder, though no less insistent tone. "We can't hole up here forever." She could have sworn she heard regret in his voice, but then it was gone as he added, "You hired me to get you to Helena. That's what I'm gonna do."

She should have been reassured by his conviction, but all she felt was a conflicting sense of loss.

TWENTY-SEVEN

LUCKILY, THE FISHING HOLE MALCOLM KNEW ABOUT proved to be a good-sized lake, and they managed to dine well that night on pan-fried fish and wild greens with elderberries. But the rest of their supplies were dwindling fast.

Over the next several days, they did their best not to burn through what foodstuffs were in the cabin, and although Alexandra still foraged for wild vegetables, roots, and herbs to add to their meals, and the fish and small game were plentiful, it was a sign that their time at Yellow Tom's was nearing an end.

As soon as Malcolm felt up to it, he started taking his horse out on short rides to scout the area and make sure no one was about. After the first time he rode out, she insisted on joining him. In part because Sibyl needed the exercise as much as Deuce did if they would soon be back on the trail, but also because Alexandra enjoyed riding beside Malcolm while they explored the various deer trails and narrow mountain passes spreading out from their little clearing.

She suspected he enjoyed their rides as much as she

did, though he never admitted as much. When they were out on what she came to see as their little adventures, everything just felt easier, more comfortable. Right.

After that first awkward morning when they woke up in each other's arms, they both seemed to put forth extra effort in keeping some distance between them—in the bed they still shared at night, as well as during the day. Conversation was kept to casual topics, and though they often lapsed into comfortable silences, it seemed to Alexandra that there was something flowing beneath the surface. An awareness or anticipation that hadn't been there before.

She told herself it was just that after being together a few weeks now, they had finally developed a familiarity. But she swore there was something else going on. Something that made her feel weak and breathless when in the vicinity of his quiet presence. Something that tightened her belly and made her skin tingle. Something that scrambled her thoughts when their eyes met across the table, and she'd become mesmerized by the way his gaze could be as hard as steel yet shine with mysterious depth at the same time.

If it wasn't his eyes making her head soft, it was his mouth. She was used to it having such a firm appearance, tense and unforgiving, but she had noticed with some surprise while they ate supper on the fifth night after he had woken from his fever that he seemed more relaxed. Alexandra found herself fascinated by the movement of his lips as he spoke, or when he found something she said amusing, and the corners would lift just a bit. She wanted to feel his lips beneath her fingers. She wondered how they would feel on her bare skin.

More than once through the meal she had to forcefully direct her attention to her plate to hide her blush and keep him from suspecting the thoughts running through her head.

That night, they lingered at the table after dinner. The fire in the hearth cast a warm flickering glow throughout the cabin, and though the hour was growing late, Alexandra was reluctant to bring an end to the quiet amity that surrounded them.

"What was your childhood like?" His low question came as a surprise, and Alexandra eyed him curiously.

Perhaps he wasn't ready for the night to end either.

"My father and I moved around a lot," she replied, glancing down at her plate. "As soon as we'd settle in somewhere, Papa would be looking toward the horizon for the next adventure. We rarely stayed in one place longer than a few months—the longest was just over a year. Papa would eventually get the urge to move on again. It wasn't until I left Montana that he finally found it in him to put down a few roots. He's been settled near Helena for nearly six years now."

She used to wonder if it was so she'd have a familiar place to return to. But after years of waiting for a letter saying she could go home—a letter that never came—she had stopped believing that to be the case.

Glancing up at Malcolm, she found him watching her again, his eyes softly reflective. "Where was your ma?"

She sighed. "My parents met in St. Louis. My father stopped there as he made his way westward and fell instantly in love with a young woman who sang at a fine-dining restaurant." She laughed. "To hear my father tell it, he was quite the charmer. He married her less than a week after making her acquaintance and swept her off on an adventure westward. But the way was difficult, and she became weakened by her pregnancy. She did not live through my birth."

Malcolm's gaze darkened, but he did not look away from her. "I'm sorry."

She'd heard the sentiment so many times through her life. But the way he said the two words—in that deep, rough voice that revealed his own experience in grieving the loss of a loved one—touched her in a way she didn't expect.

Reaching out, she placed her hand on his arm just below his elbow and immediately felt the strength and warmth—two things she had indelibly come to associate with him—contained beneath the cotton of his shirt. For a quick second, she forgot what they were discussing. Then she smiled.

"I never knew her to miss her presence, and life with my father was a constant adventure. I wouldn't trade it for anything."

"But you left."

Her hand fell away. "I did," she replied, trying to keep the tension from her voice, yet knowing she failed miserably. She waited for him to ask why, and she tensed, wondering if she'd answer with the truth or find a way to evade him.

But he didn't ask.

And Alexandra was left feeling unexpectedly disappointed. She shook it off and gave him an expectant look. "What about you? I'm curious what you were like as a boy."

He lowered his chin for a moment and brought his

hand up to brush his knuckles along his jaw. "It's not a very exciting tale. No adventure, if that's what you're hoping for."

When he didn't continue, Alexandra just smiled and waited with an expectant expression.

He sighed and leaned back in his chair. "Pa was a farmer and Ma was a farmer's wife. From the time we could walk and take instruction, my brother and I were expected to do our part. It was a lot of long days and exhausted nights. If we complained, Pa was quick to remind us that we were brought into the world to work that land."

The bitterness in his voice was buried beneath years of distance, but Alexandra heard it anyway. "It's difficult to picture you as a farmer."

"Because I'm not," he asserted. With a sigh, he shoved his hand through his longish hair, pulling it back away from his face. "Ma died of lung fever when I was twelve, and Pa passed on six years later. Gavin and I sold the farm, bought a couple of horses, and took off without looking back."

"Where did you go?"

"We never had a destination in mind, just went wherever the wind blew. Sometimes we'd stay in a town for a few days, sometimes months, working odd jobs when we could find 'em." His expression tensed as he lowered his gaze. "I think we were both just so damn happy to be free of that plot of dirt Pa loved so much, we didn't care where we went or what we did as long as it was on our own terms."

"I can understand that," she said quietly, drawing his attention back to her.

His eyes were shadowed with loss as he continued. "For more than three years we wandered free. We ended up in California right about the time I figured I wanted to become a lawman."

"Really?" For some reason, it surprised her. Malcolm just did not present himself as the deputy type, with his solitary nature and curt manner.

Then again…maybe that had come later.

"I even convinced the local sheriff to start training me as a deputy. Gavin thought I was nuts. He was only eighteen and wasn't ready yet to consider settling down anywhere. He said he had a lot more living to do first." His brows pulled down dark and heavy over his eyes. His next words sounded as though his throat was closing around them. "If I'd done more to guide him away from his reckless tendencies…maybe I wouldn't have found him shot full of holes."

Alexandra's heart ached for him. "It was not your fault," she said quietly.

His expression hardened, and he pushed to his feet. "It sure as hell was," he growled as he walked away from the table. His broad back was tense as he approached the fire and tossed another log onto the dying flames.

She knew he wanted solitude, could feel his resistance to revealing so much. She should just let him be.

But Alexandra had been doing what she *should* for too long.

Malcolm felt her come up beside him. He didn't want to see sympathy in her blue eyes, so he stared hard at the flames instead.

All the guilt and anger and regret over his brother's death were rolling through him in waves. He was usually able to contain it all, tamp it down into a tight little ball he held deep inside where it was alive but manageable. Their discussion had somehow released it, and he wasn't prepared to deal with the sickening remorse and soul-sucking grief.

"Tell me about him," she said quietly.

He stiffened, the muscles of his jaw tensing painfully as he clenched his back teeth.

It had been so long since he'd talked about Gavin.

On second thought, he wasn't sure he'd ever really talked about his brother. When Gavin had been alive, there had been no reason. After he'd been killed, Malcolm hadn't been around anyone long enough to get into such personal topics.

He muttered a curse beneath his breath. "I should have done more for him—paid more attention to him. I got so damn wrapped up in what I wanted, I didn't notice Gavin had been gambling with the kind of men he should've steered clear of."

"You couldn't have known," she offered.

"I damn well should have," he growled fiercely, turning to look at her for the first time. The misplaced compassion in her eyes infuriated him. "He was my responsibility, and I failed him. I should've kept him out of trouble. Kept him alive." He stopped, feeling the tight fist of guilt and grief squeezing his lungs, making it hard to speak.

Crouching down, he grabbed a split log from the stack and tossed it into the fire. Staring into the flames, he uttered the one thought that had gotten him over that initial wall of disbelief when he'd seen his brother motionless in the blood and dirt. The thought that had motivated him ever since. "All I can do now is make sure the four men who killed him make it to hell."

"Then what?"

"It doesn't matter," he muttered, rising back up to full height.

"Of course it does," she argued quietly, stepping toward him to place her hand on his forearm. Her eyes were deep and steady as she forced him to meet her gaze. "I am so unbelievably sorry for your brother's death. I cannot imagine the grief you have felt." Her tone was earnest and strong. Something in the low words slid past his defenses, made him feel soft inside, made the emotion rise up again. "I understand your hunger for vengeance, but you are alive, Malcolm. You still have your own life to live."

"I don't know what that means," he stated gruffly, and it was true. Life did not exist beyond the hunt for Gavin's killer. He couldn't even fathom what it would look like when this was all over. He couldn't imagine remaining a bounty hunter. He no longer wanted the life of a lawman. He sure as hell wasn't a farmer.

"What do you want for yourself?" she pressed as though she'd read his mind, her eyes flashing with purpose. "What would bring you peace?"

Peace seemed a foreign thing. Unattainable.

But as he met her blue gaze, he could think of one thing that might ease the violence inside him.

TWENTY-EIGHT

A SUDDEN, FIERCE LIGHT OF NEED FLARED IN Malcolm's eyes, sending a shot of warmth angling sharply through Alexandra's body. Then he stepped toward her and swept his arm around her lower back.

He was going to kiss her.

The astonishing realization brought her breath to an abrupt halt a bare second before his mouth crushed hers.

Shock and instant fire rushed to the center of her body. It was a powerful *whoosh* that spun every concrete, rational thought into a dizzying dance. She stood stunned and motionless as she experienced the pressure of his mouth, the strength of his arm braced around her, the solid warmth of his chest firm against her breasts. Her heart raced as she breathed in the masculine scent of him.

But then his arm tensed around her back, and his other hand came up to cradle the side of her head. A sound vibrated from his throat as he tilted his head, shifting the position of his mouth. Just enough for her to feel the odd and lovely friction of his lips moving over hers.

She melted.

Her eyes fell closed, and the shock that had claimed her evaporated in an instant, leaving behind a soft, fluid need. Curving her spine, she rose up on her toes, wanting to be closer. She wrapped both arms around his neck, trying to anchor herself to him, silently urging him to deepen the kiss.

She didn't stop to wonder why he was kissing her—didn't bother asking herself if she should be kissing him back. She just knew she was finally getting something she'd been wanting for a long time.

When his tongue swept past her teeth, the rich, heady taste of him, the luxurious glide of his tongue against hers, forced a low moan from her throat. She'd never known a kiss could be like this. So instantly deep and consuming. So physical and passionate.

He tightened his embrace, lifting her against him as though he wanted to take her into his body, meld with her. Her toes barely touched the floor.

Giving herself over to his direction—trusting him in a way she had never trusted anyone before—she softened and met his tongue with hers.

His appreciation was immediate. The sound he made was rough and erotic as he accepted the sweep of her tongue across his lips for just a moment before he took her mouth again in an even deeper kiss. A kiss of possession rather than seduction.

She felt it down to her toes. The desire to surrender. The swift and urgent need to take more from him than this sultry kiss. To give more.

Then he stiffened and lifted his head on a sharp indrawn breath. Alexandra's eyes flew open to see his features drawn taut with pain.

"I'm sorry," she gasped as she loosened her mindless grip on his shoulders.

He gave a short shake of his head, but didn't say anything—just stared at her with those intense gray eyes and his familiar stern expression. She was quite certain she had never seen a man so handsome in all her life. But even now, after the kiss they'd just shared, he couldn't seem to keep the scowl from darkening his beautiful, rugged features.

Something of her thoughts must have shown in her face, because he lifted his brows in that way he had. Then he gently brushed his thumb across her lower lip. His wolfish gaze followed the motion of his thumb with an intoxicating focus.

All further thought faded. Her eyelids fluttered, then closed, and she tipped her face toward him with a breathy sigh.

He leaned in and pressed a sensual kiss to her mouth before drawing on her bottom lip with his teeth.

Alexandra nearly fainted from the heat spreading like wildfire through her blood. Before she could fully sink into it and lose herself, he made a raw sound and pulled back. This time, he released her, slowly enough for her to regain her balance, but still far quicker than she wanted.

She opened her mouth to protest, prepared to argue against whatever reason he might have for stopping, but he spoke before she could say anything.

"I've gotta step outside for a bit." His voice sounded strange. Rough and unsteady. "I need to check the horses and fetch some water."

He was already easing past her as he spoke. Tension

rode through every movement of his body as he crossed the cabin in stiff, long strides.

Had she hurt him again?

Her willingness to surrender to all the wonderful sensations he'd inspired with his kiss had made her careless. She wanted to call him back, but the uncomfortable bite of embarrassment held her tongue as she watched him walk away, shutting the door securely behind him.

Perhaps he regretted kissing her. He'd certainly seemed in a rush to get away from her. Maybe he hadn't enjoyed the experience as much as she had. She was new to kissing after all.

Uncertainty rose within her, reaching high and tumbling over itself, bringing with it a cold and lonely feeling unlike anything she'd known before. Refusing to be consumed by it, she straightened her spine and strode to the table to clean up what was left of their supper. The activity helped use up some of the frenetic energy running through her, but not all of it.

She hated feeling unsure of herself. Hated not knowing if she was behaving as she should. Hated that she cared in the first place.

She'd never known anyone like Malcolm Kincaid. He made her feel so many things without even trying. He warmed her with a glance, amused her with his perpetual scowl, made her so angry and frustrated sometimes that she occasionally wanted to hit him upside the head.

And she couldn't imagine anyone else kissing her with as much passion.

She sat down on the edge of the bed.

When she'd accepted Peter's proposal, he had sealed the commitment with a kiss. A gentle, dry little press of his mouth to hers. The experience could barely even be called a kiss now that she knew better, and her realization of the difference only added further confirmation that she was right to call off the engagement. At her first opportunity, she would write Peter and explain that she could not marry him…that she did not expect to ever return to Boston.

She never should have accepted him in the first place. She could not be happy living as his political and social ornament.

When she married—if she ever married at all—she wanted to feel what she'd felt minutes ago.

With a shake of her head, she acknowledged that one kiss from Malcolm did not equal a proposal. He'd uttered no promises, and no words of love had left his lips.

She couldn't say with certainty what it was that had been building between them. But it sure as hell was something. And she was just bold enough to admit to herself that she wanted to feel more of it.

She looked at the closed cabin door.

He'd been gone for a while. Long enough to have checked on the horses and fetched more than one bucket of water from the creek.

She crossed to the door and opened it to stand on the threshold.

The night was quiet and dark. Clouds blocked most of the stars in the sky and filtered the moon's light to a faint glow. Listening, she heard the occasional movement of the horses behind the cabin and the rush of night wind through the trees. The chirp of crickets and the trickling sound of the creek layered in a soothing song.

But there was no sound of Malcolm.

She stood there for a while, her arms wrapped around her middle as she grew chilled. Her gaze remained steady as she searched the darkness.

He wouldn't go far. Not so far that she wouldn't be able to call for him if she needed him. But he likely wasn't planning on coming back to pick up where they had left off.

Part of her wanted to strike out and hunt him down. The more rational part had her turning back into the cabin and closing the door behind her.

But it was a brief retreat.

She knew what she wanted now. Or at least, she knew for certain what she *didn't* want: the pampered life of a Boston lady of privilege, the fearful uncertainty of a woman unwilling to trust herself.

And she was finished with running away.

TWENTY-NINE

MALCOLM RELEASED A RAGGED BREATH. ONE MORE minute, and he would have stepped from the shadows and swept her back into his arms. One more minute, and he would have had the taste of her on his tongue again, the feeling of her softness sinking into his soul. One more minute, and he would have let himself believe he could have some of the happiness she urged him to claim.

But he couldn't.

Not yet.

Maybe not ever.

Turning away, he strode silently into the night. He needed more distance, more obstacles between him and her. He had no idea how long he walked through the darkness, but after a time, the worry of leaving her alone outweighed his concerns with being near her.

When he entered the cabin, he was relieved to find her sleeping on the edge of the bed. The fire had died to a low flicker, and the chill of night had her curled tightly on her side, with her legs drawn up close to her chest and her hands tucked between her knees.

Malcolm added a few small pieces of wood to the fire before he eased himself onto the bed beside her, making sure not to wake her.

He lay on his back with his body tense and his eyes staring. Even unconscious, she got to him. The rhythm of her breathing, the soft sighs of sleep that escaped her perfect lips, the warmth of her body so close, sparking the urge to hold her.

He denied the desire to turn and take her in his arms. Denied it until his jaw ached.

Until she stirred.

With a gentle sound, she turned, rolling toward him in the narrow bed.

He knew the moment she woke. Her body stiffened with awareness, and her breath caught for a second before releasing again. She obviously knew he was there, but she continued to turn until she lay facing him.

He should have pretended to be asleep. Should have closed his eyes the second he felt her moving. Though it probably wouldn't have kept him from feeling that soft blue gaze searching his face in the dancing shadows.

For what?

What did she want from him?

He had nothing. His life had become barren and harsh since Gavin's murder. The guilt and regret had done their job in erasing what gentleness he may have had when he was younger. His anger had smothered any bit of hope for a life outside of the burning ambition to see justice meted out to his brother's killers by his own hand.

It's all he had known for a long time.

He had nothing this woman should want.

He'd tell her as much, but the words wouldn't force their way past his clenched teeth.

She shifted beside him.

His tension sharpened, but he kept his gaze focused hard on the wooden slats of the ceiling. He ached from head to toe, but it was not from pain. It was something deeper than pain, more unsettling than desire.

Then she reached for him. Her hand settled naturally over the fierce beating of his heart.

Maybe she'd be content with that. Maybe she'd close her eyes and drift back to sleep, leaving him to deal with his discomfort in solitude.

She didn't.

After a few minutes, she eased her hand up along the side of his neck, her thumb brushing over his jaw, her fingertips reaching into his hair.

Against all internal warnings, he turned his head to look at her. She was too close and so damn beautiful in that flickering semidarkness.

He should say something to discourage her, to convince her he couldn't give her whatever it was she was seeking. But words were nowhere to be found. Not when he gazed into those eyes and saw the truth.

She wanted him. Maybe even needed him as much as he needed her.

Bracing her elbow beneath her, she leaned over him. Just enough to place her lips within a breath of his as her breasts pressed against the arm lying between them like a final, inconsequential barrier.

Then she paused. Her gaze flew swift and gentle

over his face. Her expression was quiet and more serious than he was accustomed to. The moment felt weighted and uncertain.

With a flutter of her eyelids, she pressed her mouth to his.

Desire slammed through him at the tentative kiss that quickly grew bolder when he did nothing to stop her. His better judgement lost, he eased his arm beneath her, curling her into his embrace, pulling her half on top of him as he nudged her lips apart to taste her with his tongue.

She was so damn sweet. When her tongue slid eagerly along his, he was lost.

A moan rumbled through his chest, and he brought his right hand up to push into her thick, dark hair, cupping the back of her head as he kissed her with the full force of the passions running wild inside him.

She answered every thrust of his tongue with one of her own. When his hand slid down to grasp the curve of her buttocks so he could hold her more securely against him, she gasped and moaned into his mouth, her body soft yet demanding as she moved against him.

With a harsh breath, he broke from the kiss and pushed her to her back as he rose over her. She looked up at him with her breath coming swift and shallow between parted lips. Her hands gripped his biceps, as though she feared he'd leave her.

"Malcolm," she whispered on a ragged breath.

Nothing else. Just his name.

Despite his raging physical need, his fierce desire to take possession of all she offered, he held himself still and unmoving. Meeting her shining gaze, he muttered the deepest words of truth he'd ever spoken. "I can't make any promises for tomorrow."

Her lashes fluttered, and her fingers tightened, curling into the muscles of his upper arms. "I know," she replied, but he wasn't confident she understood.

Heaviness settled across his brow, and he couldn't stop it. "I've got no tenderness in me. No sweet words of courtship."

She pressed her fingertips to his lips, stopping him from saying more. Her voice was low and calm when she spoke, like the current of a deep, flowing river. "It's all right," she assured him. "I'm not looking for forever."

He didn't intend to ask, but the words came out anyway, escaping against her fingers in a hoarse whisper. "What *are* you looking for, Alex?"

She did not reply right away. On a sigh, she curved her hand around the back of his tensely corded neck. "I just want to be me. In the most true and honest way possible."

Malcolm frowned. He didn't understand her answer. Didn't see how it had anything to do with him and what was happening.

He released a ragged breath and bowed his head. His forehead nearly rested against hers, and he closed his eyes to block the light of her gaze. He was prepared to roll away—knew it was the right thing to do—but she tightened her grip on the back of his neck, drawing him in. It didn't take much for their mouths to meet. A silent breath of desire and a gentle, urgent press.

She felt so good beneath him. Sweet, warm, and welcoming.

More than welcoming.

Her body lured him. The soft arch of her back and the press of her lovely breasts, the restless shifting of her legs beneath his, and the fisting of her hand in his shirt. The more he kissed her, the more she seemed to demand he go further.

He still believed he could resist going too far.

Until she slid her hands beneath his shirt and swept her palms up the length of his back.

He wanted more. He lifted himself away so he could remove the shirt altogether, tugging it off over his head rather than wasting time on the buttons. The sound of satisfaction and anticipation that purred from her throat fired his blood, but not nearly as much as her confident caresses when she smoothed her hands over the surface of his chest.

He stilled, holding himself unmoving as she explored the contours of his torso, shoulders, and arms. Her eyes, as they followed the path of her hands, were lit with wonder and longing. She rolled her lips in to meet her tongue, then parted them to whisper on a sultry sigh, "Will you touch me like I am touching you?"

The request nearly broke him. He growled his response. "Sweetheart, there's a hell of a lot more than touching I want to do to you."

She smiled, and it was all he could do not to explode right then and there.

"All right," she murmured.

THIRTY

ALEXANDRA HELD HER BREATH AND WAITED TO SEE what he'd do.

She wasn't sure she'd survive if he denied her this when she wanted it with everything she was made of.

Her past still had to be reckoned with, and her future remained as uncertain as it had ever been. But right now, Alexandra experienced a need stronger than anything she'd ever felt before. It was a need that went beyond the sensual craving of her body, which had admittedly risen to a fever pitch. It was deeper than the longing to know who she was and where she belonged.

This was an elemental need. Intrinsic to life. As necessary and indelible as the beating of her own heart. And she refused to deny it. Despite uncertain consequences and no knowledge of where she'd be a month from now, or a week.

The only thing that mattered was this man. This harsh and competent man with his unwavering strength and rugged nobility, and his own silent pain. This man who admitted to a lack of tenderness even as he made her feel more cherished and safe than she'd felt in a very long time.

A man who couldn't look to the future until the demons of his past were resolved.

In that, they shared a kinship. Though there were no guarantees that either of them would find their peace, in each other's arms, they could at least have some of the pleasure life had to offer.

Framing his face in her hands, she drew his mouth to hers. She kissed him. Drawing on his tongue, scraping his lower lip with her teeth. She kissed him with every ounce of truth and passion he inspired, with every drop of the yearning inside her.

When he reached for her, his large hand gripping firm to the curve of her hip, she pulled back. Sitting up, she released the top few buttons of her shirt so she could lift it over her head as he had done his. She was left with only the thin linen of her undergarment to shield her breasts from the hunger in his gaze.

Alexandra would have continued undressing— was suddenly quite desperate to bare her skin and feel his nakedness pressed to hers—but he had another idea.

Scooping his arm around her waist, he rolled onto his back, bringing her with him until she lay sprawled on his chest, her lightly clad breasts hovering inches above his face. She planted her hands on the mattress to keep herself from falling on him completely.

At the same time, he smoothed his hands over her shoulders, dragging the lacy, beribboned straps down her arms. As the material slid past her breasts, he lifted his head to take one peaked nipple harshly into his mouth. He suckled hard on her flesh, as though he had been dying for the taste of her.

Alexandra's arms stiffened, holding her in place as a luscious moan of pleasure eased from her throat. The feel of his mouth on her was intense. His tongue swirled over the sensitive peak of her breast. The heat of his mouth consumed her. Her belly erupted with wild, fluttering anticipation as the reactions within her body deepened with each pull of his mouth, until she could feel every tug deep in her core.

He switched his attention to the other breast. While he tugged sensually at her breast with his teeth, then laved the flesh with his tongue, Alexandra melted over him. Her legs parted around his, her belly softened, and her back arched in a taut curve.

He moved his hands to her buttocks, gripping her rear firmly as he moved her over the ridge of his erection. When his hardness made contact with the apex of her thighs, tingling sparks of sensation flew through her deepest core. Wanting more, she bent her knees around his hips, opening herself to him.

His groan of appreciation barely registered, because he was moving her hips over him again. Her gasp at the more intimate contact dissolved into a moan as melting heat softened the flesh between her legs. The third time he slid her along his length, he simultaneously suckled hard on her breast.

Alexandra's strength evaporated. She dropped to her elbows, and her breasts flattened against his chest as she brought her mouth to his in a desperate, open-mouthed kiss. Fierce and passionate.

Her rolled her onto her back, breaking from the

kiss to reach for the makeshift belt holding up her borrowed pants. Within seconds, she was helping him shove the pants past her hips and down her legs until she could kick them away. She quickly released the tiny buttons of her single-piece undergarment and then that too was removed, leaving her fully naked beside him.

She expected him to take her up in his arms again. She nearly shook with the desire to have his hands on her while his mouth moved hungrily over her breasts.

But he chose that moment to slow down.

Braced on his elbow, he gently cupped one breast, which rose and fell with her harsh breath. Then he slid his hand down the center of her body, past her sternum, over her belly, and down the length of one thigh. Curling his fingers around her knee, he bent her leg until the sole of her foot pressed into the mattress.

She wasn't sure what to do. Her hands lay at her sides in tight fists. She wanted to reach for him, wrap her arms around his shoulders and draw him down to her until his heat and weight covered her from head to toe. She was desperate for the feel of his bare skin against hers.

But she remained still, her eyes tightly closed.

Because the tantalizing sensation of his large, rough hand moving so slowly, so deliberately over her body was a torturous pleasure unlike anything she could have imagined. The sudden patience in his touch when she wanted nothing more than for him to hurry, gave rise to an anticipation so intense it stole her breath.

As his hand slid down the back of her raised thigh, she arched, thrusting her breasts up as her hips tilted and pressed down into the mattress. And when she felt the tips of his fingers easing ever closer to the wet heat at her center, she opened her eyes to find him staring down at her, his expression so beautifully dark with his deeply creased brow and tight jaw.

He was as tortured as she was. Yet, he prolonged the moment for her. Despite the passion raging through them both, he took it slow for her sake.

Lifting her hand, she slid her fingers into his hair, cupping the back of his head to draw him down to her. The kiss began with a slow, sensual brush of their lips. But it was clearly not enough for either of them, and when his tongue swept out to tease the corner of her mouth, she opened to him.

As the kiss deepened, he slid his hand down between her thighs, easing two fingers along her aching folds.

New sensations spread through her body. Alexandra gasped into his mouth. She bloomed beneath his hand. All she wanted was to open herself to him even more. While her tongue tangled wildly with his, she parted her legs and lifted her hips. He responded with another, deeper stroke of his fingers.

Wrapping both arms around him and tucking her face into the curve of his neck, she breathed in his scent, drawing the essence of him into her own body. His mouth fell to her shoulder while his fingers caressed and teased, gliding slick along her heated folds before circling with increasing pressure over the swollen bud at the apex. The pleasure built, tension and wonder spread through her limbs, taking over her awareness until everything she knew was a shimmering, seething flow of sensation.

When he eased one finger inside her body, she stiffened. The sensation was so new. He took her mouth in another kiss as he withdrew only a little before easing back into the tight channel. The gliding friction and gentle pressure eased her initial tension. And when he pressed the heel his hand on the apex of her mound, providing a delicious immovable pressure against that tight bud, the sensations rushing through her twisted up to a fierce peak.

Her breath caught on a gasp as a fluttering started deep inside. It was as though something was releasing from her core even as the rest of her tightened and tensed. Another long stroke of his finger inside her and the feeling burst in a shuddering explosion of sensation that spread like a glittering wave. It was a pleasure so perfect it set her adrift from reality.

All she knew was that she clung to Malcolm with a mindless desperation, her fingers curled deep into the muscles of his arms. That she had lifted her hips to press hard against his hand. That her mouth was open and softly panting against the side of his throat.

Then it was easing away, with deep pulses and a heavy sigh. And she was left feeling weighted and soft. Her hands fell away from him even as she tried to curl deeper into his embrace.

He gently shifted his hand from between her legs to wrap his arm low around her back, holding her to him as his ragged breath slowed. Coming back to full awareness, she realized that he had taken her to that wondrous place alone. She tried to draw back, but he only drew her closer.

"Malcolm," she murmured, pressing her lips to his

shoulder. "Please let me… I want to…" She didn't know how to express how badly she wanted to give him the same beautiful gift he had just given her.

The low rumble of a throaty groan was his only response. Then he shifted his hold, rolling onto his back until she was settled more comfortably beside him, her head resting on his chest. Softly, he trailed his fingers along her spine. The soothing sensations eased her into a drifting state of consciousness. She didn't want to fall asleep, didn't want to leave him even in that small way, not when she still felt so much.

The last thing she remembered was wishing they could stay like that always.

THIRTY-ONE

MALCOLM WAS DYING.

He had to be.

With one foot firmly in hell.

If this was hell, he figured he could do worse than to spend eternity writhing with the pain of an unspent desire so hot and strong it threatened to break him. But it wasn't his lustful state that tortured the most. It was the emotion pressing out from his chest: the panic, fear, and longing. He had no protection, no defense built up against that moment as she drifted into sleep and he could have sworn she murmured something that sounded like *love*.

His body throbbed and pulsed. His head felt thick and heavy as he struggled to form coherent thoughts. It proved to be impossible. He kept getting drawn in by the feel of Alex's silken body against his, her soft breath on his skin, and the taste of her mouth still on his tongue.

But the thought of that word coming from her lips was more than he could take.

His arms tightened around her languid form, and he groaned. The sound was raw.

Keeping her pressed along his side, he closed his eyes against the aching throb in his shoulder. Her grip had gotten fierce in her passion. He hadn't wanted to stop her then and did not fault her the lapse in awareness now. It had been so damned worth it.

He shifted and stretched, trying to ease the discomfort in his shoulder without disturbing the woman at his side.

They couldn't stay here.

The cabin was too cozy, too intimate. The rest of the world was far away. It would be so easy to forget the vow he'd made eight years ago and make Alex his woman in every way.

And he was damned tempted.

Tempted by her ready smile and stubborn nature. Tempted by how she continually found ways to surprise him. He desired her and admired her, and could far too easily imagine a lifetime with her at his side.

But he would never forgive himself. Gavin deserved more from him.

So did she.

She may not be the fancy lady he'd first thought she was, but she was still worthy of a man with more going for him than a bounty hunter who'd been chasing vengeance for almost a decade ever would. A man tailed by violence.

Alex gave a little shiver and burrowed deeper against him. Her lips pressed to his chest for just a moment, and he held his breath, waiting to see if she was awake.

When she didn't move again, Malcolm muttered a quick curse, and he pulled the blanket up to cover her. It was best that she stayed asleep. He wasn't sure he'd be able to resist taking full possession of her if given another opportunity. He was amazed he'd held back in the first place. But something in him had fought to preserve that last vestige of her innocence even as he urged her body to sexual release.

His damned conscience, probably.

He'd never had a problem with taking a woman then leaving. It was the way of things for a man like him, who was never in a town long enough for more. But his prior companions had been experienced women who never expected promises of commitment.

Alex was different.

It the short time they'd been together, she'd managed to get to know him better than anyone else. And he'd gotten to know her.

She deserved love. The everlasting, forever kind of love. Not a few stolen nights with a man unable to imagine his own future. Knowing he couldn't give that to her cut deeper than any knife and spread an ache through his chest a thousand times worse than the pain in his shoulder.

He had to protect her.

From himself.

The way she'd responded tonight with such innocent abandon and gasping wonder confirmed that she'd never taken a lover before. That alone should have had him sleeping across the room from her. Hell, he should be bedding down with the horses.

In addition to that, and despite all her skills and

knowledge about living in the wilderness, her tales of trekking across the territories with her father, she was a lady down to her toes. If she gave him her body, she'd expect something in return. And she deserved far better than him.

It was a fact. He just didn't like it very much.

Moving so slowly and carefully that he barely breathed, he eased from the bed. If she happened to wake, he'd never make it out of there. Thankfully, she didn't stir as he leaned over to tuck the blankets back around her while resisting the urge to brush her hair back from her face. Then he stood and turned away.

Distance.

He needed distance.

Alexandra woke to the whispering rush of cold air across her bare shoulders. With a sleepy whimper, she tried to burrow into the warmth that had kept her so comfortable through the night.

But Malcolm was gone.

She opened her eyes with a start to note the hazy gray of morning filtering through the cabin. Rolling over, she found Malcolm fully dressed and crouched before the fire, adding wood to the low, glowing embers. Then he leaned forward to breathe life back into the hot coals until little flames licked up to feed on the fresh wood.

The sight of him sparked an immediate rush of tenderness inside her that flowed in harmony with her awakened sensual craving. She wanted to swing her feet to the floor and rush into his arms, clasp his head in her hands and press her mouth to his. Despite her nakedness, despite the twinge of shyness she experienced now that morning had chased away the quiet intimacy of night.

Once the fire was well fed, he stood and turned. His sharp gray eyes cut through the room to where she lay watching him from the bed. The hard lines of his rugged features were drawn into a forbidding expression, and his body was stiff and tense. He seemed unwilling to step away from the fire, as though he hated the thought of coming near her.

Then without a word, he strode to the door and stepped outside.

A sick heaviness settled in Alexandra's stomach. Something was not right. She would have expected a little awkwardness after last night, some shift in the way they interacted with each other. But she had not anticipated such coldness.

Anger flared.

He was going to revert to that old song and dance, was he? Aloof, angry, distant.

She thought they'd gotten past that. Even before the kisses, he'd at least smiled on occasion—he'd even teased her and tossed a few compliments her way. Yet, here was the gruff and prickly bounty hunter, back again.

Alexandra swung her feet to the floor and threw on the clothes she'd worn the day before with rushed and jerky movements. After securing her knife at her hip and tucking the dwindling chunk of soap into her pocket, she left the cabin.

By the angle of the sun, it appeared to be later in the morning than she'd expected—the comfort of Malcolm's arms had kept her in bed far longer than she would have been otherwise. Keeping her chin firm and her gaze trained forward, she took long strides down the gently sloping hill to the creek before she turned to walk alongside it. She didn't see Malcolm anywhere and didn't bother to look for him.

Let him stew in whatever grouchy little pot he'd woken up in. *She* was going to the lake to wash her clothes and take a bath. A real, dunk-her-head-under-the-water, float-on-her-back-and-stare-at-the-sky bath. She didn't care if Malcolm wondered where she was when he eventually returned to the cabin.

She knew how to take care of herself.

Though she understood her sudden decision to head out to the lake was in part a petulant attempt at proving to him that she didn't need him, it was also a decision based on the very basic need to be alone.

After the way he'd touched her last night, and the way she'd slept so warm and content at his side, she had not expected to be greeted by such a distant demeanor this morning.

It hurt.

And it made her question herself…after finally feeling a return of her former confidence. That bothered her most.

She refused to allow it.

She had once been a carefree, impulsive girl who lived life as it came, confident and ready. A girl who did not shy away from unexpected adventure. Of course, what had happened between her and

Malcolm the night before went a little bit beyond simple adventure.

They hadn't made love, but she would have.

She was not ignorant of the potential consequences to such a decision. Not to mention she was still technically engaged, though that issue would be remedied as soon as she could get a letter sent back East.

A more honorable woman probably would have waited until all previous ties were cut before behaving in such a way. In truth, a more honorable woman would have held out for wedding vows.

But such concerns hadn't even entered her mind last night. She had wanted him. That was all that had mattered.

She wanted him still.

Perhaps she was foolish for that, but at least she wasn't lying to herself about it. It was more than she suspected she could say about Malcolm.

She snorted.

He wanted to keep his distance today? Pretend he wasn't passionately involved in what had occurred between them? Then fine. That was his choice.

She didn't want to doubt herself anymore.

Closing her eyes, she took a deep breath of the forest air. Rich and earthy. The smell of nature grounded her. The rustle of leaves, the bubbling chatter of the rushing creek, the call of birds in the canopy overhead, and the pattern of light and shadow that littered the forest floor all helped to recall her to herself.

Stepping into the meadow that surrounded the lake, Alexandra took another deep, cleansing breath. The sun nearly topped the tree line and would likely soon burn away the hazy cloud cover that concealed the blue sky. She might just get lucky enough to be able to lie in the grass and dry under the sun after her bath.

After thoroughly scanning the area for any potential dangers and seeing none, she headed toward the side of the lake where the water lapped against the grassy shore, across from the rocky ledges where they had fished the day before.

She kicked off her boots and set them aside, then removed her stockings. After her encounter with the mountain lion, she was unwilling to have her knife out of reach for even a short time, so she tied it to her bare calf before wading into the water. The lake was cold, but not terribly so. Perfect for an invigorating swim.

She pulled the soap from her pocket and worked it into a good lather. Starting with her stockings, she washed her clothes one item at a time before laying them out on the grass to dry.

By the time she was stripped down to her one-piece undergarment, the sun had risen high enough in the sky to warm the little meadow. With another searching look around to ensure her solitude, she waded back into the water.

A breeze swept through the clearing at that moment, sending a shiver over the surface of her skin. Tipping her face to the sun, she laughed.

It felt good. The chill was a reminder that she was alive. Alive and free to exist in any way she chose. Here she stood, out in the open, wearing nothing but her underwear. Her feet were bare, and her hair was free down her back. And she had never felt better.

Sucking in a deep breath, she dove into the lake, swimming as far as she could beneath the surface before coming up for air. Surrounded in that cold nothing, she could forget.

Forget her confusion over Malcolm and his moods, not to mention her own stirred-up feelings. Forget any worry about her father and what he'd think of her return. Forget Boston and Peter. Forget the lady she'd tried to be for the last five years.

Here beneath the water, beneath the bright-blue August sky, she was Alexandra.

And that was enough.

THIRTY-TWO

❦ ❦

AFTER WASHING UP FROM HEAD TO TOE, SOAPING HER hair and dunking to rinse the suds, she tossed the soap on shore and swam out to the center of the lake.

She was reluctant to leave the water. Some of her uncertainty returned as she thought of facing Malcolm again, but she reminded herself that *she* was not the one regretting anything.

With one last dive, she headed toward shore, staying beneath the surface of the water until her lungs started to burn. When she surfaced, it was to see Malcolm standing near her drying clothes. His hat was tipped forward to shadow his face as he watched her, and his expression—stern as always—was easy enough to read.

She considered staying in the water, not sure if she was prepared for whatever confrontation was ahead. But she was shivering enough by now that her teeth had started to chatter, and her skin felt like ice to the touch. As she continued toward the shore, she remembered that her underclothes were entirely transparent when wet. A flash of maidenly modesty claimed her before she shoved it aside. She'd been bared to him last night and had felt no concern. Why should today feel so different?

With a stubborn set to her jaw, she continued toward shallower water. She kept her spine straight and her gaze focused on her clothes as she drew her hair over her shoulder to wring the excess water from its length.

Though she didn't look directly at Malcolm, she could feel him watching her, and her body warmed despite the cool morning air. She sensed his disapproval and his irritation. He thought her too bold, perhaps. Or too reckless.

Well, too bad.

As she reached the shore, she happened to sweep a glance in his direction and suddenly couldn't take another step. She was instantly trapped by the predatory gleam in his sharp eyes.

He wanted her.

Fiercely.

She could feel his wanting in a wave rushing over her. There might have been a time when such intensity—such blatant desire—would have frightened her. But not now. Not with him. All she felt was an answering need in herself. Her belly twisted with longing, and her legs went weak.

But as she stared back at him, locked in the silent track of his gaze, she realized something. She was more free to acknowledge her desire than he was. For some reason, he seemed determined to resist his attraction. He wanted her. But he didn't want to want her.

That dawning realization sparked an undeniable urge to test his limits.

With a tilt of her head, she gave him a tight smile. "Did you need something from me, Kincaid?"

His features tensed. He kept his focus strictly on her face as he replied, "It's not safe for you to be this far from the cabin alone."

Alexandra sighed and strode to where her clothes were laid out in the grass. "I can take care of myself," she assured him.

"This isn't about being able to trap rabbits or forage for plants," he said in a gruff and angry tone. "Anyone could have come up on you while you were frolicking in the water."

She lifted her brow at the word *frolicking*, but did not dispute it. She might have frolicked a bit. "Aren't you the one who said there isn't likely to be another person for miles?"

"You can never be sure when someone might happen past. It's damn foolish not to realize that."

That sparked her temper. It didn't matter that she understood his fears. She'd been well aware of the risk she was taking. But it had been worth it. She'd needed to feel surrounded by the wilderness. She'd needed the time to herself.

Apparently, he disagreed.

She tossed him a dark look. "Some risks are mine to take."

"This isn't one of them."

She turned away to swipe her pants up off the ground. "I just wanted a moment to myself."

"You don't understand how dangerous some men can be."

She spun around at that. "You think I've never

been subjected to the attentions of a man who thought he had a right to take what he wanted?" she asked in a biting tone as she stepped toward him, her pants fisted in one hand.

She sucked in a deep breath to calm her rising frustration. Her voice was surprisingly steady as she continued, "I am well aware of the dangers this world holds. Does that mean I must stay cooped up inside with people at my elbow every minute of the day? Should I never have the freedom to spread my arms and breathe and laugh and live? Should I forever exist in fear?"

Malcolm's expression had hardened to stone, and his gaze had grown impossibly dark, but he said nothing to interrupt her.

She shook her head slowly from side to side. "I did that for five years, Malcolm, and I'm tired of it. I want to live. I want to feel comfortable in my own skin. I want to be free to be myself in this wide and wonderful world," she said with rising fervor as she sent a sweeping glance around the meadow. "And if that means sometimes going off by myself, *trusting* myself, that's what I'm going to do." She paused, her breath coming fast and her heart racing from the depth and passion of her confession.

It was the truest thing she had ever said.

Freedom. Freedom to make mistakes, to go out in the world with the confidence that she would find her way and be all right in the end. That is all she wanted, and it was everything she had been missing in Boston, where life had been about carefully following the established rules and expectations.

There was little risk in a life like that and no adventure.

She stared at him as intently as he stared at her.

Alexandra wanted adventure. She wanted to face danger and head into the unknown. She wanted desire and…more. But mostly, she wanted him to understand. "And if I want to feel the touch of your hands on my body, I'm going to ask for it. And if I enjoy the way you kiss me, I'm going to kiss you back, and I'm going to want more. I won't apologize for it. If you can't accept that, then you should walk away right now, Malcolm, because I'm not going to."

He stood stiff and unmoving. His arms were still crossed over his chest, and the rolled-up sleeves of his shirt revealed the taut ropes of muscle in his forearms. The open collar of his shirt allowed her to see the swift beating of his pulse at the base of his neck. For all his stillness, there was an energy seething within him, just below the surface. It was evident in his eyes most of all, where the steely gray flashed beneath the heavy shadow of his brow with deadly intent.

He was furious, the muscles of his jaw tensing with barely contained anger. "Who hurt you? Tell me who dared try to take something from you, and I swear I'll—"

"Don't," she interrupted, her tone hard, knowing what he was going to say. "It was a long time ago."

He stared at her, hard and searching. Then he gave a short nod of acknowledgment. Taking a dragging breath, he filled his chest before expelling it again. All the while, those steel-gray eyes of his remained on her.

"You want more?" he finally asked.

The question filled her with anticipation. "I do."

He lowered his head, the brim of his hat briefly breaking their eye contact. "I told you last night I can't make any promises."

"And I told you I don't need any," she replied. Dropping her pants to the ground, she stepped up to him, pressing her hands flat against his chest. "I just want you, Malcolm, for however long that lasts."

He brought his chin back up, and the look in his eyes sent wonderful, exciting arcs of desire through her center.

"Have it your way, then," he muttered before he uncrossed his arms and wrapped them tight around her waist, drawing her in against him and up off her feet before he took her mouth in a burning kiss.

Just like last night, there was no gentle seduction, no sweet words. Just fire and passion. And it was everything Alexandra needed. Her confession had left her drained and invigorated at once, and she held him fast to her as she returned his kiss with reckless abandon. The heat of his body soaked past her cool, damp clothes to heat her chilled skin and fan the flame deep inside her. She became so instantly lost in him that she barely noticed when he lowered her to the grass.

He hovered over her for a moment, propped on his elbow, while he brought his hand up to cradle the side of her face. His gaze was intense. Though he looked like he wanted to say something, he remained silent. Then he slid his hand down the side of her throat, using his thumb to tip up her chin, before he pressed a hot, open-mouthed kiss to her waiting mouth. After a deep, drugging kiss, he slid his lips to the spot where her pulse beat swiftly at the side of her throat, sucking her flesh against his teeth.

Alexandra sighed and stretched beneath him, bringing one leg up along his until her inner thigh pressed against his hip. He dragged his lips lower, across her collarbone as he slipped the strap off her shoulder, baring her breast.

The sun, the cool air, and then his mouth covered her. She arched. Lifting herself toward him. Her arms wrapped around his neck, knocking his hat off to the side. She wanted to feel him. All of him.

With a small sound in the back of her throat, she brought her hands to his shoulders to push him away until he sat back on his heels beside her.

He gave her a questioning look. But she just smiled as she sat up and reached for the buttons of his shirt. The remaining strap slid down her shoulder, and his gaze fell to her naked breasts.

The heat in his eyes was enough to rush the movements of her fingers. She was suddenly anxious to bare his chest so she could press herself against him. Skin to skin. Heart to beating heart.

Careful of his injury, she eased his shirt off his shoulders and then tugged it down his arms until it could be tossed aside. Splaying her hands on his spread thighs, she rose up on her knees, bringing her breasts level with his gaze.

He immediately reached for them, cupping them in his large hands, kneading and lifting. He brushed his wide, callused thumbs over the peaks until she shivered at the sensation and dropped her head back with a sigh.

Then he too rose to his knees, wrapping his arms around her to draw her in close, just as she wanted. Her full breasts flattened against the heat of his skin, smooth over the hard contours of his chest covered in a crisp sprinkling of hair. She slid her arms around his neck and gave him her mouth with a low moan.

His kiss—as she expected, as she craved—was hot, open, and deep. This was no sweet seduction of soft, sipping lips. It was a passionate tangle of tongues and scrape of teeth. It was demanding and consuming.

Alexandra tossed herself into the fray. Giving of herself in a way that would have frightened her if not for the pleasure she'd discovered in the willful act of surrender.

With a harsh grunt in the back of his throat, he tightened his arm to lift and turn her so he could lay her down again. He followed her to the ground, covering her now with weighted muscle and hot skin. She parted her legs, wanting to feel him there where she ached. As he settled his hips between her thighs, she gasped quietly against his mouth. Her hands clutched his upper arms.

He lifted his head, breaking the kiss.

With a flicker of her lashes, she tried to meet his gaze, but the bright sun made it difficult to see his features. She could only hear his ragged breath and feel it warm against her face. She could also feel his heat surrounding her and his hardness pressing between her thighs.

Goodness, why did he stop?

She tried to pull him down to her again, but he resisted.

"Malcolm," she said finally, allowing her frustration to show in her tone.

His answer was a deliberate roll of his hips that had her gasping. Shifting her legs and arching her back, she tried to encourage more of the wonderful pressure and friction along the heated flesh between her thighs.

He obliged with a forceful thrust of his hips.

A soft moan slid from her throat, and she swore she heard a similar sound from him as the muscles of his arms tensed beneath her hands.

Releasing her grip, she slid her hands around his back. The ridges of muscle along the valley of his spine intrigued her, and she followed them down to the dip of her low back and then farther to his firm buttocks. Splaying her hands, she bent her knees along his hips, creating a deeper cradle as she urged him to another rolling thrust. "More," she murmured, incapable of saying anything more articulate.

The next thrust sent a rush of sensation straight through her center. She was suddenly desperate to remove the layers of clothing between them. As she reached for the waistband of his pants, intending to do whatever it took to get them off him, he pulled away.

Before she could protest, he grasped her hands in his and rose to his feet, pulling her up along with him.

"What are you doing? What is the matter?" she asked, panicked that he might think to leave her.

"We can't do this here," he replied in a low tone, thick with tension as he drew the straps of her undergarment back up on her shoulders.

"Then where?" In her lustful befuddlement, Alexandra still was not sure she comprehended. How could he stop so abruptly when all she wanted was to reach out to him again, feel his skin under her hands, his mouth on her body.

"To the cabin. Come on. The quicker we get back, the sooner I can have you naked."

The hunger, the predatory light of possession in his eyes, made her legs feel weak. "Yes," she said breathlessly, "let's hurry."

THIRTY-THREE

THEY MADE THE WALK BACK TO THE CABIN IN A silence thick with anticipation. Her hand was secure in his the entire way. Such a simple, schoolgirl gesture of affection, but to Alexandra, it was an indication that he did not want to sever their connection any more than she did, even for the time it took to wend their way along the creek.

As soon as they stepped inside the cabin, Malcolm released her and strode toward the fireplace. In swift movements, he stirred the coals to life and added some wood until the fire filled the room with warmth.

When he finally turned back to her, the heat in his gaze rivaled that from the fire, and her breath caught harshly in her lungs. His desire hadn't diminished during their walk from the lake. If anything, it had intensified.

So had hers.

She knew what she was about to do. She understood the consequences and the risks in giving herself to this man. But she could not imagine doing anything else. She needed him. And he needed her.

As if in silent communion, they started toward each other at the same time, meeting beside the bed.

Alexandra reached for the buttons of his shirt, then laughed when he simply grasped the hem of her shirt and lifted it up over her head. As soon as she could, she stripped him of his shirt as well, then switched to the belt securing her pants as he kicked himself free of his boots and began to remove his pants.

After dropping her pants to the floor, she kicked them aside, then made quick work of unstrapping her knife and removing her boots, stockings, and underclothes.

Finally, naked and breathless, she stopped to shake her hair back from her face. She hadn't bothered to rebraid it, and the length fell free and untamed down her bare back. Her breath was quite violently sucked from her body as she caught sight of him standing in front of her, as naked as she was.

Though she had seen much of his fine-sculpted torso during the days she'd treated his injury and since, it was still a shock to her system to finally see him in full.

Her eyes fell down the hard length of his body, noting his well-muscled legs and handsomely formed feet. Unable to resist her curiosity, her gaze settled on that very male part of him that extended hard and ready from his groin.

She wanted to touch him.

Taking a slow step toward him, she reached out to brush her fingers over his straining tip. He was unexpectedly smooth and so hot. Feeling bold, she ran her finger down the length of him. It was fascinating to her—how beautiful that male body part was.

Encouraged by his stillness, she stepped in closer. Her head was bowed as she gently wrapped her fingers around him. He was so hard. She tightened her grip, making him pulse and throb in her hand.

She risked a peek at his face.

He stared back at her with heavy-lidded eyes that still managed to shine brightly with his desire, while his jaw clenched with taut muscle and his breath came swiftly through flared nostrils.

The power within him—the strength and passion and fire so intently contained—overwhelmed her in a wonderful way. She felt weak and strong at once. Powerful even as her insides melted like honey. Such a contradiction. The desire to give and take. The hunger and the fulfilment.

"You still want more?" he asked, his voice thick and raw.

She tightened her grip on him, which had him sucking in a swift breath through his teeth. "I want it all," she declared.

He narrowed his eyes to dangerous slits, then grasped her hips and pulled her roughly to him. Her hand, still wrapped around him, became trapped between their bodies. She tipped her head back and offered her lips. "Now," she added.

With a growl, he kissed her. His hands moved to cup her rear, and he walked her back toward the bed. They fell to the mattress, her legs parting naturally to accommodate his hips.

He moved over her, settling his weight on his good arm, positioning himself so he rested intimately along the entrance to her body. She tried to roll her hips, wanting to feel more of him, moaning as his tongue plunged past her teeth instead. It was a fierce mating of mouths, and when he shifted his hungry kisses to the side of her throat, she gasped for breath. He scraped his teeth across her shoulder, sliding his body lower.

His lips fell to her breast. Her soft flesh was drawn deeply into his mouth as his tongue twirled over the sensitive tip. It was heaven. It was magic. A raw, hungry, wild sort of magic.

Her hands slid into his hair and her fingers curled around his skull, holding him to her.

But he was stronger and had no plan to stay where he was.

His lips continued a path down the center of her belly where she quivered deliciously inside. Then lower, where he flicked his tongue in teasing strokes of fire against the creamy skin of her inner thighs.

Alexandra held her breath. The muscles in her legs strained and tensed. Her body cried out for every bit of that *more* she had demanded. She pulled ineffectively at his shoulders, tried to shift beneath him and draw him back up to her, but he wasn't having it.

With a low sound, he hooked his arms beneath her thighs, leveraging them over his shoulders. When he paused, Alexandra lifted her head to look down the length of her sprawled and naked body to where he hovered between her legs.

Holding her gaze, he dropped a soft kiss to the apex of her mound, just above the thatch of dark curls that shielded her wet, aching folds.

She shuddered in response and he smiled. A predatory flash of teeth.

"I can't wait to be inside you, Alex. To feel your tight heat around me. But I want you pulsing when I enter your body. I want you languid and soft and swollen. Do you understand?"

She could only give a small, throaty groan in reply.

He lowered his head. At the first hot, luscious slide of his tongue, her head fell back and her hands fisted. The second tongue stroke stopped her breath and had her heels pressing into the mattress as she tried to lift herself to him.

He made a sound that could have been a chuckle or a moan, but she didn't much care, because he chose that moment to cover her with his open mouth and suckle her sensitive flesh.

She bucked her hips, but he pressed his hand flat over her lower belly, keeping her still beneath the onslaught of his mouth. Reaching up with his other hand, he covered her breast, kneading her softness before pinching her peaked and swollen nipple.

The sensations were unbelievable.

She felt entirely at his mercy. Her body, his to command and devour as he wished. Her breath, his to steal. Her blood, his to inflame.

He was relentless in his determination to bring every available sensation into play. Pleasure rippled along her nerves with every flick of his tongue and nip of his lips. Even the harsh scrape of his teeth sent shock waves of delight singing through her. He wanted something from her, and he was not going to let up until he got it.

Alexandra was helpless to fight the building of tension inside her. What started as a lovely little tingle in her core soon spread out into long spears of sensation that lifted her higher and higher. Her body became tense, and her movements were awkward. Her breath was short and shallow.

The release was so near she could practically taste it, like a sharp, metallic tang on her tongue.

She was suspended between the desire to claim that release and to avoid it, knowing that it would bring an end to the sweet fire flickering through every inch of her body.

As though he was aware of her resistance, he finally added one last, inescapable method of torment.

With his mouth sealed over the throbbing bud between her thighs, he eased his finger into her body. The glide of his touch along her inner flesh was the trigger that released the dam she'd been bracing within herself. Bright, consuming pleasure washed through her in a swift and sudden wave that seized her breath and left her trembling in its wake.

She barely had time to suck in a shaky breath before he was over her again, his mouth claiming hers as his hard length pressed hot and urgent against her entrance. On instinct, she bent her knees, drawing him into her. He moaned thickly into her mouth and pressed forward. Her pleasure still pulsed deep inside as her body softened and stretched around him. She held her breath and clung to him. Trusting him implicitly.

He initiated a slow pattern of thrust and retreat, each gliding advance reaching farther, easing the way to full possession, until finally he claimed her in one demanding thrust. The aching sensation mingled with the impossible beauty of being filled and stretched as he partially withdrew, then pushed forward again. The subtle pain became just another layer of her pleasure as she exploded in another climax. This release, however, came from deep inside and seemed to be made up of all that she was.

He continued to move in and out of her body, and the velvety friction prolonged her pleasure, sending wave after wave, ripple after ripple of delight outward from where they were joined. She loved the soft, guttural sounds that began to emerge from his throat and the strength in his arms wrapped around her. She loved the heavy beat of his heart against her breast and the warmth of his breath across her skin.

She loved the power and the tenderness that rushed through her. And the beauty inherent in being so vulnerable and yet trusting him implicitly.

She loved the sense of connection that told her he was nearing his own release.

A low sound was dragged from his throat a moment before he stiffened and pulled out of her. As he pulsed against her belly, spilling his seed, he pressed his open mouth to the soft skin below her ear.

She kept her arms wrapped tightly around him. Her breath slowed and her body softened. Part of her feared he would draw away too soon, before she was ready to give up the lovely weight of his body covering hers.

When he did start to shift his weight, she squeezed her legs around his hips. "Don't."

Braced on his elbows, he looked down at her.

She observed two things in his otherwise unreadable expression. One, that the hunger had not been completely erased from his gaze. It still crouched there in the steel-like depths, behind the flecks of black and silver. And two, his scowl had returned, tugging down at his brows and pressing his lips into a firm line.

That frown disappointed her.

She would have commented on it, but he dipped his head to press a hot kiss to her lips. It was full of the passion she'd come to expect from his kisses, but it was different now in the aftermath. More languid. More of a drawing out as he delved into her mouth with his tongue, his teeth sliding along her bottom lip before he sucked it briefly into his mouth in a way that had her toes curling.

But then he lifted his head and shifted to her side. Using a corner of the bedsheet, he wiped the remnants of his release from their bodies. When he finished, he rolled away to sit at the edge of the bed with his feet on the floor.

"Where are you going?" she asked, regretting the thickness that caught in her throat.

"Nowhere," he answered as he pressed his hand to his injured shoulder and rolled his arm in a slow circle.

"Your shoulder," she noted. "Does it hurt?"

"A bit."

Guilt washed through her. She had totally forgotten about his injury. "Why didn't you say something?"

"I didn't realize how sore it was until a second ago." Glancing back over his shoulder, he added with a tiny quirk of his lips, "I was distracted."

Alexandra warmed. "Let me take a look."

She scooted around him to kneel at his injured side. After lifting her hands to collect her hair and drop it down her back, she reached for his bandages.

It took some effort to keep from glancing down at his nude body as he sat there, exuding such a wealth of masculine beauty and power, even in the casual pose.

Focusing on his shoulder, she was surprised to find the wound itself looking quite good. There were no new signs of infection, and the skin had started to pucker around the edges as the damaged flesh repaired itself.

"You are healing very fast," she noted.

"It's the muscle beneath that's not what it should be."

She pressed her fingers into the muscle surrounding the wound. Starting in small, gentle circles, she tried to smooth out the tight bulges and taut ropes beneath his skin. After a little while, she noticed his head falling forward and his spine curving softly.

She worked her hands down the long sweep of his back and over the curve of his shoulder to the muscles of his arm and pectoral—applying varying pressure, depending on the tension she felt beneath her searching fingers. Just as her hands began to cramp from the effort, he caught her fingers in his and brought them to his lips. "Thank you," he murmured against her palm.

"Give it time," she said softly. "Your strength will return."

Lifting his gaze to look intently into her eyes, he replied, "As soon as I can draw and shoot my gun with enough effectiveness to keep us safe, we move on." His tone was low and far too heavy in the aftermath of the intimacy they'd shared.

She knew what he was saying: that they had a limited time together before they'd have to rejoin the rest of the world. Her stomach clenched, and her gaze lowered beneath his stare. She wanted to argue that there was no rush. That they could stay there together, isolated and alone, until everything else ceased to matter.

But it did matter. He would never go back on his vow to avenge his brother's murder.

And she could not ask him to do so.

The need for justice was as much a part of him as his stern nobility and the long-buried tenderness he denied possessing.

"Alex…"

When he didn't continue, she lifted her chin at a jaunty angle and flashed him a smile that she hoped didn't appear too forced. "I suppose I'd better feed you then. My father always used to say 'a man needs meat to conquer the day.' I will go check the snares."

"I can do that," he said.

"I do not mind," she replied as she slipped her feet to the floor and rose from the bed.

He caught her wrist before she could step away, and she stopped to look down at him. His frown had deepened into an expression of earnest concern. "Are you all right?" he asked.

Alexandra blushed as she realized he was referring to her lost virginity.

In truth, she felt sore but in a wonderful way. The more she thought of what they'd just done together, the more she wanted to do it again. Her skin warmed, and her body pulsed with renewed desire. "Quite wonderful, actually," she replied, refusing to be shy about it.

"Did I hurt you?"

She could see the concern hovering like a cloud

over his features. "No, Malcolm, you didn't." Bending forward, she pressed her lips to his, then flicked her tongue playfully against the firm line of his lips until she felt his tension ease and he started to kiss her back. Before she lost herself again, she stepped away. Meeting his beautiful gaze, she whispered, "I am tougher than I look."

And she hoped it was true, because even though her body felt alive and liberated and more capable than ever, her heart seemed to be developing a tenderness that could prove to be a problem.

THIRTY-FOUR

As soon as Alex left the cabin, Malcolm rose from the bed and dressed. His movements were awkward and rushed with the need still coursing through him. He'd slaked the lust of his body, but he didn't feel satiated. He felt invigorated. Virile. Hungry. And honest-to-God scared.

Because with Alex, everything was different.

She was capable, smart, and so damn beautiful. Especially when her temper was up. Her passion and fire matched something in him. Coming together with her had been unlike any coupling he'd ever experienced. Intense and fiery. He'd never been so consumed by desire that he became completely lost in a woman.

He'd willingly lose himself in Alex anytime she wanted, because amid all the heat, being with her felt like home. There was a comfort and ease to be found in her arms. And that is what scared him.

The ache in his shoulder was nothing compared to the ache in his chest as he acknowledged that there was no going back from where they had ventured together. Becoming lovers would make it all the more difficult to part when they reached Montana.

But they *would* part ways. That much was fact.

They needed to head out as soon as possible. As soon as he was capable of keeping them both alive. He'd get Alex safely to Montana, then he'd finish this thing with Dunstan once and for all.

He could have no future until the past was avenged.

After dressing, he strapped on his gun and stepped outside. He needed to get to work on restoring the full strength and capability of his gun hand.

Shaking his hands to loosen the tension in them, he eyed up an imaginary target at the tree line.

Malcolm spent more than an hour practicing his draw.

His hand felt confident and sure over the pistol grip every time he pulled the gun from the holster, but he had no speed in the draw, no fluidity of movement. He was awkward and deliberate as he tried to compensate for the weakness in his shoulder.

When his injury started to throb from the effort, he switched to drawing with his left hand, but it was going to take more work than they had time for to bring his left hand to the level of dexterity and accuracy he needed. He'd have to find a safe place away from the cabin to set up some targets. The only way to practice was to shoot.

Alexandra returned from her snares with two good-sized squirrels. Looking forward to the meal they'd share that night…and what might come after, she was smiling as she stepped into the clearing around the cabin. Her gaze found Malcolm immediately.

He stood down near the creek in his denim pants, shirt open at the throat and rolled at the sleeves, his leather vest, and that hat he always wore to block the rays of the sun and keep his features in shadow. His stance was relaxed and ready as he focused on some point in the distance.

As she watched, he went for his holstered Colt, drawing and aiming in one swift movement. He held the gun steady for several long minutes before returning it to his hip. She watched him repeat the motion several more times. He had a cross-draw, being that he holstered his gun on his left hip, handle forward, and drew with his right hand. The extra reach didn't seem to slow him down at all. She had never seen anyone draw so fast.

But he was clearly not satisfied.

Even at a distance, Alexandra noted the scowl of concentration on his handsome features and the tension contained across his upper back. He was gaining strength and increasing the range of his movement every day, but his shoulder wasn't ready for such vigorous work.

Not that he would accept her opinion on the subject.

Turning away, she set the squirrels beside the front door, then went around back to check on the horses. Leading them out to graze, she murmured a promise to give them each a good run the next day.

She lingered with the horses, feeling content, though she couldn't help but acknowledge that her time with Malcolm was limited. When the sun started to descend and the sky drifted into shades of pink, peach, and gold, she returned the horses to their shelter, then walked back around to the front of the cabin.

Entering the small shelter, she was greeted by the scent of roasting meat. Malcolm sat at the table, preparing a pan of campfire biscuits.

"You are cooking."

He tossed her a swift glance before he replied with a quirk of his mouth, "I assumed you didn't intend to eat the creatures raw."

"And more biscuits?" she asked, coming forward to peek into the pan filled with balls of dough.

"Yep, but it's the last we'll have." He took the pan to the fire, settling it in amongst some coals he'd prepared off to the side. When he turned to look at her, something in his eyes gave her warning that she wouldn't like what he was going to say next. "We'll have to be ready to head out again within a few days' time. Before we go, I need to know you're willing and able to use that rifle."

Alexandra stiffened, and her back teeth ground together.

Having a rifle within sight didn't bother her nearly as much as having a pistol around, but that didn't mean she had any intention of putting her hands on it. "I'm sure that won't be necessary. I have my knife."

His expression was almost menacing. "You want someone intent on harming you to get close enough for you to use your knife?"

No. She didn't.

But neither did she want to carry a gun. "I'm sure

there won't be anything to worry about. I saw you practicing with your Colt earlier. You will protect us."

"I'll do my best. But that's not always good enough. The men out there…the ones looking for me…" He paused before continuing. "They're not good men, Alex. You'll need to be able to defend yourself, in case I can't. Starting tomorrow, you're gonna do a little practice with that rifle."

He wasn't going to back down.

She glanced to where the weapon stood propped beside the door. Though the notion of holding any firearm made her distinctly uncomfortable, at least there wasn't a wash of cold terror through her blood.

She didn't realize Malcolm had come up behind her until he spoke in a low and even tone. "If not the rifle, maybe you'd prefer to carry my Colt. At least I know you can shoot it."

"No!" She hadn't intended to shout the word, but as soon as he suggested it, every muscle banded around her chest tightened, threatening to suffocate her. Tiny dots of light danced at the edges of her vision. The denial was as much an attempt at stopping her panicked reaction as it was to his suggestion.

He stepped around to face her, taking her shoulders firmly in his hands. The look he gave her was everything she wished to avoid. Curiosity, wariness, pity.

"Why does that terrify you?" he asked.

"It doesn't," she denied sharply.

"Liar."

She felt more exposed and vulnerable beneath his unwavering regard than she had when she'd been sprawled out naked beneath him.

"Tell me what happened, Alex. Share the burden with me."

God, how could she? She hadn't described that scene since the minutes after it happened, when she'd run the rest of the way home, the scent of gunpowder and blood in her nostrils, the sound of a man moaning in agony shuddering through her head. Falling into her father's arms, she'd stuttered and cried through the explanation of what had occurred, unsure if she made any sense beyond the phrase that kept repeating in her head and on her trembling lips: *I killed him. I killed him.*

"You don't need to carry the memory all on your own," he urged gently.

Taking a deep breath, then another, she looked down at her hands, which were clenched into tight fists pressed against her stomach. Then she lifted her gaze to Malcolm's fierce, harsh-featured face and his sharp, intense eyes.

She started slowly. "I had gone to town on some errand—I cannot remember what anymore—on a walk I'd made a hundred times. Only a few miles in full daylight. I always passed by people we knew—friends and neighbors. I'd give a wave, a smile, a quick how-do-you-do before continuing on my way. But this day was different."

She paused.

"I'd turned fifteen only a few months before, and my father had gifted me with a special modified Colt pistol. It was smaller than yours, quite a bit smaller, with a mother-of-pearl handle and a holster made specifically to fit me. I wore that gun everywhere. I was so proud to be given such a gift. I felt grown and capable and independent. Apparently, the two men I encountered that day saw something else."

Malcolm's expression tightened at her words. There was something about the sight of his fury on her behalf that angered her. She didn't want him to feel some noble craving for justice. She didn't need him to give any vow of vengeance for her. What she needed was a world where men did not think they could come upon a girl alone and take whatever they wanted.

"They laughed when I told them to stop following me," she explained bitterly. "When they grabbed for me and I struggled, trying to smack their groping hands, they laughed even harder. And when they got me down on the ground—right there beside the road I'd walked so many times—and I didn't stop fighting them, they got angry. A few hard slaps across the face ceased my frantic struggles. It also reminded me that I had a far better means of fighting them. While one held my legs and the other climbed over me, I drew my little Colt and fired. Without a thought. Without hesitation."

As she stopped to take some long breaths through her nose, she realized she couldn't shake the haze of memory crowding in around her.

"I remember the blood the most," she said softly. "The way it soaked into my dress before I managed to shove him off me and stagger to my feet. The other one had jumped back when the gun fired and stood staring at me like I was crazed. I remember thinking that odd. My gun had been on my hip the whole time, in plain view. Had they never considered I might use it?

"I lifted the barrel in his direction. I didn't need to. He took off at a dead run. The one I'd shot—the one who'd claimed the right to rape me first—lay in the dirt at my feet, terror in his eyes as blood soaked his shirt, spreading so far across his chest that I couldn't even tell where I'd hit him. Then he started making this wretched choking sound and started coughing up more blood.

"I ran. All the way back to my father. He told me to stay in the house and lock the doors while he rode out to where I'd left the man to die. He was gone for hours. I stripped off my blood-soaked clothes and burned them. I scrubbed myself with ice-cold water until my skin was chafed and bleeding. Then I sat in the chair and stared at my gun where I'd dropped it to the floor. I stared at it for hours, until the sun set and the fire died in the grate and the sun rose again the next morning. Until my father returned with a look on his face I'd never seen before. He told me to pack some things. We would be leaving within the hour. I didn't realize I would be the only one boarding that train for Boston until he said goodbye on the platform and promised to bring me home once the trouble blew over."

Alexandra blinked a few times, the corner of her mouth curling upward, though she felt no humor in her words. "I guess it never did."

She purposely looked to where his gun belt had been slung over the back of the dining chair. The glint of cold metal sent a chill down the back of her neck, and her palms grew damp.

"You shot that man in self-defense."

"I know."

"It was an act of survival."

"I know that too."

He took her chilled hands in his. "You can still hear it. See it. Smell it. Can't you?"

She nodded, then tipped her chin up to meet his understanding gaze. "Does it ever go away?"

"No. But after a time, it doesn't affect you the same," he replied, but then his brows lowered, and he dropped her hands. "Or maybe I've gathered up so many of those memories, they've lost their impact."

She arched her brow. "Are you suggesting I go on a killing spree?"

He chuckled, his gray eyes meeting hers warmly. "No. But you need to understand that your actions were justified. The reason your father likely gave you that Colt in the first place was to protect you from that kind of danger, and others. Maybe you didn't need it in Boston, but out here, a gun on your hip is a necessary aspect of life."

"Especially when there are countless men hunting you down?" she asked.

He frowned.

"You need your Colt, Malcolm," she insisted. "I'll take the rifle."

"Once you've had a little practice, I expect you'll handle it with no problem."

She gave him a half smile. "You seem to have developed an awful lot of faith in me," she teased.

"It's warranted. You impress me more every day, Alex," he replied. Then he dipped his chin, and the look in his eyes was arresting. "I suspect you could even teach me a few things."

Alexandra lifted her brows in a haughty expression. "Oh, I'm sure of it."

THIRTY-FIVE

THE NEXT MORNING, MALCOLM SET UP SOME TARGETS for shooting practice.

Though the thought of carrying a weapon caused a clenching of fear and uncertainty in Alexandra's stomach, the danger of encountering the mercenaries out there looking for Malcolm was too great. She would do her part to help protect them both until he was prepared to meet his brother's murderer on his own terms.

Just like when she'd drawn Malcolm's Colt in a split-second reaction to seeing the gun aimed at his back, the rifle's familiarity came back in an instant. The weight and heft, the smooth grip of the wood stock, the feel of it against her shoulder, and the way she had to breathe as she aimed at the target across the meadow and pulled the trigger.

A direct hit, almost dead center.

Malcolm gave her an odd look but said nothing as he gave a nod to shoot again.

Another bull's-eye and a narrow-eyed side glance from Malcolm reminded her of how her father had always been stunned by her marksmanship. She'd been a natural with a rifle since she'd first picked one up at age eight.

When the third shot joined the first two in a tight grouping, Malcolm grumbled, "I'm starting to think you don't need any practice."

"I told you I didn't."

He stepped forward and pulled her to him for a full, open-mouthed kiss that had her so breathless and weakened that she nearly dropped the rifle to the dirt. When he pulled back, a wicked smile curled the corners of his mouth. "Now try to shoot."

She brought the rifle to her shoulder. Taking only half a breath to aim, she fired.

"Aw, hell," Malcolm muttered as he turned to stride back up the hill to the cabin.

Alexandra laughed. She'd forgotten how much she enjoyed target practice.

After lunch, Malcolm and Alexandra went for a ride.

He'd resisted when she first insisted on joining him on his daily searches for any sign of Dunstan's men, but at least now she wasn't opposed to carrying the rifle. In all honesty, he preferred having her at his side over leaving her alone back at the cabin.

The rides had become an activity he looked forward to. The simple act of getting to know the land was a pleasure he'd never experienced. Though he'd always felt a certain affinity for the Rockies, he'd never taken the time to really breathe in the beauty of the mountains, but Alex's love of the Montana wilderness was obvious and contagious.

It was too easy to imagine spending every day riding beside her.

If he were a different man, that's the future he would have chosen.

But such dreams weren't meant to be.

There were a limited number of ways into the small valley, and on previous rides, they hadn't come across any indication that others had passed through the area for some time. Today, they weren't so fortunate. As they rode along a westward-facing ridge that gave a broad view over some foothills that spread out to more level land, he spotted a band of riders.

There were four of them, a rag-tag group of men, sufficiently armed to take down a stubborn bounty hunter—and they were close. Too damn close. There was no way to know if they were Dunstan's men, but a gut feeling had Malcolm quickly turning about to get out of their line of sight.

Alex kept her mare close beside him as they urged their mounts to a swifter pace. She'd seen the riders and didn't need to be told to minimize the sound of their retreat as best they could.

Despite their caution, the thunder of horses giving chase echoed from behind them. They'd been spotted.

Shit.

Malcolm looked at the woman riding beside him. Since Gavin, he'd made sure no one had to rely on him for anything. Just knowing Alex was at risk because of him made him sick.

She appeared so competent and brave as she

crouched low over her horse's neck, and when she turned her gaze to meet his, he saw nothing but fierce determination in her blue eyes. "We have to split up. I'm only slowing you down."

His gut twisted at the thought of separating while Dunstan's men were hot on their trail, but she was right. Individually, they'd have a better chance of evading their followers. She knew these mountain trails as well, if not better, than he did. Her experienced mare could head up along one of the more rough and hidden routes they'd discovered while Malcolm lured their pursuers in the opposite direction. With a little room to run, Deuce could outpace just about any other horse.

But he hated having to let her out of his sight. The thought of being unable to protect her made his chest ache with fear.

"I'll be all right," she assured him. "Please trust me. It's the only way."

He did trust her. More than anyone else in the world. She might've set out on this journey to prove something to herself, but she'd already proven herself to him a hundred times over.

"Head toward that moose trail we found yesterday. I'll try to get them to follow me, but if any of them keep after you and get too close, you find a place to hole up. Don't hesitate to use that rifle. Promise me."

She nodded, her eyes intent and focused. "Be safe, Malcolm."

"You too." He could have said so much more, but the sound of horses seemed to be growing nearer. There was no time.

Pulling hard on Deuce's reins, he spun back the way they'd come. With any luck, their pursuers would all take off after him, leaving Alex to make her way safely back to the cabin.

It took more than an hour of hard riding to finally lose sight of the men behind him, followed by another couple of hours of carefully wending his way back to the cabin by an indirect route, using every trick he knew to disguise his trail. By the time he rode into the clearing, the sun had slipped below the horizon, turning the sky a soft lavender-gray. His heart nearly stopped when Alex came running out of the cabin. Leaping from the saddle, he turned just in time to catch her as she launched herself into his arms.

"Thank God you made it," she whispered, echoing his thoughts exactly.

His relief was intense but short-lived.

He had to force himself to pull away, intentionally pushing her to arm's length. "Go back inside. I need to tend to Deuce."

By the jut of her chin and brief narrowing of her eyes, he knew she wished to say something, but she held her tongue.

He figured he knew what stopped her. He could feel the hardness spreading over his features, invading his body, preparing him for battle. The harsh, ragged edge of vengeance and fear was a raw fire inside him.

He welcomed it.

That hardness had gotten him through the years since Gavin's murder, and it would have to get him through the next several days until he left Alex with her father.

He'd allowed things to get too close. Too comfortable. Too intense.

And now it had to end.

Now that they knew he was in these mountains, Dunstan's men wouldn't stop looking for him. Eventually, they'd come upon this place and ruin the closest thing to a home he'd ever known. He couldn't let that happen.

Taking Deuce around to the shelter, he unsaddled the gelding and brushed him down. Alex had already brought up fresh water, and Malcolm emptied the last of their store of grain for both horses. Deuce would need to restore his energy before they headed out again. The dark would keep Dunstan's men from finding his trail tonight, but he had no doubt they'd be at it first thing in the morning.

Malcolm would be ready for them.

He'd done some more practice with his Colt that morning. His speed wasn't where it used to be, but he was accurate. It would have to be enough.

Coming around the corner of the cabin, he stopped when he saw Alex standing in the open door.

He said nothing when she silently stepped aside for him to enter. A sick feeling twisted his stomach as the door closed, ensconcing them in the quiet shelter. Even though Alex hadn't lit a fire, probably to avoid attracting their pursuers with the smoke, the cabin still felt homey and welcoming. "I'm heading out tomorrow at first light," he said curtly as he dropped his hat into the center of the table before removing his coat.

"You are going after them?" Of course, she would realize what he intended to do.

He wished more fervently than he ever had before that he was done tracking down Gavin's killers. The last eight years had been a vigilant study in vengeance and death. For the first time since it had all begun, he resented how he had been changed by it.

Somehow, Alex made him feel tender and full of a longing for things that could never be while Dunstan still lived.

Once he killed Dunstan, the past would be done. Then maybe he'd be able to look to the future without the constant sense of dread. Maybe he'd be able to look at Alex and see beyond the next morning.

"Malcolm?" She was still waiting for an answer.

He looked down at the table where his hat rested between the rough place settings—two tin plates, a couple of forks, and tin cups for water.

"I can't let them track me back here. Even if we leave tomorrow, they'll still be out there. They *will* catch up to us. We can't risk being caught unaware."

She came up behind him. He could feel her in the way the air over his skin became charged with heightened awareness seconds before her scent and warmth drifted through his senses.

"I'm going with you."

"No."

"I wasn't asking permission, Malcolm. You will need my help."

He turned then to look at her, his heart heavy. "I don't want you to get hurt."

She stepped toward him, and his arms came up to draw her closer. She locked her hands behind his back and tipped her head to smile up at him. "Then we will have to come up with a good plan."

Later that night, long after their cold supper had been cleaned up, Alexandra cursed herself for suggesting they get a good rest before riding out in the morning. She'd been regretting it with every breath, as sleep proved to be stubbornly elusive. She suspected Malcolm was as wide-awake as she was, even though he hadn't moved so much as a muscle since they'd settled beneath the covers—him on his back and her curled against his side with her head on his shoulder and her hand resting over his heart.

She tried convincing herself that this was enough: his closeness and comfort, the sound of his steady breath, and the warmth of his skin beneath her palm.

But her heart fluttered wildly with the yearning to be closer, to take him inside her and experience that deeply forged connection, especially not knowing what tomorrow might bring.

She trusted their plan to set up an ambush for the men who had followed them. She believed they would be able to overtake them, but the risk was great. And after that, they would be leaving this place, this quiet little meadow and cozy cabin. The silence and darkness surrounding them would soon disperse as their future spread out to encompass the rest of the world. They would never again be so ensconced in such a perfect cocoon of intimacy.

She wished she had a means of fighting against it.

She had asked Malcolm once if he would consider setting aside his vengeance for a future. She would not ask again, not now that it had become so personal to her. But the thought of losing him…

She bit her lip and squeezed her eyes shut tightly against the burn of tears as she considered the very real possibility that he might not make it through a confrontation with his brother's killer.

No. He would make it. He would see justice done, and he would live on. She had to believe it.

"If I could promise tomorrow…I would." His words were rough and barely audible as they tumbled from low in his throat.

But she heard them. And she understood.

The fist around her heart squeezed tighter as she slid her hand up to curve her fingers around the side of his throat and brush her thumb along the ridge of his jaw.

Turning his head, he pressed a soft kiss to the pad of her thumb.

Alexandra lifted her head from his shoulder to bring her lips to within a breath of his. Holding his gaze, she whispered, "We have tonight."

As she kissed him, she bent her knee and slid her leg up until her inner thigh covered his groin while he swept his hands up her back and down again to cup her rear.

She moaned softly, flicking her tongue against his.

The flash of fire in his eyes gave her a wild thrill as he rolled her beneath him.

Words of love trembled on the surface of her lips, threatening to cascade in a litany of hopes and dreams that she couldn't ask him to fulfill.

Love.

Yes, she loved him. It was so obvious, she was stunned not to have seen it sooner.

But it had been present for so long. Triggered by his noble heart and fierce desire to protect her. His acceptance of all that she had finally allowed herself to be. His encouragement and faith in her ability to get past her fears. And his trust that she would do her part in the morning, just as he would do his.

She loved him.

But instead of the realization bringing joy, it was painfully sad. Because he was not free to love her back. He would forever be chained by guilt and regret until he was able to exact revenge for his brother's murder. Despite everything that had happened between them, the day would come when he would walk away.

No matter how badly she might wish to, she wouldn't tell him of her feelings. She couldn't add that burden to everything else he carried.

Instead, she said everything she could with her body. Wrapping her arms and legs around him, opening to him, giving all that she had to give.

Or at least, all he might be willing to accept.

THIRTY-SIX

THEY ROSE BEFORE THE SUN.

Alexandra wasn't sure either of them had claimed much sleep through the night. They were quiet as they packed up their meager belongings and loaded what supplies they had left onto their horses. Malcolm made sure their guns were oiled and ready. Not just his own, but also the guns he'd gotten off the other three who had come for him. He strapped two guns around his hips and hooked another to his saddle, while two rifles went with Alexandra.

By the time they rode out from the cabin, it looked as though they'd never been there.

Alexandra refused to look back at the place that would forever hold so many beautiful memories. It was time to move on.

They were both on high alert as they retraced the route Malcolm had taken on his return to the cabin the prior day. Before the sun even reached above the tree line, they made it to a narrow ravine perfectly designed for an ambush. If any of the four men were skilled in tracking, they would eventually pass through this spot.

After scouting for a place where Alexandra could hunker down, they found one high atop a southern ridge that provided proper coverage and kept the path of the sun over her shoulder.

"You stay here. Out of sight. No matter what," Malcolm said, his eyes flinty and hard. "Your only job is to provide cover and a bird's-eye view. Nothing more."

She knew their plan well enough, but she also knew she would do what was necessary if Malcolm ended up in the line of fire.

"If things go wrong, you take off," he said. "Promise me."

Alexandra shook her head. "I can't promise that."

His frown was dark and heavy. "You have to, Alex. I won't have them taking you."

"They won't."

He stared at her for a long time, then without another word, he crushed her against him and pressed a hard kiss to her mouth. It was over too soon and then he walked away.

She watched him go with her heart filling her throat, hoping with all her might that it wouldn't be the last time she saw him.

Then she shook off the emotional distraction and set herself up. The best way to ensure his safety was to stay focused on the task at hand. Lying down on her belly beneath the shadowed cover of thick bushes, she kept one rifle in hand while the other lay beside her. Taking steady breaths, she stared at the entrance to the valley, ready for any sign of movement.

She had no idea how much time had passed when she first heard the sound of horse hooves and the creak of leather saddles. A moment later, the first rider appeared in the valley, followed by three more.

A buzz of anticipation went through her hands and up her arms. Fear and doubt crowded in for a second before she kicked them aside.

The pass was narrow, with steep-sloped sides that forced riders into single file, spreading out their resources so they would have a harder time covering each other. Malcolm was down there somewhere, waiting for the right time to bring them all to a stop. He needed her to do her part. He was counting on her to provide protection.

She wouldn't let him down.

"That's far enough," Malcolm called out. His voice bounced around in the narrow crevice and brought the four men to a quick stop, and their heads whipped in all directions, looking for the source of the order.

It also brought out their guns.

Alexandra scanned them all swiftly, looking for any sign that they might start shooting. This pass had also been chosen because the rocky sides could easily cause bullets to ricochet. A fact that the men were likely to recognize, hopefully dissuading them from carelessly opening fire. With her angle, Alexandra held a significant advantage in that her shots would be directed downward.

"Toss your weapons—all of them—off to your right," Malcolm instructed.

"Like hell," one of the men retorted as he peered toward a group of trees at the far end of the valley.

"Do it or end up with a bullet in your chest."

Alexandra shifted her aim, making sure she had clear shots of each of the men.

"Show yourself and we'll see who ends up with the bullet."

"I'm running out of patience. The first to toss down his weapons will be left with the most water."

Two of the men glanced at each other after that statement, but none made a move to follow Malcolm's order.

Her heart thundered in her ears as the talkative one suddenly leaned forward, gazing hard at the tree line ahead. Then he lifted his gun to take aim. She caught a quick flash as the sun glinted off the metal in his hands. He had spotted Malcolm. She couldn't let him get off a shot.

But as his Colt came under her sights, she felt the push of panic in her veins.

No.

She would not allow her fear to take over. Taking a breath, she stopped it on the exhale and pulled the trigger.

Her shot echoed through the ravine, combining with a harsh shout of pain as the Colt dropped from the man's bleeding grip. At the same time, his mount reared up, sending him tumbling to the ground. The riderless horse took off running, and the other men struggled to keep their own horses under control while frantically searching for the source of the shot.

"As you can see, I'm not the only one losing patience. Now toss your weapons."

The three men looked to the first, who was cradling his injured hand. "Goddammit, just do it," he said, agony loading his words.

Once all the weapons were on the ground, Malcolm

ordered the men to continue farther into the ravine before having them dismount. Only then did he step forward with rope in hand.

"You're all alive at this point, but that could change real quick, so don't be stupid."

Alexandra continued to provide cover while Malcolm secured each of the men to large boulders some distance from one another so they wouldn't be able to work together to free themselves. Then he set each of their water canteens within reach before sending their horses off on their own.

"You can't just leave us here," one of them complained.

"It won't be for long," Malcolm replied. "A day or two at most. It'll give you time to consider who you want to work for in the future."

"There are others out there," sneered the one Alexandra had shot in the hand. "Others paid to hunt you down. You're gonna get caught."

"Not by you," Malcolm said as he turned and walked away.

Alexandra stayed where she was, watching to be sure none of the men pulled any surprises.

Several minutes later, Malcolm joined her on the ridge. His expression was as hard as she'd ever seen as he walked up to her. She barely made it to her feet before he pulled her into his arms. After a quick and passionate kiss, he lifted his head to gaze hard into her eyes. "I hope to God we never have to do anything like that again, but damn, that was a nice shot."

Alexandra smiled, feeling his praise and his relief down to her soul.

"Now, let's get out of here," he said, pulling away. "The nearest trading post is a full day's ride. We'll leave word there on where to find these guys. By the time they're freed, we'll be long gone."

And that much closer to saying goodbye to each other.

The next days passed quickly—too quickly—as they made their way north to Helena.

They stayed clear of towns, which suited Alexandra just fine. She wasn't ready to enter full reality just yet. She was almost able to convince herself that these last days on the trail were an extension of their intimacy at the cabin. But there was no way to completely deny the shift between them.

There was a new barrier in Malcolm's gaze when he looked at her. And he didn't smile or laugh anymore. He was creating distance, and Alexandra was letting him.

He grew more and more tense with each day they traveled, continually raising his spyglass to scan their surroundings, seeking any sign of potential danger.

For the most part, they had fallen back into the routine they'd developed before Malcolm had gotten shot. After spending the day on horseback, they'd make camp, and one of them would go hunting with the rifle while the other tended their horses.

The difference was that they'd sit side by side at the fire while they ate and sleep side by side at night. Some nights they just held each other, savoring each other's warmth, but most nights they made love.

It was the only time Malcolm seemed willing to acknowledge what still existed between them. But it was slower, more deliberate, more tender than it had been in the cabin. Alexandra knew it was Malcolm's way of saying goodbye. If she were a smart sort of woman, at some point she would have insisted on keeping their distance from each other during the night as they did during the day.

She decided she wasn't smart at all when it came to Malcolm.

She'd gone and done the stupidest thing she could have—she'd fallen in love with him.

Knowing he would head out on his own once he left her with her father. Knowing he'd been clear from the start that he could make no promises. Knowing she still had no idea what her future looked like aside from wishing with all her heart that Malcolm could somehow be a part of it.

Far too soon, they reached Helena, Montana.

They skirted the edge of the rapidly growing city until they came to the road that led out to the home she'd last shared with her father. To get there, they had to traverse the same route where she'd been attacked all those years ago. As they approached the specific spot, Alexandra felt her body tensing with the desire to spin her horse around and fly back in the opposite direction.

She took some hard, shaking breaths and willed her hands to remain steady and confident on Sibyl's reins. When they passed the spot where she'd been tossed to the ground, where her attacker's blood had soaked into the earth, she found that she could look upon it with the understanding that the memories were just that. They couldn't touch her or hurt her or frighten her anymore.

She had defended herself. She had prevented the rape and had survived.

She breathed easier after that and managed to smile as the area around her became more and more familiar. Riding up to the tiny house with the small chicken coop and two-horse barn filled her with sweet nostalgia.

But the person who stepped out onto the front stoop was not her father.

Apparently, Randolph Brighton had moved into the next valley a while back.

Alexandra's chest tightened with the realization that her father had moved without telling her. Since her letters had continued to go to his box at the post office, she had assumed he'd stayed in the little house they'd lived in together. The fact that that wasn't the case and that he hadn't bothered to advise her of it felt like a betrayal and made her think, not for the first time, that he had no intention of ever welcoming her home again.

She grew quiet as they followed the directions to her father's new home just a short ride over the hills. Whether due to his own lacking desire for conversation, or perhaps because he sensed her need for introspection, Malcolm did not say anything to interrupt her mental preoccupation.

She hated not knowing what to expect when she saw her father again.

She'd originally intended to arrive home in her fashionable traveling outfit with her soft gloves, polished boots, and the pert little hat set at just the right angle on her well-styled coiffure. She'd intended to show him how grown and sophisticated she'd become. She'd hoped he'd be impressed. That he would declare how much he'd missed her—how much he'd missed out on over the last five years.

Instead, she was trail-worn and dusty, smelling of campfire and horse, with her hair in a messy braid down her back. She wouldn't have it any other way. She had come west to reclaim what it meant to be Alexandra, and that was what she had done.

She was proud of who she was. She could only hope her father might be too.

It was barely even an hour later that they stopped atop a small hill and looked down over a huge cattle spread.

Her heart dropped to her stomach.

This couldn't be right. They must have gotten bad directions.

Over the years, her father had tried a variety of occupations and lifestyles. He enjoyed learning new trades and developing a variety of skills. The one time he'd tried ranching had been short-lived and not very successful, because Randolph Brighton was not one to commit to anything in full measure. He had always liked being able to walk away from something without much guilt or hardship. He enjoyed living modestly and being able to pick up and move along on a whim.

The ranch spread out before them was no product of a whim.

Two good-sized stable buildings were set perpendicular to each other, with a large, fenced arena between them. To the north sat a long row bunkhouse that could easily house up to forty ranch hands. There was even an impressive-sized barn, a pig pen, and a scattering of chickens running around out front.

The house itself was grand. Painted a pale blue with green shutters, it stood three stories, with a sweeping porch that wrapped all the way around.

This was where her father lived? This elaborate place?

"Ready?"

She just shook her head, suddenly wishing she were dressed in her Eastern finery after all.

She had thought returning to her father would feel like going home, but this wasn't home. This was nothing like the life she and her father had lived together. She had changed a great deal in the years she'd been gone, but she hadn't considered that her father could have as well.

"You okay, sweetheart?"

The concern in Malcolm's voice finally cut through her mental and emotional confusion. She looked at him seated atop his horse right beside her. "It's not what I expected."

"I figured that," he replied with a half smile. "But the man down there in that house is still your pa. You came all this way for a reason. You're not gonna back down now."

What was her reason again?

To find out why her father had never asked her to come home again. To settle her past once and for all so she could look to the future without all the uncertainty she'd been carrying for so long.

"What are you afraid of?"

She breathed deeply. "That I won't be good enough."

"That's bullshit." She scowled at him, ready to argue, but he kept talking. "You're far better than good enough. There isn't another woman I know who would have stormed into a saloon, bold as you please, to argue toe-to-toe with a man like me."

"Only to accept the assistance of a thief and swindler, who left me to die in the middle of the wilderness."

"But you didn't die. You survived and convinced me to help you."

She smiled. "With you grumbling about it the whole time."

"Well, I haven't grumbled in a long while," he said gently, warming Alexandra from the inside. "How could I complain about a woman who overcame her fear to save my life?"

Her gaze dropped to the Colt on his hip.

"Don't ever doubt your worth, Alexandra Brighton." His voice was firm, allowing for no further argument. She was afraid to meet his gaze, afraid to fall deeper into the emotional snare she'd been caught in. Afraid that even after they parted, she would still be stuck in this place where she had come to need him far more than she had ever needed anyone.

"What if he tells me to go back to Boston?"

"You gonna go just because he tells you to?"

"No."

"If you go back to Boston, it'll be because it's what you want to do. But if you don't ride down there to see your pa, you'll regret it."

She nodded. "I know." Finally looking at him, she asked the question that still hovered between them. "You won't leave right away, will you?"

His eyes darkened, and he hesitated before answering.

She knew she shouldn't have asked him that. Of course, he'd want to be on his way as soon as possible now that she had reached her father's. But she couldn't bear for him to just ride away before she had a chance to give him a real goodbye. Before she was ready.

"Not if you don't want me to," he finally said.

"Thank you."

He didn't reply, and she knew that there was no longer any reason to delay her next step.

"Let's go then." She nudged her horse with her heels, and they started down the slope into the wide valley.

It was midday, so the area around the house was rather quiet. The ranch hands were likely all out on the range, and Alexandra could only hope her father wasn't with them, but if he was, surely there would be someone at the house to greet her.

Of course, she hadn't sent any word that she was coming...

Just as they passed by the stables and neared the front of the house, a shriek of childish laughter preceded the appearance of a girl around nine years old, running wildly, with two long, yellow braids flying back over her shoulders. She was swiftly followed by a boy who appeared a few years older, but with the same pale, blond hair. He was shouting words of retribution, though his expression looked more playful than vengeful.

Both children came to a skidding halt at the sight of Alexandra and Malcolm.

"Oh!" The girl said as she saw them first. Her smile was bright and her gaze curious as she approached. "Who are you?"

"Ivy," the boy said in a cautioning tone as he came up beside her. His sharp, wary gaze scanned over them swiftly before pausing for a bit on Malcolm.

"We understand Randolph Brighton lives here," Alexandra said with an uncertain smile. "Is he home?"

"Sure," the girl named Ivy replied, "I'll go get him."

The boy rolled his eyes as she turned and ran to the house in another whirlwind of flying skirts and childish energy.

Opening the door to enter the house, she let out a loud shout. "Papa! Some people are here to see you!"

Alexandra stiffened. Her heart clenched. Surely the girl hadn't been calling to *Alexandra's* father. These tow-headed children were both too old to have been born while she'd been away. And obviously he would have told her if he'd remarried, acquiring stepchildren. Wouldn't he?

She thought back through the letters he'd sent over the years, how disappointing they always were—so rarely going any deeper than courteous inquiries on how she fared with his sister and her family. There had been very little detail about his own life.

She sat stiff in the saddle, waiting for her father to appear. Hoping she was wrong in what she suspected. Though she could feel Malcolm next to her, silently lending her his strength and confidence, she was unable to look at him. She didn't want him to see the heartbreak in her eyes.

It was barely two minutes before that front door opened again and Randolph Brighton stepped out onto the porch.

He looked the same.

Same compact, wiry frame. His hair had gone whiter and there was less of it, but he still sported the thick, drooping mustache he'd always preferred. She took a moment to note his fine pants and vest, the polished boots, and the gold watch chain that looped over his chest.

"Howdy there," he said with a wide grin that had her feeling like a young girl again. "What can I…" His voice trailed away as his attention fell on Alexandra and stayed there.

Alexandra was instantly swept back to a time when she had been able to look into her father's eyes and feel that all was right and wonderful with the world. But that sense of being cherished and confident in her father's love was just a passing flash, made more painful for how quickly it flew away. So much more than years and miles had come in between them since she had been that girl.

"Oh my God, Alexandra? Is that you, honey?"

"Hello, Papa."

He let out a whoop and rushed down the steps as she swung down from her horse just in time to be caught up in his arms for a rambunctious, spinning hug.

"Goodness, girl," he exclaimed as he brought them to a stop and held her out at arm's length. "I've been worried sick about you."

She smiled back at him, though the tension hadn't left her.

"When I got Judith's telegram saying you'd up and left Boston without telling anyone, I couldn't imagine what might've gotten into you. And then when you didn't show up here, I had no idea what happened."

"I had some travel issues that caused a bit of a delay."

"I'd say that's an understatement, my dear," he admonished. "We've been wondering what happened to you."

We?

She wanted to ask who else had been worried about her, but couldn't quite form the question.

And then she didn't have to as a woman came out onto the porch. A beautiful woman with bright-green eyes and pale-blond hair, wearing as elegant a dress as any Alexandra had ever seen this far west. It must have been ordered straight from New York.

"Who is it, dear?" the woman asked before her eyes widened and she answered her own question. "Goodness me, is that Alexandra?"

Randolph's expression shifted as a blush pinkened his cheeks. This pretty woman was obviously the mother of the two children who had greeted them and, by all appearances, was also very likely her father's wife.

No wonder he hadn't asked her to come home. He'd gotten himself a whole new family.

Pain washed through Alexandra, and her chest got so tight she could barely breathe. Her homecoming was more devastating than she could have imagined. But in the next second, she realized it was about to get even worse as someone else stepped from the house to join the blond woman.

Alexandra shifted her gaze to the newcomer, and her stomach performed a plunging dive as she noted the calmly concerned expression of Mr. Peter Shaw, her still-fiancé.

THIRTY-SEVEN

THIS COULDN'T BE HAPPENING.

"Alexandra?" Peter's polished features shifted just slightly into a look of mild astonishment. "Could that possibly be you?"

Alexandra braced herself. *What is Peter doing in Montana?*

But of course, he'd come to fetch his bride. He would see it as his duty. In his mind, they were still connected, intended for each other, even though she had not thought of him as such for weeks.

She felt sick. She hadn't even told Malcolm about him. What would he think of Peter's presence?

"Hello, Peter. I did not expect to find you here."

"But of course I would come. When your aunt—who is quite upset, by the way—notified me of your rather reckless departure, I purchased a ticket straight-away." His tone was one of affront. "We have all been extremely worried for your safety. I do not understand what could have prompted such behavior."

"I am sure the reasons will be revealed," the blond woman said with a gracious smile as she stepped down from the porch to approach Alexandra and her father. "The main issue, I believe, is that she has finally made it to us safe and sound."

Alexandra glanced to her father, then at the beautiful woman who had come up to stand beside him with her arm linked through his. Her gaze flickered over the two attractive children who stood a few steps back, watching the scene with open curiosity.

Then back to Peter, still standing on the porch.

"I am sorry that my impetuous decision to come... home caused so much worry." She hated the telling hesitation in her voice. "It was something I needed to do."

"I think it's fair to say that you could have gone about it in a different way, darling," Peter declared. Though his tone was relatively gentle, Alexandra couldn't help but feel resentful of his proprietary manner, as though he had some right to an opinion over her behavior.

But of course he did. Or at least he thought he did.

She'd have to break the engagement in person now. And the sooner the better.

Alexandra struggled to find a proper response to Peter's condescending comment. But it seemed he wasn't finished. "And who exactly are you?" Peter asked, having turned his attention to Malcolm.

Everyone's gaze shifted to where Malcolm stood a few paces back, holding the reins of their horses. He'd dismounted after Randolph had come outside and remained slightly off to the side, watching the scene with his typical dark expression.

Alexandra's heart stopped.

Malcolm was staring at Peter with a glint of steel in his eyes. Peter's tone was of one accustomed to getting immediate response to any inquiry, but Malcolm said nothing, just stared silently back at him until everyone grew uncomfortable.

"Why don't we take this discussion inside?" the blond woman suggested. "I imagine Alexandra would like to freshen up after her journey. I will see her to a room, and we can all gather again in the parlor in about an hour. Is that acceptable?"

She had stepped away from Randolph when she'd started speaking and linked her arm through Alexandra's. By the time the woman got around to the final question, she nearly had Alexandra through the door and into the house.

There was only a moment to glance back over her shoulder at Malcolm, still standing with their horses, still glaring at Peter, before the door swung shut, blocking her view from everyone else outside.

The blond woman released an audible sigh and gave a side-tossed smile. "Now, that's better, I'd say. I think the men can manage sorting through the rest without us, don't you?"

"Has my father been very worried?" Alexandra asked. She felt compelled to go back outside, as though she needed to be there to protect Malcolm.

From what?

The truth of her involvement with Peter? Her father?

Or maybe she was just afraid to leave his side in case he decided to leave *her*.

The other woman gave a laugh. "From the moment he received the telegram from your aunt, he has been beside himself with excitement. Even when Mr. Shaw arrived ahead of you and we suspected that something had gone wrong in your travels, your father maintained the steadfast belief that you would be all right."

Alexandra—her thoughts still twisting in the whirlwind that had kicked up since she'd arrived at her father's new home—didn't reply, though it warmed her to know that her father had had such confidence in her.

The woman didn't seem concerned by the lack of response as she walked them through the elaborate foyer, past what appeared to be the parlor on the right and perhaps a library to the left, onward to where a lovely carved staircase led up to the second floor.

"I had the blue bedroom readied for you some time ago," she was saying. "I do think it will suit you wonderfully. Then your companion, Mr...." She paused for Alexandra to fill in the blank.

"Kincaid. Malcolm Kincaid. He was my escort."

"Kincaid?" The woman stopped to look at Alexandra in surprise before she continued. "Well, I will settle Mr. Kincaid in the green bedroom on the main floor. I think that would be best."

"I don't know if he will be staying long enough to need a room." Saying the words out loud had a crushing effect, and there was nothing she could do about it.

The second-floor hallway was wide and thickly carpeted. The blue bedroom turned out to be the last one at the end of the hall. The room itself was lovely. Decorated in a robin's-egg blue flowered wallpaper with white lace curtains and a white, lace-trimmed bed covering, it felt homey and elegant at the same time. A mixture of country charm and city finery, with south-facing windows letting in a stream of cheerful sunlight.

"Will this room suit you, dear? I can have a bath brought up right away if you'd like."

Alexandra gave a nod. "Yes, thank you." She paused, then plunged forward. "If I may ask, who are you exactly?"

The woman's green eyes widened before she tipped her head curiously. "I'm Sarah, of course."

When Alexandra lifted a brow, the woman's expression fell, and her lips formed into a downward curve. Alexandra suddenly regretted being so forward. She should have waited to ask her father.

"I am Sarah," the other woman said again, "your father's wife."

Though it was exactly what she had suspected, having it stated outright somehow twisted the sense of betrayal a bit deeper.

"Your father didn't tell you about me and the children, did he?" Sarah asked.

Alexandra shook her head. "I do not recall that news in any of the letters I received."

"I'm sure he meant to. Or perhaps the letter got lost," Sarah suggested, but they both knew that wasn't the case. "I'll have a bath brought up. Your aunt sent some of your things along with Mr. Shaw. Apparently, she was worried you wouldn't have proper attire. You will find them in the wardrobe and bureau. Please let me know if there is anything else I can do to help you settle in."

Alexandra could only manage a soft, muttered, "Thank you."

Before Sarah left the room, she added one last thing. "We are all very happy you made it home safely."

Alexandra nodded. As soon as the door closed, the tears started to come. She sat heavily on the bed, her legs no longer able to support her.

This homecoming was not at all what she'd expected. Her father, though obviously happy to see her, seemed nearly the stranger she had expected him to be. A stranger with a whole new family. A new life that he had intentionally kept her out of.

Why?

Why would he do that?

Anger and pain felt like crushing fists battering against her heart and lungs. The sobs she wanted to release were caught behind the tightness of her throat, and all she could do was gasp for breath as silent tears fell one after the other.

She felt lost and insignificant.

Then she thought of Malcolm and what he'd said to her on the ridge. She needed to remember all that she had learned about herself on this journey. She was not a child anymore. She would not shy away from her purpose in fear of what might be revealed.

Maybe this wasn't exactly the homecoming she'd wanted. But it didn't change who she was or what she wanted. Her past still had to be resolved. The present—her father's life—was what it was. But her future...

Oh God, Malcolm.

What could he be thinking right now? She needed to talk to him, explain about Peter.

Her heart squeezed tight with regret. She wished she could rewind the clock to when they'd been together in the cabin. She'd beg him to stay there with her in that safe, secluded valley forever.

But the world beyond would always exist. Malcolm would never be free until he found justice for his brother.

A knock on the door signaled the arrival of her bath.

Alexandra stood and wiped the moisture from her cheeks. She'd indulged long enough in her unexpected disappointment and loss.

She had come here to face her past and clarify her future. So that's what she'd do. Malcolm believed her to be brave and strong. Certainly, she could get through this. She'd ask her father the questions she needed answered.

And then she'd be free to move forward in whatever manner she decided for herself.

Malcolm didn't like the one Alex had called Peter. And he didn't care if everyone knew it.

He didn't like the way the fine young man had taken one look at Alex and wrinkled his nose as though he'd walked into a horse stall that hadn't been cleaned in a week. He didn't like the cold condescension in his eyes. And he sure as hell didn't like the tone in the man's voice when he'd taken it upon himself to admonish Alex like she was a child.

As soon as the two women stepped into the house, Alex's father approached Malcolm with his hand outstretched. "Randolph Brighton," he said with a smile before he gestured toward the man on the porch. "And this gentleman is Mr. Peter Shaw."

Malcolm took the older man's hand and gave a nod, ignoring Mr. Shaw altogether. "Malcolm Kincaid."

Brighton's thick brows lifted. "The bounty hunter?"

Malcolm lowered his chin in acknowledgment.

"How did you come to be escorting my daughter, Mr. Kincaid?"

There didn't seem to be any animosity in the question, just genuine curiosity. "She ran into me down in Wyoming Territory and hired me on as her guide." He decided there was no need to bring up the part about her starting off with Lassiter.

"Interesting," the older man said thoughtfully.

"And where was it exactly that Miss Brighton found you?" Mr. Shaw asked.

Malcolm answered truthfully. "In a saloon."

The other man's eyes narrowed, and his mouth pressed into a line. "Miss Brighton would not dare to step foot in such a place."

Malcolm lowered his chin but maintained eye contact with the stiff-jawed gentleman. "She's dared that and more."

Rigid anger stiffened Shaw's entire body, though his voice was fiercely controlled as he replied, "What are you insinuating?"

"Nothing," Malcolm said. "But there aren't many who'd make it through what she did without a proper dose of courage and determination."

There was a long pause before Shaw replied, "Then I am certain she will be relieved to be back within the circle of her family."

Malcolm's jaw clenched. Who the hell was this man to Alex?

Randolph Brighton chose that moment to interject. "And we are thrilled that she made it here safely." He turned to Mr. Shaw. "I'm just going to assist Mr. Kincaid in seeing to the horses. As Sarah suggested, we can reconvene in the parlor shortly."

Shaw hesitated a moment, his gaze sliding from Mr. Brighton to Malcolm. Then he gave a graceful tip of his head before he turned and reentered the house.

"Right, then"—Brighton flashed a smile—"this way to the barn."

Malcolm followed Alexandra's father with his gut clenched against the urge to glance over at the windows of the house, knowing Alex was in one of those rooms. He'd see Sibyl settled and give Deuce some water and grain, then he'd be on his way.

What was the point in one last look at her? If he took that, he'd probably end up wanting more. Then he'd have an even harder time riding out of there.

And he would ride out. As soon as possible. He had to.

He didn't get too far before his way was blocked by the boy who had first greeted them. He was looking at Malcolm with an expression that crossed between wonder and wariness. "Are you really Malcolm Kincaid, the bounty hunter?"

"Yep."

"Did you really corner Marcus Taller and his gang outside Cheyenne four years ago?"

Malcolm arched a brow. "Yep."

The boy lifted his chin—a chin that betrayed a

barely perceptible quiver—and stuck out his hand. "Can I shake your hand, please, sir? Marcus Taller's gang killed my pa during one of their bank robberies. I can't say how grateful I am that you brought him to justice in the manner you did."

Malcolm stared at the boy a moment before he shook his hand. "You're welcome."

"Thank you, Mr. Kincaid," the boy's sister added as she came up beside her brother and thrust her hand forward in the same manner. She wore a fierce frown, obviously trying to mimic her brother's stern expression, but her impishness couldn't be completely disguised.

Malcolm smiled at her as he took her small hand in his. "My pleasure, miss."

She smiled brightly as a blush pinkened her cheeks. "Are you going to stay with us for a while?" she asked with a coy tip of her head.

"It'd be great if you would," the boy added.

"I'll add my voice to that invitation," Randolph said. "Children, why don't you two run along to see if your mother needs any help with anything?"

Though they both gave groans of dismay, they did as Brighton asked and trotted off toward the house.

"I need to be moving on," Malcolm said in reply to the man's invitation.

"Nonsense. You've obviously been on the trail for some time. Have a full night's rest, some savory home cooking. It does a man good now and then," he said with a wide smile.

Malcolm hesitated.

The sooner he left, the better. Alex was safe and secure with her people, and he still had a killer to face.

But when he recalled the look of shock and hurt that'd crossed her face at the realization of her father's new circumstances, Malcolm knew he couldn't walk away without ensuring she would be all right.

He wondered if Brighton understood the pain he'd caused his daughter. Not just today, but in the years since he'd sent her east. For all that he'd seen so far, the man was very happy to have her back. But it was just as obvious to Malcolm that Alex hadn't slid back into her father's life with as much ease as she may have hoped she would.

Brighton caught his eye and gave a jerk of his head toward the barn. "Come on. Let's get these horses settled so you can come inside and clean up. Sarah's already getting a room ready for you, and I'm sure she'll be pleased to see the trail dust washed away before we all settle in the parlor."

"That sounds like a family gathering. I'm sure there's no reason for me to be there."

"Oh, I think there might be a reason, Mr. Kincaid," Brighton replied as they stepped into the hay-scented barn.

THIRTY-EIGHT

ALEXANDRA WAS WASHED AND DRESSED IN JUST OVER half the time she was given. That suited her fine, because she intended to speak with Peter before any more time passed.

While she'd soaked in the deep tub that had been brought up to her room, she'd sorted through the muddle of thoughts that had been spinning through her head since she'd ridden up to her father's door.

First things first, she needed to be up front and honest with Peter. She couldn't have him thinking and behaving as though she belonged to him.

She didn't. And she never would.

As difficult as that confrontation was likely to be, Alexandra knew it was going to be the easiest part. Because next, she intended to track down her father. She did not want to have some big family discussion with everyone gathered together in the parlor as she tried to understand why he'd never bothered to tell her about Sarah and the children, why he'd never let her come home.

She felt more betrayed and abandoned than ever,

and she needed an explanation. She deserved that much from her father. Directly. One on one. Like they always used to be.

Before leaving the bedroom, she looked at herself in the large oval mirror that hung over the small vanity in the corner of the room.

Clean and fresh and dressed in the clothes Aunt Judith had sent for her from Boston, with her hair twisted simply but elegantly atop her head, she looked like an Eastern lady again. But she didn't feel like the same woman who had followed the rules in order to blend into a society she had never truly felt a part of.

She didn't feel like the wild and impulsive girl she'd been before, either.

Tipping her chin up a notch and straightening her spine, she regarded herself carefully in the reflective glass. A smile tilted her mouth as she thought of the name Malcolm had taken to calling her.

Alex. A capable, loving, confident woman who didn't follow any rules besides her own.

In the end, being ready early didn't matter at all, since by the time she made it down to the parlor, everyone had already gathered there ahead of her.

Her disappointment at not being able to handle things her way swiftly gave way to a confusing mixture of dread and relief.

Because Malcolm stood apart from the others in the corner of the room. His gray eyes tracked her the moment she entered the parlor.

He had cleaned up and wore a fresh pair of denims with a crisp black shirt beneath his leather vest. He wasn't wearing his hat, and she noted his clean shave.

Her heart ached at the sight of him. She wished she could go straight to his side and ask him to ride out with her. Tonight. To forget about his vendetta and start a new life with her.

That she couldn't and wouldn't ask such a thing of him only made the yearning in her soul that much heavier. She had known parting ways would be difficult, but each time she had looked into his eyes, she'd seemed less and less prepared for that moment to come.

"There is the girl I know."

Oh God! Peter. She'd forgotten about him. Again.

Her soon to be *un*intended stepped toward her to take both of her hands in his. "I have to say I was shocked by your rough appearance earlier. I suppose I should have expected something of the sort, considering the mode of travel which brought you here." He gave a barely perceptible, dismissive glance toward Malcolm. "But I am happy to see your true self shining through now that you are properly attired."

He wore that easygoing gentleman's smile that had always seemed a bit off to her, and she suddenly realized why. It was too quick to appear, too easily inspired and freely given, and in that moment, it did not match the censorious tone of his words. Peter's smile lacked sincerity.

So unlike Malcolm's, which appeared when she least expected it, filling her with warmth and pleasure.

"Peter," she began in a lowered voice, "I really must speak with you—immediately, please, and in private."

He lifted a brow, but gave a smiling nod as he

released her hands. "Of course, darling. As you wish, though I believe your father desires to ascertain your well-being first."

At the mention of her father, Alex glanced to where he stood beside the deeply cushioned sofa where Sarah sat on one end. He had his hand resting on Sarah's shoulder in a casual show of connection and support.

Alex's heart gave a painful throb.

It wasn't so much that he had decided to remarry and settle in with a new family that hurt her. It was that he hadn't felt it necessary to *tell* her.

Sarah reached up to give Randolph's hand a brisk pat. Alex glanced at her stepmother's face to see that the pretty woman was looking up at her father with a stern expression.

He quickly stepped forward. "Oh, ah, yes. Alexandra dear, in the excitement of your arrival, I failed to give a proper introduction." He offered his hand to Sarah as she rose to her feet. Her smile as she looked to Alex was as sincere as Peter's had not been. "Sarah is my wife. We married more than three years ago. And those two scamps who are still washing up for supper are her children, Ivy and Jack."

Alex could have followed her aunt's many teachings about being gracious and reserved in her emotions. But this was her father. If she couldn't speak honestly to him, then more had changed than she'd thought.

"Yes, Sarah told me as much upstairs. I think we are both curious why you never mentioned it in any of your letters, Papa?" she asked with lifted brows.

Her father came forward with slightly ruddy cheeks.

"I'm sorry, honey. I didn't mention it because I wasn't sure how you'd feel. I wanted to spare you any cause for turmoil or upset."

Frustration and five years of hurt feelings boiled up inside her.

"You thought I would be upset that you had found someone to love, but didn't think I would be upset by the fact that you decided to effectively cut me out of your life? Now, that is interesting."

Randolph frowned. "Alexandra, that is not at all what happened."

"Isn't it?"

"Calm yourself, Alexandra," Peter injected in a quiet but firm tone. "Such outbursts of emotion are unnecessary and unattractive."

Alexandra took a steadying breath. She understood Peter's intention. He was likely quite shocked by her manner. It was the way of things amongst his social circles to maintain proper decorum at all times and to an almost painful degree.

Such strict moderation of behavior had benefitted Alexandra well at a time when her life had been in tumult. But it served her no longer.

"I am sorry. I am afraid I only have room for honesty. Real honesty," she added as she looked to her father again. "Can we try that, Papa?"

"That is no way to speak to your father," Peter stated in a stern, disapproving voice.

Her gaze flew sharply to the man beside her. "This is none of your business, Peter. I would appreciate it if you would stay out of it, please."

He took a step toward her, his expression stern. "As

your future husband, it is most certainly my business, Alexandra."

Indignant anger flowed through Alex, but she was careful not to show it as she replied, "We need to talk, Peter. Now and in private."

Peter's eyes flickered with subtle surprise. "You are being irrational. I insist that you apologize to your family and retire for the evening. You are clearly not yet fit to be among respectable company."

Alexandra tensed at the thinly veiled insinuation against Malcolm's character. She slid a quick glance in his direction and was amazed to see that he hadn't moved a muscle from his spot beside the fire. His eyes, however, flashed with ill-concealed fury and were aimed hard at Peter.

Returning her attention to her fiancé, she stated firmly and calmly, "I regret having to say this now and in this way, but you leave me no choice. I must end our betrothal. I have come to realize we would not be a fitting match."

"Excuse me?" His eyes had slowly grown wider and wider until she finished. "You are jilting me? Impossible," he stated with a jut of his chin.

"I am sorry, but it is the truth."

"You are causing a scene. We will discuss this further in private." He stepped toward her, and despite his outwardly composed demeanor, the hand he wrapped around her wrist was tight and punishing.

She tensed and prepared to pull away from his bruising grip, but before she could, Malcolm's voice cut swift and hard through the room. "Let her go."

Alex noted the belated wariness in Peter's eyes.

"Now." Malcolm didn't even need to step away from his position against the wall for everyone in that room to realize the threat contained in that one low-spoken word.

Peter dropped her hand as though it were tainted. He did not bother to conceal the sneering tone of his voice. "You are not the woman I thought you were."

Alexandra smiled at that. "I understand. I'm not the woman I thought I was, either."

"I am returning to Boston," he declared. "If you should think to follow me, do not expect a warm welcome. I will personally ensure that everyone learns of your disgraceful behavior."

Alex was only slightly surprised by his vindictive response. There had been a time she would have done all she could to maintain a spotless reputation. Now, it just seemed so irrelevant. She had no concern with being ruined in Boston society beyond how it might affect Evie and her Aunt Judith, but they were well connected and would surely recover from any secondary consequences.

"I need a ride to Helena," Peter declared. "Immediately." Then he stormed from the room.

Sarah stepped forward. "I will assist Mr. Shaw with his travel preparations." She gave her husband a pointed look. "You will stay here and talk with your daughter."

As she passed Alexandra's position, Sarah rested her hand lightly and briefly on her arm. It was a genuine gesture of support, and Alexandra appreciated it.

Lifting her gaze, she looked to Malcolm again, but his expression hadn't changed. The hard lines were still drawn deep and heavy over his eyes, and his lips were pressed firmly together. Her chest ached with the desire to explain herself. To tell him that she had decided to end the engagement long ago.

His eyes met hers for a long moment, but his granite gaze was unreadable.

"I'll go." His voice was low, and she had no idea if he was talking about leaving the room or leaving the ranch. Either way, she couldn't let him.

"Please stay, Malcolm," she whispered. Despite the vulnerability evident in her tone, she felt stronger with him near.

For a moment, she didn't know if he would do as she asked. Then he lowered his chin and rested his shoulders back against the wall again.

Alexandra redirected her attention to her father, who had stood quietly watching the unfolding scene. "Now, can we be honest with each other, Papa?"

His eyes lowered briefly, and he took a breath. "Alexandra, honey, I'm sorry. Sarah lost her husband some years back. We became friends."

"Papa, please. I am not upset about you remarrying. I want you to be happy, and it seems that you are. I would never begrudge you that. What I don't understand is why I couldn't be a part of it. Why didn't you tell me about it in any of your letters? Why shut me out, Papa?"

"I didn't want to, Alexandra, but it was necessary. For your own good."

"That makes no sense."

Randolph hesitated and lifted his hands in a helpless gesture. "Honey, I don't know what you want me to say."

"Why did you never ask me to come home?" Her

father glanced aside at Malcolm, but Alexandra forged ahead. "You can speak freely, Papa. Malcolm knows why I left Montana. After your letter telling me that no charges had been brought against me, that what I did was considered an act of self-defense, I kept waiting for you to say I could come back. You never did. Why?"

"It wasn't safe. It wasn't time."

"Really? Or were you happy to finally have a life without me tripping along at your heels, slowing you down?"

His look was incredulous as he lifted his hands in supplication, as though he wished to reach for her. "You never slowed me down, girl—you kept me going. Don't you know that?"

"Then why couldn't I come home? The few times I swallowed my pride and wrote to you asking if I could return, you completely ignored my pleas. Why?"

He ran his hands back through his hair. "It's complicated."

She crossed her arms over her chest.

He sighed. "From Judith's letters, it sounded like you were flourishing in Boston. You deserved to experience all the benefits I grew up with instead of the uncertainty and danger of roaming the territories on the back of a horse. I should have taken you to Boston right away after your mother died."

"Boston was never my home, Papa. You were. I loved the life we had out here. I thought you knew that."

"I did," he said quietly as he strode to the window. "But it was too dangerous. I couldn't protect you."

"I protected myself."

"You shouldn't have had to!" he shouted, turning

around again. His eyes were filled with pain and fear. "I will never forget the way you looked that day, honey. I can't forgive myself for what happened." His words got stuck in his throat, and he glanced uncomfortably at Malcolm.

"What happened wasn't your fault, Papa," she said, refusing to let him off the hook that easily. She was getting frustrated with his half answers and evasions. "But it wasn't my fault, either."

"Of course it wasn't." He looked astonished by the thought. "None of it was your fault. But you couldn't come back. It simply wasn't possible."

"Why?" she nearly shouted. "You still won't explain the reason why!"

"Because he didn't die."

THIRTY-NINE

ALEXANDRA'S HEART STOPPED BEATING, AND HER head reeled. It…couldn't possibly be true. "I was covered in his blood," she whispered. "I know I shot him."

"You did, honey. Come here and sit down before you fall over."

She stumbled forward and took a seat, reeling.

He wasn't dead? The man who had tried to rape her, the man whose blood had soaked down to her skin was still alive? It wasn't possible. She had heard his gurgling breath, saw the blood spew from his mouth, the abject terror in his eyes.

Her hands and feet felt numb. She feared she might be sick.

Then Malcolm was there, filling her vision with his stern, beautiful features and his fathomless gray gaze. Crouching down in front of her, he pressed a glass into her hand. "Drink it."

She did as he said. The glass was filled with brandy. The first sip burned a welcome path to her stomach, combatting the numbness. The second started to loosen her throat, and the third spread warmth out to her fingers and toes.

She focused on Malcolm's eyes, seeking the lovely flecks of darker gray that gave his gaze such depth, and she felt bolstered. As she reached out her hand to cover his, he stood and strode back to his spot against the wall.

The distance hurt. But she had her strength back, and she was not finished with her father.

"How could he possibly have lived?" she asked, managing to keep her voice firm.

"I'm sure you don't need Mr. Kincaid to hear of all this—"

"He stays," Alex insisted. She needed Malcolm's presence now more than ever.

Her father glanced back and forth between them before taking a breath and going on. "By the time I got back to where you were…attacked, there was no one there. I continued into town where I discovered the man's companion had come back for him and taken him to the doc's place. The sheriff was already there getting an earful. They claimed you shot for no reason."

Fury and frustration washed through her. It felt like it was happening all over again. The fear, the shame, the uncertainty. "That's a lie, Papa," she said. "They attacked me."

"I know, honey. And you remember Sheriff Tate. He wasn't one to take a man's word without coming to his own conclusions. When I got the chance to explain to him what you told me, he had no plan to register any charges against you."

"So you knew all this when you came home again? Then why did you send me away? I don't understand."

Her father came forward to sit beside her on the sofa. "Do you remember the talk of a man named Cal Dunstan up near Wolf Creek?"

Her heart stopped beating for a second as old memories tumbled one over the other through her mind. She recalled the whispered words of a wealthy and powerful man who'd practically taken over the small town to the north of Helena. A man who went to extreme lengths to get what he wanted and was well known for crushing anyone who stood in his way.

Her father took her hands in his. "The man you shot was Cal's oldest son, Walter, who had just come home after years away." His voice lowered as he continued. "We both know it wouldn't have mattered to Cal Dunstan that you were defending yourself against his boy. And we both know he would have gone beyond the law to get his revenge. He'd have had you strung up on the nearest tree before anyone could stop him. I had to get you out of his reach until I could figure how to rectify the situation."

He paused then, and she could see the truth in his eyes. "He still wants me to hang, doesn't he?"

Her father sighed. "His son lived, but the bullet severed his spine. He'll never walk again, which is almost a greater insult to Cal than if his son had died. Cal swore that if you ever stepped foot in Montana again, he'd personally see you pay for what you'd done to his boy. Don't you see? I couldn't risk having you back when that man still intends to see you suffer for his son's actions."

She couldn't believe it. All these years she'd thought she'd killed a man, when the truth was almost worse. She was essentially exiled from the land she loved.

"And then you seemed to be doing so well in Boston," her father continued, a hopeful note in his voice. "I thought maybe you were happier there."

Alex realized with a swift jolt of clarity how important that point was to her father.

At any time in the last five years he could have picked up and moved on like he always used to. He could have found somewhere to settle far away from Cal Dunstan, where it would have been safe for Alex to return.

Perhaps he'd met Sarah by then, or maybe he'd just gotten tired of roaming. Whatever the reason, though she could believe that he *thought* he was doing his best by her, she hadn't been the primary consideration in his decision to stay.

That truth stabbed deep into her already bruised heart.

"I did do well in Boston," she admitted as she met her father's familiar blue gaze, worn with worry and shadowed by regret. "But home was with you. I missed you, Papa. I missed Montana."

"Oh, honey, I missed you too," he muttered as he wrapped her in a deep hug.

She knew he meant it, but their relationship would never be as it once was.

Alexandra rested her head against her father's chest and allowed the pain and sadness of the last five years to fill her up nearly to overflowing before she let it slowly drain away.

"You could have told me the truth," she whispered. At least then she would have known why she couldn't go home. "I would have understood."

Her father drew back to set his hands on her shoulders and give her a look she had known well in her youth. "And you would have insisted on coming home to face Cal head-on."

She opened her mouth to argue, then shut it again when she realized he was right. Still... "I'm not going back to Boston, Papa."

He sighed. "I figured that."

"I'm sorry about worrying Aunt Judith and...what happened with Peter."

He shook his head. "Don't be. We all must follow where our heart leads us. Mine led me all over this great territory, trying to outrun your mother's memory. But after you were gone, all I had were the memories. Until I met Sarah."

"She makes you happy?"

"She does. And Ivy and Jack are great. Curious and full of life. They make me feel young again." He took her hands in his and looked down sheepishly. "I should have told you about them. I'm not sure why I didn't, other than I was feeling cowardly. I feared you wouldn't approve."

She shook her head. "You should have trusted me."

"I should have," he agreed. "And what about your happiness? If it's not Boston and it's not Mr. Shaw, I can support that. But, honey, I'm afraid it's just not safe for you here in Montana."

Her heart broke, but she knew it was true. She had finally made it back to Montana only to discover it wasn't her home any longer after all. Neither was it her place to be at her father's side. He had a new family, and though she was glad he was happy, it still hurt to know she wasn't an integral part of that anymore.

So where did she belong?

Her gaze slid to Malcolm's position against the wall.

He wasn't there.

Her heart stopped for the second time, only this time it held as her stomach clenched with loss and regret.

"Mr. Kincaid slipped away some time ago, honey."

She pushed to her feet, a swift panic piercing through her center. "Where did he go?"

"He stepped outside. I figured he wanted to give us some privacy."

He couldn't have left. She didn't want to think he'd just slip away like that, but he could already be saddling his horse and loading up his belongings. "I'm sorry, Papa. I have to speak with him before…before he leaves."

"Go on, honey, but dinner will be soon, and I'll expect you at the table. I think Sarah is planning a special meal to welcome you home."

Alexandra's only thought was of catching up to Malcolm before he rode away. It was already dark outside, but the moon and stars were right overhead as she rushed across the yard to the stables.

Please let him be inside.

She had no idea what she'd say to him—she just knew she couldn't let him go without telling him…

What? That I love him? That I imagine spending my future at his side?

Her steps faltered at the thought. No. She couldn't

tell him that, couldn't put that burden on him when she knew it wouldn't change anything. He would still ride away. If not tonight, then tomorrow or the next day. He would never forgive himself if he did not fulfill his vow to avenge his brother's death.

But maybe…afterward. Would he come back for her? Could she ask him to?

The barn was dimly lit with only a few lanterns set on hooks on the wall. Malcolm was in the stall with Deuce. Though he had to have heard her approach, he didn't look up. A shiver coursed down her arms from the cold night air, but it was not nearly as chilling as the fear clutching at her insides. She already felt the loss of him, and he was still here. How hard would it be when he actually rode off?

"Don't leave."

His hand stilled on the gelding's forelock. "I have to."

"I know. But not yet. Please. I haven't even had a chance to talk to Father about paying you for your services."

"Don't bother," he replied curtly.

"But I promised you…"

"I don't want it."

She bit her lip. This wasn't the conversation she'd meant to have with him.

He stood stiff and unmoving. Tension emanated from him in waves. She wasn't sure she'd ever seen him so intensely contained within himself. So much so that it looked as though even a gentle touch might cause him to crack from the strain.

Heartache, regret, and guilt filled the hollow spaces

inside her. "I should have told you," she said, the words difficult in her tight throat, "about Peter."

Malcolm turned his steely gaze upon her then. She wasn't sure what she expected to see in his eyes—anger or sadness, maybe—but it surely wasn't the flat, emotionless stare she received.

"You don't owe me anything."

The tightness in her throat worsened. She wrapped her arms around her middle as she took a deep breath through her nose. "I should have told you," she repeated. "But I knew it had been a mistake to accept his proposal. I intended to send a letter…" Her voice trailed off as Malcolm continued to regard her with no expression, not even his beloved scowl.

Something was wrong.

Something that went beyond her failure to tell him about her fiancé. Something that went far deeper and cut more painfully. Love welled in her heart, and she took a step toward him. "Malcolm."

His name was just a whisper on her lips, but it was enough of a catalyst to trigger him into motion.

He walked out of the stall, closing the door securely behind him. It seemed as though he intentionally ignored the fact that in doing so he passed close enough to her that his shoulder almost brushed hers. Almost.

"Deuce needs the rest. I'll stay the night. That's it," he said curtly.

Giving a shallow nod, she shifted her gaze and turned away.

She understood. Of course, she understood.

He was a loner. A gunman with a vow of vengeance

he wouldn't give up until he saw it through or got himself killed in the process of trying.

What did she have to offer him in exchange?

Just the love in her heart and the desire to remain at his side until the day she died.

FORTY

MALCOLM WAS A DAMNED IDIOT. HE SHOULD HAVE ridden off the moment Alex was reunited with her father. If he'd done that, he never would have learned that Walter Dunstan, the Belt Buckle Kid, the man who had killed Gavin in cold blood, had dared to place his murderous hands on Alex. She'd stopped him from raping her, but he'd still taken something from her that she'd never get back.

Malcolm had never wanted to kill someone so bad in his life. He'd left the parlor with his blood boiling, fueled by the instinctive, undeniable urge to send Walter Dunstan straight to hell.

For Gavin and for Alex.

By the time he'd reached Deuce's stall, a realization hit him that had him stopping in his tracks and cursing fate for placing him in that saloon the day Alexandra Brighton had walked in.

Killing Walter Dunstan would not stop the man's father from seeking revenge against Alex. In fact, it might spur him on even more.

Violence roared through him so fierce and hot it

was all he could do to contain it. Especially when he saw the haunted look shimmering in her blue gaze and the vulnerability she tried so desperately to conceal. He couldn't let her see the fury inside him. Didn't want her to know the connection between their pasts when it would serve no purpose.

Hell, she'd probably insist on going with him to face the bastard.

There was no way in hell he'd let her get anywhere near Dunstan. So, he'd said he'd stay the night, hoping to set her at ease.

It hadn't worked.

Somewhere along in the last few weeks, he'd become attuned to her.

She smiled appropriately through the meal and talked politely to her new stepmother of her time in Boston. She asked the children questions about their interests and was properly contrite regarding the worry she'd put her aunt through in leaving Boston. But Malcolm could see the strain beneath it all.

The tension in her shoulders was subtle, but it ran all the way up along her jaw to where her pulse beat at her temples. She sat too straight in her chair. Her hands moved too slowly and with too much thought. Her eyes kept glancing toward the window, as though seeking something outside under the moon, before they'd swing tentatively in his direction.

And whenever that blue gaze fell on him, Malcolm couldn't help but feel too much.

By the time dinner ended, he was ready to bolt from all the tension built up inside him. He wasn't sure if Randolph Brighton sensed his discomfort, but the man stood and gave Malcolm a short nod. "Come on outside, Mr. Kincaid. I like to enjoy a smoke before settling down in the parlor after dinner."

Intentionally not glancing toward Alex, Malcolm followed her father out to the front porch.

Brighton took a seat in one of the rocking chairs set off to the side, while Malcolm preferred to stand looking out over the ranch yard as he withdrew his pouch of tobacco and quickly rolled a cigarette.

"Alexandra mentioned you'd be heading out tomorrow," Brighton said in a conversational tone.

"Yep."

"Where are you going?"

Malcolm turned to meet the older man's curious gaze, leaning his hips back against the porch railing. He considered his answer carefully before deciding on the truth. "Up near Wolf Creek."

Brighton's features tensed. "Is that so? Business or personal?"

"Very personal," Malcolm replied. "There's a wanted man hiding out up there. A man who murdered my brother in cold blood, and only a few years later attacked a young girl walking home alone."

Brighton's eyes narrowed, but he didn't reply.

Silence fell then as Brighton packed his pipe and lit it. After taking a few deep puffs of the sweet-smelling tobacco, he shifted his gaze back to Malcolm. "Does Alexandra know?"

"She knows what she needs to know."

"Cal won't make it easy."

"It's never easy," Malcolm countered, flexing his gun hand.

"And after?"

Malcolm didn't answer. The thought of sweeping Alex up onto his horse to ride off for parts unknown sent a swift, sharp edge of anticipation up his spine. But any time he rode into a dangerous situation, he was aware that he might not come out alive. He figured that's what made him good at what he did—the fact that he was willing to do what it took to see the thing through, despite whatever threat there might be to his own life.

This time was different. He wanted to ride out after the gun smoke cleared. But he wasn't sure all of that was any of this man's business.

"I don't want to see her hurt."

Now it was Malcolm's turn to narrow his gaze. "Then you shouldn't've sent her away."

"I did what I had to do to keep her safe," Brighton stated sharply.

"Seems to me there might have been other ways to do that."

The other man rose to his feet. "Listen, Kincaid. And listen good for a minute. I know you've earned your reputation as a fast-draw bounty hunter with a talent for putting away dangerous men. But you've never come up against someone like Dunstan. Now, I'm talking about the old man, Cal, not his cowardly boy. Cal Dunstan has men all over this state—powerful men—tucked deep in his back pocket.

"You go after his boy, you bring down on your head the kind of wrath only limitless wealth and unending spite can buy. You may be prepared to face that brand of consequence for whatever justifies your craving for blood. But I'd ask you to think real long and hard about dragging my daughter into the mess with you. Because it won't end with the boy's death, and you know it."

Without waiting for a reply, Brighton turned and headed back inside.

The older man hadn't said anything Malcolm hadn't already been struggling with in his own mind. By some terrible twist of fate, his vengeance had become inexorably intertwined with Alex's future. How could he live with himself if by killing Walter Dunstan, he only spurred the old man on to seek retribution now that Alex was back in Montana? And if something went wrong, Malcolm wouldn't be around to protect her.

He refused to accept that. There had to be a way to avenge his brother without putting Alex in greater peril, but right now, he couldn't see it.

He waited several minutes before following Brighton inside. He was careful not to look too long in Alex's direction for the remainder of the evening. Part of him was afraid of what he'd see in her eyes if he did. Another part was afraid of what she'd see in his.

Luckily, the hour grew late quick enough, and Sarah shooed the children up to bed. Alex followed soon after. As she turned to leave the room, she glanced toward Malcolm, but he looked away, not wanting to see what might be in her eyes.

Tomorrow, he would be gone. There was no point in saying goodbye. She knew it as well as he did. He told himself it was better this way, though he wasn't looking forward to the sleepless night ahead.

He'd tried to say he'd be fine in the bunkhouse with the ranch hands, but Sarah had insisted he stay in the house. The room he'd been given was small, but far more comfortable than what he was used to. A large bed nearly filled the space. It had a plush feather mattress covered in soft linens the color of Texas sage bushes right before the flowers bloomed.

Sitting on the edge of the bed, he tried not to think about Alex being so close and so out of reach at the same time. He took off his boots, then removed the rest of his clothing before he lay down between the cool sheets. Though the night held an autumn chill, his body was overly warm, heated from the inside by his perpetual craving for a woman he shouldn't want this bad.

He pressed his eyes closed, determined to at least give sleep a shot, but after an hour, he knew it was impossible. He'd gotten too damned accustomed to having Alex tucked under his arm, her warm breath spreading across his skin. The beat of his heart was an empty echo without the weight of her hand resting on his chest.

He needed her at his side. It was that simple. But it wasn't possible. Not yet. Not until they were both free.

With a grunt of frustration, he sat up and swung his feet to the floor. Running his hands through his hair, he huffed a breath through clenched teeth.

Then he heard the faint click of his door opening.

His breath stalled as Alex slid silently into his bedroom and closed the door behind her.

She was dressed in a dreamy white nightgown that covered her from neck to toe. Her thick, dark hair fell in soft waves down her back with one long tress resting over her breast. Her hands were knitted together in front of her, as though she had to keep them locked together to keep from reaching for him.

Malcolm was grateful for her restraint. Seeing it bolstered his own.

"You shouldn't be here."

Her body stiffened at the intentionally harsh tone in his voice, but she didn't answer right away. Instead, she just looked at him. In the quiet, moonlit bedroom, she stood with bare toes peeking from beneath the white gown and her hair free down her back, and she looked at him.

She had always done that.

In a world of stronger, rougher, more dangerous men who avoided looking Malcolm in the eye, she did so readily. And she saw him. His past and pain, his narrow future.

Yet she was here anyway.

"Why not?" she asked.

It took Malcolm a moment to form the words, though they were true in almost every sense. "I don't want you here."

There was a barely noticeable flicker of hurt in her expression. Malcolm saw it and hated himself for it. Then she lifted her chin and spoke in a dark but urgent whisper. "I was afraid you'd left."

"I said I'd stay the night."

Her words were raw with an emotion he didn't want to recognize. "Then stay the night…with me."

His heart ached so bad it took everything he had to stay seated on the edge of that bed. There was no promise he'd make it through the next day. What good would one more night of holding her in his arms accomplish? It could only add to the pain of parting, and everything already hurt too damn much.

"Malcolm."

He couldn't hold back the regret in his reply. "It won't make it any easier when I ride out tomorrow."

On a shaky exhale, she started toward him, stopping only when she stood close enough that the swirling hem of her nightgown teased the tops of his feet. "I know," she whispered. "But right now, I need you more than life itself."

His stomach twisted into a fine knot. "I know the feeling," he said in a raw murmur that almost didn't make it clear of his tight throat.

"I'm here," she said with a breathless little smile.

He took a long, slow breath to calm the fierce racing of his heart then he rose to his feet slowly, holding her gaze.

Malcolm slipped his hand beneath the fall of her silken hair to curve around the back of her neck. He brushed his thumb across the crest of her cheekbone, then down the slope of her nose to her mouth, where he rubbed back and forth over the lush cushion of her lower lip.

Parting her lips, she sighed in a warm caress against his thumb, sending a shiver of anticipation down his spine.

The blue of her eyes wasn't evident in the darkness, but he knew the color intimately. Pure and deep. Beautiful and strong. He hoped to God he'd see those eyes again after tomorrow. Lit with joy or sparked with annoyance. Sharp and determined and so damn smart. But if he didn't...

Shit.

If he never saw this woman again, he needed her to know how he felt.

He cradled her face in both hands and lowered his head, stopping just shy of putting his mouth on hers. The sweep of her lashes was dark against her skin as she closed her eyes in anticipation of his kiss and she slid her hands around his back, bringing her body flush against his.

Her softness contrasted painfully with how he felt inside, like a machine whose gears had been wound too tight.

"I love you." The words slipped from his mouth before he'd even formed them in his mind, but that made them no less true. He couldn't deny it a second longer. Couldn't hold it in to save his miserable life.

Her arms tightened around him, and she took a breath to speak. Before she could, he kissed her. He didn't want to hear the same words from her lips. It would break him when he needed to be strong.

For her. For Gavin. For the future.

The kiss was soft and achingly sweet. He would have liked it to go on forever, but he had more to say. Lifting his head, he tried to memorize the look of her right then. Everything was softened by the darkness around them, but he saw her no less clearly than if it were broad daylight. He knew her skin was a soft golden color and her mouth curved perfectly for smiles and his kisses. He knew the arch of her brows and the way her eyes flashed with life.

"Alex, I want you to promise me something," he began in a raw whisper. "I need to know you'll keep on searching until you find what makes you happy." She tensed and tried to draw back as her eyes flew open, but he held her with his gaze. "You belong out here. Where you can be free. Where you can explore all the beautiful things life holds. I want that for you."

"I want that for *us*, Malcolm," she murmured thickly as her hands curled over his shoulders as though she would anchor herself to him. "Together."

His throat started to close, making it hard to go on. "I have to see this through or I'll never be free. I swear I'll do everything in my power to come back to you, Alex. But if I don't…"

"You don't have to go alone, Malcolm. I can help. We are so much better together." The suggestion of tears glistened in her eyes. He hated seeing it.

And she was right. They were great together.

But she didn't know all that was at stake. She didn't know Malcolm intended to face one man who'd attacked her as a child and another who'd forced her exile from the land she loved. There was no way in hell he was letting her anywhere near the Dunstans.

"I'm going with you," she murmured, and though the words were soft, they were filled with conviction.

"We'll talk in the morning." He regretted the lie as soon as he uttered it, but it had to be said.

He kissed her again, with all the passion and fear and love he possessed. He had no idea he could feel so much for one small woman, but he poured every ounce of himself into the kiss. Though he could feel her resistance at first—her desire to argue her point further—he was relentless, and she soon softened. Her body arched against him, and her tongue played passionately with his.

In a rush of desperation, Malcolm grasped handfuls of all that white cotton swirling around her and lifted it off over her head. Her naked body gleamed in the moon-light. Wrapping his arms around her, he lifted her off her feet. Then he lowered her to the mattress, covering her body with his, settling one of his thighs high against her heated core while his arms caged her shoulders.

He soaked in the sight of her beneath him—the most beautiful thing he'd ever seen.

Looking into her eyes, he kissed her again. Long, slow, luxurious kisses that sapped them both of strength. Gentle nips in her full lower lip, the tip of her nose, and the corners of her eyes where her lashes fluttered against his lips. Suckling kisses that lapped up the unique salty, fresh, feminine taste of her skin below her ear, over the pulse at the base of her throat, and across the crest of her shoulder.

He wanted to taste every inch and explore the different sounds she made. He wanted to remember every shiver that coursed through her body, every arch of her spine and tug of her hands as she silently urged him to more.

Dipping his head, he placed a quiet, gentle kiss on the inner curve of her breast. Then another one on her belly. Next her hip. Her inner thigh. She writhed and sighed with every light touch of his lips, murmuring pleas for more, more, more.

He had every intention of giving her more. So much more. Until she was limp and exhausted and so damned satisfied she'd sleep through the morning and awake with memories of love burned so deep in her soul she'd never forget him.

Because he'd never forget her. Not for the rest of his life…however long that proved to be.

FORTY-ONE

ALEXANDRA WOKE WITH A SLOW SIGH AND A LONG, toe-tingling stretch, followed by a helpless grin as memories of the night before flooded her consciousness.

A perfect, tender, loving night.

Malcolm had been different. Attentive and delightfully determined. Not a single inch of her body, heart, or soul went untouched—unloved—by him.

She felt complete in a way she hadn't known was possible.

She felt glorious.

Rolling onto her back, she cracked her eyes open as the light from a full morning sun fell on her face, bright even through the drawn cotton curtains. Panic lanced through her center, and she sat up to see what she already knew was true.

He was gone.

Her heart squeezed tight. She clutched the bedclothes to her chest and took a deep, slow breath through her nose. But the room smelled like him—like them together—and it made her heart ache even more.

That scent was the only thing left behind. He was gone for certain this time. Without her.

She should have known he would sneak away, but still it hurt like hell. She wanted to huddle under the covers and sleep for a week, or however long it would take to forget the feel of Malcolm's hands gliding over her body, or the way her insides trembled when he turned his steady gaze on her, or how she warmed when he smiled.

She wished she had made him smile more.

The sense of loss burned through her like a wildfire. With an odd numbness, she pulled herself from the bed and dressed in her nightgown. The house was quiet as she tiptoed upstairs. Everyone else had probably already started their day, going about the tasks and chores required by a ranch this size.

She almost made it to her bedroom unseen, but just as she stepped into her room and was about to close the door behind her, a small, pert little face framing large, hazel eyes appeared in the open crack.

"Good morning," Ivy declared with a sunny smile. "You slept late. Are you getting up now? I have so many questions about your journey from Boston. I bet it was a grand adventure. I've never been farther from home than Helena, and that doesn't count much."

Alexandra could only blink at the girl. She remembered having such boundless energy and curiosity when she'd been the same age.

"So are you?"

"Am I what?"

The girl tossed her a frustrated little scowl. "Are you getting up? We've all had breakfast hours ago."

"Hours ago? What time is it?"

"Past nine, I'd say."

"Goodness." She hadn't slept so late in ages. Then again, she and Malcolm had been awake through most of the night. "That is late. I will get dressed and be down in a few minutes."

"All right," the girl replied brightly before skipping away.

A quarter of an hour later, Alexandra went downstairs, but Ivy was nowhere to be seen. She did find Ivy's mother, however, coming from the kitchen.

"Oh, there you are," Sarah said with a welcome smile. "Are you hungry? We all ate breakfast, but I can fix something up for you quick."

"That's not necessary."

"I know, but come along to the kitchen anyway." The older woman turned and headed back the way she'd come, with a wave over her shoulder indicating Alexandra was to follow her. "Have a seat at the table," she said as they entered the kitchen. "I can fry up an egg or two, and I have fresh bread with butter or plum jam."

"That sounds fine. Thank you."

Sarah insisted Alexandra take a seat while she moved efficiently around the kitchen. Within minutes, a lovely breakfast was set before her.

"Do you mind if I sit with you?" Sarah asked.

"Not at all," Alexandra replied, sensing the other woman's need to say something.

Now that the initial shock of her father's new family had passed, Alexandra was surprised to realize that it didn't upset her as much as she would have thought. There may have been a time when Alexandra would have rebelled against the idea. But that had been long ago. It had become obvious to her yesterday that her life had diverged significantly from what it had been when she'd traveled at her father's side.

As had his.

"This is a lovely house, Sarah," she said with genuine warmth, feeling a desire to put the woman at ease if she could.

"Thank you," Sarah said with a smile as she glanced around. There was a slightly wistful look in her eye. "The kids' father, Evan, built it for us when we were first married. This was his family's cattle ranch. I was a city girl from Helena, but he wanted to make me comfortable." She glanced at her hands as she continued. "Evan was killed nearly six years ago, during a bank robbery."

"I'm sorry. That must have been terrible."

"Yes, well, I learned right quickly how to run a ranch," Sarah said with a rueful smile. "Not always well, but I learned. Mr. Kincaid was the man who tracked the gang down in Wyoming and brought them to justice."

Alexandra wasn't surprised. "I didn't know that."

"He seemed in a pretty big hurry to be on his way this morning."

"You spoke with him?"

"Only briefly. He wouldn't even grab a bite to eat before he headed out."

Alexandra got the sense she should say something to that. "He has a job to finish up north."

"Yes. If he is successful, I imagine it will make a lot of Wolf Creek residents very happy."

Wait a minute. A sick sense of dread suddenly weighed down her limbs. "Wolf Creek?" Cal Dunstan's estate was not far from there.

Sarah must have heard the odd note in Alex's voice because she tipped her head, and a frown curled her brow. "Neither of them told you?"

Alexandra could only shake her head as a horrid suspicion took hold in her mind.

"Will men never learn?" Sarah muttered angrily before she reached out to place her hand over Alexandra's, which had fisted against the table. "From what your father told me, Mr. Kincaid is seeking revenge against Walter Dunstan for killing his brother some years ago." She paused. "I understand he's also the man who…"

Alexandra nodded. Her mind was in a whirl.

The man Malcolm had been hunting for so many years was Walter Dunstan.

How was it possible that the same man who had attacked her, the one she thought she'd killed, had also shot and killed Gavin Kincaid?

It seemed unfathomable.

Alexandra rose to her feet. "I have to go."

"No, Alexandra, you can't. It's too dangerous. There will be violence. That is no place for a young lady."

Alex met the older woman's concerned gaze. "Then it's a good thing I've never been much of a lady. Malcolm needs me," she said then turned and left the kitchen.

Sarah shouted after her, but Alexandra was already halfway up the stairs.

Malcolm—the stubborn and infuriatingly honorable jackass—thought to protect her by not letting her go with him after Dunstan. He should have known by now they protected each other, especially against a shared enemy. And she sure as hell couldn't do that from here. If he had left at dawn, he was already several hours ahead of her. But she knew this area; she could get there. She had to try.

She changed quickly into her split skirt and button-down shirt. She wished she still had her pants, but they'd been left behind in the cabin. After unpinning her hair, she braided it in a long plait down her back, then strapped her knife on her hip.

Rushing through the house, she'd almost made it out the front door when Sarah stepped into her path.

"I'm begging you to wait for your father to come in from the range so he can go with you."

"There's no time, Sarah. Malcolm needs my help. I need to go now."

"Take this food, at least," Sarah replied, worrying her bottom lip with the edge of her teeth as she handed Alexandra a small sack. "And there's something else you'll probably need."

She went into a cupboard in the hall and reached up onto the top shelf to pull down a wooden box. "Your father said this was yours. He kept it safe for when you might want it back."

Sarah set the box on a table, and Alexandra approached to see what it held. As soon as she caught a glimpse of the contents, she sucked in a hard breath.

It was her modified Colt.

To her amazement, icy fear did not course through her at the sight of it. The old terror had been replaced by a new sort of fear. Fear for Malcolm, fear that he would be killed and she'd never see him again. Fear that she wouldn't make it to his side in time to help him. His injury still slowed him down, and Dunstan would have too many men for him to take alone.

Frankly, the gun would help.

Without another thought, she took the Colt and custom-made leather holster out of the box. Strapping the weapon around her waist, she gave Sarah a quick smile. "Thank you. The rifles I rode in with—do you know where they are? And my ammo?"

Sarah looked reluctant to reply, but something in Alexandra's expression must have convinced her. "They were put in a back room in the barn."

Alexandra gave a nod and turned to rush out the door, but she was stopped short by Ivy, skipping happily into the house. At the sight of Alex, the girl came to a quick stop, and her eyes went wide. "Are you leaving?"

"I am sorry, Ivy. I would love to talk to you of my adventures, but it will have to be another time. I have to ride out."

The girl's attention fell to the Colt. "Are you going to fight bad guys?"

"Yes, and I really do have to hurry." Alex crouched down and gave the girl a quick hug and a smile before rushing past her and out to the barn as the little girl gave a whoop of excitement.

She had Sibyl saddled and ready within minutes. The mare seemed just as eager as she was to head out. Her heart beat as fast as her horse's hooves on the earth as she rode away from her father's ranch, but she had no regrets.

Alexandra had come home to find her future, and Malcolm was it. She just needed to make sure he stayed alive so she could convince him of that.

FORTY-TWO

Malcolm crouched behind the brush and boulders on the northwestern ridge overlooking Dunstan's estate.

The place was unlike anything he'd ever seen. From the front, it had the look of a prosperous ranch, with barns, stables, and bunkhouses spreading out behind an elaborate mansion surrounded by fancy gardens, a gazebo, and a pond.

But from Malcolm's perspective, the place looked more like a fortress. Armed men, clearly not ranch hands, strolled about from building to building in groups of two or three. Seven men in total, by Malcolm's count. And that was just the men who showed themselves.

After a couple of hours of watching the place through his spyglass, he saw a wheeled chair pushed from the house onto the wide back porch, and he finally got a look at the man he'd been hunting for eight long years.

Walter Dunstan.

Malcolm squinted against the sun. Every muscle in his body tensed. His heart pounded, and his hands itched to grab his gun and take the man down. He'd expected to see a murderer who'd run roughshod over the western territories and California, killing at least two people Malcolm knew about.

What he saw instead was the man who'd attacked a defenseless girl along the side of a road.

Not defenseless.

Fierce.

Smart. Proud. Capable. Beautiful.

She deserved to live without this mess hanging over her head.

The Dunstans weren't going to keep hold of her future—or his—for another day.

It would be so damn easy to shoot the bastard from where he was. He'd just need to raise his rifle, get the man in his sights, steady his breath, and pull the trigger.

Except Malcolm wasn't a murderer. Every man he'd killed had been given a fighting chance.

For years, Malcolm had imagined walking up to the Belt Buckle Kid and calmly reminding him of the young man he'd killed for a hundred dollars in poker winnings. Then he'd order him to draw. Malcolm would be faster, and that would be it. Justice served.

But justice had gotten a lot more complicated.

Walter Dunstan wasn't holed up in some shack with a few other outlaws. He was sitting in the middle of a damned fortified compound.

How the hell was he going to get close to Walter Dunstan without losing the upper hand?

When Walter was wheeled back into the house, Malcolm realized he had only one way to see this to the end. He'd have to take his chances on a direct approach.

That always seemed to work best anyway.

Of course, in the past, he'd always been prepared for the potential of his own death. That fearlessness had given him an edge over his opponents.

This time was different. He was terrified.

Because he wasn't content with the thought that if he died, at least it would be in the pursuit of vengeance for his brother. This time, he wanted to make damn sure he lived. More than anything, he wanted to be free of the chains vengeance had wound around him. And he wanted to explore that freedom with Alex. For the rest of their lives if he had his choice.

Returning to where he'd left Deuce to graze, he double-checked his Colt and his rifle. He had to get some of those men away from the house. Riding around to an open pasture extending from the rear of the estate, he found a good spot to gather up some dry brush and prairie grass. Then he waited for the angle of the sun to come around to where he wouldn't be riding up to the house at a disadvantage.

The fire would burn swift and fierce, creating a lot of smoke and hopefully drawing the attention of Dunstan's men. But he'd only have so much time.

Just as the first licks of flame started to dance against the brush, he heard a footstep behind him.

"What the hell do ya think yer doin'? This here's private property."

Without pause, Malcolm drew his gun and whirled to face a young man who stared back at him with wide-eyed shock. Malcolm could see right away that the kid wasn't experienced. He hadn't even had his gun drawn, for God's sake, though the idiot went for it now.

"Don't," Malcolm said.

The kid blinked at him a few times, then dropped his horse's reins and lifted his hands into the air.

Well, his approach to the house just got a little easier.

Malcolm made the kid dismount and discard his weapons. Then he tied the hired gun's hands behind his back and stuffed his handkerchief in his mouth. Back on horseback, Malcolm forced the kid to walk in front of him as they skirted back around to the main road and the drive that led up to the front of Dunstan's grand estate.

One way or another, this would all be over soon.

He heard the shout go up around the bunkhouses as someone noticed the fire. Though he couldn't see how many rode out to deal with it, he hoped it would be enough to better his odds a little bit.

Keeping his gaze sharp and his mental focus even sharper, Malcolm rode up to Dunstan's front door. His Colt was trained on the kid's back as he walked out in front of him. Before they got to within twenty yards of the house, a man came out onto the porch.

"That's far enough," he said with his gun already in hand. As far as threats go, it wasn't a subtle one.

Malcolm came to a leisurely stop. Another gunman stepped out from around the western corner of the house, and yet another came out of the bunkhouse to the east to stand beside the door.

Well, that was three. Not too bad yet.

"I am here for Walter Dunstan," Malcolm said to the hired gun on the porch.

"And who might you be?"

"You know who I am."

The hired gun laughed. "I woulda thought you'd be smarter than to ride up to the front door like this. You make my job easy, mister."

Malcolm smiled. "Happy to oblige. Now, from what I understand, Dunstan wants to kill me himself. I'm not saying he'll get the chance, but it sure as hell ain't likely to happen if he stays holed up in that house. Why don't you call him out here?"

"Do you think I'm a goddamn idiot, Mr. Kincaid?" This was spoken by a tall, slim-built man with silver-white hair and a long-grown mustache loaded with enough pomade to make it curl at the corners. He'd stepped from the house wearing a fancy, brown-and-red plaid-patterned suit with one thumb linked in the watch pocket of his vest, and in his other hand, a thick cigar.

Malcolm's hostage tugged at the rope as he shifted position. The appearance of his boss seemed to make the boy nervous.

"You must be the old man," Malcolm said with no surprise.

The old man's small, dark eyes narrowed. "I am Cal Dunstan, if that is what you mean."

"You know why I'm here, Dunstan?"

Dunstan waved his cigar in a half-dismissive gesture. "Feel free to explain, if you wish."

"Eight years ago, Walter Dunstan sat down to a card game with four other men in Sacramento. When

the game didn't go his way, he and three others followed the winner into an alley and killed him in cold
blood for the hundred-dollar pot. The man they killed
was my brother."

"Seems your bother was in over his head," Cal
replied callously.

Malcolm smiled as icy fury spread through his
veins. His fingers flexed on the reins, making his horse
sidestep. "Your son's wanted for murder. The papers
in my bag and my certification as a bounty hunter say
I can take him dead or alive. How do you suppose I'd
prefer it?"

"You want revenge," Dunstan sneered. "Such a
petty motivator."

"You'd know all about that, wouldn't you?"

That comment made the older man's gaze flicker,
but only for a moment before he gave a sweeping gesture at the three hired guns currently eyeing Malcolm.
All they needed was one word from Dunstan, and
they'd happily open fire.

"Look around you, Kincaid. This isn't a low-
budget operation you walked into."

Malcolm flicked a dismissive glance at the hired
guns, then swept his gaze around to see if any other
gunmen had decided to show themselves. If there
were more about who hadn't run to put out the fire,
they remained out of sight, but Malcolm suspected
their guns were at the ready.

Curving his lips in a half smile, he said, "I noticed
you've got a few men strolling around the place.
Worried about something?"

Malcolm swept his gaze over the windows in

the house, wondering if the Belt Buckle Kid was watching them right now. He would have liked to draw him out into the open, to look into the man's eyes until the bastard realized Malcolm held his life in his hands.

With a snort of disappointment, Malcolm dropped his attention back on the older Dunstan. "It must be Walter's lucky day, because I've come to negotiate an agreement with you, Mr. Dunstan."

The old man laughed. "Negotiate? Boy, are you stupid? You have no leverage to negotiate. Your hostage is useless. I've got a dozen other guns to do what he can't." The young gunman in question made a muffled sound of distress or protest, but Dunstan paid him no mind. "You've got nothing, Kincaid. You're going to die today. End of story."

Malcolm smiled. A slow grin that held no humor. "Maybe so, but I bet I can put a bullet between your eyes before I do."

Dunstan's expression didn't change as he calmly held his hands out to the side. "I am an unarmed man, Mr. Kincaid. That would be outright murder."

"You'd still be dead."

"I do believe I will rely on the skills of my men here. You cannot defend against them and kill me at the same time."

"Try me."

Dunstan stared him down. Malcolm was taking a risk not knowing where the other men were or how many there might be, but he was tired of the talking. Action was his leverage.

"Dammit. Might as well," Dunstan muttered after a

minute. Then he gave a small nod to the man standing beside him. "Kill him."

The hired gun cocked back the hammer of his pistol.

Malcolm immediately shifted his aim from his hostage to the gunman and fired, sending a bullet into the man's chest. Though his shoulder was well on the mend, his movements still weren't as fast or smooth as he needed them to be. As the first gunman fell, the other two went for their weapons.

Malcolm swung to the one on the left, taking him out just as the man's gun cleared its holster. Continuing his momentum, Malcolm leapt from Deuce's back and dropped to the ground as a bullet whizzed past him from the one on the right. In a crouch, Malcolm took aim below Deuce's belly, hitting the third man before that one could get off a second shot.

At the same time, another shot came from somewhere behind him, followed by shattering glass as one of Dunstan's men fell forward through a window in the bunkhouse. His cold gun landed in the dirt beside him.

Malcolm had no idea who'd shot the fourth man, but he had no time to be grateful as the sound of more breaking glass drew his attention to an upper-floor window in the house where the barrel of a rifle appeared.

Unable to see the rifleman, Malcolm took blind shots at the window as he ran and dove to the ground behind a water trough.

Malcolm had released his hostage when he'd leapt from his saddle and he saw the boy running in a crouch for the tree line, the tail end of the rope trailing in the dirt behind him. He had just a second to hope the kid made it.

Then all hell broke loose.

There were more men in hiding around the house than he'd thought as bullets rained down, sending dirt and rocks flying in all directions. The explosion of gunfire was sure to draw the attention of those who'd gone to fight the fire, but Malcolm had every intention of being outta there before then.

Swiftly reloading his Colt, he noticed that whoever had shot the man in the bunkhouse was continuing to provide cover for Malcolm. The scene felt sickeningly familiar to when Alex had kept a bird's-eye view over the ambush in the ravine.

The woman better not have followed him.

Even as his gut churned at the thought, he knew it was a likely possibility. She wasn't exactly the type to sit back at her father's house and just wait for Malcolm to return. All he could do was pray he was wrong and finish what he came here to do. His focus needed to be on taking out the rest of Dunstan's men.

Scooting to one end of the trough, he took a swift glance out toward the house. Cal Dunstan was nowhere to be seen. Neither was Walter, though Malcolm expected such cowardice from that one. The rifleman in the upper window hung limp over the sill, while two more bodies lay in the dirt near the bunkhouse. But three other gunmen had joined the scene and were still standing. They continued to send fire in Malcolm's direction while scanning the area for the location of the second shooter.

If it was Alex out there, Malcolm couldn't let them take any shots at her.

Two more well-aimed rounds from his Colt took out a gunman hunkered down by the porch.

Malcolm sent a couple more shots toward the other two, hoping his ally might have time to get repositioned for a better shot at them. While he slunk down behind the trough to reload yet again, he heard a shout of pain. They were down to one, but the last of Dunstan's men stood around the corner of the house and was hard to get an angle on. It was Malcolm's turn to get into a better position. Trusting the rifle fire would keep the man pinned down, Malcolm dashed from behind the water trough, running full-out toward a pile of barrels near the bunkhouse. From there he had a clear shot at the last man. Standing, he took aim over the top of the barrels and pulled the trigger.

He knew he'd hit his target but didn't have a chance to see the man fall as another shot hit too damn close to where he stood. He spun around to see someone had managed to sneak up behind him.

Before Malcolm could re-aim his Colt, a rifle shot sounded. A look of shock crossed the man's face, and he fell forward into the dirt.

Then all became eerily quiet.

Malcolm continued to scan for activity around the house, but nothing moved.

After a while, he heard the sound of a horse riding in from the western tree line. It was risky to take his eyes off the enemy, but he couldn't stop himself from a quick glance as Alex rode up beside him—unharmed, thank God!—with her rifle raised and ready and a modified Colt strapped to her hip.

He fought against the fierce urge to sweep her from her horse and plant a hard kiss to her mouth and the desire to grab her shoulders and shake her for putting herself in the middle of this. The feelings rushing through him were such a jumbled mix he couldn't figure out which reaction should take precedence.

"What the hell are you doing here?"

"Helping," she replied easily without interrupting her steady scan of the area. "Or didn't you notice?"

Her sassy reply nearly had him smiling, but just then Cal Dunstan shouted from inside the house. "I'm coming out. Unarmed, so don't shoot."

Malcolm leveled his gaze and his gun on the old man as he stepped onto the porch.

Just because the hired guns had been taken care of didn't mean the danger was over. Malcolm was not about to underestimate the old man, and Walter still hadn't made an appearance. It was time to end this. "Ready to hear my offer?"

"Goddammit, spit it out then," Dunstan growled, clearly not pleased by the swift and complete shift in power.

Malcolm kept his gun and his gaze on Dunstan as he reached into his vest to pull out a set of papers.

"These are the documents ordering the capture or killing of the Belt Buckle Kid under sanction of law. I'm willing to leave these with you and forget I ever heard the name Walter Dunstan."

Alex drew a swift breath that caught on a tight sound in her throat. Malcolm wished he could tell her to trust him—assure her he knew what he was doing. Then he realized he didn't have to. She might not know his plan, but she trusted him, just as he should have trusted her when he took off from her pa's without a word.

"I'll discontinue my pursuit of justice regarding your son's past crimes if, and only if, you both give up your vendetta against Alexandra Brighton."

Malcolm watched Dunstan's face. It went from surprise to seething wrath.

But before he could reply, the front door of the house swung wide-open. Walter Dunstan wheeled himself onto the porch with a roar of fury. "It's you! You little bitch!" He lifted a rifle from his lap and took aim at Alex.

The pure terror that shot through Malcolm nearly made him blind.

But it didn't slow his reaction time as he adjusted his aim and pulled the trigger.

With a strangled cry, Walter dropped the gun.

His father muttered in disgust, "You damn idiot," while Walter cradled his injured arm against his chest.

"I repeat my offer one last time," Malcolm shouted. "Drop your vendetta against Miss Brighton, or Walter dies."

"I'll never give up on wanting that bitch dead," Walter snapped. Though his body's weakness was evident, and the fresh gunshot wound was still bleeding, the man looked as though he wanted to fly out of his chair and wrap his hands around Alex's throat.

Malcolm cocked back the hammer on his gun. His trigger finger was itching to squeeze.

"Shut up," Dunstan growled. "We accept. Now, get the hell off my property."

Malcolm stared at the older man, noting the murderous fury in his eyes. Dunstan was not one to easily concede defeat, and he clearly loathed having to do so now.

The old man was everything Malcolm had expected him to be. Dunstan hadn't amassed the kind of power he maintained by keeping his word when it didn't suit him.

Malcolm was counting on that.

Without shifting his gaze, Malcolm gave a shrill whistle. A moment later, Deuce came running from somewhere behind the bunkhouse. Keeping his gun at the ready and knowing Alex did the same, Malcolm mounted his horse.

"You make any move against the Brightons, I'll hear about it," he said in a final warning. "And I won't need any damn papers to see justice done."

Dropping the documents he held to the dirt, he drew on his reins to turn Deuce toward the trees, putting himself squarely between Alex and the two men on the porch. Malcolm was supposed to be the only one at risk today. With Alex beside him, the whole situation was that much more perilous.

He hated turning away from the Dunstans, but it was the only way to play this thing out to the end. Instead of heading down the long drive, he directed Deuce westward, keeping the Dunstans in his peripheral vision.

They didn't get far before he saw what he was waiting for.

Walter proved himself to be the idiot he was and couldn't wait more than a minute before making a move toward his rifle. Malcolm spun around just as a gunshot rang out. But it wasn't from Walter, who was still in the act of raising the rifle. It was the old man. He'd been carrying a gun the whole time.

Malcolm fired his Colt, hitting the old man square in the chest. Dunstan's body stiffened in shock before going limp as he dropped to the ground. By then, Walter had the rifle in hand. Two shots rang out in quick succession. Walter's went wide, hitting the dirt to their left.

Alex's shot was deadly accurate.

FORTY-THREE

ALEXANDRA TOOK A GULP OF AIR, TRYING TO EASE the fiery pain searing her side. She twisted to look down and pushed her coat aside to see a small patch of red soaking into her shirt. Reaching with her hand, she pressed her fingers against the sticky warmth of her blood.

Just a graze.

She scanned what she could see of Malcolm and saw no injuries.

"Alex. You all right?" His voice was hard as he looked back at her.

"I'm fine," she assured him, tucking her coat over the wound in her side as she met his glinting gray gaze. Damn, but she loved that fierce scowl of his.

"We gotta ride. And hard."

"Let's go," she answered, kicking Sibyl straight into a gallop.

Once under cover in the forest, they slowed their pace, but only a little. Alex understood that Malcolm wanted to get them as far from Dunstan's place as possible. She'd seen the fire he'd started and knew there were likely to be more men swarming the place in minutes, though she had to wonder what they'd do once they saw their boss dead on the porch.

Her stomach rebelled at the memory of how much death littered the ground behind them, and much of it by her hand. Though her body shook in the aftermath of what she'd done, she felt no regret. Malcolm had given the Dunstans a chance. They'd opted for violence.

The sun was getting low by the time Malcolm slowed and started scouting for a place to make camp. He found a nice spot tucked in between some rocky hills where a narrow river cut a deep path. "We should be safe here," he said, swinging down from his horse. "At least until we can figure out what comes next."

When Alex dismounted, her clothes shifted over her wound, making her suck in a swift breath at the burning pain.

"Christ, Alex, you were shot."

Malcolm was beside her in an instant, scooping her into his arms and carrying her to where he could set her down with her back resting against a rocky outcropping.

"Why the hell didn't you tell me?" he grumbled as he started to strip her clothes away.

"It is just a graze. I barely feel it."

Giving her a sharp look, he started removing her coat and lifted the hem of her shirt to get a better look at the injury. A shallow trail had been seared across her ribs.

"See," she said lightly. It hurt like hell, but it certainly wasn't life-threatening. "Just a scratch."

Malcolm said nothing to that, but the look on his face probably would have scared just about anyone other than her. Luckily, she knew it was worry and love making him so angry. He strode back to Deuce and grabbed a canteen of water, then returned to her side to wash the wound.

She sat still and quiet under his attentions, allowing herself to soak in the fact that they were both alive and likely would remain so for some time to come.

"Well, I guess I've seen worse," he mumbled.

"So have I," she replied, bringing his gaze up to hers.

"You shouldn't've been anywhere near that place. It was too damned dangerous, Alex." He hung his head as he pressed a clean cloth to her side and tugged her shirt back down to cover it. "You could've been killed."

"You could have been killed too," she murmured, bringing her hand up to the side of his face. Then she smiled. "I'm glad we weren't."

"I wanted to save you from that, not drag you right into the middle of it."

Alex tipped her head and gave him a hard took. She knew it wouldn't be nearly as effective as his steel-like glares, but she did her best. He needed to understand how it was between them—how it was going to be. "You didn't drag me into anything, Malcolm. I was in it long before I met you. The important thing is that we got out of it. Together."

"You shouldn't have been in that position."

"But I was," she answered sternly. "And I'll damn well do it again if it means keeping you safe. Just as I know you'll do the same for me. I heard your offer to Dunstan. I know what you were willing to sacrifice for me. You cannot expect me to do any less for you."

He stared at her. His eyes flinty and deep and unreadable. His jaw tense beneath her hand.

Then he sighed—a heavy, weighted sound that seemed to come from deep inside. Grasping her wrist in his fingers, he turned his head to press a kiss into the center of her palm. "You're right."

She smiled again. "I know."

His answering smile was sweet, but still tense.

She had to ask. "What will happen to all those... men we left behind?"

"We'll stop in at Wolf Creek and let them know what happened. The other hired guns will likely disperse now that they don't have a paycheck coming to them. Men like that are only loyal to themselves."

"Won't you need those documents you left behind to claim the bounty?"

"Those were decoys. I still have everything I need."

Alex sucked in a breath. "You knew they would renege on their word, didn't you? As soon as they shot at us, you had justification to kill them both."

There was a long pause as the weight of what they'd gone through settled around them.

"It's finally over," he said in a low, gravelly voice. "You're free, Alex."

Firelight danced over his rough-hewn features and made his silvery eyes shine all the brighter. But the tension across his brow, though familiar, was not what she wanted to see at all.

"We are both free, Malcolm."

He glanced away from her questioning gaze. "I imagine you'll want to go back to your pa's house."

Alex tipped her head. "No. I don't," she answered quietly.

The muscles in his jaw bunched. "Isn't that why you were so determined to get to Montana?"

"All I really wanted was to figure out where I belong, and that isn't with my father. I hope to have opportunities to visit and get to know his new family—my new family—but my place isn't with them." She lifted a hand and pressed it to his chest, covering his heart. Waiting until he lifted his eyes again to meet hers, she took a breath and said, "I want to be with you, Malcolm. Wherever you go, whatever you do in life, I want to be with you."

His eyes darkened as she spoke, but he remained stiff and unmoving. She held her breath. She thought he wanted the same—she felt in her bones that he did—but something still held him back.

"You're not safe with me." His words were tight and gruff, like they were getting choked in his throat. "Violence has attached itself to my life. I'd die if something happened to you while you were under my protection."

Alexandra's heart shuddered at the loss and fear in his voice.

This was it. The reason he resisted. He was afraid.

She rose up and repositioned herself to straddle his lap. Taking his handsome, ornery face in her hands, she looked intently into his eyes. Love flowed through her when his arms came around her hips, holding her tight.

"Life holds no guarantees, Malcolm," she

whispered. "We both know that. But I'd rather spend a thousand dangerous days and nights with you than one perfectly safe—horrendously lonely—day without you. I love you too much to be apart from you, Malcolm Kincaid."

His arms doubled around her back, drawing her in snug against him. She slid her arms around his neck and closed her eyes as she squeezed him back, feeling the tension and resistance slowly easing from his body.

He released a deep and long-drawn breath against the curve of her neck. "I've been chasing demons so long, I don't know how to do anything else."

"We'll figure it out together. It will be a grand adventure," she suggested. "I'll have to send word to my father that I'm all right. And my friends back in Boston are probably dying to find out what happened to me. I doubt they'll believe any of it," she added with a grin before she gave him another squeeze. "I'm afraid you're stuck with me, Malcolm."

His expression was still a little troubled, but his mouth slowly curved into a smile. "Not yet," he replied in a low murmur. "I reckon we better make it official. You'll have to marry me."

Her eyes widened before she curled one corner of her mouth in a teasing smile. "I just got out of one engagement—I'm not sure I should jump right into another one," she teased.

A low growl rumbled from his throat as he lifted her and turned to lay her back on their spread bedrolls. He was so careful, it caused only a slight twinge along her side.

"Then we'll forego the engagement and visit the

justice of the peace in the morning," he said as he lowered his head to press a hot kiss to the side of her throat.

She sighed and arched her head back as tingling shivers coursed through her. "In the morning," she murmured in agreement.

His fingers began to make quick work of the buttons on her shirt and then the tiny buttons of her undergarment beneath. He paused for a moment at the sight of the cloth pressed firm to her wound.

Lifting his head, he looked at her with his gaze bright. "I love you more than anything in this world, Alex. I vow to do whatever it takes to keep you safe and make you happy."

She framed his handsome face in her hands and lifted her head to press a kiss to one corner of his mouth and then the other. "And I vow to do the same. You deserve happiness more than anyone I know."

"This makes me happy. Being with you," he said in a rough murmur, sending warmth through her body. Warmth and delicious waves of desire. "But I have no home to take you to."

"Home is wherever we are, Malcolm. Our future together is as wide-open as the Montana sky. And if we get tired of exploring, we can stop to rest in a little cabin I know of hidden deep in the mountains."

He chuckled. "I think I know that place."

"You should," she assured him. "It's where you fell in love with me, after all."

His laughter then was warm and deep. It was everything.

WANT EVEN MORE AMY SANDAS?
DISCOVER HER FALLEN LADIES

When three sisters are dragged into London's underworld of gamblers, prostitutes, and thieves, it will take all their ingenuity to save themselves before they are ruined forever.

LUCK IS NO LADY
In the dark underworld of high-stakes gambling, Emma discovers that in order to win the love of a ruthless scoundrel, she has to play the game...

THE UNTOUCHABLE EARL
Sold into the glittering world of the demimonde, Lily comes to the attention of a devilishly handsome earl with a tragic secret...

LORD OF LIES
Determined to save her sisters, Portia descends into a world of cutpurses and thieves, running afoul of a mysterious confidence man known only as Nightshade...

ALSO BY AMY SANDAS

Fallen Ladies
Luck Is No Lady
The Untouchable Earl
Lord of Lies

Christmas in a Cowboy's Arms anthology